Kitchen Boy

Sanford Phippen

Blackberry Books

Nobleboro, Maine
1996

Best wishes!
Sandy Phippen

Grateful acknowledgment is made for permission to reprint excerpts from the following copyrighted works:

"THE GLORY OF LOVE" from "Guess Who's Coming to Dinner," words and music by Billy Hill, copyright © 1936 Shapiro, Bernstein & Co., Inc., New York, copyright renewed, International Copyright Secured. All Rights Reserved. Used by Permission, p. 132.
"JUST A GIGOLO," by Leonello Casucci and Irving Caesar, © 1930 (Renewed) Chappell & Co. (ASCAP) and Irving Caesar Music Corp. (ASCAP) All Rights on behalf of Irving Caesar Music Corp. administered by WB Music Corp. All Rights Reserved. Used by Permission. WARNER BROS. PUBLICATIONS U.S., INC., Miami, FL 33014, p. 32.
"LIFE GETS TEE-JUS DON'T IT," Words and Music by Carson Robison, © Copyright 1948 MCA Music Publishing, a division of MCA, Inc. Copyright Renewed. International Copyright Secure. All Rights Reserved. Used by Permission, p. 38.
"SOUTH AMERICA, TAKE IT AWAY," words and music by Harold Rome, © 1946 (Renewed) Warner Bros., Inc. All Rights Reserved. Used by Permission. WARNER BROS. PUBLICATIONS U.S., INC., Miami, FL 33014, p. 26.

Chapters from this book were previously published as adapted stories in the following magazines and book:

1. "Chauffeuring in the Summer," *Portland Monthly Magazine*, September 1995.
2. "Crazy Yankee Bellhop," *Portland Monthly Magazine*, September 1991.
3. "Going for My Interview," *Puckerbrush Review*, Orono, Maine, Vol. IX, No. 1, Fall/Winter 1989.
4. "Hot Action in the Pickin' Room," *Portland Monthly Magazine*, June 1994.
5. "From *Kitchen Boy*, A Novel-in-Progress," *Puckerbrush Review*, Orono, Maine, Vol. XII, No. II, Winter 1994.
6. "From *Kitchen Boy*," *Puckerbrush Review*, Orono, Maine, Vol. XIV, No. 1, Summer/Fall 1995.
7. "The Lobster Stomp," *Puckerbrush Review*, Orono, Maine, Vol. IV, No. II, Winter 1982; and *The Police Know Everything*, Puckerbrush Press, Orono, Maine, 1982.
8. "Mattress Moving," *Portland Monthly Magazine*, July/August 1992.
9. "Mrs. Lawson Arrives for the Summer," *The Police Know Everything*, Puckerbrush Press, Orono, Maine, 1982.
10. "One of the New England Treats," *Puckerbrush Review*, Orono, Maine, Vol. XI, No. 1, Summer 1992.

ISBN 0-942396-77-4

Blackberry Books, RR1, Box 228, Nobleboro, Maine 04555

Book design by Christopher Smith
Cover design by Stephen Shedd

Printed in the United States of America
Thomason-Shore, Ann Arbor, Michigan

TO

Annie Larrabee
Susan Springer
Condon Rodgers
Susan Young Webber
Mary Lou Tracy Hodge
Jane Dickson Pezzullo
Carol Melin Connolly
and
All the Other FBL gals

and
in memory of
Isabel Farnsworth and Jane Miller

Also by Sanford Phippen

Fiction

The Police Know Everything (1982)
People Trying to be Good (1988)

Essays

Cheap Gossip (1989)

Editor

The Best Maine Stories (1986)
with Martin Greenburg and Charles Waugh
High Clouds Soaring, Storms Driving Low: The Letters of Ruth Moore (1993)

Plays

The Straight And Crazy Doped-Up World (1973)
Agreen and Us: A Revue (1978)
The Police Know Everything (1992)

History

A History of Hancock, Maine: 1828 - 1978 (1978)
with the Hancock Sesquicentenniel Committee

Video

A Century of Summers: The Impact of a Summer Colony on a Small Maine Coastal Town (1987)
with the Hancock Historical Society

Audio

The Police Know Everything (1995)
for Voices for the Blind

Anthologies in which Phippen's work appears

Inside Vacationland (1985)
Maine Speaks (1989)
A Lobster in Every Pot (1990)
The Quotable Moose (1994)

Acknowledgements

I didn't mean to take twenty-three years in which to write this novel. However, that's how it turned out. I began it and wrote the bulk of it in Syracuse, New York in 1972, after I had received my Master's degree at Syracuse University and before I became a regular columnist for the *Tuesday Weekly* newspaper in Ellsworth, Maine, in 1973. Busy since then with my teaching and other writing projects, I didn't get back to it until 1993-95. The title has undergone several changes from *Swift Journeyings* to *Hot Flashes and Cold Chills* to *Summer People and Some Are Not* to *Six Summers* to *Kitchen Boy* to *Mainiacs and Foreigners* and finally back to *Kitchen Boy*.

The following friends and relatives, both living and deceased, helped me to persevere and to point me in the right direction with sound advice, good information, emotional and financial support, good humor, and love. Such perceptive and keen listeners and readers I've had! My eternal thanks to all of you: Ted Adams, Jane Colwell Alley, Lew Alley, Virgil Bisset, Farnham Blair, Peggy Bowditch, Cathy Whitehouse Buzwell, Shirley Chase, Carolyn Chute, Robert A. Clark, Robert W. Clarke, Steve and Myrna Coffin, Margaret Colwell, Leo Connellan, Carol Melin Connolly, George Daniell, Richard and Karen Dickson, Walter Dickson, Janet Chase Fickett, Mary Ann Fiorenza, Virginia Flynn, Nancy Gilbert, John Gould, Harriet Gundersen, Sturgis Haskins, Chuck and Mary Lou Hodge, Edward M. Holmes, Constance Hunting, Thom Ingraham, Alice Dean Janick, Stephen and Tabitha King, Annie Larrabee, Marilyn Laufe, Gary Lawless, Toby LeBoutilier, Gerald E. Lewis, Wayne Mayo, Robert and Elaine McConnachie, Mark Melnicove, Gene and Mary Monahan, Ruth Moore, Lawrence Moores, Dave Olson, Jane Dickson Pezzullo, Elizabeth Phippen, Anne Pomroy, Condon Rodgers, Floyd and Jackson Rodgers, Betsy Graves Rose, Mark Rose, Colin Sargent, Marcia Savage, Bea and Scott Shablak, Steve Shedd, Christopher Smith, Susan Springer, Ruth Stein, Roslyn Targ, Robert Taylor, Cindy Todd, Janwillem van de Wetering, Susan Young Webber, John A. Williams, Dennis Young, and Elizabeth Young.

——— Sanford Phippen
Hancock and Orono, Maine, 1995

Prologue

I am the detective of my life, and the case is never closed. I probe on paper the whys and wherefores of my existence, examine as carefully as I can the myriad clues to the mystery of me, and follow up on whatever leads come my way. I wish to know as much as I can about myself before I kick the bucket, so that I won't be saying good-bye to a complete stranger.

To that end, I want to focus here on the crucial years from ages 16 - 22 when I was associated with a small summer resort hotel on the Eastern Coast of Maine. As it turned out, Frenchman's Bay Manor provided me with the gateway to the greater world, the way out from a dead-end life, the escape route from provincial Downeast.

On a more literary note, it might be said that the Manor was my raft down the Mississippi, my Pency Prep, the wedding of which I became a member, and, perhaps, even my *Pequod*. It's where I met Thomas Wolfe who became my guide and helped me find the key that started unlocking many doors.

——— Sanford Phippen
Hancock and Orono, Maine
December 1995

"Gawd, didn't we have a riot down at the old Frenchman's Bay Manor on Granite Neck! Those two old birds from New York were hilarious: Madella and Jean were so much fun to work for. I mighta bitched and complained some from time to time, and even quit on 'em for a spell or two, but I'd always go back. I couldn't stay away, and when I look back now honestly--and ya have to get old to get really honest--they were probably the best people I've ever worked for in a lifetime of trying to make do, going from job to job. When ya hear all this talk today about women's lib and people asking, 'Would you like to work for a *woman*? Would you want a *woman* for a boss?' Well, I think of Madella and Jean, and I answer right off, 'Damn right, I would!'"

——— Alberta Ficket
Commonrest Convalescent Care
Route One
East Hamlin, Maine
August 1995

"We Mainiacs, born and raised in the State of Maine, like to be called Mainiacs, because we know we're crazy; but the foreigners don't know what they are."

——— Fat Moon
Taunton Ferry, Maine

June 1960

1

I was down on my hands and knees scrubbing with a scrub brush the vast, cracked, warped, and worn linoleum reaches of the kitchen floor of Frenchman's Bay Manor one early Saturday afternoon in June 1960, when my portly bosslady, Mrs. Madella Richmond, hailed me from her favorite perch, the captain's chair at the kitchen table, about six feet away.

Looking down at me from over the tops of her bright green-rimmed spectacles, her blondish-gray hair frizzed about her round pink and rouged face, her jowls at rest, and her great body straining the seams of her light green summer suit, she pronounced, "You'll never get married!"

I must have looked up at her like a startled deer: a tall, skinny, seventeen-year-old geek with a blond crew cut and what must have been a surprised and quizzical expression upon my beak-nosed mug. I didn't respond and I didn't stand up—I remember that—and I was probably even grinning at her in agreement. Such was the depth of my good servant's complex, and lifelong working class training: always fearful of being let go, of being found wanting, of getting a bad reputation, always willing to serve and to do a good job, no matter what, and never questioning my boss to her face.

Without further explanation, Mrs. Richmond went back to her reading of *The New York Times* and the sipping of her coffee; and I returned to my scrubbing, but inside I was in turmoil.

After two summers of working at the Manor, I was used to Mrs. Richmond's having strong opinions and making such startling comments to me and about me, leaving me usually in a puzzled state; but this declaration really rattled. I was so unsure of myself in all respects. What was it she saw in me: a seventeen-year-old virgin, that would make me unmarriageable? What the hell was my destiny supposed to be in her sophisticated eyes? Was I some kind of freak? An artist-in-the-making? Some other kind of loser who didn't have what it takes?

I wish I could go see her right now, or call her up, after all these years, so I could ask her just what she meant, what she saw in me that dreary day when I was helping her open up the Manor for yet another season by the sea.

When I had scrubbed up to the table at which she was sitting, I did stand up; and since I am over six feet tall, she did have to look up.

"Yes?" she asked, and then coming to realize why I was so close to her: "Oh! You'd like me to get out of your way."

"Well, I could finish it later."

"No, no," she said, attempting to extricate her huge body from the armchair, pointing at the knees of my faded jeans, which were wet from the floor. "Finish now—while you're in the mood."

She laughed, shaking the bread crumbs from her dress, and then clomped away in her fat lady's high-heeled shoes down the hall to her office.

"Time to go juggle me books!"

She had picked me up the afternoon before, a Friday after school, to accompany her to Granite Neck, the exclusive summer colony of Summer Harbor where the Manor was located, to work around the place, weed the petunia beds, run errands, and help with the big dinner party planned for Saturday night.

Even though the Manor wasn't officially open for the season, she did book dinner parties if she could get the help.

"Who are these people?" I had asked.

"Oh, rich Bangor business types out for an early summer sail. Actually, I think they're coming on some fancy cabin cruiser. They're scheduled to dock at the yacht club, then walk up here to meet with some friends coming by car. Oh, I know it's a big bother for us all, while we're trying to open; but I could use those Bangor bucks to get this joint spruced up; and if they like their time here, they might just come back and bring their pals. Business is business, ya know."

"Who's coming in for help?"

"Hattie Pinkham will be doing the waitressing as usual, and I've engaged Alvina and Cliff Masters for help in the kitchen. Cliff will play bartender, too, while Alvina can heat up the dishpan. You, of course, will be in charge of the lobsters. Berter can't help out tonight, except that she's promised to drop by with a few dozen home-made rolls and three or four lemon meringue pies. Cliff is to make his famous fish chowder as a first course."

Berter Fickett was the cook in Mrs. Richmond's absence and an all-purpose general handywoman who came and went at all hours, not only at the Manor, but at cottages all over the Neck. She was known far and wide.

The summer of 1960, Mrs. Richmond had planned to show me how to drive and take care of her car, a silver '57 Oldsmobile 98, a car I loved and could hardly wait to have the care of. After school got out—and graduation ceremonies were over—in another week or so, I would be at the Manor full-time, living up in the attic room where I had first stayed the summer before in 1959.

In the fall, mid-September, I would be a college freshman at the University of Maine. Mrs. Richmond was very pleased that I was graduating fourth in my class and going to college on two small scholarships and a government loan.

"What I'd have given to be able to go to college at eighteen!" she'd often say. "As it was, I ended up taking courses in New York at the New School, at NYU, and all over the city. I studied everything from hooking rugs to Chinese literature—and I loved every minute: but there was never any degree program."

"Why not?" I asked.

"I was married by the time I was eighteen, Andy."

"Mister Richmond?"

"Yes. Dear old Ralph. He was forty-five and a good-looking Lutheran minister. He was the first good man who came along and asked me. And he was on his way to New York City and that's where I longed to be—way beyond the Kansas wheatfields—so I climbed aboard the fast express and never looked back."

"You grew up in Kansas?"

"Yes, deepest, darkest Kansas with a goddamn German farmer for a father, too stubborn to even learn English, and where there were no lucky rainbows, only tomatoes and working from dawn to dusk in the fields. In case you haven't noticed, my boy, I warn't cut out to be no cow milkin' farm gal!"

And so she wasn't. The only other time I remember her mentioning a return to Kansas was when she was one of the first passengers on a cross country airplane trip in the 1920s.

"What was it like?" I asked.

"We were just like chickens in a coop!" she said. "You see, we passengers were seated down below the pilot, who perched above us; and every now and then, he'd open up this little hatch through which he'd peer down and ask us how we were doin'. We'd only fly a little way, then land in some field, and everyone would try and get to the one phone to let our relatives and friends know we'd made it twenty more miles. I remember at one stop, I asked the airport manager, who was picking his teeth with a knife, if he'd be kind enough to direct me to the ladies' room, and he pointed to this field of tall grass!"

"Top-notch accommodations."

"Well, we were pioneers. I was in my twenties in the Roaring Twenties, and, God, was New York fun! My ancestors had been pioneers out west, but I was a pioneer back in the east—I was a liberated flapper if there ever was one. I drank so much of that bathtub gin, it's a wonder I'm not blind as a bat!"

Later that afternoon, I was out in the petunia beds in front of the Manor when Hattie Pinkham arrived to begin preparations for the dinner. She had on her close-fitting waitress uniform as she walked towards me across the lawn from the service entrance where she had parked her '52 baby blue Plymouth sedan. Even as a middle-aged and rather plump woman, Hattie was good-looking and sexy, always full of fun.

"Listen, you handsome young devil, when are you going to grow up and take me away from here?" she asked, laughingly.

"I'm headed to college now, Hattie," I said.

"Well, can't I go with ya and help ya with your studies?"

"I'll be living in an all-boys' dorm, I'm afraid."

"Wow! That's even better. I could be the housemother, and you

KNOW how well I keep house," she said with a wink.

She stood over me as I crouched there by the beds with a trowel in my hand and with boxes of new little petunias surrounding me, waiting to be planted. Hattie reached down and rubbed my head.

"I'm glad you're back for another season, old boy. That was fun last summer."

"Yes, it was; and I'm glad, too, Hattie. I look forward to more of our mattress moving."

"Ya remember the mattresses, huh, An-day? . . . Whoops! Gotta run! I can hear the Kansas Tornado herself clompin' her way towards me! You get those pretty posies all lined up and watered down. We don't want to greet our dinner guests with dead and drooping flowers!"

Hattie turned and started walking toward the back porch steps.

I called after her: "She's hired Alvina and Cliff to help out tonight!"

"Oh, Jesus!" Hattie said, turning around to look at me. "You had to ruin my evening! I'll have a good drink before, during, and after to get me through this party!"

I had to finish with the planting, and then go get cleaned up myself for my work with the food. First, a quick trip down to the shore where I filled up a couple of buckets with sea water and seaweed for cooking the crustaceans. About the time I returned to the Manor, I met Hick Young, a local lobsterman, who liked to make his weekly deliveries to Mrs. Richmond (usually Friday night was lobster night), for they always had a cocktail or two before he went on his way. Hick was no hick, far from it. Good-looking in a hairy, craggy sort of way, he knew how to get on the best side of the summer people, especially the ladies, and was well-liked. He had no formal education to speak of, but he was bright, ambitious, and had charm.

"How many lobsters did you bring, Hick?"

"Two dozen, mostly pound-and-a-half, and all hard-shell. Mrs. Richmond said they were expecting as many as fifteen people." He handed me two large, double-strength paper bags crammed with live lobsters.

"That ain't all of 'em. There's another bag in the truck."

"O.K., I'll go get it."

And while I was getting it, Hick went in the house, as I knew he would. Mrs. Richmond and Hattie were both at the kitchen table, which was of the aluminum folding variety, smoking and nursing their drinks. The peas were simmering in a double boiler on the stove, and the potatoes to-be-baked were lined up and greased-to-go. Preparations were well underway.

Mrs. Richmond got up to greet Hick, a local man she greatly respected.

"Hick Young, it's so good to see you again! Wontcha have a drink?"

"Don't mind if I do," said Hick. "It's good to see you again, too, Madella."

They both sat down.

"What are you having, Hattie?" Hick asked.

"Tonight, it's an old-fashioned, because I guess I'm feeling old-fashioned. What can I get for you, Mr. Young?"

"I'll try one of those."

"I was hoping you'd say that. I just happen to have made a pitcherful."

I'd listen to such kitchen talk while I went about my business, in this case getting the lobster kettles out and on the gas stove. I only put about an inch of the salt water and sea weed in them. Just before the first course was being served, I'd start boiling the lobsters. We'd boil them for twenty minutes.

It was also my job to get out the heavy blue glass lobster plates and cut up the lemons into wedges to stick on the bony spurs between the lobsters' eyes when they were served. Between the claws, we placed little bowls of melted butter. The crystal finger bowls were prepared with warm water with lemon. Before arranging the lobsters on the plates, I had to crack the claws and the tails for our guests, even though we provided nutcrackers and picks for everyone.

Soon after Hick sat down, Alvina and Cliff arrived with some liquor, drink mixers, and a big pot of Cliff's fish chowder.

"I've been cooped up all winter, so I'm ready for a good party!" exclaimed Alvina coming through the back door.

She was on the pudgy side and loud, brazen, and blonde; she took the lead with her faithful husband Cliff following on behind, his arms loaded with bags of stuff and the chowder pot.

Alvina kissed and hugged Mrs. Richmond.

"Hello, dear," Mrs. Richmond said, and then to Cliff: "Cliff, thank God, you brought more booze! I told this Bangor crowd that we provide set-ups, and they should bring their own bottles. But, of course, ya never know; and it's only being friendly having some stuff on hand. Say, is the chowder all made and fit for a king?"

"Just needs to be heated up!" said Cliff.

"Great. Now if only Berter would get here with the rolls and pies."

"I AM here!" exclaimed Berter barging through the back door with a bag of rolls and one of the pies. "Still warm from the oven! Anday! Go out to my car and git the other pies! Don't try to bring 'em all at once!"

Berter was red-haired and sloppily attired; but she was good-natured, a hard worker and a wonderful cook. Her hair was always a mess, but with a good hairdresser, she could have been a most attractive woman.

I came back with the pies, two at a time—Berter had made five—and placed them on the large zinc-topped table in the middle of the kitchen which served as a chopping block and now accommodated the lobster plates, lemon wedges, and bowls for the butter.

Hick took his leave when Berter did; Hattie disappeared into the dining room; and after another round of drinks, Mrs. Richmond, Alvina, and Cliff, were well into entertaining each other with nostalgic tales from the Manor's past.

"Remember that high society doc you found in the bushes one night, Cliff?" asked Mrs. Richmond. "He was well into his cups and was stumbling around back of the garage trying to relieve himself when he lost what footing he had and decided to lie down and take a nap!"

"Yes, I remember what a time his foolish wife had when she missed him. She sent out this drunken search party with flashlights!"

"They made the acquaintance of some raccoons, didn't they?" asked Alvina.

They all laughed in reminiscence.

"Here come the guests!" hollered Hattie, who had been looking out the window in the butler's pantry, which faced the front entrance of the Manor.

Ultimately, there were two carloads of nine people and six men walking up the road from their boat. The people from the cars were dressed up, but the six seafarers were in jeans, shorts, and boating togs. A lively crew, they wanted music and I was summoned into the huge living room to put some LPs on the record player, and to fetch trays of goodies and set-ups for their drinks. Lots of haw-haw all around, with the middle-aged Sunday sailors recounting their cruising tales from their recent trip along the coast.

One of them, a beefy, boisterous Bowdoin man in plaid Bermuda shorts and a white sweater asked me: "Hey, son! Wasn't this house built by a Maine sea captain?"

"Yes," I said. "He founded this Neck and laid it out. He was an Irishman named Moore. All of the furnishings here, like the inlaid tables and cabinets, he brought back from his trips to the Orient."

"See what I told ya?" Beefy Boisterous said to his friends. "These old Maine sea captains, who sent their sons to Bowdoin and Harvard, had it all! That wild adventurous spirit! They went all over the world, saw everything, and built mansions like this magnificent one for themselves to come home to—talk about the good life!"

Hattie rang the gong, I moved back the oriental screen that separated the living room from the dining room; and Hattie announced, "Dinner is served."

And, as always, the dining room with the large windows overlooking the full length of Frenchman's Bay with the Mount Desert Hills on the other side, was warm and welcoming with the glittering glassware, fine china, silver, and candlelight. The brass plates on the walls glowed, and the fire in the fireplace, which I had set, crackled and snapped.

Soft instrumental music was playing as the guests with their drinks in hand entered, with one of the ladies exclaiming, "Isn't this a beautiful room!"

Standing by Hattie, who was smiling, Mrs. Richmond herself greeted her guests. "I always try to give a good party," she said. "Do enjoy yourselves."

After her gracious greeting, when we were all back out in the kitchen rustling up the grub, Mrs. Richmond said, "Oh, how amusing that Bangor crowd can be! You'd think to hear them talk they were still chopping down the woods, stealing the Indians' land, and building Bangor into the Lumber Capital of the World. But all they ever did was go to college, to Boston shopping, and get a good job back home with granddaddy's company. They're way too soft to be real pioneers, but, oh, how they love to effect the image, and wax nostalgic for that romantic past that never was."

"What do you mean 'wax'?" I asked.

"Look it up in the dictionary, Andy! To wax means to increase, to exaggerate, or if you will, to lie!"

Summer 1959

2

That's how the summer of 1960 began at the Manor, but that's not how I began. Mrs. Richmond did not hire me; it was her partner, Miss Jean Meyer, who did the year before in 1959.

My mother, Eleanor, nicknamed Sid, got me up early that day, and we were spinning the retreads on the big '51 Mercury Downeast on Route One by 8:30 a.m. The interview was scheduled at 9 a.m.; and I didn't want to be late. Of course, Sid wouldn't let me drive, even though I had been practicing all spring. She was at the helm, and as she drove, I dreamed of a new and more glorious life for myself as a budding bellhop at the summer hotel, meeting rich, glamorous, and influential people who would take an instant liking to this nice Maine boy.

We did talk a bit. Sid said, "If you do get this job, you know you won't be able to go back and forth."

"But I'll get my license in July," I said.

"How do you know you'll get it? Anyway, your father wouldn't let you have this car every day."

"Would you let me?" I asked.

"No, I wouldn't. The car's already eight years old. We have to nurse it along now. It can't stand much more wear and tear. You'll just have to ask this woman to give you a room."

"O.K., I will," I said.

I had been to Summer Harbor many times over the years to visit friends, to go to parties and on picnics, to play basketball and baseball, and to feed the seagulls down at the mainland section of the National Park. But I didn't know the summer colony of Granite Neck all that well. All I'd ever known really was that it had bigger summer cottages and richer residents than Taunton Point, the summer colony of my hometown.

Following the green-and-white hotel signs, shaped like arrows, we drove off Route One and along a winding, narrow backroad that took us through a couple of small villages and gatherings of buildings, many of them surrounded by stacks of lobster traps and fishing gear, by an old millhouse and water wheel with a pond and ducks, by the road leading down to a defunct sardine canning factory, up hills and around bends, by a stone library, a combination grocery store and post office, a couple of churches, a small, rocky sheep farm, some fine homes and some tarpaper shacks, through beautiful stretches of field and woods, beyond which lay the nearby ocean and cliffs.

All along this familiar road scene from my childhood, I wondered if there would come a time in my grown-up life when I wouldn't have to work all summer long, wondering if I could achieve somehow a life like I imagined the summer folk led: forsaking their fancy apartments in the city for their Maine cottages by the sea in the summer, where, as one of my caretaking uncles used to say, "They play at their work and work at their play."

After a couple of miles, the road we were traveling became two, the wider stretch continuing onto Summer Harbor Proper, the U.S. Navy Base, and the National Park, while the narrower and rougher route, which we followed, led more directly to Granite Neck and The Manor. This road curved dangerously at points where there was really only room for one car to pass. I liked it; it seemed a properly adventurous way to my new life. I only wished we were speeding along in a low-slung European sports car instead of timidly hedging forward in our rusted-out hulk of a Merc. My mother said that she wished we had gone the other way, that this road was too dangerous with its steep grade and sharp turns.

While she uttered her fears, I wondered (for I was such a wondering boy) at a stone wall that stretched for a few yards up this hill in the middle of the woods and which was evidently built to serve as a fancy guard rail. I wondered who had built such an artistic, protective bulwark and when and how long it took them. The rocks used in its composition were large and it must have taken a great deal of effort to drag them in through the woods here and set them into the wall.

My mother commented that in this thick-wooded section she wouldn't be surprised to see a deer leap out at us.

As Sid maneuvered the Merc expertly, I grew increasingly nervous and excited as we drove past more and larger elaborate summer estates, all landscaped and impressive in their upkeep. We passed a golf course by the sea and a beautifully designed little Episcopal church nestled at the road intersection to Granite Neck Proper and where the last green arrow sign for the hotel read: FRENCHMAN'S BAY MANOR 1/4 Mile. By each of the private home entrances were little red-and-white wooden flags with the owners' names on them. "These people are well-organized," I thought, and also couldn't help thinking if these were only their summer houses, what in hell must their more permanent residences look like? Granite Neck, my mother said, is like the way Eden Street in Bar Harbor used to look before the Great Conflagration of 1947 leveled many of the estates.

Finally, the main entranceway to the Manor-of-my-Dreams lay before us, wide and graveled and winding its way alongside fancy formal flower beds and spacious, manicured lawns with bits of ledge sticking out here and there. My mother pointed out the handsome gray granite *porte-cochère* under which guests' cars could arrive and depart without any raindrops plopping down on their heads.

"What does *porte-cochère* mean?" I asked.

"Oh, it's French for something like front entrance, I guess," she said.

Frenchman's Bay Manor had two large double-story wings that extended outward at a slight angle from the center tower that reigned solidly over the majestic main entrance. The paint trimmings, to offset the grayness of the weathered shingles and stone work, were painted, appropriately enough, a forest green similar to the green of the road signs. They must have gotten a bargain price.

My mother, worried that we should have driven to the servants' entrance instead of the front, didn't dare to pull up under the *porte-cochère*. Instead, she parked the powerful Merc machine off to the side, sort of tucked inconspicuously under some lilac trees near what appeared to be the back entrance, where, after the usual cautions from her to be pleasant and polite, know my place and mind my manners, and not forget to ask about a room for myself, I apprehensively entered.

I had forsaken my faded Roebuck jeans for a pair of tan chinos and a cheap but neat blue-and-white checked short-sleeve shirt, so I'd look like a nice and clean All-American goofball with a crewcut. As soon as I was in the building where my mother couldn't see, I stuck my glasses in my shirt pocket. One of the girls I knew well at home in Taunton once told me I looked cute without my glasses. My mother was always saying, "Where are your glasses? Why don't you wear your glasses?"

I was surprised as I ascended the stairs to the enclosed back porch to see, beyond the typical old-fashioned black sink and zinc-topped table loaded with cleaning paraphernalia, the hills of Mount Desert at such a different angle. They were as impressive and beautiful here as from Taunton Point, twenty or so miles up the coast, but Granite Neck juts out into the bay further so that the gentle pink granite mountains appear not as rounded humps but more angular, climbing a more graceful curve to a sharper summit.

After pausing for this new change in the old view, I opened the over-sized screen door (everything at the Manor seemed over-sized) and entered what appeared to be a back dining room with a laundry room off to the left. I peered hesitantly about, but no one seemed to be at home. Tip-toeing in my loafers across the red-and-white tiled floor, I knocked at the entrance to the immense kitchen, but still no answer. So I probed further and further into the heart of the Manor.

The kitchen ran the width of that side of the house and harbored the two biggest, blackest cookstoves I'd ever seen. There were also several table areas, cupboards and shelves everywhere crammed with cooking utensils and crockery. There was a shelf just for cookbooks with fancy bindings and titles. Two shelves over one of the stoves were stocked with spices I had never heard of. The windows over the sink area looked down a back lawn to the cliffs and ocean; and to the right of the sinks was a wall of pans, colanders, egg beaters, and the like. On the opposite side of the room, between the windows overlooking the front lawn and driveway were five large black armchairs surrounding an aluminum folding table upon which were scattered notebooks, a couple of detective novels, part of *The New York Times*, ashtrays solid full of butts, and an empty Miller High Life bottle. To one side of the table stood a huge freezer and an upright refrigerator. What a kitchen! The biggest one I'd ever been in.

Not daring to call out, I proceeded to knock at every door I came to, and there were three more between the kitchen and the main living room. There was a small pantry attached to a larger butler's pantry which was filled with fancy glassware. Beyond that was a cozy little office, no doubt the financial focal point of hotel operations, for there was a safe in the corner; and physically the office was nearly at the center of the building in the tower, tucked off a dark, narrow hallway furnished with a telephone and stand at one end and a bookcase at the other, and illuminated by a heavy metal, Spanish-looking chandelier whose arrangement of side openings cast a romantic but also rather spooky pattern of light on the hall's walls. From the dark passageway, I entered the handsome dark-wooded foyer with a tinkly crystal chandelier and from the foyer crossed into the most impressive and large living room I had ever been in. There was nothing on Taunton Point as grand as this.

Dark paneled like the foyer with huge beams criss-crossing the ceiling, the living room had an impressive granite fireplace at one end and throughout bright-colored furniture offset the darkness of the walls and ceilings. The setting reminded unworldly me of pictures of ritzy ski lodges one might see in the Alps. In the center of the room was a large plate glass window which framed the same handsome view of the Mount Desert Hills and sea that one could see from the back porch balcony. On a beautiful, round, inlaid-wood coffee table was a huge vase full of fresh flowers.

Looking warily about me, I wondered if anyone at all was about, and worried that I had come on the wrong day. It was so still and quiet. Finally, I summoned enough courage to call out in my screechy teenage voice and awful Maine accent, "Hello? Is anybud-ay he-ah?"

My call was answered by some scuffling around from above me upstairs, followed by a door's opening and closing and rapid footfalls coming along a carpet. I turned towards the handsome staircase which was wide and bounded on either side by dark wooden railings which extended to a balcony above.

Right down the middle of the staircase, where one would be expecting a mysterious, beautiful, other-worldly woman to appear, hurriedly clopped a middle-aged woman with frizzy salt-and-pepper hair pulled back from her homely face and held in place by a tight, wide elastic band. Her dress was a shapeless, sloppy one like my mother would embarrass me by wearing as a housedress. The woman stopped suddenly on the middle landing with one hand on her left hip, half-akimbo, and the other holding a cigarette. Her blue-and-white sneakers were toeless and the toenails that showed were painted red.

"Errr. . ." she cleared her throat before speaking. "What can I do for you?"

"I'm An-day Harrison," I explained. "I was sent here by Mrs. Madeline Dow of Mollusk Memorial High School to see about a summer job."

She descended the remaining stairs, taking a dramatic drag on her cigarette, like Bette Davis, throwing her head back as she did so. It was a mannerism which from a movie actress would have seemed special, but which, coming from her, a homely, dumpy woman, seemed both ludicrous and affected.

"Errr. . .yes, I've been expecting you," she said. "Your teacher gave you an impeccable reference. Won't you come over by the window and sit down, so that we might discuss terms?"

Her voice contrasted sharply with her amorphous appearance. She was so unattractive, but her voice was cultured and classy-sounding, like that of the summer ladies from Taunton Point. She had to be from New York or Philadelphia, probably some heiress from a rich, old family. She led me across the living room to an overstuffed sofa in front of the big picture window.

"Errr. . .this window isn't new," she said. "It's just one of the many unique features of this grand old house. It was installed at the time when the house was built in the late nineteenth century by a sea captain who then owned this whole Neck. Now, let's see: how old are you, Andy?"

"I'm sixteen, but I'll be seventeen in a few days."

"Errr. . .I see. Do you have a driver's license?"

"No, but I'm going to try and get one the first of July," I explained, worried that for the job she needed someone who drove.

"Errr. . .have you completed Driver's Education?"

"No, they don't offer Driver's Ed. at my high school, but my parents, who are both good drivers, have been teaching me."

"Errr. . .I suppose I should tell you," she said with a big Cheshire cat grin, "to whom you are speaking. My name is Miss Jean Meyer, and I'm the co-owner of the Manor. My partner is Mrs. Madella Richmond who'll be coming up from Connecticut later on, but she generally concurs with my choice of employees."

"Concurs, eh?" I thought. That was one of our junior year vocabulary words, along with "loquacious" and "akimbo," but I didn't remember what it meant exactly.

Miss Meyer chose her words carefully when she spoke, and this made me a mite nervous. After each statement or question, she would take another long drag on her cigarette, and clear her throat before beginning another sentence. It was an awkward interview because I sensed that she was as nervous as I was. She came off better, however, for she had more experience in such matters, a much larger vocabulary and a hand-dandy cigarette with which to gesture and punctuate. I don't know why it is but people who smoke always seem to be more thoughtful and intelligent, maybe because while they're taking a puff, they can think out what they're going to say next.

"Errr. . .let me tell you something about the nature of the job before we go any further. It consists primarily of helping around the kitchen before, during, and after mealtimes; washing dishes, keeping the stoves and pantry refrigerator cleaned, the coal stoves down in the cellar going, helping the cooks, that sort of thing. You'll be expected to help the guests with their luggage and set-ups for drinks; you'll have to carry wood to various fireplaces and light fires. It's largely a general handyman type of job, a little bit of everything. I'll prepare a weekly schedule for you so that everything doesn't come at once. You have afternoons off most days for a few hours between luncheon and dinner and one night off a week. The pay is eighty dollars a month plus tips. Errr. . .do you have any questions?"

The job description sounded fine to me, but what did I know? I wasn't sure what "set-ups" were then, but I decided not to look too ignorant and ask. Instead, I inquired, remembering my mother's concern, "If I get the job, will I be able to live in? It'll be hard for me to go back and forth every day to Taunton."

"Errr. . .well, I have two more boys to interview before I can be definite about anything. Could you possibly come down here next Saturday morning and stay over? Then we could see about a more permanent arrangement."

"Yes, I think I could," I said, wondering if she were planning to have the other two boys down also, all of us furiously competing to see who could wash dishes and stoke the coal stoves faster and more efficiently.

"Errr. . .Andy, did your mother by chance bring you down?"

Not by chance, but by Merc, I wanted to say.

"Yes, she's out in the car," I did say.

"Errr. . .you should have brought her in."

Suddenly, I was angry with Miss Meyer. Why should I have brought my mother in for her to meet? What's my mother got to do with my getting this job? Does she want to check on my working class background? See if I'm good enough to work here? See if my mother is a true Downeast hick? See my mother in her proper kerchief and housedress? So she can have a good sophisticated laugh to herself? Run and call Mrs. Richmond in Connecticut about this local hick Maine boy and his quaint Mom?

Anyway, whatever it was, at that point, I wanted to be done with the interview and on my way.

"I think I better be going now," I said. "My mother and I have to go to Ellsworth shopping."

Miss Meyer cleared her throat for the thousandth time.

"Errr. . .all right. I'm glad to have met you. Thank you for coming down. I hope to see you next Saturday morning. Don't forget to call me if you can't make it. Errr. . . what time do you think you could be here?"

"What time would you want me?"

"Errr. . .well, I think it's best to get off to an early start. There's lots that remains to be done and the first guests of the season arrive that afternoon. How about eight a.m.? Could you be here by then?"

"Yes," I said. "I think I can."

"Errr. . .good, then; it's settled. I expect you at eight on Saturday morning." She smiled her big grin again and shook my hand.

I walked quickly and self-consciously to the massive front door and opened it, remembering at that moment that it was too late to ask her if it was all right that I use this exit. I turned to look back across the room at Miss Meyer, who stood there fully akimbo, the smoke from her cigarette in her hand appearing to be wafting upwards from her hip.

Smoking from the hip, I thought to myself.

"Bye," I said.

"Errr. . .good-bye," she said.

I liked the way the big oversized door clicked shut behind me. It sounded as solid as it looked, and was rich and hand-carved. I didn't know if it was walnut or oak or mahogany; but it had been made to order, as was this kitchen boy job for me. I was very excited at my exit and rushed pell-mell across the graveled driveway, flinging myself onto the front seat of the Mighty Merc.

I told my mother right off that I was to come for an overnight the next weekend, and then added, "I think she liked me," realizing that that made all the difference in the world in getting a job or anything.

"Well," Sid said, "she asked you to come down again. That seems like a good indicator, but don't get your hopes up."

3

For the second time in a week, Mother Eleanor (I can't call her Sid now that I'm employed by such a posh place) delivered me via the plug-ugly driving machine to the Manor's back door once again.

"Don't let your big mouth get you in trouble now," my mom advised from the driver's seat. "Do what she tells you without acting as foolish as you usually do."

"Don't worry about me, toots! I'll bring home the bacon, and it'll be a fancier brand than Armour ever created! Thanks for driving me down to my destination. . .maybe even my destiny!"

"Maybe even your doom!" she said. "You call and let us know when they're through with you."

"Why, by tomorrow, my de-ah, I plan to be transformed from this ugly teenage duckling you see before you into a truly handsome and sophisticated swan prince!"

"Don't be smart now!" my mother intoned in her Voice of Correction, unimpressed by my bird imagery.

"You, too—and don't let the bucking Merc throw ya!"

"You'll probably be canned by this afternoon!" she hollered in retort; and even though I yelled back, "You believe in failure too much, Sid!" she didn't hear me, for the Merc's bald tires were spinning about in the gravel. She sped off through the long back driveway of cedar trees in the family coupe, the rear of which resembled a sad-faced fat cartoon car that had just been squashed in a demolition derby.

Then, stumbling, as an awkward and lanky teenage lout must, into the great kitchen, attired in my blue-and-white high school jacket with my cross country letter stitched on and toting my gym bag, I came face to face with Miss Meyer again. She was having her toast, coffee, and cigarette, taking the morning sun at the aluminum folding table. She asked me if I would like to join her. I said sure, and she poured me the best-tasting coffee I have ever swilled: strong, delicious, and as they say on TV, "full-bodied," or as my father would say, "a meal in itself." She even gave me real cream to go with it, unlike my parents who used canned milk. The toast was made of Pepperidge Farm bread, which I had never heard of before, and the plum jam that went with it was from England and came in a little tin bucket.

Speaking of buckets, Miss Meyer had her frizzy hair pulled back with a different colored hair band, but she still sported her toeless sneakers, which she probably thought were cool and sexy for the summer. I wondered if she thought the enormous bunions on her big toes were cool and sexy? Puffing furiously on one Marlboro cigarette after another, she told me next time definitely to have my mother come in so that she could meet her.

Next time? I asked myself. Was I definitely the New Boy in the Kitchen? Did I have the job?

After our toast and coffee and rather strained conversation (I could sense it was going to take some time before I could be myself with Miss Meyer), she showed me up to my room, which turned out to be this elegant guest room on the second floor. I was thrilled. I expected a cot behind the kitchen stove, or some other such third-rate accommodations good enough for a working class Maine boy who wouldn't know any better. The Number Nine Room, so named, overlooked the lawn down to the cliffs and bay and was decorated with oriental stuff like much of the rest of the Manor.

I didn't bother to unpack, for there was nothing to unpack except for the raggedy-ass cotton pajamas and equally ragged change of underwear and socks. Instead, I spent the allotted couple of minutes looking around the room and out the windows down at the ocean scene beyond the lawn, trees, and cliffs. Ah, what a view! And all mine for an evening! The ocean was much more spectacular from this location than it was from the cove at home up the coast.

Catching a glimpse of myself in the floor-length mirror, I sighed, "What's wrong with this picture?" Teenage goon stumbles by mistake into the Emperor Ching's Hotel! Mildly depressed whenever seeing my reflection so accurately and clearly displayed, I left the room, located the backstairs which led me down to the kitchen, and hurried down for further instructions.

My new bosslady, peering through her bifocals at piles of what appeared to be files of old recipes, and surrounded by dozens of brass and copper pieces, greeted me again with a list of what had to be done before lunch. First, there was the painting of the back porch toilet seat (I wanted to ask her if the guests were to be using it); then, there was the wood to be carried from the cellar to the various fireplaces throughout the house; and, finally, all the brass and copper andirons, decorative kettles and plates, and what-nots gathered about the kitchen tables had to be cleaned, polished, and put back in their respective places. Miss Meyer, in her nervous, fidgety way, impressed upon me the need to be hasty and efficient and correct as possible. She said if I needed anything she would be in her office near the lobby; and Hattie Pinkham, the head waitress and a long-time employee, would be upstairs making beds and cleaning bedrooms. Lunch would be served at the aluminum folding table for both Hattie and me at noon.

I finished the toilet painting in an hour and then began hauling the wood for the fireplaces. There were five such in use at the Manor, and these almost solely for decoration, since there was a coal furnace for central heat. What had to be done that first morning was not only to lay all the fires, but to stock all the window seats with a ready supply of dry firewood and kindling. In all the rooms, except the dining room, where there were fireplaces, there were these cushioned window seats under which were spaces for this extra wood, kindling, and newspapers. It took me a good hour and a half to finish the wood job.

After that I returned to the kitchen to begin work on the brass before lunch.

I started polishing and then Hattie joined me.

"Ain't this fun?" Hattie asked in this sarcastic voice, while snapping her chewing gum.

"Well, it has to be done," I answered in my good servant's voice.

Hattie, who was dark-haired like my mother and about the same vintage, lifted an eyebrow, and said, "Why, you must be sold on doin' your duty."

"Well, I want to work here."

"Oh? Hasn't she hired ya yet? I thought you were a foregone conclusion."

"No, I'm just here this weekend to see if I work out."

"Gee, do I get to pass judgment on your brass polishing? I don't know of anyone else she's mentioned except you."

"What about the other two boys?"

Hattie laughed. "Oh, no! Did you fall for that old one? She always says things like that to make ya think there's standing room only around the sink, dozens of hopeful people clamoring to wash the dishes. She thinks it's a good business practice. She's from New York, ya know, where they like to keep people guessin'."

Hattie had me confused, but I liked her very much right off.

"Here," she said, "give me a lobster pick, so's I can go after some of this green crud that's choking off the life of this bee-u-tee-ful artifact."

I handed her a pick from the silverware tray. "What causes crud, anyhow, Hattie?"

"Why, m'dear, it's that Maine salt air! It'll corrode anything!"

As she rattled on, I learned that Hattie had worked at the Manor for seven summers and had the run of the place. She was a little plump and old enough to be my mother, yet voluptuous (one of my favorite vocab. words) with big breasts. Her white waitress uniform fit snugly with not much room for breathing space, and she seemed to like it that way. When she brushed by me, or bent over me, she was so warm and smelled good.

She made her friendliness known to me through song. She started humming and then singing right there in the kitchen. As she polished a poker suggestively in front of me, she sang, "Take back your rumba, aye! Your samba, aye! Your mamba, aye yi yi!"

It was aye yi yi all right, I thought to myself. I might just be getting quite the education without even leaving the kitchen.

When we finished the brass, we gathered up all the pieces and Hattie, leading the way, showed me where things went.

"Walk THIS WAY, hon-ay!" she called back to me, swinging her hips and laughing.

"They say everything has its place, ya know," she said, "and that goddamn thunderjug you're toting can be shoved upstairs in the Number Five Room, or Pink Room, as Miss Meyer calls it. And God rest anyone's soul who dares to thunder in it!"

"Now, ya take them period pieces you're carrying—one of 'em goes in the guests' dining room and the other one goes in the living room. Don't get your periods mixed up with your pieces; if ya get things out of kilter, there's apt to be repercussions!"

Handing me a brass Buddha, Hattie said, "Put this old sourpuss in his place by the front door. He's too damn mean to smile from within, so we have to hope that the sun, or at least a GE light bulb, will do the job!"

And so it went, upstairs and down and all around. When we had finished, and were glancing around the lobby and living room, I learned the value of a pretty shining object in a darkly wooded place, like the brass Buddha glowing from a corner of the richly carpeted entranceway.

It was afternoon by then, and Hattie and I went to the back dining room. After fixing our grub, Hattie sat across the table from me, a sandwich in her right hand.

"Get the logs laid, An-day?"

"Yes," I said.

"Well, when ya get 'em laid right, there's apt to be a good blaze," she said, her words dripping with double entendre.

"That's what they tell me," I said, realizing that I wasn't much of a match for her in the word play department.

"Oh, An-day, I hope you don't have to be told," Hattie said with a mischievous wink.

"Hattie, you're incredible."

"I'm glad you think so, m'boy. Others say I'm simply impossible."

We schlurped the soup, first hot, then warm, then cool. But Hattie couldn't stand even partial silence for long.

"You attend Mollusk Memorial High, the clamdigger's prep school, dontcha?"

"Yeah," I said. "I'll be a senior in September."

"Well, whoop-de-do! Do you happen to know a tall, dark, and handsome lad named Arthur Heckman?"

"Yes, somewhat," I replied. "He was in my phys. ed. class last year. He's a year behind me."

"No kiddin'! Well, I could tell you're way ahead of your time, An-day, old boy; but you don't have to brag. I just wanted to know if ya knew my one and only son." And then, she added quickly, as if to explain the difference in surnames, "I've been married twice. Twice-burnt, that is."

"Do you have any other kids?"

"Glory Smith. She lives up the road apiece in the Maine Native Section of town with her fisherman husband and her two kids—my grandchildren! She was at Mollusk, too, for a while, but she got too big for her little schooldesk. Like mother, like daughter, you see. Both of us would have been val-a-dick-torians if we'd used our brains instead of other parts of our anatomy."

At this point, a car drove down the front driveway. We heard the gravel crunch under the wheels, and Hattie jumped up and went to the window.

"Good gawd almighty! They're here already and it's not even one o'clock! Put on ya red cap, An day!"

"What red cap?"

"Just an expression, hon-ay! The porters on THE BAR HARBOR EXPRESS wear red caps, ya know? The guys who tote the luggage? Just like Maine guys hunting in November."

"Who just drove in?"

"Why, it's the WONDERFUL WERTSES, the first guests of this and every season! Wait till ya see 'em, but don't wait around for any tip! There's only one reason why guests like them come off-season: off-rates! They only come in June or September, never in July or August. Finish eatin' quick, An-day! You won't feel much like it after you've met the Wertses!"

I didn't even have time to do what Hattie suggested, because at that moment Miss Meyer rushed into the room all aflutter.

"Errr. . .Andy, take off your apron, right away, and come get some bags, will you?"

"Yes, be right there," I said, wolfing down the remains of my sandwich and slipping off the gray kitchen apron.

The greeting of actual guests to the hotel seemed to unnerve Miss Meyer as much as an inexperienced actress before the curtain goes up. She scurried before me like a funny, plump, little mouse-woman as fast as she could go, swaying from side to side, puffing on her

Marlboro, hurrying to the front door; and I rushed after, tucking my shirt into my jeans.

Just as Miss Meyer opened the front door, a shiny gray Mercedes-Benz pulled under the *porte-cochère* , and from its passenger side, almost before the car came to a complete stop, emerged the bright red-haired Mrs. Wert, hailing Miss Meyer by her Christian name.

"Jean! We'd better be FIRST! We're ALWAYS THE FIRST, you know!" she exclaimed. "We've been the first since 1947!"

"Errr. . .so nice to have you back, Esther."

Mrs. Wert rushed up the front steps to where we were standing and took Miss Meyer's hand and pumped it excitedly.

"SUCH a trip we had, Jean! Everything was so GREEN and FRESH! This is THE TIME to travel, before the summer press is really on! The roads are so CLOGGED in July and August and it gets worse every year, like a SWARM OF LOCUSTS who leave a path of UTTER DESTRUCTION in their wake! DIXIE CUPS line the highway! Now, Jean" (she said, looking up at me), "is this the NEW BOY, standing by, on call, ready to help us this time around?"

Mrs. Wert turned toward me, towering above her, and Miss Meyer said, "Errr. . .yes, this is Andrew Harrison, Esther. He'll be with us this season."

"So I got the job!?" I almost yelled aloud. What a way to find out.

"So NICE to meet you, Andrew," said Mrs. Wert. "C'mon down to carside and meet THE OLD GRAY DOG!" She chuckled before and after everything she said, as if everything she said was marvelously amusing.

Mrs. Wert had tight red curls in her hair, and like many other redheads I've known, she often wore green and purple. That day she was attired in an expensive-looking, well-tailored green suit and green hat with matching green pumps and handbag. She could be called Mrs. VERT (one of my French vocab. words). Her husband, the old gray dog, who is also known as Fred, finally emerged from the driver's side of the Mercedes. I was beginning to think he was her aged chauffeur or a cripple who had to be helped from the car.

"Fred, here's ANDY to help us with our ENTOURAGE," said the Female-in-Charge.

"Hiya, Andy!" said Mr. Wert, putting all six-foot-something of him behind his crushing handshake.

"Hi!" I said, meek and mild in the presence of one of the best-dressed and most self-assured gentlemen I had ever seen up till then. He was the living and breathing illustration of "urbane," one of our junior year vocab. words. Fred Wert the Dog was so urbane that with a patch over one of his eyes, he could have modeled Hathaway shirts.

Mr. Wert opened the trunk of the car, which glistened with cleanliness even from the inside. Even his jack looked freshly polished. Arranged neatly in the center of the trunk were three compact bags to be handled.

"I think you're a strong enough lad to tote these three at once, eh?" he asked, grinning his manly grin at me.

"Oh, sure," I said.

The bags, however, were packed with cement. I managed to carry them upstairs to the Number Four Room, the best suite in the house and one of only three with its own private bathroom. As soon as the guests were sufficiently greeted, Miss Meyer had disappeared into some hole in the wall. At Number Four, I placed the suitcases on the racks at the foot of each of the twin beds, as Hattie had instructed me. Mr. Wert placed a quarter in my hand; we said thank you together, and he asked me to bring "set-ups" right away.

I still didn't know what "set-ups" were. I knew from reading Dick Tracy comics and crime novels all my life that people were always being "set-up" by someone wanting to do them harm; but I hurried downstairs to the kitchen and told Miss Meyer I needed set-ups right away for the Wertses. She told me to get a small tray from the butler's pantry and to ask Hattie for the rest. The mystery as to what exactly constituted set-ups was being unraveled as I raced about the kitchen and pantries following Mrs. Pinkham's instructions.

"Out back, An-day, in the back fridge, grab some splits of ginger ale, tonic, and soda."

"What are splits?" I asked.

"Well, they ain't banana, I can tell ya! Try the little baby bottles of ginger ale, club soda, and Schweppe's tonic water—the six packs—on the floor under the onions."

From the back pantry I procured the splits, and then the cocktail glasses, ice and an ice bucket, napkins, crackers, cocktail shaker, a plate of fresh lemon, lime, and orange slices, a small dish of olives, onions, and cherries. The way Hattie arranged everything on the tray, the set-ups looked very inviting.

"O.K., An-day, them's set-ups! Now ya know, to make it easier next time on both of us, be sure to ask what types of drinks they're planning to get juiced on so's we can spare the soda or whatever. It seems to me that he likes martinis and she likes Manhattans, but I can't remember. This way, without knowing, we had to set up for the works; and there'll be a lot of waste. Any questions?"

"Nope. Looks good to me."

"What wouldn't to you? Why, you're just a poor little Downeast herring chocker who's never even sipped a martini!" She laughed and shoved my shoulder. "Say, whisk that stuff away to the Wertses before the ice melts! They probably need a few drinks before they have to watch each other get dressed for dinner!"

After I returned from this delivery with another quarter, Hattie asked me how much of a tip I received for services rendered.

I showed her the total of fifty cents with which Mr. Wert had greased my palm.

"My God, could they spare it? Don't spend it all in one place, An-day, unless you're only shopping in Summer Harbor where there IS only one place!"

"At least they tipped. I thought at first he was going to lug everything in himself."

"He's got enough to support with that dizzy dame he's hitched to. Don't she just love to hear herself talk, though? You'd think she had just regained her powers of speech!"

"She laughs at her own jokes."

"She has to! They're far too witty and subtle for the rest of us to get! She's a phys. ed. teacher at Smith College, after all!"

"Oh, she probably means all right," I said.

"Are you kidding? Take a good look under those dyed-red curliques some time. There's a bitch of the first water."

"What do you mean by 'first water'?"

"Well, I suppose, the first water would be the water drained off the top. So, she's top bitch. I don't know; it's an old saying, and I'm just an old sayer. All I know is what I half-read in the *Reader's Digest*, and that's condensed! Remember, star pupil, I never got through high school, so don't expect no fancy translations. I have to get by on my beauty and charm!"

We had hardly turned around when the other expected guests arrived: two spinster ladies in a green '58 Chevy Custom Tudor, Miss

Bolster and Miss Gentle.

"Off with the Wertses and on with the old maids!" Hattie said, as we watched the Chevy pull under the *porte-cochère* . "Get out there, An-day, and strut your stuff!"

"Yeah, right."

"C'mon, boy! You've got some cute stuff there to strut. Ya just gotta learn how."

"You'll teach me?"

"Well, I don't know how much time I've got for tutoring these days!" Hattie laughed her great laugh, which, when she did it, made you want to laugh, too. "Just walk tall, An-day. You are tall, so keep your shoulders upright. Don't hunch over. Don't scamper like Miss Meyer! Show some class and masculine cool." She winked. "And make sure your fly is zipped up."

So I tried walking tall and cool down the hall, and this time the tip was bigger and so were the suitcases.

Upon returning to the kitchen, I called out, "Hey, Hattie! My stock has risen!" I showed her the two dollars.

"Oh, these old maids will always shell out their pension money on you young bucks. It's as if they're still hoping against hope."

"Hoping for what?"

Hattie laughed. "Oh, An-day, YOU ARE JUST SIXTEEN, ain't ya? Haven't you ever heard of a gigolo?" And she started singing, "I'm just a gigolo, everywhere I go . . ."

"Spanish dancers? Italian gamblers, or con men?"

"Could be. They do come in all shapes, sizes, professions, and nationalities; but they're more apt to be just no-good bums."

"But why would such ladies hope that I was a bum?"

"Because bums are more fun," Hattie said.

Puzzling over that idea, I stood there in the kitchen for a few minutes watching Hattie and Miss Meyer begin dinner preparations. Miss Meyer suggested that I go in the living room and light a fire, turn some of the lights on, and put some dinner music on the record player.

"And that don't mean Bill Haley and the Comets!" said Hattie.

The record turntable and speaker were cleverly concealed in this massive, hand-carved wooden sea chest which stood nearby the dining room entrance. With soft music, a few soft lights, and a fire flickering from the fireplace, the atmosphere of the Manor became steadily more warm and romantic as the sun went down beyond Mount Desert

Island.

Before the scene became so cheery, though, I had trouble lighting the fire. The guests were already there, arranged in their chairs about the hearth, watching every move I made, which made me nervous. Since this was the first fire I had had to start up to this point, I was none too sure of my materials or techniques, and hardly in need of an attentive audience. I struggled a while with the kindling, the logs, the newspapers, the bellows and poker, piling, stuffing, and rearranging and nursing the tender little flamettes with every bit of Boy Scout craft and common sense I could muster.

When the four guests saw I was having difficulty, everyone offered suggestions or explanations of what I should do. Mrs. Wert said, "Andy, dear, perhaps the wood is TOO WET. You know, it has to DRY OUT before burning; maybe it's TOO GREEN. . ."

"No!" I wanted to yell, "YOU'RE TOO GREEN!" She even had on this green silken cocktail gown.

"Haw, haw!" shrieked Miss Bolster, one of the old maids, but more like an old man, I thought. "I thought these Maine woodsmen could start a good fire in a blinding snowstorm with just a rock and a couple of twigs. Aren't you a good Maine woodsman, Andy? Haw, haw, haw!"

"I guess I'm not as much of a man as you are, Bolster Baby!" I said to myself.

Mr. Wert intervened. "Here, let me have the poker. It's not a very good one. Here, I'll stir it up some more. I think you've got too much newspaper and not enough good pieces of kindling."

"Yeah, that's it, Fred!" said Bolster, clutching her drink, which I had just learned was what they called an old-fashioned, full of orange peels. "Stir 'er up, poke 'er where it'll do some good! We longs to roast our tootsies! Haw, haw, haw!"

Miss Gentle, the only one not offering me any advice, sat ramrod straight on the edge of one of the big bright chairs, simply smiling at the proceedings.

Frustrated as hell at this point, I remembered the kerosene pot by the fireplace and doused the highly flammable liquid over the smoldering blaze. It worked—too well! There was a brilliant flash of light, which probably singed Mr. Wert's well-knitted eyebrows, caused a loud whoop from Miss Bolster as she nearly got more than her tootsies roasted, and sent a gigantic roar up the chimney. For one horrible moment I thought that the chimney would catch on fire.

"Man has always had to help nature along, it seems," said Mrs. Wert chuckling.

"Here's to man's ingenuity and especially to the man who first refined kerosene!" guffawed Miss Bolster, raising her glass.

"You know, Andy," said Mr. Wert, placing his mighty hand on my bony shoulder, "that was the lazy man's way of getting the fire going, and a very dangerous thing for you to have done." His face was a mask of Sunday school seriousness. Mr. Wert, I could tell, always knew best. That's why he drove a Mercedes-Benz.

"I know, sir," I said. "I'm sorry."

I was seriously beginning to question my Boy Scout inventiveness at this point and fully expected to be canned on the spot once word got back to my boss. Instead, much to my relief, he patted me on the back.

Hattie rang the dinner gong, which was like a baby xylophone played with a leather covered drumstick. For my entertainment, she threw in a few extra notes. By nine p.m. or so, my duties for my first day on the job were done. I had finished up the kitchen pots and pans and taken the garbage out.

Hattie went home to her "little divorcee's shack," as she put it; and Miss Meyer, relieved to have some paying guests in the house, sat nursing a bottle of Miller High Life while smoking her hundredth cigarette of the day.

I climbed the back stairs to my fancy room, exhausted but satisfied that I had learned the ropes and had passed inspection pretty well. And delighted that I had the job.

So it came to pass that I, Andrew Francis Harrison, spent my first overnight in a real honest-to-goodness mansion by the sea, enthralled by the sumptuous appointments of my elegant suite, soothed by the restless roar of the primeval ocean, fascinated by the lights a-twinkling from Cadillac Mountain and Mount Desert Island, transfixed by the flashing red light from Egg Rock out in the bay, and excited as hell about working and living in such a fabulous joint. Ah, yes, I thought to myself, while snuggling amongst the fanciest sheets, blankets, and bedspread I had ever had the pleasure of rolling around in, this is the life for me.

Of course, I hardly slept a wink, but I slept NUDE! My raggedy cheap cotton pjs simply didn't look right in such fancy digs. Ruined the whole spell, so I cast them off, threw them aside, stuffed them into my all-purpose gym bag (my luggage!), put the bag and all my other poorboy clothes in the closet and closed the door. Banished from sight—for the night at least. I was coming naked into my new life.

4

I went back home to Taunton on Sunday. I had been chosen by the seniors as the junior student to lead them as class marshal down the aisle at graduation. I also had final exams, the end of school; and after that about two weeks in which to finish up with my lawn-mowing customers and help my parents and relatives open up and clean a number of summer cottages on Taunton Point.

Miss Meyer wanted me back to the Manor for the rest of the summer just before July Fourth, at which time the hotel, she promised, would be teeming with well-heeled guests desirous of my humble services and ready with handsome tips.

That particular night Mother Sid, Father Frank, and I dined on fried tripe and stewed tomatoes. Chomping away at one point, I told Sid that no one had to tell me what the expression "tough as tripe" means.

"Just be sure you eat everything on your plate," she replied tartly.

Of course, both my mother and father knew how ultra-excited I was to be leaving home and being gone for the summer, being on my own. While we supped on cow's stomach, all white and rubbery and vinegary, I got 'em talking about their earliest jobs as Maine kids in the Mount Desert Island area. Dad was a dockhand at fourteen, and even a life boatman, on the Maine Central steamboats on Frenchman's

Bay. He quit school at the end of the eighth grade to work on the boats and there he stayed until he was into his twenties and the steamboats were a thing of the past.

"I'd always hung around the Mount Desert Ferry dock," he said, "and the train station, too, and knew all the men who worked there. When I finished grade school here in town—there was no high school here in those years—I was ready to work on the boats, and at fourteen I started as a deckhand."

"Did you have to have an interview?" I asked.

"Hell, no. I showed up one Monday morning, and they put me to work. That would have been June of 1921—almost forty years ago!—and I worked for the Maine Central Railroad Company until 1930 when the boats stopped running on Frenchman's Bay."

"What did you do on the boats?"

"Oh, the things they'd let a kid do. I helped keep the decks cleaned, emptied the garbage, helped load and unload the freight, helped the cooks. We had to keep the passenger area nice and clean. They gave ya all kinds of jobs at first to see what you were good at. I watched the men and saw how they did things, and little by little, they let me do the harder jobs."

It always amazed me, when I stopped to consider it, just how many jobs my father could do. He was like so many Maine men that I knew growing up: very self-sufficient, largely self-taught, and incredibly capable. Besides being a crack shot with a deer rifle, he could splice a rope better than anyone around town. Lobstermen and other boat owners were always asking him to splice some of their rotten ropes together; and he always did it so they looked brand-new. He had learned how to splice ropes and caulk boats when he worked for Maine Central. My father also did most of his own car repair, carpentry, electrical work, and plumbing. He shingled our roof, painted the house, and cut up his November deer kill with minimal help from his sons.

My mother was no slouch either when it came to multiple skills. I asked Sid when she first left home to work on Taunton Point, and she said she was eleven when she started baby-sitting for a rich Bangor lumber dealer's son, who was about four.

"Did you have to go for an interview?"

"Heavens, no. The Point people all knew our family, so this woman asked my mother; and they decided I was old enough to baby-sit. The first day, and this would have been the summer of 1927, they came and got me; but for the rest of the summer, I walked back and forth from the Ferry to the Point—a daily walk of four miles round trip."

From that summer until age seventeen, Sid began her life of working away from the family farm where she had learned to be an expert cook, seamstress, and housemaid. By age fifteen, as an assistant to a cook, she had learned how to set a table for an elegant dinner party on Taunton Point; and by age seventeen, she was a cook herself in a summer place that also employed two maids, a nanny, and a chauffeur.

"Did you ever serve tripe to the summer people?" I asked Sid.

"No. Tripe's kitchen food for us kitchen folk."

Expanding on that theme, my father, with what was left of his hair hanging in his face as usual, expounded upon his negative philosophy of life, telling me I shouldn't get myself all worked up over some lousy, low-paying job in a summer hotel, since I would soon find out that there was not much future in it and that most jobs in the world "for people like us" are pretty goddamn tedious.

"You mean," I asked, "like in the song 'Life Gits Tee-Jus, Don't It'?" And I started imitating singer Tex Williams:

> Ya open the door, and the flies swarm in.
> Ya close the door, and yer sweatin' agin!
> Life gits tee-jus, don't it?

"Don't start being a smartmouth!" warned Dad.

"But I am a smartmouth!" I protested. "My teachers have always told me so, and treated me accordingly. They call me An-day Smartmouth, the smartest boy in the Class of 1960!"

"Just keep it up," growled the Old Man, his mouth rubbery with tripe, his fangs dripping juicy red with succulent tomato parts, brandishing his stainless steel fork in my youthful countenance.

After the tripe and tomatoes on that sultry June night in 1959, I couldn't rush right back upstairs to my teenage haven with my 45s, my magazines and books, and my writing journal of wet and dry dreams; but had to accompany my parents once again to Taunton Point where they would deliver laundry and check out the pipes under one of the summer cottages. Besides driving an oil truck as his regular job, my father also gave haircuts on Sundays to neighborhood men, and was the caretaker for two summer places. My mother also took in laundry and did sewing jobs, as well as cleaning cottages, working as a cook and housekeeper for the summer people.

Frank, Sid, and I motored down to The Point in our luxurious '51 Mercury, which my brother Bobber had bequeathed us in 1956 when he left for his three-year stint in the Air Force stationed in Germany. Sid and Frank, as usual, were dressed like immigrants from the Old Country. She had on her multi-purpose, shapeless housedress and kerchief and he sported his best undershirt with complementary baseball cap. They stayed in the car while I tripped down the graveled path with the laundry to this ultra-modern summer beach house perched on the rocks overlooking Frenchman's Bay. What a shock greeted me right after pressing the doorbell (one of the very few to press in Taunton at that time) for that night I caught my first glimpse of a real-life cocktail party on Taunton Point. Both nervous and excited, I stood there in the doorway a-trembling, looking like a total teenage goofball with this laundry basket with a bill from my mother pinned on the top.

"Make sure she sees that," my mother had forewarned from the car. Luckily, Mrs. Vera Anderson, one of my favorite summer women, answered her own door, saying with a great grin, loudly to my super-sensitive ears, "Oh, for heaven's sake! It's Andy Harrison with the laundry! Just in time for a fresh change!"

While she went for her pocketbook, I stood there awkwardly gawking at the handsome men in dinner jackets and the lovely women in cocktail dresses, all of them with fancy-looking drinks in their hands and framed by the floor-to-ceiling windows against the brilliantly blue background of the bay and the Mount Desert Hills at early evening, the lights just beginning to twinkle from across the water. I felt very shabby, out-of-place, and utterly unworldly. My parents, our relatives, and friends never held such parties at set hours all dressed up. They would get together in our kitchen on a Saturday night or on some special occasion, like someone's anniversary, and drink Narragansett Beer and Four Roses whiskey served with ginger ale in all purpose tumblers or in paper cuts. The men would often excuse themselves to take a piss off our porch or out on the lawn under the locust trees.

As soon as Mrs. Anderson had paid me, I scrambled back up the bank from the elegant cottage (designed, I found out years later, by some noted MIT architect who had built the first "modern house" north of Boston) to the roadside where my parents were waiting. I must have looked as if I had just gazed upon the Forbidden Society, because of the way my parents looked back at me. I gave my mother the money, crawled into the back seat and exclaimed, "Wow! You ought to see the party they're having. What an impressive-looking group of cool people!"

All my father said, with a grump, as we drove away, was, "They take a shit the same way we do!"

While my father was right in the biological sense, I remember thinking to myself, "Yes, but these types don't defecate in the same places. They have marble bathrooms with a view of the sea. And their fecal matter, I'm quite sure, is made up of fancier waste products."

Anyway, that evening, once again, I caught a glimpse of the world I wanted to join. But how to get there? I was sure by getting a job at the hotel where such summer folk came and went from all over, where I'd be living in close proximity to them, I'd find the key.

On our way home from the Andersons', we stopped briefly at the Connellys' summer cottage, so my multi-talented Dad-of-all-Trades could check his latest plumbing job. He had tried to fix this pipe under the kitchen sink a couple of days before, and he wanted to check it to see if it was still dripping. I had to go with him and hold the flashlight under the house so he could see, for the electricity hadn't been turned on for the summer. "The Connellys" were actually three old maids from New Jersey, two of them schoolteachers, and one of them, Evelyn Connelly, the vice president of some big company in New York City. Evelyn actually owned the place, which included land that stretched from one side of The Point to the other, but it was her younger sister Laura and Laura's friend Cora Evangeline Braley who spent most of the summer at "Geranium Cottage." The Connellys' nephew Tommy, who was about my age and size, would send me a box of his discarded clothes at the end of every summer for use as my "new school clothes" in the fall. In my senior year in high school, my classmates were to vote me "best-dressed boy" on the basis of Tommy Connelly's discards.

At the height of the summer season, our house was turned into a laundry. I would eat my breakfast under the overhead racks of dripping underwear and linen. My mother's huge white mangle, a professional ironing machine and one of the prized appointments of our kitchen, was always humming away, pressing the dozens of sheets, napkins, and pillow cases. Because we had to be careful in our old house about not putting too much strain on the few electrical outlets and extension cords, my father was always hollering upstairs to me, "Turn off your radio! Your mother's on the mangle!"

5

In making the big move from home to the hotel, I had some trouble with a few disgruntled lawn-mowing customers who didn't want to lose me—and with the Mermaid of Warren Cove, Essie Torrey, the girl who thought I was cute without my glasses and the bane of my growing-up years. I called her "The Mermaid" because that's what she seemed when I first met her. My cousin, Lillie Partridge, and I, who were swimming one summer afternoon in Warren Cove, an inlet of Frenchman's Bay named for our ancestors, when who would dive off her father's lobster boat and swim underwater but Essie.

She emerged out of the freezing salt water covered in seaweed and throwing small live crabs at us.

"Hey, who are you?" Lillie asked.

"If she's a mermaid," I said, "she ought to have a tail."

"I AIN'T GOT NO TAIL, BUT IF YOU DON'T GIT OFF MY FATHER'S BEACH, I'M GONNA THROW CRABS AND SEA-WEED AT YA!" she yelled.

We laughed at her. "This beach belongs to our grandparents!" I yelled back, and then started wading in waist-deep water out towards her. She dove under again and came right at me. I yelled when she grabbed my crotch and pulled me under. I came up spouting sea water, splashing about and gulping for air. She was up on the shore by then pointing at me and laughing.

"YOU MIGHT BE A BOY, BUT I CAN BEAT YA!"

I scrambled out of the water ready to bash her brains in on the rocky beach, but Lillie, ever the peacemaker, persuaded us both to settle down and to have some picnic lunch with her. I think I was about to go into the fourth grade that fall, while Essie, who had just moved to Taunton, would be in the third grade with Lillie. We munched on our peanut butter sandwiches and Devil Dogs while swilling soda pop and finding out about each other.

Essie told us that her father had built the new one-story house with the big picture window up on the shore road overlooking the Cove. He was a fisherman and had bought the land, two houselots, from our uncle, Oliver Warren, for $300. She lived there with her parents, and two younger brothers. The Torrey house was new but already there were piles of junk, as well as stacks of lobster traps, a couple of overturned rowboats, and assorted pieces of machinery around it.

Even as a child, Essie was striking looking. She was tall for her age and very tan. Her thin lips would break into this great wild grin. After first meeting her, Lillie said, "I think she looks like an Indian."

That fall, Essie joined us at the Taunton Ferry School; and one of the first things she did to me one recess was to pull my pants down out in the woods behind the school's outhouse. Out on the playground, she proved she could also play baseball better than most of us boys. She was always whooping, yelling, speaking out of turn, and getting into trouble. And she was always at me: winking at me from across the multi-graded classroom, grabbing at me at recess, hauling me down into the woods, peeking at me in the boy's room when I was trying to change into my basketball uniform or swim trunks. "I see you, Anday!" she'd say with a giggle. She could be a lot of fun, but I was such a serious and studious boy, trying to get "A's" from my teachers and make my mother beam with pride over my perfect rank card. And I was always working.

When I wasn't mowing lawns and helping my parents with their care-taking chores on Taunton Point, I'd be helping my Uncle Oliver on the "Milk Drive," delivering milk, cream, and eggs from his pickup truck around town; or I'd be cleaning out the barn at my grandfather Warren's farm; or helping my Uncle Owen in his saw mill. And even in grammar school, I was saving my money for college, because I wanted to go; but my father said we weren't rich, and I'd have to pay my own way.

One time I was scraping the cow manure down the trough behind the cows in my grandfather's barn when who should hail me from the entrance into the barn proper but Essie. Her father was visiting my Uncle Owen and Essie found out that I was there.

"Come wrestle in the hay, An-Day!" she hollered.

"I've got cow shit and piss all over me, Ess-ay," I said.

"Oh, you've always got some excuse for not playing with me. You're such a mama's boy and always just with Lill-ay."

"I've got to get this barn cleaned up before the cows start shitting again."

"OH, SHIT! SHIT! SHIT! MAMA'S BOY! MAMA'S BOY!"

I dropped my shovel and went after her; and we did wrestle in the hay. I tickled her all over until she screeched and howled. Then, I stopped and she started kissing me. We had hay all over us. Suddenly, she pulled away from me and said, "Gawd, An-day! You DO stink!"

"Well, no worse than you do after you've been out on your father's lobster boat with pails of rotten bait."

She laughed. "I smell like fish bait and you smell like cow shit."

"So, together we oughta smell pretty good," I said.

That became our little joke. From then on our terms of endearment for each other were "Fish Bait" and "Cow Shit."

When I was in the ninth grade at Mollusk Memorial High, and Essie was in the eighth grade, we both were invited to this birthday skating party at the Rainbow Roller Rink on the Bar Harbor Road near the bridge to Mount Desert Island. It was 1957, and I was wearing my first brand-new pair of Levi's and Essie was in one of her cowgirl outfits with a fringe skirt and blouse with a neckerchief and cowboy hat. We had fun trying to out-race each other around the rink.

There was an undercurrent of heat at the rink with the continuous whir of the wheels on the hardwood floor. The place was overheated with four huge oil stoves going full blast. With the organ music playing, the whole place reeked of popcorn, hot dogs, mustard, sweat, and cheap perfume. There was a penned-in area where one put one's skates on and waited before all the young animals were let loose upon the floor.

That night Essie skated up behind me and yelled, "Hey Cow Shit! Watch out for Fish Bait! I'm gonna stink ya out!"

Later in the evening, when we were having a break sipping our Cokes, she suggested that we go outside in the parking lot, where most of the older teenagers were half the time, smoking, drinking, and necking in the cars.

Essie led me to our Taunton neighbor's Pontiac station wagon that we had come in with a few other kids. We climbed in the back seat and I didn't even protest. She said she wanted me to see something. Before I knew what was happening, she had her cowgirl blouse opened up, her bra off, and had taken my hands to feel her breasts. She had really developed in a year, and had a great-looking body for a fourteen-year-old.

"Look at these tits I've got!" she said. "Are they better than Lill-ay's? I'm sure they're bigger."

As I fumbled with her breasts, she started kissing me; and then she said, "I've showed ya what I've got; now let's see yours."

"You've already seen me."

"Not hard, and you've got a hard-on, haven't ya? I can feel it."

She already had my Levis unzipped and her hand on my erection, pulling it out, with the exclamation, "An-day! You've got the biggest dink! Yours is bigger than any I've seen yet!"

"Have you seen all the boys' dinks?"

"In your class and mine," she said, squeezing and pulling on my manhood.

"Don't pull so!" I protested.

"Oh, I'm sorry. I didn't mean to hurt ya! It's just so exciting. I love dinks! Can I kiss it?"

I let her kiss it, but that was all.

"Stop it, Ess-ay! We shouldn't be doing this!" I started to tuck myself back into my tight Levis, quite the difficulty in the back seat of a car.

Essie protested: "Other boys would want me to suck on it! What's the matter with you? You're not like other boys, An-day! You must save it for cousin Lill-ay! Or those smart girls you're always with. I'm not good enough!"

I struggled out of the car, trying to zip up my pants, walking stiffly back toward the roller rink, with Essie behind me laughing at the way I looked.

"You better not go in the rink looking like that, Cow Shit! They'll know that the Mama's Boy has such a hard-on he can't walk straight!"

I didn't do any more skating that night. I stood around on the sidelines eating hot dogs and drinking Coke, watching Miss Mermaid go sailing by, giving me the finger, and yelling at me at one point, "Hey, Mister Super Dink—you stink!"

Up until that night, the only other girl I had really been naked with had been Cousin Lillie. As childhood companions, we had gone swimming naked together, gone through puberty together, played with each other. Because of the closeness of my relationship with my cousin, I hadn't ever really needed to be with other girls. She was the most attractive, intelligent, and humorous girl I had ever known. And even though Essie realized how very close Lillie and I were, she kept trying to make a difference.

By the time she was a freshman in high school, Essie had quite a reputation; but it didn't seem to cramp her style. She'd strut down the hall in her cowgirl boots and hat grabbing all the guys by their crotches. She stopped grabbing me, however; but on the schoolbus she'd often slide into the seat beside me and we'd have these little private talks and jokes with each other. I was a college prep. student and she was a vocational student, so we had different friends and different worlds that seemed to be growing further and further apart. She was already going out with guys who had cars, Navy Base boys from out-of-state. By the time she was sixteen, she was a tough-looking babe, tough in all ways. She was a great but undisciplined athlete. She hated the way girls used to have to play basketball, only allowed to run for half the court. She was always fouling out of games and getting into know-down, drag-out fights. Essie was a good fighter.

One night as I was getting off the Taunton schoolbus to go for my piano lesson, Essie and her low-class gang, smoking cigarettes, started making fun of me, calling me "Liberace."

I couldn't believe it when I turned around and looked her in the face, and she and her leather jacket crowd were mocking me. She kept it up until I picked up my physics book, and let her have it as hard as I could right in the face. That shut them all up, no one on the bus said anything, including the bus driver; and I just gathered up my books and got off.

That summer of 1959, I was mowing a lawn down at Taunton Ferry near Essie's house, when she came up behind me and grabbed the ass of my Levis.

"Oh, An-day, you should wear tight Levis, because you have a great ass and legs! Guys' asses in Levis are so great-looking."

"Oh, Ess-ay."

"I just want ya to know, Mr. Cow Shit, Mr. Vice President of the Junior Class, that even though you'll be way down at Summer Harbor all summer, that you won't be escaping me. I'll be down there, too, as much as possible, since my new boyfriend is from there. So plan on seeing me, when I can sneak away from him. I plan to haunt you always!"

That's all I needed to hear—her continuing to bother me even when I was living at the hotel.

"Ess-ay, don't you understand how I have worked as hard as I can to save money for college? That's what I'm doing. It's not that I don't like you, or don't want to fool around with you. YOU ARE INCREDIBLE; and I want you to be happy. It's just that I can't be with you all the time; and I want to leave Taunton Ferry and even Eastern Maine. I don't want to live around here."

"You mean you don't want to live *like we do*? You don't want to live in a shack by thc shore digging clams for a living? You want to be rich and get to wear a suit to work and be with all the fancy intellectual-type people?"

"Yeah, I'm afraid I do."

"Oh, An-day! I wish I didn't like you so much. You really can be such a goddam prissy snot! And you're just a truck driver's son! Your relatives are fishermen and dig clams, working class people, same as mine! What are you—*ashamed of your heritage*? Well, I've always known I wasn't good enough for you. I don't fit into your upper-class plans!"

We stood there in misery and frustration. She finally walked away, and I started up the lawnmower again, thinking to myself that she must understand, but that maybe she couldn't see how I equated having sex at an early age with how so many Maine people ended up. My own mother had to leave school when she was a junior and pregnant. There went her dreams of going to college and becoming a teacher. My parents, neither of them high school graduates, were always encouraging me to get as much education as possible, to get a good job, and not to end up living like they had to; working hard at physical labor for low wages. Every time I fooled around with Essie, and we were getting all excited, I could see my mother's frowning face; and I could hear my father, and other relatives saying, "If you don't get out of Maine by eighteen, you'll never get out."

6

Unlike the fancy guest room I stayed in for my first night at the Manor, my permanent room for the first four summers at the hotel was on the third floor at one end of what was actually the great, long attic which ran the length of the top of the house. Two flights up from the kitchen, the room was painted a sunny yellow with a gray floor. There was one window overlooking the garage roof; and if one craned one's neck, one could see the ocean, as well as the patio down below of the cottage next door. There was a single Hollywood bed with a night table and lamp; also a chair, a bureau, and a hat rack, all painted white. A small mirror was nailed on the wall above the bureau and on the floor was a small white throw rug.

Ah, my writer's roost! My artist's lair! My garret!

My books-to-be-read-by-the-end-of-the-summer were piled by the bed along with my Voice-of-Music record player and a few favorite LPs and 45s. There wasn't to be a typewriter until the summer of 1960 when I was trying to teach myself to type, so there were only my cheap notebooks and journal into which I was scribbling and making lists all the time.

Hattie helped me get my room set up. She brought me blankets, a bed spread, and showed me which linen and towels I was to use from the dozens of neat piles of such stored in the large closets on the second floor hall.

Hattie said, "Be sure you stick to the worn-out and ragged stuff, An-day, m'boy. We couldn't have you scrubbin' your be-hind with the same towel used by Lady Quality from Tuxedo Park." Hattie loaded my arms with sheets and towels, and then asked, "How many pillows do you need to dream on? Since you read so much, I imagine you need at least two."

"Two will be plenty," I said, as she piled them on top of everything else.

"Don't forget, when you are 'making your toilet,' as the French say, to use the bathroom at the end of the back hall over the garage which is for the exclusive use of Miss Meyer and her slaves. Of course, you can also take a whizz whenever you need to in the back porch john, you know, the one you painted. Of course, you males can relieve yourselves any old place, but we gals have to be careful where we scooch down!" Instead of my toilet, I made my bed, and came downstairs. It was about eight a.m. and I was ready to start my regular routine for the summer.

Miss Meyer had my schedule for the week all ready. She was a very nervous person, an addicted smoker and drinker, but she always had things organized clearly and on time, no matter what. She informed me that every morning as soon as I got up, even before I had breakfast, I was to rush down cellar and check the coal stoves. THE COAL STOVES MUST NEVER GO OUT!! This rule number one for the kitchen boy became my guiding principle for all my summers there. I'd wake up in the middle of the night worrying whether or not I'd shaken down the coal stoves and banked them properly. There were two of them: a little pot-bellied one named Jennie, which was used for heating the water; and a big black one called Bertha, which was used for heating the house. As I soon discovered, both were goddamn finicky monsters to nurse along. My first attempts to keep them going were futile. Hattie and Miss Meyer had to keep helping me.

That first day I was back and forth between the coal stoves and the kitchen dishpan. It was a delicate operation starting up the stoves. The drafts had to be opened wide, much newspaper had to be crinkled up and placed loosely enough about the kindling to allow for air passage, and then once the blaze was roaring, the cover or grate had to be left partly open. I had to keep feeding the fire until the time seemed right for the application of the coal itself. There was big coal for Bertha and small coal for Jennie, and even different-sized shovels and bins for both. I had to guess about how much coal to heap on each blaze at first, because I didn't want to smother the fires right off. While the little shovelfuls were catching on, I'd run back upstairs and start the morning pots and pans. It took all morning, several shakedowns, several more starts, and assists from Hattie and Miss Meyer to get the damn fires actually going simultaneously. Then, throughout the day, I had to be extra careful about shaking them down too much and putting more fresh coal on top.

Over my kitchen sink were two small windows through which I could observe the action on Frenchman's Bay and the sea beyond while I was washing and scrubbing the kitchen pots and utensils. It helped to have such a view to return to; and at night what wonderful sunsets over Mount Desert of red, orange, pink and purple reflected on the water. Just after nine p.m., as I would be finishing the third pile of pots and pans for the day, the *Bluenose* Ferry would be crossing the bay on her return to Bar Harbor from Yarmouth, Nova Scotia. She'd be all lit up, just as the Manor's brochure described, "like a birthday cake." I'd fantasize about taking a trip to the Maritime Provinces aboard her.

7

Besides Miss Meyer and Hattie, my co-workers that first summer in 1959 included Caroline Cole, the chambermaid and part-time waitress, a girl from my high school who had just graduated and was planning to attend the University of Maine in September. Caroline and I had been rather close acquaintances in high school and I was glad she was at the hotel, too. She commuted to work since her family lived nearby up the peninsula. She couldn't spend many afternoons off with me, because it seemed as if she always had errands to run or visits to make with various relatives and friends. We did eat lunch together every day, and many times she came to work early enough in the evenings to share an early supper with Hattie and me.

Thanks to her folks, Caroline had the use of two cars: a beat-up but fast-moving, black 1947 Chevy coupe to bomb around in and a sexy, forward-looking, turquoise-and-black 1957 Dodge four-door sedan with fins and push-button drive. She promised to drive me places; and after I got my license, even let me drive her cars.

Caroline, Hattie, and I got along well and enjoyed our many meals and wonderful story telling sessions together. We ate in the servants' back dining room off the kitchen, and there were always delivery people coming and going. If it wasn't Hick Young with the lobsters, it would be the laundry man from Mount Desert, somebody with some specialty item Miss Meyer had ordered, and even Passamaquoddy Indians with their sweet grass baskets for sale. Both Mrs. Richmond and Miss Meyer were suckers for those baskets, so the Manor was full of Indian baskets for laundry, shopping, floral displays.

Almost every evening, Hank, the thirty-year-old grocery boy from Blackstone's Grocery in Summer Harbor, would arrive with a "rush order." Miss Meyer would telephone her order in every morning, but she'd always forget something; or by early evening, there would be more guests for dinner whom we didn't expect and would have to stretch the food.

Hattie had known Hank since he was a boy, and she loved to joke with him, as with everyone; so just as he came through the screen door one suppertime, she asked, "Whatcha got in the bag, Hank?"

"All kinds of goodies, Hatt-tay," he said with a boyish grin.

"Goody goody for us," Hattie said, winking at Caroline and me. "I hope you plan to dole out them goodies in equal parts, so that we all get our fair share."

"I believe in democracy," said Hank.

"I don't care about your political beliefs, Hank. I want to know what you've got for me."

Hank then plucked a green pepper out of the bag and shoved it in Hattie's face. "I've got a nice hot pepper for you, old girl!"

Hattie laughed and then said, "Is that all? Just one little wrinkled green vegetable? I'm very disappointed, Hank."

Hattie had such a good voice and mannerisms for comedy. She sounded like a Downeast version of Mae West; however, more feminine and better-looking. I remember the first night I was on the job and had to pick up all the garbage after dinner. Hattie was washing dishes at the waitresses' sink when I entered the pantry with the big pail and asked her if what was deposited in the little dining room pail was all the garbage.

"That's all we're throwing out!" she said, raising her right eyebrow the way she could.

One of the regular guests for many summers was a Philadelphia lawyer named Harvard Sizer. He'd stay at the Manor while visiting with his important clients who summered at Granite Neck. A great golfer, he'd be up early teeing off. He adored Hattie and the two of them had practically a running comedy routine.

"Oh, that old Ha-vad," she'd say. "He might have graduated summa cum lordy lordy from Yale, but I can give him tit for tat, and I've got the tits to prove it!"

Every night after dinner had been served and we'd cleaned up everything, and the dining room tables had been set for breakfast, Hattie would sit with Miss Meyer at the folding table in the kitchen and they'd have a smoke and a drink together while talking the day over. At such times, Hattie would let her hair down, be quieter, more low key, and sometimes rather sad sounding. One night, when I returned to the kitchen after having deposited the garbage and secured the cans from the raccoons with chicken wire, I could tell that Hattie had been crying. When she saw me standing in the doorway, she brightened up and said, "Into each life some rain must fall, and recently I've been experiencing a goddamn downpour with no let-up." She didn't explain further, but just said good-night.

Another co-worker was Mrs. Sabina Spurling, the pastry cook and laundress, an old lady who came once a week to make pastries but also to help with the ironing. With her curly white hair, short and stout body, big red cheeks, and old-fashioned spectacles, she looked like Mrs. Santa Claus, which I sometimes called her. In the laundry room off the kitchen, she'd sit while she ironed the table cloths, napkins, and aprons and read from novels that she'd prop up on the window sill by her ironing board. When she was in the kitchen baking, she'd wrap her hair in a bath towel, while she bustled about dusting, kneading, and pounding the piles of dough that she'd have all over the kitchen tables and sideboards, making as much of a mess as Miss Meyer and Alberta Fickett put together. She hummed as she worked, the bath towel flapping about her head.

Something about her serious demeanor and her lack of a sense of humor brought out the bad boy in me. With that towel draped over her head, she reminded me of some middle-Eastern woman and I'd call her "The Shriek of Araby" and "Madame Nasser." She'd bustle about me and snap, "You just keep it up, sonny boy! Just keep out of my way, or I'm liable to bake ya!"

Her biscuits, breads, cakes, and pies were wonderful; but one time she did have a baking failure and she was beside herself with grief and humiliation. Luckily, I, the hapless kitchen boy, was her only witness. She had accidentally let three pie shells for lemon meringue pie stay in the oven too long and they became too brown to use. Sabina sputtered and grunted in a fury, the towel flapping even faster and more furiously about her face, as she rushed to dispose of the evidence before Miss Meyer found out.

"Here, kid!" she said, handing me the three hot shells. "You take 'em!"

"What do you want me to do with them?"

"Don't be smart!" she commanded sharply. "Run away with 'em quick! Or take some jam and go eat 'em like tarts!"

I opted for the latter course of action, lugging the steaming hot pie shells up the backstairs with a jar of S.S. Pierce red raspberry preserves. There I crouched on the attic part of the staircase that led up to my room, destroying as much of the delicious evidence as fast as I could eat. The one shell I couldn't finish I stuck in an outdoors garbage pail.

After that incident, Mrs. Spurling was noticeably nicer to me.

Hattie was the head waitress, but there was another full-time waitress named Greta, a Navy wife from the base, originally from Germany. She was very pretty, petite, extremely efficient, neat and bossy. I loved Greta's accent, and Miss Meyer liked her because she was such a good worker and because she was German. However, by the end of July, she had to let Greta go because of a big rift with Hattie.

I didn't want to get involved in the spat between the two of them, but being around the kitchen all the time, I got told things; and even if the people involved in a discussion weren't directly addressing me, it was relatively easy to overhear a conversation on the other side of the room, particularly if the debaters were hollering at each other. At any rate, at the beginning of July, Greta would rush out to tell me, while waiting on a breakfast order, that Hattie and Miss Meyer "ver in zee dining room making fun of her vile she served zee guests. Vell, she vould show zem!"

Greta moved quickly and with purpose, and while there was alacrity in her style, there were also a lot of broken dishes in her wake.

Miss Meyer did ask her several times not to greet the guests in the morning by asking, "Vatcha Vant?" She told her to at least preface that important question with "Good morning." She had also instructed Greta several times in my presence not to place the forks at the heads of the plates like they evidently did in Germany, but Greta persisted in setting the tables her European way.

Greta also had the disturbing habit of not using the serving stands for her trays as she was supposed to. She would plunk the tray right down on a guest's table and serve from there. Miss Meyer hit the ceiling over this practice.

Finally, at the end of our first month together, the tension peaked and Hattie came running from the pantry into the kitchen one morning to greet Miss Meyer, Mrs. Spurling, and myself with this message: "Let me tell you now what that LITTLE BITCH has done!"

"What happened?" our faces must have inquired.

"Look at the front of my uniform covered with coffee and marmalade and then look in there on the floor! I thought Miss Krauthead was holding the swinging door for me with her heel like we are supposed to do for each other, when I'll be goddamned if she didn't let it fly in my face! And me loaded down with a full tray! No, whataya say, Miss Meyer!? Am I exaggerating? Is it HER OR ME?"

Miss Meyer took charge immediately, and after a few loud German exclamations emanating from the recesses of Miss Meyer's office, Greta was seen leaving the Manor for good.

She paused in the kitchen, where I was working alone, to tell me that she didn't blame me for "vat had happened, zat she hoped I vould only think vell of her, but that I should be avare of zat bitch Hattie, who vas a very vicked voman if she couldn't get her vay."

Later, at the end of the summer, Miss Meyer did confide in me her doubts that Greta was not entirely at fault. "Errr. . .Andy, in any relationship," she said, "it's never just the one person's fault. It takes two, and Mrs. Pinkham can be very difficult to work with." Being of German stock herself, Miss Meyer had not appreciated Hattie's calling Greta a Krauthead and making anti-German remarks.

The only other male on the premises nearly every day was old Gus Finney, the caretaker. He lived in Summer Harbor for half the year with his son and son's family and then the rest of the year he went back to New York City to which he'd come from Ireland to work and live in the late 1930s. "I'm a goddamn summer person, too!" he'd say with a laugh. Miss Meyer was always sending me outdoors to look for Gus, when she'd miss him. He was supposed to be watering the flowers or doing some edging along the driveway, but he'd usually be asleep in the big wheelbarrow in the garage or on one of the settees or lounges about the grounds. Gus liked his grog, as he called his beer. He was always jolly and in a good mood.

He'd feel the muscles in my arms to see how strong I was getting. "Yer skinny now, Andy, but yer gitting to be a real strong guy. Yer going to be a big man." Gus was one of the smallest men I'd ever known, but he'd say, "I'm little, but I could take guys bigger'n me! I was a good fighter. I broke a guy's jaw once!"

In later summers, when I'd be driving Mrs. Richmond's Olds, chauffeuring and running errands for the Manor, I'd take Gus home; and he'd tell me his stories of growing up dirt poor and tough in Ireland and then his struggle in New York to make a living and raise his family. Gus's son was the dentist at the Navy Base, and they lived in Navy housing in the middle of Summer Harbor—this whole little development of pastel-colored, lookalike modern two-story houses plunked down in the midst of old Maine farm houses, shacks, and boat sheds.

"Like a wee bit o' Levittown, ain't it?" asked Gus.

"What's Levittown?"

"A big suburban housing development on Long Island."

"Do you like it here, Gus?"

"Oh, sure. It's cooler than in New York. It's been great to be here summers; but when I walk downtown to the barber shop, to the poolroom, or down on the town wharf, I'll be damned if I can get these goddamned Maine guys talking with me! They are nice enough fellas, but I miss me old pals in the city."

He asked me if I had ever done any boxing.

"At high school, we have this punching bag, and we have some boxing gloves, too; but that's all I've ever done—punch the bag, and I wasn't much good at that."

"I used to box quite a bit," he said. "Course, I was a lightweight."

"Gawd, Gus! I'd guess you were more of a featherweight—or maybe a leprechaun weight!"

"By Jesus, I knocked out a couple of guys in my time! I'll have to show ya how to use yer mitts!"

"Us boxing out in the garage?"

"Why not? Wouldn't ya rather be doing that than washing dishes with the women?"

"Maybe, but I like working with Hattie and Caroline."

"Oh, sure! That Hattie's a great-looking woman! But women

don't understand a man's need for violence, for bloodthirsty killin', for excitement and adventure! God, how I loved hanging around the ring, watching the boys take each other on. I saw some great fights. Great fun after working on the docks all day."

"Is that what you did, Gus?"

"I was a fuckin' longshoreman, that's what I was. Being an immigrant, first generation, you can only go so far, ya know? It was a tough life, but I made a decent livin' after a while. And I had a good wife, a good son, and I had some good pals to hang around with. We understood each other, knew what each other had gone through; but these guys up here in Maine, they've been here forever, many generations. They don't have to prove nothing to nobody. They aren't hurryin' around and hustlin' tryin' to make it. And they won't talk to me. I don't know how to begin to talk to 'em. I can't get 'em to talk."

"Maybe they can't understand you. You have a heavy accent, you know, both Irish and New York. You have to listen carefully to you. Also, Maine men won't talk easily with any strangers. You've got to win 'em over. They'll talk after a while."

"Christ, I've been trying now for the past two summers; and you talk about ME ACCENT?! You should hear the goddamn accent you Maine guys have got! Jesus Christ! The communication is damned difficult both ways, now that I can tell ya!"

I had to agree with him there.

Another co-worker, on and off, was Alberta Fickett, the cook and handywoman of Granite Neck; but my reminiscences of her deserve a full chapter.

8

"Berter," as nearly everyone around the Neck called her, was the living opposite of all the taste, class, and shiny brass that Frenchman's Bay Manor represented. Every time before she opened her lips to speak, she would whine, with the most incredible Maine twang, "Waa-all." Clad in her husband's slippers or boots, white socks, shapeless meal-sack frocks, ragged sweaters, slips that hung a half-foot or more below her dress hems, Berter would slouch in and about the kitchen cooing and caterwauling, her mop of red hair held partly in place by bobby pins.

What she was doing there, coming and going at all hours, seemingly whenever she was pleased to do so, was evidently anyone's guess. She was like an employee-at-large. Once I did manage to ask her just what her job was.

"Waa-alll," she whined, "I'm whatcha might call a jill of many trades! You name it 'n I can tackle 'er! When Miss Meyer here gits overworked, or. . .(she leaned towards me, her eyes wide, whispering in a conspiratorial rasp). . . overtight, I comes right down and pitches in. Usually, I cook. I'm a good roundhouse cook, as they say."

"What does 'roundhouse cook' mean?" I asked.

"Oh, I guess it means a cook that can go 'round, cook anything, anytime, under any conditions, and I can! They used to have roundhouses on boats and in the trainyards where they fixed the trains. I've worked in all the houses on Granite Neck. They all know me. Faithful old workhorse Berter! They know ma quality. I been in all the kitchens 'round here and then some. They know what to expect from me! I don't just quit at four o'clock."

Working as Berter's kitchen assistant often proved dangerous. She was constantly muttering to herself, messing up the place, knocking things about, breaking stuff, and making great crashing noises. She broke more dishes in a night than Greta smashed in her whole month at the Manor. I'd be at the dishpan scrubbing a baked-on pot, and she'd scale a ladle steaming hot from the soup into the sink beside me, and then hoot, "Ha! Missed ya that time, An-day!" She was always saying how she like to "git the job done in shot aw-dah!" Usually, she did, leaving me to pick up the pieces and clean up the debris. While stirring, tasting, and hovering over her bubbling and steaming concoctions, she'd be smoking one cigarette after another and swigging beers. "You'll see, An-day, in this business, we chefs drink a lot of beer. It's because we're always bending over a hot range."

Sometimes, I'd come upon Berter standing in the middle of the kitchen with a crazy, wide-eyed, vacant look on her face, while tapping her thigh with a ladle or large cooking spoon.

"What's the matter, Berter?" I'd ask.

"Oh, I'm trying to remember where I put the christled bowl of potatoes I just peeled!"

Miss Meyer was usually nervous when Berter was in charge of the cooking; but she always seemed to appreciate Berter's presence and be somehow comforted by her. "Errr. . .she comes in handy," she'd say. "And she's dependable."

When Dependable Berter was cooking the main meal for the evening, she would stand there whooping, slapping her thighs with her hands, with flour or bits or food on her face and apron, adjusting her bra straps, and yelling out to the waitresses, "Waa-alll, I gis we better git this show on the rud!"

Just before serving time, she'd taste everything on the stove with the same spoon one more time, usually adding more salt or pepper. "Iffin it don't taste jes right, you kin always throw in another slug-a-salt!"

All the time Berter was doing the cooking, Miss Meyer would stand by, nervously pacing the floor between her office and the kitchen. Sucking on her cigarette and then on her cocktail, expecting at every moment for everything to go to hell. With her, especially at dinner time, a crisis was always pending.

"Don't git hyper, Miss Meyer! Don't git hyper!" Berter would yell. "The christled cream sauce didn't burn on this time, and the jeezley tomato aspic is jelled okay, so have another highball and enjoy ya-self. The customers is paying ones, ya know."

Berter taught me how to properly shake down the coal stoves, better even than Miss Meyer or Hattie; and also how to shake down the Manor itself. Her questionable morals were evenly matched by her long fingers. One night, when Miss Meyer wasn't looking, Berter helped herself to a fancy decanter of Old Forrester whiskey from off the kitchen sideboard, saying to me, "Waa-alll, I need it more than she does! She's got a whole goddamn case in her office. Her private stash!" She took a big swig, turned to me with a grin and declared, "Good stuff!" Then, she packed the bottle into the huge canvas bag she always carried and wished me a loud good night.

Berter robbed the Manor regularly like a good many other Downeasters who slaved for the summer folk and lugged off this and that from their places of employment. It was an accepted practice at least on Taunton Point and Granite Neck. The stealing was rationalized, as Berter said: "They'll never miss it. They don't need it as much as we do. They come up here and expect us to work for them for nothing."

Once a week, the order came from S. S. Pierce, the fancy food distributor in Boston; and it was another of my jobs to open up the boxes and check off the list what arrived and re-stock the shelves in the food locker down in the cellar.

One night after the order had come, and I had spent the greater part of my day opening the boxes and re-stocking the shelves with jars and cans of blue-and-red-label produce, Berter came to me, her lips smacking, her face aflame, her red hair full of snarls and bobby pins, and rasped in my ear: "Waa-alll, listen, An-day, when ya git the chance, grab a few of them nice big S. S. PURSE cartons and put 'em in ma wagon out back."

I agreed to do so since I thought Miss Meyer trusted Berter and had no use for the extra boxes, but, somehow, back in the recesses of my unformed mind, I knew I should have cleared this clandestine operation with my boss, and not take what a fellow employee suggested as a command. But Berter was older and "my kind of people." I had to trust her more than my summer employer from away. Berter was a Downeaster like me, after all, and we lived here year round. We looked out for each other, whether we liked each other or not. The summer folk got to leave. We didn't.

Anyway, that night, after I had finished cleaning up the kitchen and had secured the garbage from the raccoons, I transported the cartons to Berter's '52 Chevy beach wagon parked in the servants' back parking lot.

Silhouetted by the light from the Manor, she came barging out to me in her mis-matched and ragged charwoman's outfit and floppy shoes, slambanging about, muttering to herself, and overloaded with Pierce produce, consommé madrilene and all.

"Waa-alll, quite a haul, wouldn't ya say?" she asked me with a hoot. "Ever try any of this watermelon pickle? It's a taste treat all right! Working all these years down here on the Neck has ruined ma taste buds forever! Every time the S. S. PURSE order comes, we Ficketts have a great feast, now I'll tell ya! I even let Sir Phil, my DARLIN' HUSBAND, have a bite or two. Now, look, to git the rest that I couldn't carry, let's just back the wagon down around the garage to the back door that goes to the cellar."

My face must have betrayed my feelings, because at one point as we packed the cartons in the wagon, Berter said to me, "Waa-alll, ya know, An-day, this is part of our pay. They expect it and we earn it!"

Right then, after Berter had driven off up the back driveway, I wanted to go and tell Miss Meyer about the heist, but I didn't. I decided to wait until the subject came up. That night I just went upstairs to my room and my reading and records.

Come to find out, Berter had even stolen the company beach wagon! It had once belonged to the Manor to be used for shopping and chauffeuring. Still written on both sides in fancy lettering was FRENCHMAN'S BAY MANOR, GRANITE NECK, MAINE. Miss Meyer told me that Berter used to use the car more than anyone else, so after a while, she just naturally laid claim to it. Miss Meyer said she didn't mind except that she wished that if I ever got the chance, I would paint over the lettering. She didn't think Berter's racing around the area, looking like she did, in such a battered old junk heap, was a very good advertisement for the hotel.

Berter usually traveled in the beach wagon all over Maine with a "bunch of desperadoes," as Hattie named them. One member of this ragtag band was Berter's mother, who was stark bald and wore a flashy bandanna wrapped around her head to conceal her misfortune. She was as silent as Berter was loud and would creep into the Manor when Berter was cooking and just sit for hours by the kitchen window, not saying nor doing anything. She was one of the strangest people I've ever known. She always wore this heavy wool coat, even in August. When she did speak, her voice was like a ghostly rasp. She usually only talked with her daughter, however, and whenever I asked her a question, she'd simply smile at me and nod her head.

"Is Berter's mother retarded?" I asked Hattie one day.

"Probably no more than the rest of us," Hattie said. "She's just plain worn-out, An-day. She's still cleaning cottages and cooking for the summer people at her age. She's raised seven kids, while married to a bum, and worked all the time down here on the Neck, or in a fish factory, or some place. She's known nothing but work, just like Berter. If you notice it, Berter, when she's working, works hard, too."

One time the old lady actually laughed! That was the afternoon when Berter brought more of the Desperadoes into the Manor when she was working. Berter's tall, muscular, dark-haired teenage son, Bertram, who was handsome L'il Abner-style, and the love of her life, was among this group of young, wild males who often accompanied her in her beach wagon travels. The two other boys that day were two of her nephews from "up Millinocket way." One was short and tough-looking; in fact, on probation from some criminal activity. He showed me a freshly-severed squirrel's tail which he had in his pocket. "I like to kill squirrels," he told me with a gap-toothed grin. "They ain't much good anyways." The other nephew was a clean-cut, dark-haired, but shifty-eyed fellow who was illiterate. "He can't even spell 'cat'," said Berter. The boys lounged around the kitchen for a while as Berter started dinner preparations and I continued washing the pots and pans.

When Berter stepped out into the back pantry for a minute to get some potatoes and onions, the three desperadoes rushed over past me to the swinging door which separated pantry from kitchen and held onto the knob from the kitchen side. When Berter tried to re-enter, the boys held tight to the knob and each other, giggling and tee-heeing. As the tension grew and finally peaked, the boys let go of their side, sending her sprawling with her potatoes and onions all over the pantry floor. The boys ran lickety-split to the other side of the kitchen, all excited, cowering expectantly by the silent old lady, scooching down by the kitchen table and freezer.

Berter picked herself up, swearing her head off, and came out of the pantry like a pitcher from the dugout. And she let them have it with a wild barrage of potatoes. She could not only steam them on the stove, but steam them with deadly accuracy across the room. She could pitch like Sandy Koufax, and beaned every one of the boys before she was done, and knocked an ice bucket off the shelf. I had to duck a couple of times, too. I was afraid there'd be some broken windows before she was through.

"Goddamn ya, boys! Goddamn ya!" she yelled; and when it was all over and there were spuds everywhere, I looked around to see Berter, panting and gasping, her flaming hair in a furious snarl, her eyes bugging out of her head. Across the room, as the boys were still crouching about the floor, there sat the toothless old hag over in the corner by the window cackling her head off, her purple and red bandanna shaking so hard that it was beginning to unravel.

Two summers later, in 1961, I timidly approached Mrs. Richmond one night after Berter had lugged off even more than usual. Mrs. Richmond was in her office juggling the books while I stood there in the doorway.

"Yes?" she asked, looking at me over the tops of her glasses.

"Mrs. Richmond, I'm sorry to bother you, but did you know that Berter is frequently stealing stuff from the hotel?"

Mrs. Richmond sat back in her swivel chair, broke out into a wide, wonderful grin, and then started laughing.

"My God, Andy! Bert has been robbing this place blind regularly for nearly twenty years!"

"Why do you keep her on?"

"I have no choice. I can't run the joint without her. The woman is incredible, fearless, and indispensable. I can call on her at all hours, and she'll show up. She's a good cook, and she'll do the dirty work no one else will. She knows, even in her rough and tough way, how to get things done; and she can do anything. I also like her company. She'll take a drink, and she generally makes sense when she talks. So, whatever she lugs off is the price I pay for doing business on the Maine Coast!"

9

Officially, the Manor opened for the season on Memorial Day weekend; but it wasn't until the Fourth of July that things were really humming and the rooms were full.

The evening of July 4, 1959 most of the "July regulars" as well as a few irregulars were assembled on the great winding front porch facing Frenchman's Bay, having cocktails, and awaiting the fireworks display from Bar Harbor, which began as soon as the *Bluenose*, all lit up, passed by the Porcupine Islands. It was a beautiful, clear, and warm night with the car lights twinkling from the road up to the summit of Cadillac Mountain across the bay. It was my job to flit about seeing to the whims of the guests, answering their calls for more soda water, soda crackers, orange peels; or just lending my attentive young ear to their chatter. As usual, they supplied their own bottles of spirits; and most were well-spirited before the festivities got underway.

"Here, boy!" an Old Gent would call, rattling the ice in his glass. "We seem to be out of tonic!"

"Yes, sir," I'd say. "I'll get you a bottle straight away!"

"My dear young man," a Grande Dame would call, "how I'd relish a fresh slice of lime. I'm afraid I've squeezed the one I have bone dry."

"I'll get you one right away!"

"*Vite! Vite!*" she exclaimed with a laugh.

As I rushed back and forth between the porch and the kitchen, I'd catch snatches of their reminiscences of Fourths from their pasts. One Old Fart, an irregular on tour with his wife, said, "The Fourth I remember best was in Rome the summer of 1946 when a few of us Americans gathered to celebrate in the ruins of World War II."

"I was in Vienna that summer when my husband was still in command of the allies in that city," said Mrs. Julie Lawson from Tampa, Florida, who always walked on tip-toe presumably to strengthen her calf muscles. "It was very difficult arranging the Russians, British, and Americans around the dinner table," she said. Since Mrs. Lawson had been a guest at the Manor since the first summer the hotel opened its doors in 1947, and because she stayed for the whole season, she was accorded top status. She had the number one table in the dining room with the number one view of everything.

Hattie had told me that Mrs. Lawson's teenage son Parker stayed at a boys' camp down near Deer Isle; and usually, at the end of August, he would join her at the Manor for a week or so before they both returned to Florida.

I remember the afternoon she arrived on July 1 in her 1956 two-tone blue Ford Fairlane because she tried to put the car through the hedge that separates the servants' entrance from the main entrance. For some reason, Mrs. Lawson preferred to park with the help and to live upstairs in the Number 12 room with no bath and to share our bath with us over the garage.

I was just finishing up the luncheon pots and pans when Julie flounced, because she never just walked, into the kitchen.

"Hi!" she breathlessly exclaimed, bouncing up and down on her toes; but because she came in the back way, I wasn't sure if she were to be accorded guest status or what.

She was so girlish-acting, even though one could see from her graying brown curly hair that she was not really young. She was dressed in blue flared trousers with white blouse and sneakers. Her hair was pulled back by her ears. Except for her face, she was tanned and pretty, and looked like she had just been sailing. She radiated energy and seemed never still, always moving about. She jounced across the kitchen on her toes to greet Miss Meyer.

"Jean!. . .so good!" she said, taking Miss Meyer's hands in hers and holding them for what seemed an inordinate amount of time, all the while looking into Miss Meyer's face, giggling through a smile which lit up her face, but saying nothing more, as if she were too overcome for words.

"Errr," said Miss Meyer, "it's good to have you back, Julie." My boss then pulled her hands away, but all the same trying to be naturally friendly, which was hard for her. Perhaps she had been an old maid secretary in New York for too many years. She always was awkward and mannered, particularly when greeting someone as effervescent as Julie Lawson.

But Julie didn't seem to mind or notice any such awkwardness. "So good," she repeated in her whispery voice; and then she tip-toed across the kitchen to me. "Hi!" she exclaimed again, extending her hand. My hands had been in the dishpan, and she didn't give me time to wipe them, but she didn't seem to mind the suds. She seized upon my right hand and squeezed it, looking like a little girl discovering something brand-new and exciting. "You're the new boy!" she said.

"Yes," I said.

"Errr. . .his name is Andy," said Miss Meyer.

"Andy," Julie repeated with what I determined had to be a southern accent. "Will you help me. . .when you can?" she asked in a pleading tone.

"What?" I asked in return, not understanding exactly what she meant. I found out soon enough that Mrs. Lawson hardly ever completed her sentences when she talked. And her fragmented speech was often vague and inexplicit. She evidently expected people to garner the gist of her communication through osmosis.

"Errr. . .he's about done and will be right out to help you, Julie," Miss Meyer said, clearing the whole matter up.

"Good!" Julie exclaimed, for she was full of exclamations. "I'll go, and Andy will come. . ." She started to tip-toe away, only to run into Hattie emerging from the dining area.

"Hattie!" she whooped, bouncing over to her, giggling and taking her by the hand, saying, "I'm back! You're here!"

Hattie laughed and said, "Yes, I guess we both are. Ready to go another round, Julie. It's good to see ya."

"I need your help, Hattie," said Julie.

"I know it, Julie, you always have."

"Will you sew?" Julie asked.

"When I get time. What do you need sewed?"

"Things. Many little things. Everything's falling apart."

"Don't I know it!" Hattie exclaimed.

"Good, you'll sew then?" Julie turned to leave. "You'll come, Andy? I'll be by the trunk."

"Yes, right away," I said, assuming that she referred to her car's trunk, not that of an elephant, tree, or steamer, but not altogether sure. She did seem magical, after all.

"Is there juice, Jean?" Julie asked Miss Meyer from the doorway.

"Errr. . .there's some orange. Could I get you a glass?"

"Please! I need it. The trip was hot. . .I could drink a jug!"

She had two tall glasses of orange juice which she seemed to relish as her life's blood, giggling at all three of us, and looking wild-eyed about the kitchen, while she sipped from her glass. Then, all of a sudden, finished, she plunked down the empty glass, jumped up, and danced out of the room.

"Well, An-day, was that your first real-life glimpse of a tip-toeing southern belle?" Hattie asked.

"I guess so. You both had mentioned her, but I didn't really expect anyone so. . ."

"Nuts?" Hattie asked. "Listen, if she didn't have the millions she's supposed to, they'd lock her up in a padded cell. You ain't seen nothing yet, honey chile!"

"Why does she walk on her toes?"

"She's floating on air — the air between her ears, that is! But don't worry; she tips, when you remind her what planet she's on."

"Errr. . .you'd better go help her now," Miss Meyer suggested, evidently wishing to discourage any more of Hattie's comments concerning the Manor's longest-paying, full-season guest.

"Yais, and go easy with the hoop skirts, high-protein cereals, and magnolia blossoms, An day, hon-ay!" mocked Hattie, executing a tip-toeing imitation of Mrs. Lawson back to the dining room.

Peering into the trunk of Mrs. Lawson's Ford, I was curious to see how she packed or didn't pack, as the case seemed to be. There was only one old battered suitcase; everything else, including underwear and melted chocolates, was wrapped in plastic or paper bags or in newspaper or just lying free on top of everything else. The rear seat had been removed and therein lay more of the same: another battered suitcase, a half-dozen floppy wide-rimmed picture hats, one with little red balls decorating its rim, half-eaten boxes of "health" candy, petticoats, bundles of dead, dry foliage, magazines, books, swim suits, bottles of lotion, and a partial set of weights.

"Trunk first," Mrs. Lawson instructed, beginning to remove things from the rear of the car and placing them in little piles on top of and beside the Ford. As I began to help her, I noticed what looked to be an expensive cocktail dress stuffed about the spare tire as if it were used to wipe some grease monkey's hands.

"Oh, it's bad," she said, "do you know someone who cleans?"

"My mother. She takes in washings."

"Good. Could you take it to her?" She held the greasy gown out to me. "And does she sew? Mrs. Pinkham's always so busy. . ."

"So is my mother," I said to myself. "Yes, she does, and very well."

"Then I have a few things," she said.

She held up a piece of white canvas which turned out to be a cloth helmet cut to fit her head when swimming. "I can't have the sun strike my face when I'm in the pool," she explained. "But I need wider nose holes and mouth opening. I nearly choked and drowned last week."

It looked to me like the Phantom's head covering; I was thinking to myself what my mother would say when she saw this. She was always joking over what "little jobs" the summer people had her do, like the time Ambassador Sedgwick's wife from Taunton Point brought her Burmese draperies to my mother to be made into a gown. It was amusing to me, imagining Mrs. Lawson with her canvas helmet on at the Granite Neck Pool down the street, midst all the royal blood.

She also handed me a ripped pea-green bathing suit for my mother to repair; and then we began the unpacking of the car in earnest. She busily tried to arrange and organize her stuff into little piles about the car and parking lot while I began transporting things upstairs to her room where I was instructed to make other little piles. At one point, I was carrying a bag of Florida oranges, a make-up kit, a bottle of Poland Spring water, and a plastic bag of bathing suits.

All during this process, which took over an hour, and which more or less continued throughout the rest of the summer, she would pause and ask me questions about my health and hobbies.

"Let me see your teeth," she said.

I did as I was commanded and she put her hand into my mouth

and examined my teeth, finally declaring, "They seem strong. Are they?"

"I think so. I've only had about two cavities ever."

"Do you chew?"

"Things that need chewing."

"Chewing is good. Chew always."

"Do you break bones?" she asked.

"No, not if I can help it."

"Don't drink Coke," she said, and returned to her unpacking.

After the car, she told me to go up into the attic and fetch a steamer trunk she kept there filled with her summer frocks.

"I purchased these dresses in New York in 1947 for my first season here. . .it's been thirteen seasons, but they'll still do fine. Isn't this one lovely?" She held up this light green, full-skirted, padded-shouldered monstrosity for my praise.

"Yes, it's held up well," I said, convinced of her insanity, and waiting, now that the errands had been done, to see if there would be any tip.

"Ohhh!" she finally exclaimed, rushing to her pocketbook on her dresser, fumbling through it, scattering credit cards, twenty and fifty dollar bills, finally handing me a five, the biggest tip I had ever received from a summer guest up till then.

"Here!" she said, crumpling the bill into my hand. "From a very grateful Mrs. Lawson."

"Thank you," I said. "See you later."

"Ummmmm," she hummed, smiling her funny little quivering smile, closing the door behind me.

I returned to the kitchen and there sat Hattie and Miss Meyer having a cigarette as they often did in the early afternoon after lunch was out of the way, and before they both went their separate ways before dinner preparations began in earnest around four p.m.

"Get much?" Hattie asked.

"Five big ones! See what I'm making while you're just sitting around?"

"Whataya mean? We were just figuring out how we were gonna roll Miss Julie some dark night when she's out on one of her nature hikes. Did ya know she climbs trees?"

"No, I just met her, Hattie, and that ability doesn't always show up on first meetings."

"Well, your innocent eyeballs will be opened more clearly by tomorrow, no doubt. First, she does her breathing exercises out on the front lawn for all the world to see. Then, she's off to the pool down the street for twenty-five laps; and she doesn't drive there; she tip-toes! With a towel over her head so the sun won't crack her face-lift. Then, she tip-toes back here for breakfast, always late and always with nutty demands, like no spices, no poisons. She doesn't want anything that's good to eat or tastes good. Then she washes her undies in the back porch sink, brushing her teeth at the same time. In the afternoon, she does yoga exercises followed by a nap. And just before supper, off she goes again to the pool for more laps. Of course, like everything else, she's late for dinner. For about an hour beforehand, she races around upstairs nude from the bath to her room. I suggest, An-day, if you really want an education, go upstairs about five-thirty and be on the lookout. She's got a good body for a dame her age, but she's got nothing else to do except take care of it."

"Errr. . .she always pays her bill in advance," said Miss Meyer, "so I don't care if she stands around nude in the front hall."

"Oh, now, Miss Meyer, you know you do," said Hattie, chuckling.

It was true what Hattie said about Mrs. Lawson and her daily routine. She was out on the front lawn early the next morning clad in a white playsuit and sneakers, holding an umbrella over her head, doing her breathing exercises.

Right after breakfast, Mr. Lyon, who was with the French embassy in Washington, came bursting into the kitchen, dramatically demanding from Miss Meyer in a very loud voice, "Who ees theese woman geemnast?"

"Errr. . .it's Mrs. Lawson, Mr. Lyon. Is she bothering you?"

"No. Not at all. I'm rather enchantée by her performances. I want to talk weeth her."

"That should be cute," Hattie said afterwards. "He'll find out how enchantée she is right after she checks his cavities."

All that day, Caroline Cole, the chambermaid, and I watched Mrs. Lawson, whom we'd affectionately dubbed "Twinkle Toes" as she went about her daily rituals. While she was washing underwear on the back porch, she would clean her teeth with some rubbery substance she chewed furiously in her mouth, twisting and contorting her face as she did so.

After she finished her undies, she would bend over the balcony above the clothesline and toss her foundation garments to the lines, not bothering to go down around and hang them up with pins. Sometimes her clothes hit the lines, and sometimes not; and if the wind from off the water were strong enough, some days, her things would be blown into the hedges and bushes.

One morning the milkman came into the kitchen with a grin on his face and carrying some of Mrs. Lawson's underwear with his milk. He looked at me and Mrs. Spurling, and said, "Must have been quite a party here last night. I found these panties in the bushes halfway up the driveway!"

In the evenings, Twinkle Toes would enter the dining room late, dramatically pausing in the entranceway, before going to her table. She was always attired in one of her 1947 get-ups, usually wrinkled and unironed, rips in her hose, and the straps of her high heel shoes undone. She'd often have flowers in her white-gloved hands for which she would request a vase.

"Flowers must always accompany me," she'd say, "even if just a bunch of ragweed." And the flowers, she ordered, were to stay on her dining room table or bedroom dresser until she herself threw them away, which meant never. Hattie, Caroline, or Miss Meyer would usually wait until the old flowers had become as crisp and brown as toast and then give them the heave-ho.

Anyway, Julie would pause in the dining room entranceway, looking quite lovely in a faded sort of way with her hair pulled back and her skin deeply tanned. She'd tip-toe across the room, greeting the other diners with her funny, little eccentric smile, and assume her position at her corner table.

As soon as she sat down, Hattie would announce to the kitchen staff, "Bring on the wheat germ and alligator milk! Scarlet O'Hara's ready to be served!"

Julie Lawson had let us all know that she wished no spices in her soup or food, no white bread, no ice cubes, no gravy, no rare meat, no rich desserts. She loved fresh fruit and wheat germ. She always had milk with her meals, no coffee. She had Kellogg's Concentrate sprinkled on top of everything.

After dinner, she walked around "the oval," as she called the Neck, and after that, she sat alone by herself, reading. She'd curl up on a couch or chair with her pumps off and peruse a book, but she'd hardly ever finish one. It became one of my daily duties to go about the house and grounds and pick up all of her unfinished books and put them back on the shelves. She took copious, hard-to-decipher notes on her readings and left them stuffed inside the books. I removed them and left them stacked on her bedroom dresser.

At the end of July, Mrs. Lawson spent a weekend away from the Manor down at Deer Isle at her son's camp. At the end of August, and her stay, Parker Lawson III joined his mother at the Manor. He was a tall, handsome, sandy-haired, blue-eyed fellow, as athletically inclined and eccentric as his mother. He went swimming, exercising, running, and walking with her. He lifted weights and did not tip-toe. She measured his biceps and chest regularly and they climbed trees together; they were frequently closeted in the bathroom giggling together. It was like Jane and Boy without Tarzan.

While Parker was around, Mrs. Lawson was always radiantly happy; her sole offspring was obviously the love of her life. Daily, she left him notes on their dining room table, under his door, by his bed. She made lists of books for him to read and rules for him to follow. She clipped dozens of magazine articles for him to read while meals were being served. She was constantly intent on every facet of his education. And mostly he obeyed her; but I remember one evening, when Mother wasn't around, when Parker invited me up after work to his room for a talk. His room, like his mother's, was a mess with piles of underwear and socks in one corner, a stack of books and magazines in another, things scattered all over, the bed clothes rumpled. He offered me a drink; I could have grape-flavored Zarex or a Budweiser, both discouraged by his mother. He also showed me his suitcase collection of comic books and sex magazines. We sat there for a time ogling the girlies and sipping our Buds, Parker informing me what a cultured man should be looking for in a woman.

"I attend military school like my father did," he told me. "I will try for West Point in two years."

"You really like the Army, huh?"

"I have an obligation. The Lawsons have always been Army men."

He didn't speak with me the way he did with his mother and the other guests. With me, it was strictly man to boy. He lectured me, told me what life was all about. He assumed the military man-of-the-world stance, as my superior in all things. And I let him, because to my mind then, he was superior. I was lucky to be in his presence, to be considered good enough for him to spend time with. He was handsome and his body, with all the daily exercise and milk-drinking, was very muscular and tanned. He wore jeans, t-shirts, and sneakers like I did; yet he looked far healthier, more capable, more ready and assured. He puzzled and intrigued me the whole time. He was so close with his mother, and yet he could be so tough. He drew a sharp line between the World of Men and his private existence. I thought then that a person who changed his behavior as radically as Parker did that evening with me had to have psychological problems, but I didn't tell him that. He did most of the talking anyway, and the talk centered around his great respect for his father and his father's supposed military exploits.

"Why doesn't your father come up here in the summers with you and your mother?"

"He was here once, but he doesn't share mother's appreciation for Maine or any other northern climate."

"How come?" I asked, not accustomed to hearing of someone disliking my native land.

"He's a southerner. The farthest he will go north is Washington where he visits the Senate. He took me to the Senate with him last year."

"Is he in politics?"

"All rich men are in politics. They have to protect their money."

And so it went. The next day I told Hattie about my evening as Parker's guest.

"What a little jerk that poor boy is," she said.

"Jerk! He's rich and smart."

"He's queer like his mother. Haven't you heard 'em giggling together? He'll never break away from her. She won't let him."

"But he admires his father a lot."

"His father is a handsome snob. He came up here a few summers ago and strutted around like he was reviewing the troops. I could go for him physically, but he was crazy, too, like the whole lot of 'em. Julie herself says that he married her for her money. The Lawsons were broke and he didn't want or know how to work, so he married her and can sit around in his Army uniform on his veranda down in Tampa, sipping his mint julep. He thinks he's still commanding over in Europe like he did in the War. There's no love there; she says so. All her love goes to Junior and that's the boy's problem. She'll never let him grow up on his own. He'll be queer, you'll see."

"He drinks beer and reads girlie magazines," I noted.

"Thank God for that much. The poor boy's trying, but it's a lost cause, I'm afraid. He pretends, but he's in need of a lot of help."

I really didn't see what she meant, for I was blinded by Parker's dashing appearance and by my own unworldliness. I really thought looks and money like he had were enough. If he were queer, as Hattie said, then I wanted to be queer like that.

That last day, the Lawsons started leaving early in the morning, but didn't actually pull out of the back parking lot until mid-afternoon. Things were re-packed the way they came, wherever they fit.

"We drive to Portland," Julie told us, the entire staff assembled there for the occasion. "Tomorrow, we pick up Eric, a college boy who drives us to New York and Tampa. I hope the trek won't prove too ravaging. . .Parker and I wish you all. . ."

She never finished what she was wishing us. Typical of Mrs. Lawson.

"Look, Julie, you and Parker drive carefully. We'll see you next summer," said Hattie.

"Ummmmm," hummed Julie, smiling that funny little smile.

Driving out, she managed to take only half of the cedar hedge with her.

"I'm glad to see Julie really listened to my advice," said Hattie.

10

The regular guests for July included Dr. Morris Fidelstein and the Levys, all three from New York and all Jewish.

Dr. Fidelstein was an owlish little man with very thick glasses. He was very quiet and kept to himself; but he must have discovered Mrs. Lawson's nightly habit of tip-toeing nude down the hall, because at that hour, he'd usually be in his room which was next to hers with his door ajar. When I reported my finding to Hattie, she said, "Well, I'm glad to know that! Dr. Fiddle-dee-dee is a nice little fella, but he's so quiet. Not much fun. Even with all my farm gal charms, I can't get much of a rise out of him!"

"Is he married?" I asked.

"Yes, but I believe his wife is in Europe this summer. Usually they come up here together in July, and then go to Europe together, too; but for some reason she had to go there early this year. She's very nice, attractive, and red-headed, quite a bit taller than the Doc."

The Levys ruined one of my afternoons off. Miss Meyer told me that morning, "Errr. . .the Levys of New York City are expected this afternoon, Andy, so don't go down to the rocks or off some place. Stay around here, will you?"

"Who are the Levys?" I asked.

"They're rich Jews," Hattie exclaimed, "so don't expect a tip!"

"Errr. . .I believe Mr. Levy is an executive at Ginn and Company, the book publishers," Miss Meyer said.

"Well, I'll be up in my room reading," I informed both women, "unless you want me to do something else."

"Well, An-day, now that you brought it up," Hattie said with her raised eyebrow. "What do you do up there in that teeny little room so many afternoons by yourself?"

"You are welcome to visit me, Hattie, any time."

"Your time is my time, huh? Maybe this would be worth an investigation. Maybe, if I can sneak by Miss Meyer's ever-restless eagle eyeballs, I'll join ya a little later in one of your readings; but don't count on it, 'cause she's drivin' me today something wicked."

"Errr. . .you do get compensation for overtime, Mrs. Pinkham," said Miss Meyer with a smile.

"Don't I know it!" Hattie said. "I can have as much S. S. PURSE coffee as I can swallow!"

I left them to their usual banter and went upstairs where I lay down on my bed, and started reading *Anatomy of a Murder* from where I had left off the previous night. Miss Meyer had recommended it from the Manor's library. She always recommended mysteries because that's all she read. While reading, I'd play music on my record player, trying out various artists from the Manor's collection. Miss Meyer loved George Feyer's piano music and his whole series of Vox recordings: "Music of Broadway," "Music of Latin America," "Music of Spain," and so on. I was listening to the "Music of Broadway" when the Levys arrived. Miss Meyer hollered up the back staircase, "Errr. . .Andy! Andy! Come and get the bags!"

I made sure my shirt was tucked in, that I looked halfway presentable, took a quick peek at myself in the mirror on my little bureau, passed a comb through my crewcut, and rushed downstairs to greet the rich Jews.

The Levys drove a '55 Dodge Coronet and I was very disappointed, since I expected rich Jews from New York to arrive in a brand-new Cadillac.

At that point in my life, what did I know about Jews? What being Jewish means? I'd just begun to learn about the Holocaust, had read *The Diary of Anne Frank* when I was a freshman. The Jews seemed exotic to me, like the gypsies. I had just finished *Battle Cry* by Leon Uris for a book report at the end of my junior year; and I had loved and even identified with the sensitive Jewish boy's plight in that novel. I knew Eddie Fisher was Jewish because one time when he was singing on his "Coke Time" TV show, my father arrived home from work and said to my mother, who loved Eddie Fisher, "Is that curly-headed Jew boy moaning again?" My mother's reply was: "Do you think you can sing better?"

I knew there had been Jewish peddlers on the Maine coast, that there were Jewish stores in Bangor, and that Jake Kaplan, my grandparents' friend and cattle dealer, was Jewish. Many of my favorite comedians on radio and TV were Jewish; but I didn't know about the Jewish families that had lived right up the road in Taunton, the summer folk who were Jewish, and my own relatives who were Jewish. Actually, I had never heard many anti-Semitic remarks when growing up. Most of the prejudiced comments I had always heard in Eastern Maine were directed at the French, the Catholics, the Blacks, the Indians, and people from Massachusetts.

So, I greeted the Levys, pleasantly but on the lookout for tell-tale clues as to the depths of their Jewishness. They both had the requisite beak noses all right (but so did many of my relatives and me); they wore glasses and looked serious; but they didn't talk with any pronounced Brooklyn, New York accents. He was quite bald with grey sideburns. They were nicely and conservatively dressed, but then so were most of our guests. She was a bit grouchy right off, complaining about the trip, the road, the car, her husband, the weather, her multitude of aches and pains. She didn't seem much like Molly Goldberg to me.

"I'm to bed right away," Mrs. Levy said. "And, please, Miss Meyer, send my dinner up. I couldn't make it downstairs tonight. I must lie down from this highway ordeal. Route One has become impossible. The trip seems to get longer and longer every year. Except for dinner, I don't want to be disturbed."

Having made her intentions known, she brushed right by Miss Meyer and me and went right upstairs to their room.

Mr. Levy seemed worried and tired, maybe from riding so far with his wife. He was not pushy or obnoxious like he was supposed to be. He was very soft-spoken, thoughtful, and very nice to Miss Meyer and me. He didn't shout or make demands. He even smiled at us; and after I had carried all of their luggage to their room and the car was parked, he gave me a dollar tip.

"You were wrong, Hattie," I said upon returning to the kitchen, waving the greenback in her face.

"Have you scrutinized that bill under a magnifying glass? It's probably freshly minted, you know, just to hand to young suckers like you. It's either that, or that's the tip for all of us for the next two weeks. So don't spend any of it; two-thirds may be mine!"

"Oh, Hattie, I don't believe you. They seemed just ordinary people to me. And he's no Shylock."

"Appearances are deceiving. We shall see."

But for the two weeks of their stay, we heard more than we saw. For her entire visit, Mrs. Levy stayed mostly confined to her room, coming out not more than a dozen times for a meal, a walk about the Neck, or a ride in the car. Caroline, the chambermaid, said she had to practically make the bed around her. Often the breakfast trays taken up to her room were returned with most of the dishes smashed all to pieces. When this happened, Miss Meyer would instruct Caroline or Hattie to make a list of what was broken and she would add it to the Levys' bill.

The Mystery of the Smashed Crockery was solved one morning when Caroline was cleaning the hall near the Levys' room. She reported to us that she could clearly hear Mrs. Levy yelling and screaming at her husband, and then the sound of breaking glasses as if she were throwing the dishes at him. Occasionally, Mr. Levy's voice would also be raised in anger. Evidently, all was not total happiness within the rich Jewish confines.

Every day Mr. Levy was up early and would come to see Miss Meyer about what his wife would like for her meals that day. She was a finicky eater and wished everything just so. But he was completely the opposite: he seemed grateful for whatever we set before him and always complimented us on our service and on the quality of the food. He spent his days wandering about the Neck, climbing the rocks and ledges down by the sea, walking to the village and back. Once in a while, I'd see him reading in the hotel library.

One afternoon, when I was down on the rocks sun-bathing and reading one of my books, after having had a bracing dip in the ocean, Mr. Levy appeared from the underbrush above the ledges and sat down beside me for a talk.

"Do you like to read?" he asked.

"Very much," I answered readily, glad to be able to talk with a guest like him.

"Books are a solace," he said.

"I'm trying to read a couple a week this summer."

"Good for you. They can't take that away from you. You'll have your knowledge, your learning, no matter what happens. It'll be something to fall back on."

He was such a sad man, like somewhere, sometime, he had lost something. Everything he said seemed weighted with tragedy, like he had suffered terribly for a long time. I had never met anyone like him before.

"This is beautiful here," he said, looking out at the bay, and to the hills of Mount Desert. "It's life-saving. You could come here and get religious."

"Yeah, it's nice," I said, having known no other area of the world with which to compare it, except northern Maine and Quebec, both of which I had only visited once on school and Boy Scout trips. But every summer I'd hear from visitors like Mr. Levy how beautiful the Maine coastal scene was. To me, then, an anxious and romantic teenage dreamer, the canyons of New York City seemed more beautiful, exciting, and beckoning.

"Where do you go to school?" he asked me.

"Mollusk Memorial High School, near here, up on Route One in East Hamlin. I'll be a senior this coming year."

"What are you going to do after you graduate?"

"I want to go to college. That's why I'm working here, to save money."

"Good for you! You're a smart boy to do that. You want to improve yourself. Good for you." He smiled at me. "What college would you like?"

"Bowdoin or Colby, but I'll probably have to go to Maine."

"The University of Maine in Orono?"

"Yes."

"Well, you get your education. Don't give up and work hard. Keep reading your books. They can't take that away from you, remember. I'll go now, so you can read." He got up from his crouching position and started to leave.

"Good-bye," I said.

"It's not good-bye. I'll see you back up at the hotel, right?" He walked away from where I lay on my towel in my swim trunks, picking his way carefully along the rocks.

With his going, I checked the book cover to see if the publisher was Ginn, his company. It wasn't. It seemed to me that Ginn published mostly schoolbooks.

Later that afternoon, while preparing for dinner, I asked Hattie about the faded numbers tattooed on Mr. Levy's bare arm.

"What do you suppose they mean, Hattie?"

"Well, he was a prisoner in a Nazi concentration camp in World War Two. He lost his whole family and everything. They numbered the prisoners like that," she said. "Also, if you notice, I wait on the Levys, Dr. Fidelstein, and all the other Jewish guests this summer, because Greta doesn't want to. So, Miss Meyer and I had a little talk about it. Miss Krauthead is prejudiced! As if she's got anything to feel superior about!"

"What about Mrs. Levy!" I asked.

"She's an American, his second wife, I believe, poor guy."

A few summers later, one day, when Miss Meyer was reading *The New York Times* at the kitchen table, she turned to me, still at the dishpan, and asked, "Errr. . .Andy, do you remember the Levys who stayed here a couple of weeks in 1959 and again in 1960?"

"Sure."

"Errr. . .well, she died in a terrible way. She evidently choked to death on some meat while flying enroute to Israel."

11

Many afternoons I wouldn't go down to the rocks for a swim, or walk up to the village drug store for a sundae with homemade chocolate sauce, or stay up in my room reading and listening to music. I'd hang around downstairs in the kitchen listening to Miss Meyer talk with some of her local cronies, people who had either worked at one time at the Manor, or were former guests, neighbors from around the Neck, or had serviced the hotel in one capacity or another.

Some of the most interesting gossip sessions for me were held between Miss Meyer and her good pal and frequent dinner guest, Dolly Hillock, whose real Christian name was Edna, and who functioned as the editor, chief reporter, and publisher of the *Summer Harbor Gull*, a weekly local newspaper, which became defunct the next summer of 1960 when Dolly married for the fourth and last time. The ceremony was held upstairs in the Round Room of the Manor, a beautiful circular chamber with a fireplace in the center section--or tower--of the building, from whose five large windows one can see nearly the whole length and width of Frenchman's Bay.

Dolly had a husky, deep, and dramatic voice like Tallulah Bankhead. Her mannerisms even reminded me of that famous actress for she wore sunglasses all the time, and wore her grey hair long and straight and parted on one side. Her laugh was raspy and guttural and her wit sophisticated. She had Maine blood, having been born and bred in Livermore Falls; but she had been around a lot since then and was well aware of the world's possibilities, and she had taken advantage of several of them.

In the course of one or two conversations, she had told me about her music studying days in New York and Europe and how she had once played the piano in Vienna with some orchestra. She had also studied dance under Martha Graham and in Europe had been personal friends with Roland Hayes, the black American singer. He had nicknamed her and her two American girlfriends, who followed him to many of his concerts, "The Three Musketeers." Probably, then, though, to me, since I had never heard of Graham nor Hayes, the most impressive fact of Dolly's career was that she once had played the organ at Radio City Music Hall and on Broadway. I knew without her telling me that she had written two books about Summer Harbor and her life with her first husband in a lighthouse just before and during the years of World War II. Several of my classmates had made book reports on her writings, and we had about a dozen copies of each of the books for sale in the Manor's lobby. And Dolly kept saying she still had a closet full.

She would pull her jaunty green-and-white Jeep with colorful canopy in close by the lilac trees surrounding the back door, entering the hotel accompanied by her huge Chinook dog whom she told me not to bother because he hated males. Over their conversations and jokes, she and Miss Meyer would share drinks and cigarettes.

Dolly would frequently pause to ask me a question or two, not just to be kind or because she was a newshound, but out of genuine interest in me and all people.

"Andy, dear, do you like music?"

"I like the 'Valse Bluette,'" I said.

Dolly laughed. "Oh, my God! That's rich, Jean! Andy liking the 'Valse Bluette!' This big, tall boy! Andy, dear, do you know that was a very funny thing to say?"

"No, not really. It's true. I do like it, at least the version I just heard on an album of Miss Meyer's called "Music for Romancing." I'm trying to learn about great music and that's one of the pieces I like very much so far."

She took my arm. "I'm glad you are, dear. You know. . .you're going to be a big man, when you fill out. Strapping, as they say. Do you know you're going to be strapping?"

"I'm awful skinny."

"Yes, but you've got the frame; all you need is the added muscle, and then you'll be strapping, and women will go crazy over you. Say, would you like to have a nice, cold drink with us? Jean, can Andy have some pop on the rocks?"

"Errr. . .of course. He can take whatever he wishes from the pantry refrigerator. He knows that."

"Yes, I dare say, Andy knows. He must by this time. . ."

From the way Dolly sat in the chair, it was hard to tell whether she was slouching or was round-shouldered. She always did seem sort of bent over.

I didn't know it at the time, but Dolly had quite the scandalous reputation around Summer Harbor. She not only reported the news; she made it. In the war years, when her husband was away fighting for the country, she was not just writing books and giving piano lessons while living in her lighthouse. She had had affairs with some of the local men; and at the end of the war she divorced her husband and married some guy people called the "Amazon Kid."

I asked Hattie who he was.

"Oh, some gink from Canada," she said. "Dolly married him after he'd only been in town for a few days. He told everyone he was on his way to the Amazon to strike it rich, and she had a wild time with him. The marriage didn't last long and then he left town. She had to go back to her lobster fishermen then."

When I came back from the pantry that afternoon with my pop on the rocks, Dolly bent forward over her drink, leaning conspiratorially towards Miss Meyer and me, saying, "Listen, you two. I've got the scoop of the week, and you'll be the first to hear! You've doubtless been hearing all the rumors about who is moving in next door to you, to the old Captain Jones estate?" Jones had been another 19th century Maine sea captain who had built a similar mansion adjacent to the Manor of Captain Moore.

Both Miss Meyer and I nodded, for we had heard the stories, as Dolly continued relating the scoop.

"Well, just as rumor had it, IT IS somebody important from Hollywood, but it's not Zsa Zsa Gabor nor Orson Welles."

"Who?" I asked right away, always excited by Big Names from

American Public Life.

Dolly, always the mannered, but never really phony, actress, deliberately and dramatically paused, sitting back in her chair, taking another sip from her cocktail, keeping us waiting, just a moment more for The Name.

"Hugh Robert Fitzpatrick," she said to my keen disappointment and puzzlement, for I had never heard of him.

"He's a famous movie writer. His scenarios have included such famous movies as *Black Ball Express*, *Seen Through the Binoculars*, several films by Alfred Hitchcock, and most recently, *Plainville, U.S.A.* In fact, while they were filming that infamous movie here in our own state of Maine, Mr. Fitzpatrick, so enamored by Maine's scenery, heard about the Captain Jones place here on Granite Neck, and without coming down the coast here to see it, bought the place, sight unseen, for eighty thousand dollars. Nice what real money can do, isn't it?"

"What's a scenario?" I asked.

"A film script, dear. That's the fancy name for it. I'm an aficionado for fancy names, aren't you? When television has finally succeeded in erasing all the fancy words, along with all the delicious dialects of our language, then I shall want to be long gone!"

"Errr. . .when is Mr. Fitzpatrick supposed to be moving in?" Miss Meyer inquired.

"In two weeks or so, I believe," said Dolly. "He's already been here for a short visit with his beautiful but rather ethereal wife. That's when he was gracious enough to grant me a little interview and that's when I found out all. Rushed right over here to the Neck in my Jeep. He's really quite nice, and handsome in a squinty sort of way. He plans to live here year-round which is quite possible nowadays with a man of his stature. The old Hollywood is no more, I gather; so he doesn't have to be around a studio all the time. He's now working on a film for Elizabeth Taylor, which should interest you, Andy."

"Why?"

"Liz is a sex symbol, dear. One of the world's great beauties. Along with Monroe, she makes males froth at the mouth. Now, I shouldn't have to explain any further. And, well, look, you two, I've got to be running along...the press, that is, mimeograph, must roll. . .and I must join a lovely old lady for dinner. Anybody newsworthy staying here at the Manor this week, Jean?"

"Errr. . .I don't think so. No, not really."

"Well, then, thanks again and again for the spirits, liquid and otherwise. Andy, dear, you are a charming fellow, soon to be strapping. Don't forget, either of you, to hawk *The Gull* to all of your guests Surely they can part with fifteen cents for information and entertainment about this wonderful part of the world! And I do need to eat. . . so, HAWK *THE GULL*! Toodle-oo for now!"

Our new neighbor, Mr. Fitzpatrick, I first met in person one late afternoon several days later in the back parking lot while attempting to change a flat tire on Hattie's Lulabelle, the mufflerless '52 Plymouth, but I didn't know it was he at the time.

For one thing, with my unsophisticated hick's romantic imagination, I didn't expect a famous Hollywood screenwriter to be dressed as a cowboy. He came through the white picket fence garden gate surrounding his backyard sporting a white Levi outfit of jeans and matching denim jacket. He wore fancy boots and a cowboy hat. At first, I thought he was one of the workmen or gardeners who always seemed to be doing something around the Fitzpatrick place, and then I decided he must be a guest of the writer's, maybe even a fledgling cowboy star. He came up to me and asked if I needed any assistance in changing the tire. I said no, even though I had only helped my father change about two tires ever; and so he walked away.

A week or so after that, he and his family held a birthday party for one of his three children at the Manor and I recognized him as the back parking lot cowpoke, even though this evening he was all dressed up, animatedly presiding over the affair. He seemed too young to me to be a famous writer for Alfred Hitchcock.

Anyway, for Caroline Cole and myself, Fitzpatrick-watching became something of a daily sport the rest of the summer. If he was out on his patio, no doubt busy creating clever lines for Liz or Lawrence Harvey, her co-star for the picture, we'd try improvising some "dramatic dialogue" while hanging out the clothes or dumping the garbage. We did a lot of shouting, exclaiming, crying, and carrying on those days just for Mr.Fitzpatrick's benefit; but Hattie told us to cool it for we were just being crazy. "Listen," she said, "even if he could get you two into the movies, which is surely a major doubt in my mind, he wouldn't be about to, with you wrecking the very peace and quiet he needs to work here."

Mr. Fitzpatrick had a beautiful German Shepherd dog whom he kept tied up in his backyard, and who barked a great deal. Caroline and I felt we should try and free the dog; and after lunch one day, we were down on our hands and knees reaching with some leftover meat under the fence, trying to get the pooch to come closer to us so we could unfasten his collar, when suddenly, our eyes met with a pair of fancy boots. When we looked up to see whose feet occupied the boots, it was Mr. Fitzpatrick.

"What do you think you're doing?" asked the Great Master of Movie Dialogue in a not exactly loving tone of voice. "You're not supposed to feed him this stuff," he said. "This dog is a thoroughbred. He eats a special diet, so don't feed him like this again!"

"O.K.," we both said, getting awkwardly to our feet.

Retreating to the Manor to hide our embarrassment as quickly as possible, Caroline said, "Some diet! That man should be reported to the S.P.C.A.! The way that dog ate those leftovers, I'd say he was being starved. No wonder he barks like he does."

When Hattie heard about this latest incident with our celebrated neighbor, she laughed and said, "For God's sake, leave Wee Hughie alone, and let him finish Liz's love scenes!"

"Errr. . .I did hear from Dolly," added Miss Meyer, "that Mr. Fitzpatrick was having his troubles with this current scenario."

"Well, it's no surprise to me, with him being so distracted by the beautiful Maine scenery and these damn kids who pretend to work at the Manor!" Hattie said.

My favorite encounter with Mr. Fitzpatrick occurred at the end of that summer in Merle Bamford's Barber Shop on Main Street in the village. In one part of his shop, Merle had a pool table upon which a number of local men and boys, when they weren't busy fishing or doing something else, used to while away their time and have some fun with the cue sticks and taking bets. Merle also sold penny candy and tobacco products. He and his shop were right out of a Norman Rockwell painting of small-town America. Merle himself could have posed as the prototype of the typical taciturn Yankee stoic so often imitated in books, films, and advertisements. He was just the type of Downeaster the tourists were looking for. Merle stood well over six feet, so he didn't have to adjust his barber chair down much. He had a long, serious face to go with his lean and lanky body. He hardly ever smiled as he clipped and shaved away; and when he spoke, he chose his few words carefully.

Anyway, the conversation in the shop between Merle and the old fellas who sat around in straight-backed chairs in the window and between the older men and the younger men playing pool was often a linguistic treat. The heavy Maine accents mingled with those of the nearby Navy Base sailors from all over the country combined in turn with those of the summer people from Philadelphia provided quite a symphony of strange, and often humorous, sounds. "Some of the chuckles you're apt to hear in my shop," Merle once said, "come from the way some of these fellas put things."

I was in Merle's barber shop one August afternoon when Mr. Fitzpatrick and his little boy, inexplicably nicknamed "Mr. Callahan," happened by and sat down to wait their turns.

Right away, Mr. Fitzpatrick's smile of friendliness faded to an expression of puzzlement. I could tell that he was having trouble deciphering what the old fellas by the window were jabbering about. After all, even as a Maine native, I often had difficulty in understanding the same old fellas, and even the younger fellas. In my area of Maine, the older people had grown up in small towns isolated from each other, and so there would be different expressions and ways of speaking from place to place, just as in the old ethnic neighborhoods in New York. I was thin-skinned, too, when it came to the manner in which some Maine people like Merle, with their often perverse pride, used to sharply and rudely reply to honest questions. For instance, one time, I asked Merle, "What are your hours?" And he snapped, "Can't ya read English? Tells ya right on the door!"

Anyway, that afternoon, one old man was talking in Mr. Fitzpatrick's presence about his "bot dun th' rud" and what not, when the queerest expression appeared on the face of the movie writer, earnestly searching for a clue as to the nature of this version of English he was hearing. He looked from man to man, his ears cocked for part of a word he recognized. He was sort of half-smiling, but not really comprehending.

Merle kept saying "ayuh" no matter what they were discussing. At one point he swung me around in the chair so that I was directly facing Mr. Fitzpatrick, and since it bothered me to see how nonplussed he was without any help from the old fellas who weren't about to include such a stranger in on their secrets, testing him the way they did with all newcomers, I said to him, "They are talking about a boat down the road."

"Oh, yes, thank you," Mr. Fitzpatrick said, fully smiling.

I wanted to know someone like Mr. Fitzpatrick very much and get the chance to talk with him about his work, about Hollywood and the movies, and so this little bit of communication we shared in the barbershop pleased me immensely.

"You're done!" Merle announced, unclasping the hair-covered cloth from about my neck.

"I guess you're next, Mister Callahan," Mr. Fitzpatrick said to his son.

"Not by a damn sight," said Merle. "Ole Alton over here has been waiting his turn all week."

"Oh, excuse me; I thought all of these men were just talking," Mr. Fitzpatrick said to his son.

"Well, the others are," Merle said, "but Alton ain't."

12

Ever since I began working at Frenchman's Bay Manor, I had heard much talk, many jokes, and reminiscences about the fabled Mrs. Madella Richmond, co-owner of the hotel and Miss Meyer's beloved friend of many years. She obviously had a great impact on many people, especially Miss Meyer, Hattie, Berter, and Dolly Hillock, who were always making references, mostly humorous, to her. I really didn't know what to expect upon meeting her, because I had never even seen any pictures.

I was sweating profusely over the kitchen sink one of the hottest and busiest nights of the summer when Mrs. Richmond came waddling through the back dining room into the kitchen, which was a wild scene because the hotel was packed and we were in the middle of serving dinner. I say waddling because Mrs. Richmond must have weighed about 250 pounds or more.

We were having two settings that night in the main dining room in order to accommodate the large overflow of non-hotel guests who had dinner reservations. The hotel people had already eaten and we were in the midst of rushing about the kitchen and pantries, helter-skelter, getting the hot, expensive food to our patrons as soon and as properly as possible without messing up and getting on each other's nerves. With the temperature in the kitchen hovering around the ninety-degree mark, the fan blowing on high, the windows wide open, all of us sweating like stuck pigs, all we needed was to be distracted by someone like Mrs. Richmond, who stood there filling up the kitchen doorway: this round and jolly heavyweight of a woman, dressed in a fancy but wrinkled pink summer suit, with her curly gray hair framing a really quite lovely, happy, fat face bright pink with rouge. Right away, her laughter at the scene of us scurrying madly about under her nose, was booming and infectious. Her eyes twinkled as if she were Burl Ives dressed up as a woman; but when she finally spoke, it was more like Orson Welles playing God.

"Ye Gods and little fishes!" she roared. "The yoke of mammon weighs heavily on their muddled course!"

Her speech, I soon came to realize, was often thus: full of pompous sounding phrases, literary allusion, lusty statement, florid vocabulary, hyperbole, puns, and clichés (I could throw away my high school vocab. lists and just listen to Mrs. Richmond). How she loved to roll her tongue around words, spewing and belching them at us. She treasured a good line or word.

"Errr. . .Madella," said Miss Meyer, "you've arrived earlier than expected."

"Now, that's a fine, rousing way to greet me, Jean! But I can see why you don't want any more excitement at this point. Why, the joint is jumping! We must be in the chips! Now, I'll jes' sit me-self down over here out of harm's way, and watch you people maneuver the *viands* and *hors-d'oeuvres*. Don't anybody bother with me for the moment. Pretend I'm nothing but a local Downeast washerwoman resting from her daily toil. Finish up with the paying guests, and then we'll all have a nip together!"

"It's wonderful to see you, Mrs. Richmond!" Hattie said, hugging our co-boss lady.

"Dear Hattie, it's so good to be here, back in my spiritual home. I got on the road in Greenwich in my merry Oldsmobile and the vision of these haunting tidelands drove me on! Didn't even notice the Merritt Parkway. There was no stopping!"

"Didja have a good trip, Madeller?" asked Berter, who was cooking that night, from the stove.

"My God, Bert, the Olds drove like a Cadillac. And it should! The goddamn thing has a Caddy engine in her!"

Mrs. Richmond may have set herself out of the way, but she certainly never left the action; she commented and laughed about everything. She had to see, feel, smell, and taste everything around her. At one point, Caroline passed by her with a bowl of coffee mousse. Mrs. Richmond stuck her finger in it, tasted it, and declared, "Not bad, Jean, for some old egg whites you whipped up! And say, speaking of that, is that the new whipping boy we've hired, over yonder there, tending the sink?"

She had noticed me finally and told me to come over and meet her across the room.

"Andy, as soon as you have finished up walloping those pans, you want to come out to the car and help me bring in a few things? There'll be a beer in it for ya."

Miss Meyer interrupted before I could answer.

"Errr. . .yes, that's a good idea. Why don't you, Andy, just go right now? Then we can have dinner for Madella ready when you get done."

"Did you get the impression she was trying to get rid of both of us, Andy?" asked Mrs. Richmond with a loud hoot.

I accompanied her outside to her beautiful 1957 Olds 98, silver gray with a red streak along the side, which was parked in the back parking lot; and there she gave me my red cap instructions.

"Deliver them goodies in the front seat, Andy, to the kitchen and pantry cupboards; and that includes the decanters of demon rum lying here and there; they're for us all for our nips. But the stuff in the back seat and trunk lug directly to my quarters over the garage. STEERAGE, I calls it."

The driver's side of the front seat was littered with the crumbs and crumpled wrappings of a variety of sweetmeats. Half-opened and half-eaten boxes of cookies and crackers lay on the passenger's side along with straw baskets and gift packages of fancy jellies and jams. There were several bottles of liquor, the labels of which I couldn't pronounce or understand—liquor was even spelled in a fancy way: "liqueur." And all over the car was strewn a mélange of magazines and paperbacks "for my summer's readings," as Mrs. Richmond said.

First trip, with my arms laden with booty, I trailed after my portly co-boss, she grunting under the weight of her great body up the back porch steps. I felt like some ancient European slave returning with my Queen from Asia bearing a rich haul of spices and jewels with which to fatten our larder.

Once back in the hotel, and busily storing the haul on the shelves in the back pantry, I heard Mrs. Richmond call out to Miss Meyer, "What's for dessert, Jean—apples of discord?"

Instead of apples, we offered our guests a choice that night: the aforementioned coffee mousse served on cut glass plates with fancy cookies, or German chocolate cake *à la mode*.

After dinner, while Caroline, Greta and I finished cleaning up, Hattie and Berter joined Miss Meyer and Mrs. Richmond in the servants' dining room for drinks and joke-telling. Greta resented Hattie's being invited and not her, but Caroline and I tried to explain that she shouldn't feel that way because Hattie and Berter had worked for the Manor for many years. But Greta kept bitching anyway and went home as soon as she could.

I tried to hear the jokes Mrs. Richmond was telling with such success, but the clattering from the cleaning-up was so great that I could only get a spotty account. I remember one punch line to an evidently very humorous "Southern-style" story which Mrs. Richmond told in a mock Southern accent: "And then when the minister in this Baptist church asked all the virgins in the congregation to stand, a man got up with a baby in his arms and said, 'She ain't old enough to stand by herself.'"

At this, there was a lot of laughter from the ladies, but mostly from Mrs. Richmond herself, who had a very loud, infectious whoop of a laugh, one that went right along with her live it-up attitude.

The night after she arrived, Miss Meyer wanted me to dress up in my white dinner jacket and black bow tie (both belonged to the Manor) and get used to helping Hattie and Greta in the dining room as a bus boy; so I was standing in my fancy duds by the back dining room door in late afternoon when Mrs. Richmond banged open the door, nearly slicing off my nose. She was wearing the same pink suit but had freshened up her rouge. I greeted her by smiling and meekly saying, "You look very nice tonight, Mrs. Richmond." And she replied, "I bet!" And clomped on by into the kitchen.

With the arrival of Mrs. Richmond, what a change in the atmosphere! While Miss Meyer had always taken time to relax a bit after the work was done for the day, Mrs. Richmond was apt to take a break in the middle of everything and start telling us stories or giving us lectures on all manner of subjects. Everything that would happen in the course of a day would remind her of something from her past history. During the two weeks she was at the Manor that summer, Mrs. Richmond would take turns with Miss Meyer in supervising the meals and help.

In the mornings, she, too, would sit for lengthy spells in the kitchen in one of the big black armchairs around the folding table reading *The New York Times Book Review*, which she called her Bible, and other literary journals and newspapers, and eating goodies and drinking whatever took her fancy. She had about ten pairs of eyeglasses, and was always trying to find a pair, slapping her hands around and about the mess on the table top, and hollering, "Where's ma specs?"

As she read, she'd talk back to the writers.

"Oh, for God's sake! Clare Boothe Luce, you really are a fool! No wonder you became a Catholic!"

"Who's Clare Boothe Luce?" I asked.

"Oh, I suppose some would say she was the most important woman in America, or some such bull. She's the present wife of Henry Luce who started *Time* magazine."

Then, in the middle of such talk, she'd holler across the kitchen to me at the dishpan, and command, "Say, Andy! Have we got any of that there PEACH SU-PREME, or whatever-in-hell Jean called it, left over from last night? And how about some of that cold cream of leek soup? There must be a cup of that on ice. Do what you can for me, huh?"

One day Caroline was expressing her grief over accidentally breaking a champagne glass, and Mrs. Richmond simply said, "Listen, honey, they used to pitch them things in the fireplace after a nip!"

When Miss Meyer was telling about these guests who were leaving earlier than they had planned and had complained about a number of things, Mrs. Richmond, without looking up from her newspaper, said, "For this relief, much thanks."

I loved her attitude and the way she dealt with the world. One afternoon, she said to all of us, "Ya gotta cut through the crap, or stand the chance of choking to death on it!" She clomped about the Manor in her big, square, white high heels, bellowing and barking like the captain of a ship, which she was in a way.

"Listen, it's all stuff and nonsense! Don't whine and carry on so. You'd think this was the Wailing Wall of Jerusalem! So what if the peas didn't get pureed right!"

One busy week during lunch, she waited on us, her servants, even bringing food to our table, saying, "Here ya go—crumbs from the rich man's table!"

With the trouble and bad feelings between Hattie and Greta coming to a head near the end of July, I'd overhear Miss Meyer and Mrs. Richmond discussing the situation. "Greta has no sense of humor," Mrs. Richmond declared, "and she's too damn German, and I guess we both know enough about that." Both Mrs. Richmond and Miss Meyer were German-Americans.

Then, there was the afternoon, when Caroline and I were just coming in the hotel from having been swimming and sunning ourselves down at the rocks. Our bosslady was at the kitchen table sipping a beer and invited us both to join her.

"Did you kids have a good dip?"

"An-day did," Caroline said, "but I can't swim in the ocean. It's too cold."

"Ah yes," she said, "I remember when Jean and I first moved in here, and I could still scramble down the cliffs to the beach and back. It was on the occasion of the hottest afternoon in July, and I decided to brave the brine. My God, I think I got one toe in! But not much more—that was enough for a farm gal from Kansas! I guess I may have squatted down in a tide pool or two over the summers since, but never again did I take the Atlantic straight on!"

She talked a great deal about her love for New York City, the theatre, and the opera. "I was eighteen when I arrived in New York in 1920, and I've never really left. Oh, it was such a grand time, and the theaters were packed. Two hundred new shows a year then, and I tried to see 'em all. I can't tell you the thrill it was for me to see my first opera at the Met! After that goddamn isolated childhood out on the plains, I felt like I'd been born for the first time. Either of you kids ever been to New York?"

"Nope," I said. "I haven't been much beyond Bangor."

"Poor boy. You must be as hungry as I was," she said. "How about you, Caroline?"

"Well, I did get to Boston once," she said, "but not to New York."

"Well, as soon as we can arrange it, you've got the perfect enthusiastic guide in me! I'll prepare you for the sights you'll have to see some day soon!"

By the time her visit had ended, I had become as big a fan of Mrs.

Richmond's as any other employee of the Manor. Upon her departure, her Olds loaded down with more stuff than when she arrived, she kissed us all good-bye, laughing and bellowing to Miss Meyer, "Jean! The spirit of the troops is excellent! Don't drink too much, honey, and keep the books in the black! I'll be back in September. Keep laughing, everyone!"

With this characteristic advice, she floored the car in her getaway, spinning dust and debris all over us as we stood there waving her on, watching her narrowly miss tree limbs and rock walls, roaring away up the back driveway to the main drag.

13

Oh, what confidence I was gaining, learning to make my own decisions living away from home and my parents. Having just turned seventeen, I was ready to take on the adult world; but I needed that ultimate passport to freedom: a driver's license. Mrs. Richmond had told me before she left that if I'd get my license, she'd maybe let me drive her Olds the next summer.

My test was scheduled for a weekday afternoon in July, so I wouldn't miss any work.

The test was to be administered in Ellsworth, the capital of Hancock County, approximately twenty-five miles from Summer Harbor. My mother picked me up and we drove to the city hall parking lot, where the officer-in-charge greeted me, along with a dozen other prospective drivers. First, along with them, I had to enter the city hall basement to take the written part of the test. I had studied my booklet backwards and forwards, so it was a short and easy affair; they corrected it while you waited, and I passed. From the basement I proceeded back to the parking lot and our family driving machine, the fabulously engineered '51 Merc, to await my turn. All the time I kept worrying about parallel parking, for I didn't feel that I had practiced enough. At nights, all spring, after work, my father would drive with me here to Ellsworth to this same place and I would practice until we were shouting at each other; but at those times the lot had been empty. Now, in the summer rush, the traffic was very heavy. There was hardly a place left to park. And it was very hot.

My examiner arrived with a crunch. The car in which he was testing a young girl about my age came speeding into the parking lot and didn't stop until the front end rammed into the high banked city hall lawn. Evidently, the girl forgot to use her brakes. The policeman got out, fuming and swearing at her. She was in tears, and I assumed she didn't get her license. The incident seemed a bad omen for me.

This same officer who accompanied me on my trial was like every other Downeast cop I had encountered up until then. He was all-business with no perceptible sense of humor, with no special compassion for the shortcomings of humanity. He displayed no wit and made no jokes. He was law and order, right or wrong, black and white all the way. He gave directions clearly and well. Going up State Street Hill by the Congregational Church, which people had warned me about, I didn't pull on the emergency brake hard enough, and we started rolling backwards. I pulled again, harder this time, hoping that the old Merc hadn't slipped too far to flunk me. This second time, to my relief, it held.

I was embarrassed about the age and rusty condition of our car; everyone else who was scheduled for a test that day drove much newer and shinier models. The paint job on our old roadster was so worn that it wouldn't shine. My father, for some reason, had hooked on the fender flaps over the rear wheels that made the fat, hoggish monster look like some hot rodder's racer, which was certainly far from the case. To my way of thinking, he couldn't have done a more stupidly unaesthetic thing, except perhaps to add a raccoon tail to the radio antenna. The rocker panels were all rusty, so he had painted them over with a shade of green darker than the car's over-all pale green color. But in the interest of actually getting my license, I surmounted my feelings of shame, and drove the old Mercury as if it were a brand-new 1959 Chrysler Imperial with push-button drive.

I was lucky, however, during my test when my rigid examiner twice became distracted: first, over a woman jaywalker's suddenly jumping in front of us, and second, over a Greyhound bus almost sideswiping us.

"Get back on the sidewalk, you goddamn fool, and watch where ya going!" he screamed out the window at the woman; and to the backside of the bus, he yelled, "Goddamn idiot ought to be run in for that!"

During these distractions, he didn't notice that I signaled the wrong way when making a turn back to the parking lot whence we came.

As I pulled the car around by the City Hall steps, I was surprised to see my father in his Texaco uniform and cap standing there supervising my ordeal. Evidently, he was in Ellsworth making a fuel oil delivery. He stood there next to Sid, both of them unsmiling, as grim as the couple in the painting *American Gothic*. He was smoking a cigarette while my mother clutched her handbag and tried to be brave for me, trying to compensate as she always did for my father's negative outlook, egging me on to succeed, at least a little bit.

I was sweating at the wheel, listening to the gruff and officious Officer Rigid order me, not to parallel park, as I expected; but to back the car into a very narrow parking space at an acute angle to the edge of the City Hall lawn, right in the path of busy two-way traffic. I was petrified, and wanted to ask him, "Are you crazy? No one in their right mind would back into a space like that! They'd have trouble nosing in, even in a compact car." It didn't even look like an official place to park.

Directly across from where I was trying my best to park the Merc sat this old white-haired codger in the front seat of a brand-new Plymouth trying with his hands and facial expressions to show me how I should cut 'er. He made me more and more nervous every time I noticed him with his furious hand and arm signals and his twitching face. At first, I thought he was having an epileptic seizure, but then I realized that in this foolish, wild way he was trying to help me. I was later grateful to him, but as I glanced from his face to my father's to my mother's to Officer Rigid's and then again through the side mirror and rear-view mirror and out the back window towards that narrower-than-narrow space and realized the limited clearance to either side of me, I became nearly hysterical. I backed back a bit and than I went forward, backing and filling, whenever the traffic flow let me. Cars kept coming by all the while, hindering my delicate maneuvering. And then, after what seemed a great length of time, Officer Rigid Himself began to squirm. He turned and twisted his head with me to look first front and then back and then to either side; but he didn't say anything, which was good.

Finally, after what seemed an eternity to all five of us involved in this little scene, and after I had the car lined up in the best position I could manage, I drove forward one more time, put the shift into reverse, glanced back for the last time, closed my eyes, and shoved down on the gas. The Merc lunged backwards, and I prayed, expecting to hear this dreadful crunch of metal against metal, from one side or the other; but I did it! With hardly two inches to spare on the passenger's side. I knew after seeing how close I had come to the other car, that I hadn't passed the test.

Officer Rigid looked at my papers, and asked, "Do you always close your eyes when parking your car?"

I wanted to scream at the bastard, "Look, no one with half a brain would back up in this narrow space in the middle of July on a hot busy day like this!" But I said nothing.

"You need to practice your parking," he said, sounding the death knell, "but. . .you passed." He handed me my temporary license. "Send this paper to the Motor Vehicle Bureau with your fee."

Relieved and happy, I took the paper from him.

"Thank you," I said.

"Don't thank me. Just practice your parking."

Then he looked out the window on his side which was almost one with this other car.

"I'll have to get out your side," he said.

When I got out of the car and met with my parents, I realized how wet my shirt was from all my perspiration during the ordeal. It was sopping.

"Did you pass?" asked my mother.

"Yes," I said. "Isn't that amazing?"

"I'd say so," my father said.

"That was an awful spot to try and back into," my mother said.

"Sure was," I agreed.

My father went back to his truck, off to make another delivery down on Mount Desert Island; and on my way back to work with my mother, who let me drive to celebrate, she said, "Just because you got your license now, don't get the idea you're going to be on the road all the time."

And when I returned to the Manor that afternoon, Miss Meyer and Hattie, who were having coffee at the kitchen table, congratulated me. Hattie said, "Now, An-day, you can really start your love life, soon's you get a car to go with your license!"

14

Most guests at the Manor arrived during the afternoon, but occasionally we had a night time arrival. One of our regular Night Hawks was Miss Betsy Jane Rousseau, society editor of one of Canada's major newspapers. She arrived in July 1959 in a little red Renault Dauphine accompanied by a middle-aged girlfriend, a much younger boyfriend, two suitcases, and a bag of liquor. As I helped them unload their car, they giggled with each other continuously. I wondered if all three of them were to occupy the same room. Naive of me to wonder.

Betsy Jane was like a breezy, brash heroine of a 1930s Hollywood comedy. Sporting black-and-white spectator pumps, a black-and-white suit with red lipstick and red accessories, she was very blonde and thin. Always in a mad rush with her heels clicking up and down the stairs, she spoke both French and English fluently and rapidly. She told old, mostly vulgar jokes and she evidently liked her booze.

Her girlfriend was a round complement to Betsy Jane's sharp angles. The girlfriend was brown-haired, soft, pretty, and dressed all in pink. She adored Betsy Jane, you could tell, and chuckled at every quip that came from the saucy society columnist's lips.

The boyfriend was male-model handsome with a deep tan, and he spoke only French. His well-tailored clothes fit him like a glove and his job was evidently to keep looking cool and to keep the ladies amused and in a state of excitement with all his pinching, tickling, grasping, and fondling.

The three of them had, from all appearances, been on an extended joy ride all the way from Montreal to the Maine coast. The whole weekend visit to the Manor seemed some kind of joke.

I stood out in the parking lot with them with a flashlight as they giggled and fumbled about with the keys and coats, while Miss Meyer stood silhouetted in the hotel's front doorway, awaiting their entrance. She had roused me from bed when they arrived.

With the front-end trunk finally open, Betsy Jane pointed at the suitcases and bag of liquor and exclaimed to me, "*Voilà*! Those, *Cherie*. Please bring those!"

I followed them inside, the boyfriend in the middle, holding both women who found it difficult walking on our graveled driveway in spike high heels. As they stumbled, however, they laughed.

"Errr. . . what a smart outfit, Betsy Jane," said Miss Meyer.

"Black and white and red all over! Just perfect for a newspaper woman, wouldn't you say?" said Betsy Jane.

They were to occupy the Number Two and Three rooms, which actually constituted a suite with bath between the two bedrooms. One room had twin beds and the other a double. It was the perfect set-up for peccadilloes. And speaking of set-ups, I had to fill a rush-order immediately for them. Betsy Jane hoped I wouldn't mind a tip with Canadian coins.

"This whole trip was just so spur-of-the-moment," she said. "The only kind of trips to take!"

Every morning of their three-day stay, Caroline found at least two empty liquor bottles occupying their wastebaskets along with other interesting and exotic items. The three were not very discreet in their intentions, and this bothered Miss Meyer who said at one point, "Errr. . . I may have to speak to Betsy Jane about her future stays here."

The morning they left, Caroline came downstairs with a cocktail shaker that came from their suite.

"Would you look at this tip!" she said to Hattie and me in the kitchen.

We looked. In the bottom of the shaker, a most fancy piece of glassware and Miss Meyer's favorite for mixing her own drinks, someone had deposited a stool of excrement.

"My God, a turd!" Hattie said. "Now, who do you suppose had the most delicate rear end—that pretty French guy?"

"I don't know," Caroline said, "but I'm not going to stand around and smell it any longer. I think it's disgusting."

"It's certainly a conversation piece," said Hattie. "Maybe one of them was just too drunk to crawl into the bathroom."

"They couldn't have been that drunk without hurting themselves," Caroline reasoned.

"You've got something there, Kar-O-line," Hattie said.

"I sure have. What am I bid?"

15

When he could get away from his own jobs, Lester Moon, my best pal from Mollusk High since our freshman year, would drive down to the Neck, and we'd go on adventures together.

Les had a boat and a few lobster traps that he hauled, but mostly, he worked as a caretaker's assistant for the Mirbach estate, a summer villa made possible by Mr. Mirbach's liquor importing business.

Les got his driver's license our junior year in high school, and soon after, his own '52 green Ford Tudor sedan with which he had managed to extend the boundaries of his social existence. We had double-dated a couple of times, and to hear him tell it, he had girlfriends all over Hancock County, and he did have a couple, which was two more than I possessed.

Standing a little under six feet, Les had black hair and blue-gray eyes. He was as skinny as I was but he had much better skin and tanned better than I did. He always wore Roebuck jeans and flannel shirts. He had a deep voice and a wonderful Downeast twang. I treasured him for his dry sense of humor, his jokes and his good stories. For the four years in high school, we took all the same classes.

Whenever Les visited me during those summers at Granite Neck, we'd most often end up cruising around the area in his car, listening to rock-'n'-roll music from WMEX in Boston, swapping jokes and stories, talking about cars, school, our summer jobs, mutual friends, our families, and plans for college.

One such afternoon that first summer, we joined forces with another school classmate, Cal Burpee, in his Jeep for a wild tear down a rough road that led to the run-down summer estate of Mrs. Electra Danforth and her prep school son Whitney, who had just dialed an emergency call to Cal. It seemed that Whitney had mired his mother's new Lincoln Continental in the clam flats and the tide was coming in.

By the time we had arrived at the head of the point several miles up the peninsula from Granite Neck, the Lincoln was already up to its rocker panels in salt water. Whitney with his tangled hair and patrician features was stalking the beach with his cigarette, bottle of beer, and latest girlfriend, who was standing around all pouty in her short shorts and halter.

Whitney, in soaking wet tee-shirt, jeans, and moccasins, looked as if he'd been trying to free the car from underwater.

"Jesus fucking Christ, Cal!" Whitney greeted us, "I hope to hell that Jeep is strong enough to pull out this car!"

"We might have to dig out the tires a bit more, but the tide coming in will help loosen 'er," Cal said.

As Cal, Les, and I got out of the Jeep and began to connect the chain to the front end of the Lincoln, Whitney said, "We've got to be as quiet as possible, too, since Mother's room is right up there facing us, and she doesn't know how we got her car stuck!"

"Well, we'll try and spin the tires on the Jeep as quietly as we can!" said Cal with a wink to Les and me.

Whitney never did introduce his girlfriend to us. She just stood by, as if in a catatonic state. Whitney's mother had been a beautiful high-fashion model in New York with her picture in many national magazines; but after she had divorced Whitney's father, she went from man to man, and around the world; but she always returned to the Maine coast in the summers.

On Cal's first attempt at freeing the Lincoln, the mud and sea water and sand were flying every which way; and it took several more tries and a lot of tugging, pulling, pushing, chain slipping, with us all wet and muddy, before the car was actually loose and free, the sea water swirling about our ankles.

Whitney thanked the three of us, and invited us over for a beer "real soon," obviously too busy and too concerned about his girl and his mother to do so right then. "I hope to hell the old lady's still knocked out," he said.

"You better hose down your car to get the salt off," advised Les, as we drove by Whitney up the road that went down to the beach.

"Yes, O.K.," he said, waving good-bye to us.

"He won't bother," said Cal. "He doesn't care if his mother's car rusts.

"How old do you think that girl is, twelve or thirteen?" asked Les.

"Oh, I'd say she had to be at least fourteen," said Cal, "and stupid enough to think that Whitney Danforth is a great guy!"

As we drove by, I took a good look at the old Danforth mansion-by-the-sea. Then it was in sad shape, rotted and dilapidated; and I was reminded of a story my mother had told about the place. A few years before, Mrs. Danforth had invited all the Pilgrim Guild ladies from our Taunton Congregational Church down for a Sunday afternoon tea, but the Saturday night before, Mrs. Danforth had held another party with one of her men friends that had progressed into the wee hours. When the good church ladies arrived for their tea, they found empty whiskey bottles, broken glasses, leftover food, and cigarette butts all over the messy living room. The place was a shambles, and the ladies, according to my mother, were deliciously shocked. They actually found the aftermath of just what they wanted and all the rumors about Mrs. Danforth were instantly confirmed. The Lady of the House did make a brief appearance in her dressing gown at the head of the stairs, where she informed the women that she was unfortunately in no condition to proceed with the discussion of the final plans of that summer's annual flea market and rummage sale.

After I recounted this tale, Les and Cal added their much saltier reminiscences of the Danforth clan, and by the end of our drive up the private dirt road to the main highway that headed back down the peninsula to Summer Harbor, we were all laughing, taking pleasure, as did our elders, in feeling slightly superior to these crazy, outlandish summer neighbors of ours.

"You know, Mrs. Danforth was once a high-fashion model in New York," I said.

"Now, she's just high all the time!" said Cal.

"Christ, she doesn't even wear a bra!" said Les. "And she fucks half the lobstermen down at the Co-op."

"All she's good for these days is fucking and drinking," said Cal, "but she's probably all stretched out. With her, a guy would just fall in."

"Oh, I think there's more to Mrs. Danforth than that," I said. "She's a pretty sharp dame."

"Christ, An-day! You always take up for the summer shitheads, don't ya?" Cal asked.

"Not exactly," I said, "but I don't think they're all as bad as you always paint them."

"They're worse!" said Les. "They save up all winter to come here and pay us as cheaply as possible, or not at all, so they can live their high life with their boats and booze while they look down their goddamn noses at us!"

At such moments, to me, Cal and Les sounded just like so many of our elders, full of resentment and bitterness, always accusing the summer people of drinking too much, screwing around and being lazy, while conveniently neglecting the fact that such accusations could be applied to a number of natives as well. Local mythology had it that these foolish, impractical, wasteful summer people were always getting themselves into silly scrapes and had to be rescued and set aright by the more practical, sensible, and self-righteous natives, who knew right from wrong, and knew enough not to tamper with Nature's laws. In the case of Whitney Danforth, no self-respecting Downeaster with an ounce of common sense would be driving a new Lincoln Continental on the clam flats with the tide coming in; but then, most Downeasters we knew would be able to meet the payments on such a car in the first place. And if a local boy was after a girl like that, he'd have done it in the bushes or in the field, not down on the beach in his mother's car.

"You did notice, An-day," said Cal, "how Whit asked me how much I owed him for pulling him out? Maybe a beer some time! I'll never get a cent out of the bastard! That's just typical of the way they are!"

16

Mrs. Richmond and Miss Meyer were always fuming about the lack of business from their neighbors on the Neck. My bosses refused to join the local "Improvement Association" and Yacht Club, because they felt the annual fee was exorbitant; but they still expected association members to patronize the Manor. There were occasional guests who were relatives or friends of people on the Neck; and there were also several regulars who ate at the Manor on their cook's day off, one of these being the richest person in the neighborhood, as well as one of the world's richest women. She'd be driven to the Manor every Wednesday for luncheon in her Bentley by her chauffeur. She'd also have lawyers, various financial advisors, and even hairdressers flown in from Philadelphia who'd stay at the hotel until summoned for their audience.

One Philadelphia lady whose relatives owned a large summer cottage on the Neck was Mrs. Rosie Talbot, who stayed at the Manor every summer for the first two weeks in August with her driver and companion, Mrs. Ruth Tainter.

Miss Meyer prepared me for meeting Mrs. Talbot by telling me a story that went something like this: when she was a rich little girl growing up in the City of Brotherly Love, Rosie had gone traipsing through Africa on a safari with her intrepid Daddy, a big game hunter, and there she was bitten by the tse-tse fly, or whatever bug it is said to cause sleeping sickness. However, Rosie did not succumb to this "deadly disease," which is the usual case. She survived, sort of; but was left crippled in mind and body. But she was still very rich, so much so that some strange man married her for a while and lived off her trust fund until Rosie's family could get rid of him, no doubt leaving him in a more fortunate position than when he entered the picture.

I met Rosie knowing this story, but still not prepared for her looks. I was simply standing there, waiting patiently in my usual position with Miss Meyer, under the *porte-cochère* for the long, black, gaudy 1958 Mercury to pull up where I could perform my, by now, very familiar bellhop routine.

What a shock! She looked like a monster to me: this deformed, huge woman hunched over in the front seat with a little dinky hat perched on the back of her head and a large silly grin on her face. She was in late middle-age and she wore glasses. Her voice in greeting Miss Meyer and me was like a drunken, raspy, nearly unintelligible slur. Her declarations were exclamatory.

"MIZ MEYER! SHO GOOD TO SEE YOUSE, MIZ MEYER!" she yelled out the car window.

"Err. . .good to see you, too, Rosie," said Miss Meyer.

To look at Rosie when she spoke was enough to turn one's stomach. She frothed, drooled, hummed, smacked and seemed always to be chewing or chomping on something, which often turned out to be the case. Most of the time she carried with her a half-melted and messy box of expensive candies which she generously offered to anyone present. Right away to me, she proffered the box of assorted chocolates. They looked as if someone had tried to make a mud pie with them, in their frantic search for a favorite flavor.

"YOUSE WANNA PEECESSE OF CANDY, BOY?" Rosie asked me.

"Sure," I said, trying to smile at her. I picked out a piece while she tried to hold the box steady that didn't seem too squashed or half-eaten or drooled upon. "Thank you," I said.

"THASS O.K.," she said, grinning. She stared at me while I ate it. I found out she talked so loudly because she was deaf. She also watched people's lips so she could tell what they were saying. She was very good-natured and wildly enthusiastic about life, like an oversized child. At such moments, everything seemed to excite and please her.

She grabbed my hand at one point and started pumping it up and down. "ANDY NICE! ANDY NICE BOY, MIZ MEYER!"

"Errr. . .yes, he is," said my boss.

Mrs. Tainter, Rosie's companion and keeper, and a Philadelphia doctor's widow, could have been played by Olivia De Havilland as she appeared in the film *Hush, Hush, Sweet Charlotte*, being extra sweet to Bette Davis' demented frump. Mrs. Tainter was a handsome, carefully composed, and precise woman who not only did the driving; she controlled and managed Rosie's every waking moment. Mrs. Tainter also evidently wore a very tight constricting corset, for the movements of her torso were incredibly restricted. From the waist on up she seemed unnaturally erect and moved the upper part of her body as if robotized. She had a wealth of long blondish gray hair done up on top of her head. She was very gracious in her statements and appearance, but one could detect an air of craftiness about her. She treated Rosie like a little child.

"Now, Rosie," she would say, "let's put the messy chocolates away while we unpack the car."

As soon as Mrs. Tainter spoke to her, Rosie's sunny grin and happy manner faded. She became suddenly silent and pouty, like a scolded, spoiled youngster.

While Mrs. Tainter, with Rosie and Miss Meyer helping, unpacked the Mercury, I started upstairs with some of Rosie's luggage. Since it was to be a three-week stay, they had a lot, and there were several trips to make from car to room.

Rosie was being installed in the Number Nine Room where I had spent my first night in the Manor. Just as I was placing the two heaviest bags on the luggage racks, I heard this incredible noise as if a horse were loose and galloping and banging up the stairs and down the hall. Suddenly, Rosie appeared in the doorway of Number Nine, her misshapen hulk of a body draped in an ill-fitting but expensive suit. In her hands dangled her handbag and the ever-present box of crushed candy.

"WHERE'S MA DUDS?" she asked. "WHERE'S MA DUDS?"

"Your suitcases are right here, Mrs. Talbot."

"THASS GOOD, ANDY!" she slurred, grinning and smacking her

lips, staring right into my face. "THASS GOOD, ANDY!"

I started to step by her to return to the car, but this female Frankenstein shoved the chocolate box in my face again.

"WANNA PEECESSE OF CANDY, ANDY?" she frothed.

"Another one? Sure, O.K.," I said, even though I didn't. I reached in for another unsquashed piece.

"THASS DELISHSHUS, ANDY. THASS DELISHSHUS!"

"Sure is," I said, smiling through my chewing, trying to show her how pleased I was for the sweet.

Despite her grotesqueness, I liked her. She was a good person, and not at all childish, more child-like; and there's a difference. I sensed that she knew what was going on all right, and that her mind wasn't all that atrophied. She was making the best of an awful situation. She seemed like a prisoner in her own body, like the Beast in *Beauty and the Beast*, transformed from a kind and loving human into an ugly monster.

That evening, after Rosie had been put to bed, Mrs. Tainter came downstairs to the kitchen to have a nightcap with Miss Meyer. She had literally let her long hair down and was attired in a fancy housecoat. Her corset had evidently been removed also, for she moved about much more freely and normally. After downing one drink and beginning another, her mouth loosened up, too. She bewailed her station in life as Rosie's constant companion. She seemed to resent the poor lady and had very little sympathy for her; but she stayed on the job, she said, because of the security and benefits. Rosie's family had evidently set her up nicely so that Mrs. Tainter's comforts were assured forever.

"All these years, I've never really been able to completely enjoy my vacations here in Maine or down at Palm Beach in the winter, because I've had to keep DEAREST ROSIE on her schedule. We have to have tea every goddamn afternoon with more of her boring Philly relatives and friends, none of whom really want to see Rosie for more than ten minutes here or any other place. If only they could see what I have to endure every day. If only my dear late husband could see how I ended up! The tantrums she throws when I'm trying to get her into her nightie! And the hell she raises when I'm trying to get her to take a bath. She throws soap and water at me! It's such a nightmare sometimes, with those damn chocolates and her painting crap!"

Mrs. Tainter was referring to the fact that every afternoon before tea, Rosie painted miniature water colors. Sometimes she'd do ten or twelve a day so that by the end of their Downeast sojourn, there's be dozens of these little, child-like painting of rocks, trees, lighthouses, ocean waves, blue skies, and what not. There was an exhibit of them one afternoon that August in Rosie's room and all of the staff was forced to attend. Some of the guests were there, too, and lemonade and cookies were served. The overall effect of her works, I felt, was light-hearted and optimistic. Things looked pretty and bright to her, but her technique was simple to the point of resembling grammar school efforts.

Everyone said something nice to Rosie, anyway, and a couple of guests actually bought a few samples. Rosie signed her name to her pictures with just her initials. Hattie kept raising her eyebrows and winking at me throughout the exhibit.

Afterwards at supper, Hattie asked, "How come you didn't blow your paycheck on a painting today, An-day? Art's a good investment, they say; and I thought you were a connoisseur."

"What I know about art, Hattie, could be printed up on a tiny postage stamp."

"Well, I've seen tiny postage stamps that were more artistic than Rosie's offbeat view of the local scene."

Besides painting on paper, Rosie also indulged from time to time in the more kinetic art form of interior decoration. She particularly favored bathrooms. One disastrous evening, Caroline came running out to the kitchen to tell Miss Meyer that something had evidently overflowed upstairs and water was dripping from the ceiling into the butler's pantry right onto the dessert trays.

Miss Meyer said to me, "Errr. . .Andy, run upstairs, will you, and see if anything is wrong?"

"Sure," I said, abandoning my dishpan for the back stairs.

When I reached the second floor hall, I located the trouble right away, in the bathroom across the hall from Rosie's room. Opening the door, I stepped into a puddle almost an inch deep. From the bits of paper and fecal matter floating all over, and from the smell, it was obvious that someone had plugged up the toilet, which had overflowed, and was still overflowing.

As I rushed about procuring a plunger, a mop and a pail, my report to the troops downstairs was greeted by a laugh and comment from Hattie. "Every time the old gal gets a few boxes of those chocolates in her, she explodes! Happens every summer."

And it didn't just happen once that summer. Unfortunately for me, it was a rather frequent occurrence for a week or so there. We learned to keep a close check on Mrs. Talbot's movements to and from the bathroom.

Coming downstairs any time, Rosie sounded like a party of four youngsters clomping and clattering as fast as their wooden shoes or logging boots could carry them as if pursued by wild animals. Rosie's noisy descent was a daily irritation that several of the other guests didn't learn to appreciate. There were a few complaints and Miss Meyer finally requested that Rosie use the back staircase as much as possible.

Julie Lawson was probably the most pleased of our guests to have Rosie around, for in Rosie, Julie found a constant walking and talking companion, someone who could more than keep up with Twinkle Toes on her nightly jaunts about the Neck.

Together, they'd explore the roads and walks of the peninsula each night after supper. Julie would be in the lead, dancing along animatedly on her toes, chattering girlishly and continually over her sweater-draped shoulder to Rosie, the hunch-backed giantess, clomping right along after Miss Southern Belle. Rosie would have her little hat on the back of her head and her dinky little pocketbook dangling from one of her paws. She didn't carry her chocolate box at night, because Mrs. Lawson had informed her how neither of them should be eating such a thing.

"How would you like to run into those two some dark night in the woods?" Hattie asked me.

17

After work, I spent as much time as I could with Caroline Cole and her family. Her father owned a garage in Westbay just up the peninsula on Route One and their house was on what was called the Guzzle Road. Several afternoons I went with Caroline to her uncle's camp on nearby Smith's Pond in the middle of the peninsula where we went swimming and boating with her two younger brothers and sister and her cousins, all of whom were younger than we were. Her uncle had a miniature sailboat big enough for one person and a kayak with which we had a lot of fun. There was always plenty of picnic food, soda pop, and good storytelling among the Cole clan that I enjoyed.

Caroline had the use of her family's '57 Dodge which I thought was the ultimate in car design. It was painted turquoise and black with fins and push-button drive. She also had a '41 black Chevy coupe which she drove more than the Dodge. The Chevy's front seat was permanently stuck way back from the steering wheel, so that a short person, like Caroline's mother, had trouble reaching the clutch and accelerator. When Caroline or her mother, whose great sense of humor could always regale me, would be driving, the old car would jerk this way and that with the uneven pressure applied to the gas pedal by someone's uncontrolled foot. Whenever this happened, which was almost every time we went for a spin together, it would always get worse before it got better, for the jerking of the car would make us laugh harder. Several times we almost combined with a tree or two beside the road when we were in that jouncy condition.

One night when Caroline had invited me to go home with her after work and stay overnight, we shared a memorable little scene with the Chevy. As we were driving down the back driveway toward the road, Caroline said the car was steering hard, that something must be wrong and that maybe we had a flat tire. She stopped by the side of the road right across from the main entrance to the Manor which was all lit up for the evening, the way Miss Meyer liked it to look. I got out, looked, and found Caroline to be correct in her estimation of our trouble: the front tire on the passenger's side was as flat as an Aroostook County potato field. We had been driving practically on the rim. Since she did not have any tire-changing tools in the trunk, I had to return to the Manor's garage, but searching there was to no avail. Luckily, Mrs. Lawson was just returning from her nightly hike about the oval, when she noticed our predicament.

"I have tools," she said. "Come. . ."

Caroline did have a spare tire, and Mrs. Lawson's tools worked well enough; but at nine o'clock at night, after a long day's work, I wasn't in the mood to try and change a tire. With the weight of the car and the softness of the pavement, the jack sank into the road. The washers on the wheel were rusty and hard to loosen, and the wrench was old and awkward. The whole operation, illuminated by Caroline's holding a small flashlight, took quite a long time.

"Gosh, Caroline," I said, "couldn't you have found a smaller flashlight?"

"This one is awful teeny, isn't it? I'm sorry, An-day, but this one fits into my handbag better than a big bulky one."

Beyond Mrs. Lawson, we attracted attention from one other night person out walking his poodle. Just as I was hammering the hubcap back on the wheel with my fist, Mr. Lyon, the guest from the French embassy, happened by.

"You have feenished? Praise the Lord," he said.

"And pass the ammunition," whispered Caroline to me.

With Caroline and her jovial mother Elsie, I saw two movies the summer of 1959, which I loved: *Some Like It Hot* with Marilyn Monroe and *Gigi* with Leslie Caron and Maurice Chevalier. They were both shown at the county's only drive-in theater on the Bar Harbor Road, a little over twenty miles from the hotel, so we really had to rush after work, racing with the receding sun before it became too dark, to make it just in time for the beginning of the show.

Only once did Caroline stay the afternoon with me to go swimming and sunbathing down on the rocks in front of the Manor. I was pleased and excited for I wanted her companionship. We were teenagers of the opposite sex, after all, and she was only a year older. I was ever anxious, if also ever-shy, to find out more about sex. I had even bought some daring new swim trunks that I hadn't worn in front of anyone else before.

Until 1959, my mother had bought me regular elastic-band, boxer-style, plain-colored trunks from J.J. Newberry's, the type of trunks with built-in support; but this summer on my own, I had clandestinely sent away for some "Riviera Style" trunks, as advertised in the back pages of a body building magazine. Surely, anyone seeing someone clad in these trunks would realize, as the ad had proclaimed, that the young swaggerer was "ready for action."

Right after we finished with our luncheon duties, I rushed up to my room and put on the new trunks. They had no protective pouch or inside support, because they were reversible: black on one side and white on the other. While not as revealing as briefs, the trunks fit much more snugly and lower on the hips than boxer-style. They had no fly flap either; there was a zipper on one side, and this bothered me because it seemed rather feminine to have a side zipper. The new trunks felt good, however, so much so that I became aroused. Trying to take my mind off such an embarrassing situation, I quickly slipped my jeans over the new sensation, pulled on a tee-shirt, grabbed a towel, my suntanning lotion, my sunglasses, and my usual book, and went back downstairs where I met with Caroline on the back porch for our trek to the cliffs.

One didn't rush down to the ocean from the Manor, unless one wished to break one's neck. It was an arduous trip picking one's way down to the cliffs and an even more arduous climb back up. Most of the trees had been cleared so that there was a more unobstructed view of the water from the hotel's windows, but there were boulders, outcroppings of ledge, and a lot of neck-high puckerbrush with only the slight rudiments of the path that hadn't been kept up.

Caroline and I picked up the trail at the edge of the back lawn and followed it through crab grass, blueberry and blackberry bushes, across two broken-down little wooden bridges that spanned usually dry streams, finally arriving on a beach of small pink granite boulders bordered on either side by the lovely sloping pink cliffs of the same substance. I learned later in geology class at the University of Maine that this is the "Bar Harbor Granite."

Perched high above the beach on one ledge was erected the shell of a fancy little beach or tea house, built of the same materials and in the same shingle style as the Manor itself. Vandalism and nature had reduced its beauty to a state of broken-down disrepair. Miss Meyer had told me that the boy students at the exclusive remedial Three R's Summer School located on the other side of the Neck from the hotel were responsible for much of the damage; and, indeed, I had seen several teen-age lads lurking about and within the structure a few times when I had been down on the cliffs. They, or someone of little wit or originality, had carved the usual banal obscenities upon the walls of the little house.

It was in the shadow of the wrecked beach house that Caroline and I removed our outer garments for our proposed afternoon dip in the brine.

I showed her how I used to love to sit on the edge of the cliffs, especially when it was very windy and rough, and have the waves sweep over me and sweep me off into the ocean. She thought it was dangerous, but I thought it was exciting; and in my haste to show off my athletic prowess, I plunged too quickly off the cliff, slicing my foot on a sharp edge of rock or some barnacles. I yelled out and not just from the freezing temperature of the water. Crawling ignominiously out of the water and back up to where Caroline was sunbathing, I noticed how badly I had cut my appendage. The blood was running freely and we had nothing but my tee-shirt with which to bandage it.

"My mother always wears light sneakers when she swims in the ocean," said Caroline.

"Yea, I know some people who do that, too; but sneakers feel so clumsy when you're trying to swim. I guess I can see why, though."

I must have looked like such a stupid fool. We sat there a few minutes longer admiring the view and the ocean waters slapping around us and the rocks, but my foot continued to bleed through the cloth; and we presently returned to the hotel.

Caroline had noticed my new bathing ensemble, but she hadn't said anything; and now, because of my blood-soaked loafer and limping up the cliffs, I felt I had taken more than a reckless dive.

What could have been going on in my head at that point? I knew I had to do something about my virginity, but I wasn't sure how to proceed, especially with nice girls like Caroline. I was certainly hornier than a Maine barn cat, jerking off two or three times a day to all manner of masturbation fantasies. But how to put them into practice with real, live people? There had been furtive, exploratory forays with my cousin Lillie Partridge; but Essie Torrey seemed to be the only real possibility for sex; and I was scared to death of Essie. It was the late 1950s, after all, and if a boy got a girl pregnant, he married her.

18

Leading with her buck teeth, Mary Treat burst through the screen door on the back porch of Frenchman's Bay Manor one dreary afternoon and spied me sitting at the table in the back dining room writing.

"Oh, Andy! I so hoped I'd find you here. With the impending downpour, I thought you might be in."

"Certainly a poor day for a stroll, Mary. What brings you down from the family estate--going slumming?"

Mary was a classmate from school who lived year-round on Granite Neck and full-time in a fantasy world. She told wild tales about her international connections and the alleged loss of the Treat family fortune in 1929 that had left them virtually penniless, except for their Maine summer cottage, which had to then become their winter home as well, and which now stood in a sad state of neglect. Mary herself, she would readily admit, had never known money, only the vestiges of what money had once bought; but she compensated, she thought, for her homely physical appearance—she was over-tall, gawky, gaumy, and overweight besides being buck-toothed—by telling these incredible tales about her family's legendary fall from financial, political, and social grace to anyone who would listen. Her name-dropping and acting superior to us local yokels did get tiresome.

As far as I knew, her father repaired TV sets and radios and held some kind of part-time electrician's job at the Navy Base while her mother was a substitute English and French teacher at Mollusk Memorial High. And so it had been for some time; they were no more aristocratic than my parents. But Mary persisted in and even strengthened her belief that she had more class and knowledge by natural birthright than the rest of us, and would doubtless rise again back to her deserving state in a matter of time. "It's a matter of making the right investments," she'd say.

She sat there in the servants' dining room across the table from me while I was trying to answer a letter. She had on one of her father's old sports coats which she often wore because "they were so fun." Actually, she probably couldn't afford many new clothes for herself so she wore his cast-offs and started another of her one-girl eccentric fads. As usual, she reeked of body odor.

"What are you doing?" she asked.

"I'm composing a thank-you note to the Empress of Mozambique and the Supreme Potentate of Zanzibar who were both so kind to me last weekend."

"Oh," she said. "I just returned from Washington, D.C."

"How is Ike?" I asked, in reference to the President.

"I didn't see him, but I was with Senator Muskie. In his office for a moment. He gave me a Senate pass. When he saw my name, he asked right away, 'Are you one of the New England Treats?' Of course, I told him, which is true anyway. The Senate debate I witnessed was really thrilling. They were discussing urban problems. I think I may major in political science."

"When you get out of high school or before?" I asked.

"Oh, Andrew, really. . .I'm not sure where I wish to attend. Possibly Wellesley where Mother went. We may still have some pull there. But I know one thing: I'M DEFINITELY NOT GOING TO COLLEGE IN MAINE!"

"Why not? What's wrong with Maine colleges?"

"I crave intellectual nourishment! And Maine is sadly lacking in that area."

"Even Bowdoin?"

"Andrew Harrison! I may be wearing my father's jacket, but I haven't undergone a sexual transformation! Bowdoin, in case you haven't realized, is still for males only."

"Oh, I know, Mary, but you do act very aggressive; I thought you might be able to get by."

"Someone with my background is naturally aggressive. The Treat women were always strong. Look at my mother, reduced to such a lowly station in her middle age! What she's had to endure and suffer through! The power she has, however, is hard to detect on the surface."

It was indeed. I had just bumped into Mrs. Treat a few days before up in Summer Harbor village and she looked shy, withdrawn, and sad as ever with her cheap blonde wig that she wore to cover up her baldness. She was just getting out of her old, rusted-out Studebaker, when some boys I knew from school came by and started slamming their fists down hard against the ancient fenders and hood of the car, yelling, "Hey, Mrs. Treat! This is sure one hell of a Cadd-ee-lack ya got here! Shit, what I wouldn't give to own 'er! Bet ya can really goose 'er! Take us for a spin, huh, Mrs. Treat?"

Mrs. Treat, who was much more of a lady than her cloddish daughter, ignored these young hooligans as best she could, and greeted me with a gracious invitation to come and visit some afternoon at the Treat cottage.

But, besides her mother's hidden strengths, Mary had come to talk of other matters.

"Who's here now for guests?" she asked, forever on the lookout for Important Contacts, VIPs who might be good for a free meal or a stroll along the ledges, people whom it might help to know, stepping stones paving her way back home to the lost aristocratic position on Beacon Hill.

"Oh, let me see now," I began. "There's the Shah of Lapland in Number Four, and a Texas nabob and oil tycoon and his actress mistress in Number One. They always travel with a couple of torpedoes. Barbara Hutton will be joining Mrs. Merriweather Post for dinner, and if he can tear himself away from his Seal Harbor Compound, Nelson Rockefeller has promised to put in an after-dinner appearance."

"Andy! Be serious, please! You are too funny, as usual, but I really do want to know who's around. There may be someone who knows Mother."

"I doubt it, Mary; I really do." Mary did resemble Eleanor Roosevelt as a young woman.

"Well, what do you know? Have you ever read the *Who's Who*?"

"In your mother's case, wouldn't it have to be *Who WAS Who*? Are there any Treats doing anything now, occupying important positions in our culture or government?"

"Of course; cousins and uncles, numerous other relatives whom you've never heard of, not all of them named Treat, of course."

"Of course. Well, I won't press you for specific names and addresses. We are all cousins and uncles under the skin. Even the ape is our brother—or is it step-brother?"

Mary never really did get to meet or become acquainted with any of the Manor's prominent guests except the effervescent Julie Lawson. Mary and Julie would often visit together, go on hikes, recommend books to each other. Mrs. Lawson seemed genuinely fond of Mary and was frequently presenting her with little gifts, and clipping newspaper readings for her.

Sensitive about my own background, I was probably too sharp and mean to Mary when we were teens. She provided me with the opportunity to get back at the summer people who made me feel inferior. One time near the end of the summer, Hattie and I were out running errands in Lulabelle, her car, when we ran into Mary who was hitch-hiking along the road.

"Hey, An-day, shall we give your girlfriend a lift?" asked Hattie, turning to me with a laugh.

"No! She drives me crazy."

"Well, isn't that whatcha want? Someone to drive ya crazy?"

"That's not what I meant. Let her get another lift with a millionaire friend of her mother's."

"Well! I don't call that being very cordial. And her being a neighbor and classmate and all. I think I'll stop and give her a ride."

"Have your fun, Hattie. She can sit in front with you and stink ya right out. I'm getting in back."

But it didn't work out that way, to Hattie's delight. Mary accepted the offer and immediately jumped in back with me. She was wearing a bright plaid pair of Bermuda shorts.

"What do you think of my summer shorts, Andy?" she asked. "I picked them up at Bloomingdale's in New York on my way back from Washington. They were a bargain I just couldn't pass up. Marked down from thirty dollars to fifteen! They're originals."

"They're O.K. for thirty dollar shorts, but they're not even at the sides. The pattern doesn't match where the seams come together."

"Oh, that's not important. Plaid doesn't have to match, not this type of plaid. Just feel the material."

I touched Mary's plaid thigh, acutely aware of Hattie's wild giggles from the front seat. I thought she was going to have trouble keeping the car on the road.

"Feels comfortable," I said.

"From Scotland," Mary said.

It was an agonizing journey back to the Granite Neck and the Manor for me with Mary chattering on and on about her life and plans, pressing her plaids against my jeans, and Hattie's choking and wheezing over the sight of Miss Bucktooth and me together in the back seat.

"Oh, An-day, I think you two make the cutest couple!" Hattie said upon our return to the hotel.

"You just wait, Hattie! I'm gonna get back at you for this!"

"Don't be so revengeful-sounding, boy. I was just trying to fix up something nice for ya. Mary's such a nice girl from such a rich and important family. You could be living in the lap of luxury, An-day, with your own pair of thirty-dollar Scottish summer *shots*. You wait, and I'll go get some bagpipes and pipe you and Miss Mary all over the Neck. I think you're made for each other!"

19

One Saturday night, Hattie asked me to go to The Lobster Stomp with her and Glory, her married daughter. Since I hadn't been to a dance all summer, I agreed to the proposition. We drove in Hattie's '52 Plymouth up Route One to West Hamlin to the old Sorosis Hall which had been recently and generously rebuilt and refurbished by one of the benevolent summer folk, a doctor, I believe, who had entertained some noble vision about founding a cultural center for the area which would incorporate a library, a woman's club, a youth organization, a place for year round concerts, lectures, parties, art exhibits, and a host of other activities for the benefit of the surrounding coastal communities. Translated, however, into Downeast practicality, the new center became as the old: a dance hall. And the Navy boys from the Summer Harbor base who frequented the place every Saturday night had christened the handsome new Recreation Center "The Lobster Stomp." The orchestra that was giving its concert that evening was a motley get together of local musicians who called themselves "Pearly Allen and His All-Stars."

When we arrived, the joint was jumping, out in the parking lot as much as in the hall. And what a strange mixture of people was present. Along the sidelines, seated on the folding chairs, milling about the kitchen area, hanging around the front hall were native Mainiacs and summer foreigners, local bums and Navy boys. They all stood ogling, watching, sipping their beverages, smoking, talking about and to each other, and occasionally asking each other to dance.

Since this was a dry dance by law, the locals had to bring their booze in Canada Dry Ginger Ale or Pepsi bottles which they passed back and forth out of the light, grinning and giggling over their naughtiness.

As we entered the hall itself, Hattie turned to Glory and me and said, "I love to dance, so let's hope this week I can find another two-legged animal who can at least swing me around the floor without busting my kneecaps."

Blond and pony-tailed Glory, as amusingly tough as her mother, replied, "You sure are choosy, Ma. I'll be happy if I get someone who can stand up straight."

"What are you talking about?" asked Hattie. "Who wants to dance with a straight man?"

"You're the lucky one, An-day," Hattie said. "At least you get to ask."

"And get refused," I said.

While Hattie and Glory went their separate ways amongst the crowd, I looked around to see if I could find anyone whom I knew. To my relief, there were several familiar faces, but they did not belong to close acquaintances.

There was this one creepy bespectacled fellow who had been in several of my classes at nearby Mollusk Memorial. He had on a baggy brown suit and held a Pepsi in his hand. He accosted me first at the edge of the floor. His name was Uriel Martin and he was known about school as a very odd character, hung up on religion.

"I'm not supposed to be here, ya know," he told me, his eyeballs nearly bulging out of his head.

"No, I wasn't aware of that, Uriel; why not?" I asked, trying to sound bored, to get him away from me. All I needed was to be identified with this freak to be ostracized for the entire evening.

"I'm a hard-shell Baptist," he said. "We're not supposed to play cards, go to the movies, or dance or drink. I'm sinning tonight!"

"Then why did you come?"

"Because I'm weak, just like my foster mother said."

"Then you don't really believe in your religion."

"Oh, yes! I do! I'm a very strong believer, and I know right now that I'm standing in a house of sin with sinners all about me. And I'm sinning! I would not complain if we were all to be wiped out this instant by God, because this is a wicked, evil place!" Uriel took a swig from his Pepsi bottle.

"Is your Pepsi spiked, Uriel?"

"Of course not!" he said. "But even without the taint of liquor, it's still a strong, filthy stimulant not fit for human consumption!"

"Then why in hell are ya swilling it?"

"I told ya! I'm very weak. I have relapses unless I have constant guidance."

"Have you danced, Uriel?" I asked. "I think it's fun."

"Well, you're an infidel to begin with and don't know your head from a hole in the ground! You're in the dark!"

"All the better for dancing."

As the All-Stars were playing an unreasonable facsimile of "The World Is Waiting for the Sunrise," Hattie swung by me in the arms of some old gray-haired codger, looking very young, pretty, and happy, calling to me, "An-day! Give one of those girls on the sidelines a chance!"

Glory, like her mother, was dancing with a man I hardly considered her equal. How could really smart women like them let such men buy their affections? Did they want to dance that much? Glory's partner, for instance, was a local sometime-lobsterman who always had a stubble of beard on his face, and who always wore cheap cotton work clothes, even to a Saturday night dance. But Glory seemed, like her mother, to be making the best of it, and giving him a good time. Perhaps I shouldn't be so bothered by it all, I thought.

But I didn't want to dance with just anyone. I wanted to have the guts to ask one of the summer girls. There was this one in particular that evening, a pretty, well-tanned, brown-haired girl who had on a white party dress and who sat against the wall with another pretty blonde and an older, handsome man who looked as if he might be their father. They had class, I could tell. The way they looked; they seemed amused in their slumming experience. I reasoned that people like them couldn't have come to the Lobster Stomp for reasons other than curiosity. It would be fun to go home and tell about this hick joint. For a while, I sat near them. The brown-haired girl was one of the prettiest girls I had ever seen and I loved the way she laughed, talked, and moved.

To my shock and disgust, Wendell West, one of my classmates who affected one of the then current Downeast imitations of Elvis Presley, asked Miss Brown Hair to dance, and she accepted! Wendell was good-looking and muscular in a greasy sort of way. He had on his usual tight Levis which he wore beltless and low on his hips, and he had on a silky, bright-colored shirt open to the waist, and no undershirt so that everyone could see his chest. His long black hair was combed into a well-oiled D.A. and hung in his face. The girls at school had labeled him arrogant, cheap, rough, and over-sexed; and as far as I knew, not one of them had ever refused an invitation to date him. When Wendell danced, even with this classy summer girl, he struggled as close as he could without suffocating his partner; it was obvious that Wendell considered his dance only a prelude to the main event in the parking lot.

In my nice boy's delusion, I just couldn't understand why Hattie, Glory, and Miss Brown Hair would dance and keep on dancing with this inferior type of male person. Couldn't they see, as I thought I did, that they wouldn't amount to anything?

Perley's All Star Band was hopelessly outmoded and behind the times. They didn't play any rock-'n'-roll. Their repertoire consisted mostly of variations on "Blue Moon," "Stardust," and for a fast beat, "The Beer Barrel Polka." They did play a couple of Virginia Reels, one of which I danced with Gracie Ray, a buxom, middle-aged bleached blonde from my hometown of Taunton who was always dressed as a cowgirl with fringe on her sleeves and skirt and with fancy high heeled boots. Every Fourth of July, Gracie led the Bar Harbor parade down Cottage Street astride her proudest possession, her golden palomino horse. She was a great and lovely character with her teased blonde hair, her dangling earrings, and her raspy voice. Dancing a reel with her was one of the two good moments for me in the evening.

The other moment came when I danced with Linda Terrapin, a pretty, tall, long-haired girl, who was a year behind me in school, an intelligent girl who came originally from out-of-state. She was very witty, an excellent science student (her homemade tarpaper telescope had won her a prize in the preceding year's county science fair at Ellsworth), and she liked me. We danced several dances and I bought her several Cokes. We sat for quite a while talking and making each other laugh on the sidelines. I imitated some of the summer people in deriding my local neighbors, poking fun at their antics, laughing at this or that "character," like Uriel.

The worst moment for me in the evening came when I asked this other girl to dance. She had been a freshman at Mollusk, two years behind me, and was cute. I thought she'd be very glad to dance with a prominent junior honors student like me, but she refused! I felt humiliated and angry, and didn't understand how such a dumb little bitch like her could refuse me, the vice president of the junior class, and not only one of the school's best students, but a member of our state champion cross country team and soon to be a college man at the University of Maine. My confidence had increased after time spent with Linda, who was much prettier and sexier than this freshman, so I was really crestfallen and confused by this refusal from someone so obviously inferior to me. I thought I was doing the little freshman a favor.

Leaving the dance that night, I walked by a little commotion out in the parking lot, and there at the heart of it was Essie Torrey! I had thought she might be at the dance, for she loved dancing, and would get boys to drive her for miles to a hall; but I hadn't seen her inside all evening.

She was with her boyfriend Vaughn Bishop, a brown-haired, curly-headed, handsome, and wild lobsterman in tight jeans. They were wrangling with Vaughn's lookalike brother Victor and his girlfriend, squabbling loudly enough so that everyone could hear them. They all had cigarettes in their hands, and both boys had obviously been drinking quite a bit. I caught Essie's eye, as I went by; but she couldn't or wouldn't divert herself from the argument at hand. She didn't let on to them that she had seen me, but she had.

"YA GODDAMN FOOL!" I heard her yell at Victor. "YA COULD HAVE KILLED US, THE WAY YOU WERE DRIVIN'!"

Just as Hattie, Glory, and I were getting into Lulabelle, however, who should run over to us but Essie, wild-eyed with a cigarette in hone hand and a bottle of beer in the other.

She yelled at me. "LOOK AT ME, AN-DAY HARRISON! DRUNK AND STILL DRINKIN'! AIN'T I JUST THE MOST SINFUL GIRL YOU KNOW!" And then, looking at Hattie and Glory, she said, "So, you're keeping company with older women now, huh?"

"Ess-ay," I started to say; but before any of us could say anything, she dashed back across the parking lot to her boyfriend, laughing and throwing herself about. "O.K. VAUGHN! LET'S GO DANCE OUR ASSES OFF! That is, if you can still stand up straight!"

"Is she a good friend of yours, An-day?" asked Hattie in the car.

"She's Essie Torrey, a girl I grew up with in Taunton Ferry."

"Oh, so that's Ess-ay Torrey. I've heard quite a bit about that young woman!" said Glory. "All the fishermen talk about her. I guess she'll do anything with anybody. I've heard she's even taken on two guys at once. You better watch out, An-day."

"I have been."

On the way back to Summer Harbor that night, Hattie and Glory made me feel better with their constant joking. When we pulled into the yard of Glory's house, every light in the house was on, and her lobsterman husband was drunk and waiting for her in the doorway.

"Oh, gawd," she said, when she saw him. "He must have his dander up."

"That might be exciting," said Hattie.

"Are you kidding?" Glory asked, as she got out of the car. "Good night, Mama. Goodnight, An-day. See ya later."

"I hope so, Glor-ay," I said.

"WHERE THE HELL HAVE YOU BEEN?" shouted her silhouetted and shirtless husband from the house as she walked towards him.

"Oh, shut up! I've been out with Mummer!"

"Jesus H. Christ! This is a fine goddamn thing! Git in here where ya belong before I kick your ass!"

"Had enough to drink?" Glory asked to his face, standing up to him on the doorstep, finally shoving him inside with one hand and closing the door behind them with her other.

Hattie began to back Lulabelle out of the driveway when I asked her, "Will Glor-ay be all right, Hattie?"

"Hell, yes. Don't worry about them. That's the way they make love."

20

So that the Titcombs, our most prestigious guests of every season, could visit with us in the comfort they had come to expect over many summers on the Maine coast, Hattie and I had to move mattresses.

Miss Meyer told us that Mr. Titcomb had back trouble, so we had to exchange the mattress from his twin bed in Number Four, which he and his wife would be occupying for the whole month of August, with another from down the hall in Number Eleven. His back required the firmest mattress we had.

After a summer of such exchanging and moving things around, Hattie and I had dubbed ourselves "Fox and Ginn" after a prominent moving van outfit in Eastern Maine.

After breakfast that day the Titcombs were due to arrive, and while Caroline was busy attending to all of her regular chambermaid duties, Hattie and I vacated our downstairs posts to assume our moving men positions on the second story.

"She would pick a room ten miles down the hall to switch with!" Hattie exclaimed.

"Maybe the mattress in Number Eleven is just right for Mr. Titcomb's back," I said.

"Who measured and tested? All the beds in this joint feel the same to me."

"Have you slept on them all, Hattie?"

She regarded me with a sarcastic grin.

"No, but we had a chambermaid here once who did. Miss Meyer would miss her after she didn't appear for lunch, and someone would run up here and check and usually she'd be in slumberland in one of the guest's beds. Guess she must have had trouble sleeping at home."

Mattresses, as well as anything else big and bulky, were awkward to move through the narrow halls and doorways of the old house, especially if the people moving them were laughing their heads off.

Hattie would sing, "Ya Gotta Give a Little, Take a Little. . ." or to the tune of "Frankie and Johnny," a suggestive melody, particularly when moving mattresses, such as "Ro-ll me o-ver easy. . .ro-ll me o-ver slow. . ."

When she had me laughing so hard that I couldn't function, Hattie would chuckle, raise her eyebrow, and ask, "What's ya problem there, Ginn? You've dropped your end! You better watch it or you'll find yourself working for Cole's Express. Say, let's get this bag of goose feathers on the road. One, two, three—hike! Don't wet your pants now, Dearie! I sure don't want to stand here all day stuck in a door sill. God knows, I got other things I could be doing. . ."

At one point in our mattress-moving, on a job other than that for the Titcombs, Hattie and I had a lot of trouble getting a box spring for a double bed shoved through another narrow doorway. The thing stuck halfway through, and with us tugging and pulling every which way, Hattie started singing, "Something's Gotta Give."

That day, though, finally, the mattress was moved, the room was set in order, the same room the Titcombs had been renting for years, with fresh flowers and plenty of wood for the fireplace; and we awaited the encroachment of our perfect guests.

They arrived exactly when they said they would, and paid two weeks of their month's stay in advance. They were always so grateful-appearing for all that we did for them, and kindly in their comments, that we always did more for them than anyone else. They left large weekly tips for the entire staff. They were always pleasant, cordial, and thoughtful to everyone at the Manor, guests and staff members alike. I saw them as "rich people with class." They often had influential, and, as I found out later, notable people to dine at their dinner table frequently. They also had a tragic past for us to gossip about. I had read about it in *Who's Who* or *Current Biography*, where under Mr. Titcomb's name, the story was briefly told of his coming home one night in New York to find that his first wife had killed their two children and herself. The present Mrs. Titcomb, the second wife, had been his secretary.

Theirs appeared to be a deeply loving relationship. And with Mr. Titcomb, as an ex-head of one of the world's mightiest foundations, and brother to one of our country's most well-known and important theologians, they were celebrated and famous people themselves, to be nurtured and cared for most exactingly.

I had never seen Hattie as respectful towards anyone as she was to the Titcombs. "I love these people," she said. "They've got real style. Nothing phony about 'em. They know what life's all about, and yet they keep their dignity."

Every morning it was one of my duties to deliver *The New York Times* to Mr. Titcomb as soon as it came in, a day or two late. He studied the *Times* like a Bible or a law book.

They used the telephone more and received more calls than any other guests, for they seemed to know everyone who was someone in the Mount Desert Island area. Every afternoon, the Titcombs missed lunch because of their busy visiting schedule. But before they left for the day, they'd always pay their respects to the staff, an act that endeared them to us, letting us, their servants, in on their lives that way.

Mrs. Titcomb, who was much younger than her husband, did the driving of their Oldsmobile, another '57 98 like Mrs. Richmond's, but every night when it came time for them to put their car in the garage—the only guests at the Manor who ever did so—Mr. Titcomb assumed the position behind the wheel. It was a funny little ceremony to see him doing this every night, as if he were proving to himself and others that despite his advanced age, he could still park his own car in the garage.

Mr. Titcomb loved Mrs. Spurling's graham cracker pie. She was the pastry chef; and she'd make at least one pie a week especially for him. He always ate every crumb of the large piece she served him, except for one time when he returned half of his pie uneaten. Upon examination the reason for this inexplicable action became disgustingly apparent with the find of a dead fly in the remaining portion of the dessert.

"Errr," said Miss Meyer, "this is awful. An immediate apology must be made. Hattie, would you go at once to the Titcombs?"

"Sure, but what do I say—how did you like the little extra-added attraction in your pie? We're experimenting, folks! You've heard of Shoo-fly-pie? Well, we thought we'd try Graham Cracker Fly Pie!"

"Errr. . .no. Just tell him how very sorry we are and how it will not happen again."

"Right. We'll now add fly-inspection to our list of dinner duties."

But Mr. Titcomb was a gentleman with a sense of humor, and he laughed off the whole incident the next day in the kitchen in the fearful presence of Miss Meyer and Mrs. Spurling.

"Please don't be so upset by the fly in my pie, ladies," Mr. Titcomb said. "Worse things have occurred in my life, you may be assured. I have not lost faith in the quality of your meal preparations. In fact, I look forward to the menu for this evening."

21

After Greta had been fired at the end of July, we had no steady replacement to help Hattie in the dining room through the busiest month of the season, so most often Caroline would help out and Miss Meyer and I would do the chambermaid's evening chores of turning down the beds, fetching fresh linen, turning on the bedside lamps. But when we were very busy, which was most every night in August, other ladies had to be hired to help with serving dinner or washing dishes.

One of these women was the daughter-in-law of Mrs. Spurling. Her name was Charlene and she worked days in the kitchen of the Three R's Remedial School for Rich Boys on the other side of the Neck. An attractive and quick-tempered redhead, Charlene had grown up and gone to school with Hattie in Summer Harbor. They had much in common, including the fact that they had both been married twice. Often times I would walk in on them in the dark of the butler's pantry—it was kept dark so that the waitresses could watch the guests without being seen through the small pane of glass in the swinging dining room door. They would frequently be convulsed in fits of laughter over some joke or story about one of the guests or old times in Summer Harbor.

"Remember, Hattie, when my house burnt flat?" Charlene asked one night.

"You're always having an accident of some kind, Charlene," said Hattie, with a mischievous wink to me.

"No, you remember, a few years ago. When Boyd got out of the Navy. He just got home and we just got into bed when the goddamn oil stove blew up! All we had time to grab was the TV set and my Playtex girdle. And when I got outside in that christled cold, Boyd had me giggling about that! He said I dreamed I was watching TV in my Playtex girdle!"

"Boyd could be a lot of fun," Hattie said, "even under the worst circumstances."

"I'm sure you know! Just like every other woman around here. All he ever did was drive around town in the summer with no shirt on in that Galaxie convertible, even after we were married."

"He was the brightest star in or out of the Galaxie!" said Hattie. "He was also built as good as Tarzan, and he sure looked sexy down on the wharf piling up lobster traps."

"He was an asshole, Hattie. You should have been married to him."

"Well, I tried," Hattie said, laughing.

"Don't think I didn't know it! You're right, though, he was fun, but he couldn't be loyal to just one woman. He couldn't even support one! He was just a good-looking playboy, and I'm better off now with Monroe."

"Well, if you say so, you probably are. I'm glad you've got yourself convinced."

Monroe Spurling, a used car dealer, and big and fat as he was loud-talking, would pick Charlene up after work many nights when she was at the Manor; and one night, he came in the wrong car.

"Monroe!" Charlene screamed, looking out the window at the back parking lot. "Where's my Retractable? I don't see my Retractable!"

"Got a good price for that Ford, Charlene," said Monroe, in reference to the hard-top convertible that the Ford Motor Company used to make.

"You big fat shithead! Don't joke about something I care about! You know I love that car. That was my car. So where is it?"

"No joke, honest injun, Charlene. I got a price and I sold her out from under your ass. I'm sorry, but now we can go to Portland or Boston for the weekend and have a toot!"

"Jaysus Christ, the only toot you could have would be out your ass! That was my Retractable, Monroe! The only thing you've given me that was any good!"

"Get your sweater on, de-ah; it's chill-ay out tonight, and I wouldn't want you to catch any more cold." Monroe instructed his wife and winked at me, as men like him do with other males, suggesting some kind of male understanding about how stupid and crazy women can be to make such a fuss like this over nothing.

On their way through the back porch screen door, Monroe said, "Lissen, de-ah, you just ride in 'em. I pay the goddamn bills. We got a real sweet deal on this one. There'll be other cars. I'll try and get ya another Retractable."

"Fat turd! I always thought you looked just like a swollen red prick dressed up with a hat on!"

"The better to make love to you, my de-ah."

"You're sleeping on the couch tonight, you goddamn thing!"

Charlene slammed the door behind them and she and Mr. Spurling roared up the back driveway in a simple Ford Fairlane sedan.

22

Early in the morning before the guests were served breakfast and right after I had had my breakfast and had stoked the coal fires, I had to walk the grounds and pick up the trash, sweep both the front steps and the two sets of steps that led from the huge back porch facing the bay down to the back lawn. Some mornings I had to polish the carriage lamps by the front door. I'd straighten up the lawn and porch furniture, too; and, if it was a stormy cold day, I'd have to light the fires in the dining and living rooms.

Some mornings guests would be around, and some times they would engage me in conversation. One late August morning in 1959, two ladies, and aunt and her niece, whispered *sub rosa* to me on the enclosed porch off the hotel's library while I was taking cushions outside for the lawn furniture. Actually, the aunt did all the talking. The niece just sat there smiling and nodding in agreement with everything the older, but not much older, woman said.

"Now, I don't want to say anything," the aunt whispered to me, "but I don't think we'll be coming here another summer."

"Why not?" I asked.

"Well, it's so cold; there's no heat in our room, and yesterday morning there wasn't enough to eat. For me, there was, that is—I don't need to eat that much, surely—but not for my niece here. She leaves the table every meal, her stomach rumbling. And for the price we pay, I guess, we just expect more."

"I'm sorry. Why don't you speak to Miss Meyer? Or to Hattie Pinkham, the head waitress? I'm sure they'd give you seconds."

"Oh, I don't think so. We're quite disenchanted really. We've been coming here for several years. Maine used to be so beautiful in the old days, so peaceful and lovely. We used to come up to Ogunquit, but that became too busy and commercial. Then we summered at Castine, but that didn't work out. Bar Harbor was too commercial and crowded, too, and filled with families camping out in the Park; and Boothbay Harbor is just for boating enthusiasts and far too crowded. We don't care for any more boat trips. We do love this coast so, but it's simply too hard now to find the perfect type of accommodations. When we first came here to the Manor, we thought how wonderful it was, so neat and simple and quiet. Relaxing, the way we like; but now, this summer in particular, something's changed. We're really very disappointed. I don't know where we'll go next summer. Probably not here to Maine at all. We just won't be coming here any more after this week is up. It's been really quite uncomfortable. Now, don't you tell anyone, young man."

But, of course, I did, and right away. That very afternoon at lunch I told Hattie and Miss Meyer both. For one thing, it was the novelty of the aunt's remarks; only once before had I ever heard any complaints all summer about the Manor and its fare. Everyone always came out to the kitchen, out of their way, to praise Miss Meyer and her staff for our efforts. Miss Meyer received letters from former guests signing up for their rooms a year in advance.

Hattie said, "Sure sign that there won't be any tip from them. They've just let us know through our cute little kitchen boy, who just wouldn't tell a soul, that they are a couple of old maid, whining, conniving cheapskates. The nerve of 'em! They've had good service and plenty of food—up till now!"

Miss Meyer, who looked especially serious at such news times, said, "Errr. . .Hattie, are you sure you let them know each time that they could have seconds on anything they wanted?"

"Sure I did. That's always been one of your Golden Rules, and I follow it with every guest, no matter how obnoxious they are. By Jesus, they knew it! But they're just too damned cheap and searching for excuses. They've got to find something to complain about so's they won't feel too bad about not leaving a tip."

Miss Meyer considered this and then turned to me. "Errr. . .Andy, the next time any guests wish to discuss such complaints with you, please direct them to me right away. Don't you say anything. Don't encourage them to use you like this."

"Tell 'em nothing!" added Hattie.

"O.K.," I said.

When the aunt and her niece left, never more to return, Hattie's prophecy turned out to be unfortunately correct. None of us received a tip for our daily services rendered. The two complainants even carried their own luggage down to their car so they wouldn't have to face me, say good-bye, or part with a quarter.

"Have a lovely trip, ladies!" Hattie hailed them from the kitchen window. "Off the nearest cliff!"

23

For three weeks in August, a Doctor Olive Garland occupied the Number Ten room, the most cramped, least luxurious, least expensive of our hotel rooms.

"She picked Number Ten because she's a poor, starving teacher," Hattie said, "or maybe because she's such a timid old maid she likes sleeping in closets."

Whatever the reason behind her choice, Dr. Garland had to be the most private of our guests that summer, which was rather irksome to those of us servants who took a great deal of pleasure in learning as much as possible about our guests' habits and lives. Knowing something awful, or at least "secret," about people always makes them more interesting, or at least more human. But that first week, Dr. Garland was a bore to us, because she kept to herself entirely, never came out to the kitchen to compliment or complain about a meal, never was drunk or disorderly in the living room or library, never left her room in an interesting mess with tell-tale clues for the chambermaid to find. She went on walks and drives, but spent most of her time in her tiny room reading and typing.

Of course, what she was typing became the focal point of our interest in her. Caroline reported that it seemed to be something about

Maine, for there were Maine books in her room and she had read a paragraph or two concerning the Maine coast. Was she an author? Caroline never had time to really do a good, thorough investigation, because Dr. Garland was never out of her room long enough.

One morning when Caroline had been cleaning, and Dr. Garland returned from breakfast before Caroline had the bed all made, they had a chat about the Doctor's work. She told Caroline that she was writing a book about Maine and would appreciate the loan of any materials concerning studies, histories, or reports of local Maine towns that we could find for her. Caroline told me, and together throughout the final two weeks of her stay, we became busy researchers for Dr. Garland.

Physically, she was a lovely lady, tall and rather imperious-looking. Her long gray hair she wore in braids piled up on top of her head and held in place, like ladies of old, with fancy combs. Her suits, which she wore even in August, were plain-colored and very smartly-tailored. She was what so many writers have termed a handsome woman. She drove a brand-new, fancy, baby blue Oldsmobile covered with chrome, which surprised me, because it seemed incongruous to my teenage mind that an old maid professor would be driving such a gaudy, powerful car.

Caroline and I scoured the Manor's bookshelves, rooms, and closets, finding some helpful Maine material in the attic archives where Miss Meyer and Mrs. Richmond had stored hundreds of imposing-looking notebooks and many other volumes, mostly of a religious-philosophical nature, and many of them written in German.

When Caroline went home and I had my days off, we widened our search to the homes of our families and friends, returning to Dr. Garland in her little room with a treasure load of books, magazines, and pamphlets. Near the end of her stay, her room was becoming very cluttered with piles of materials by the side of her bed, on top of her writing table and bureau.

"I couldn't have asked for a better research team," she said to us one day. "I'm glad you both plan to attend college, for you should do well, if your interest in my writing project is as acute in the other academic areas."

Dr. Garland talked a great deal with us at such moments, letting us know that she was a history professor at Pembroke College in Rhode Island and had never married. She was "married to her work," as she put it. She had traveled widely but had visited Maine nearly every summer since she was a teenager. Her father had been a history professor, too, and she mentioned him with great reverence. He had obviously been an important influence on her life. She loved teaching, she told us. And, as we joined her more and more frequently for discussions, we began to think of her as a great, natural teacher, inspiring and fascinating to listen to. She came alive when she talked of history.

"We are the results of history," she'd say. "How wonderful if each man could tell and know and care about how he came to be, what forces and influences on every level of experience were working to produce him, by what flukes and designs he was born."

Afternoons after we got to know her she would often work with the door to her room open and would call out to us if we happened to be passing by.

"Andy," she'd say, "come in here and hear what I've just learned about the original settlers of Lubec!"

Or she'd ask Caroline and I if we knew this or that fact about our native Downeast, and when we shook our heads no, as we inevitably did, she'd scold us. "Honestly, such ignorance of important human history! You'd better read some of these books, if you're to refer to yourselves as true sons and daughters of Maine!" One of the books that we brought her and that she especially enjoyed reading was *The Meddybemps Letters* and *Maine's Hall of Fame Memorial Addresses*, a satirical collection by Maine newspaper writer and humorist, William Pattangall. Dr. Garland termed the book "a rare find. At his best, Mr. Pattangall can be as funny and as wise as Mark Twain." Caroline had picked the book up at a local rummage sale.

By the end of her stay, Dr. Garland had become one of Caroline's and my favorite guests. We had such a good time being with her and doing research for her. She had a good time with us, too, and showed her feelings by leaving us both a ten dollar tip with nice little messages about how much she appreciated our thoughtfulness and kindness on her behalf and how she wished she could give us more money. She mentioned again the value of a good education and how we should get the most out of college. "Remember," she emphasized, "it's YOUR LIVES that are most important when you are dealing with teachers and classrooms; don't let either interfere with your real education, like Mark Twain said."

In return for her gifts, we wished her well and told her how excited we would be to read her book about Maine.

But there never was to be a book. About a week after she returned to Rhode Island to begin preparations for her fall semester at Pembroke, she died of a sudden stroke. Miss Meyer sat Caroline and me down and told us the shocking news by reading us Dr. Garland's brief obituary from *The New York Times* which stressed her prominence among scholars of New England history.

"Now I see why you read *The New York Times* every day so faithfully," said Hattie later that morning, "so's you can find out why so many of our guests never return!"

24

So many things happened in the back parking lot between the hotel and Mr. Fitzpatrick's house. Nights, after I had dumped the garbage behind the garage and secured the pails with chicken wire and rope from the ever-scavenging raccoons, I used to play tricks on Hattie and Caroline.

Once I tied both of their cars to the cedar hedge and laughed my head off watching them from the darkness of the garage trying to back their cars away from the hedge. I also tied tin cans and brooms to their back bumpers and put grease on their steering wheels. They, in turn, got even with me by going up to my attic lodgings and sewing my pajama bottoms together at the waist, short-sheeting my bed, and filling my sneakers with rice and flour.

Many nights after work, to get away from the stifling kitchen, I'd take a walk through the back parking lot, up the back driveway, and out and around the Neck. If the moon were out, I'd frequently walk down by the ocean before returning to my room for the evening.

Captain Moore, the old 19th century Irish sea captain, entrepreneur, and principal architect, beyond God, of the Granite Neck layout, had built a wonderful trail that circumvented the whole top of the peninsula, parts of which, like the path that connected the yacht club with the tennis courts, were lighted. Where the paths or roads led down to the sea, there were little parks with hedges and granite benches.

I'd roam these paths, usually ending up sitting on one of the stone benches, staring out at the black ocean, watching the winking lights from across the bay, listening to the breaking of the waves in the dark.

In my nocturnal excursions, I'd sometimes meet other people, and we would furtively glance at each other as we passed.

Luckily, the students from the Three R's Remedial School for Rich Boys weren't allowed out after their study and sleeping hours had commenced, so I had no fear of their bothering me.

Mostly, I'd encounter guests from the Manor, most notably "Twinkle Toes" Lawson herself; and sometimes she'd ask me to "go the oval" with her. She would usually have a raggedy sweater thrown about her shoulders and a picture hat on or a scarf tied about her head. Usually, she was alone, but sometimes she was with Mary Treat or Rosie Talbot. When she'd spot me, she'd grin and make a strange little noise in greeting; or sometimes, she'd whisper in a very soft, girlish Southern voice, "Hi, Andy. . ."

One night, after one of my hikes, when I was returning to the Manor through the back parking lot, I noticed a shiny blue, brand-new Chrysler New Yorker parked in the most secluded corner of the lot. Because of my love of cars, I walked towards the Chrysler to look it over, to perhaps get inside and behind the wheel, when I suddenly noticed that there was a couple "doing the dirt," really going at it, in the back seat. I turned immediately to retreat, when in one of those proverbial seconds that lasts much longer, my eyes met Hattie's. She was making out with the Commander of the Navy Base! I was sorry to have seen her with him like this, and she looked equally sorry. I could tell by her eyes when she saw me looking on. The stories that Greta had told all summer, the nasty rumors I hadn't wanted to believe, were suddenly made true. I didn't hate Hattie, though; she had never denied the rumors, after all, and had never tried to cover up anything from me. So she was dating a married man.

The next day we hurried about, doing our jobs as usual, but not joking as usual. We didn't even have a talk until just before lunch when Hattie caught me alone in the kitchen. Coming over to me at the sink where I was scrubbing some caked-on pans, she leaned over the sink, grinned at me, and said, "Hey, ya know, the Navy sure has a lot of brass!"

"Yeah, it sure looks like it," I said, relieved and grinning back, letting her see that I wasn't all that angry at her.

"I'm sorry for last night, An-day. We grown-ups sure do stupid things in stupid places sometimes. . .but these things happen, ya know? In this life, you take love where you can find it. . ."

"Do you love him?

"Maybe I should have said you take sex where you find it. . .let's say I love the way he needs me and I love being physical with him; but he is a married man with kids, so I don't want to fall in love with him. And I couldn't stand it, if you wouldn't forgive me. . ."

"I forgive you; it's O.K. . . I know. . ."

"Well, you don't really know, but you are learning, and I'm glad we're still friends and you aren't so upset with me that we wouldn't speak again. . .why I'd have to spend the rest of the summer eating lunch with Miss Meyer!"

25

The summer of 1959 ended and I moved home to Taunton Ferry to begin my senior year in high school; but I hadn't been home for a week when Miss Meyer called to ask if I might come back to the Manor for the first weekend in September to help her and Hattie wait on a crew of Harvard boys.

It was a tradition, I soon found out, for this geology professor to have a Downeast outing with about a dozen of his past and present students before fall term began in Cambridge.

I don't know what I expected Harvard men to look like, but like so many other places I had over-romanticized in my head, I pictured Harvard as this awesome seat of highest learning where demi-god-like young men and their peerless professors magically communed with each other in darkly paneled, richly carpeted clubs and dens. Men and boys alike would be attired in handsome tweed jackets and wool ties; and would be lounging around discussing politics, sports, the arts and sciences, and world problems, gesturing thoughtfully with their pipes, sipping their brandy, laughing and being witty with each other, in a sensitive and intelligent but manly way.

So, I was nonplussed, once again, as I watched a couple of old Jeeps and a Dodge station wagon pull up to the Manor loaded with a rather tough-looking crew of young roughnecks dressed in faded Levis, old corduroys, red-and-black hunting jackets, and heavy boots. They could have been so many pulp-and-paper workers standing around in the driveway the way they did with their hands in the back pockets of their jeans, canvas hats perched on the backs of their heads, before unloading their packs and gear.

"Poor little rich boys out on a jaunt in the backwoods!" Hattie said as she heard them arrive. She kept on with her kitchen work as I dropped whatever I was doing to run to the window and look out to see what Harvard men looked like.

"You better run out and help 'em with their bags, An-day."

"Miss Meyer told me that since they were a bunch of men, they would probably carry their own bags."

"Ha! That's a good one! Wait till you see how helpless these types of males are. They're trained to be dependent. Every year they leave this place a mess; don't know enough to pick up their clothes off the floor. They might go to Haa-vard, An-day, but they ain't so smart. They're lucky they're rich. They can afford to be noisy and sloppy and stupid."

"Hattie, you sound so bitter, and here you'll be surrounded all weekend by a bunch of good-looking men, and you the only dame!"

"Aren't you funny, now, calling me a dame? What would these little millionaires' sons see in an old workhorse like me? I'm a slave to them, a butt for their wisecracks. They go over to Mount Desert or down to Schoodic every day and bring back piles of rocks and leave them all over their rooms for me to trip over. You'll see; it's such fun!"

"I think you're just tired, after a long summer."

"I'll buy that all right, but it's like being tired after a long life of never having anything extra. I'm tired of slaving for nothing. It's too much to put up with for a quarter tip here and there. Surely, I keep telling myself, there's more to life than this!"

Miss Meyer bustled into the kitchen at about this point. "Errr. . . Hattie, could you and Andy fix enough set-ups for Doctor Mountenée and the twelve boys?"

"That's not a question but a command, right?"

"Errr. . .right!"

"Hadn't we better check those boys on their ages? It's still 21 here in The Pine Tree State, ya know; and I don't want to be carried off in a paddy wagon at this point. . ."

"Or even off this Point!" I added.

"Errr. . .I think most of them are twenty-one or close enough to it. They aren't freshmen; and I haven't seen a state police car down here all summer."

"Whatever you say, ma'am," Hattie said and began gathering the high ball glasses together.

"An-day, sweets, you can help me. You haven't had the extreme pleasure yet of serving a bunch of Haa-vard men. Go get some splits of everything. There's no telling what they'll be sipping. Probably some exotic thing we never heard tell of just to prove how superior they are."

"You know, Hattie, you're really being bitchy today."

"Yeah, I know. Feeling sorry for myself. I'm letting things get to me. My dog days. Sorry, An-day. I'm just all worn-out and sick of this foolishness. I know it's sort of fun for you at your age; and it used to be for me, but now I'm older and I haven't gone any place. I see these people come here and then get to leave. My life is a rut. I need a change. I'm becoming a 'quaint Maine character,' for God's sake! I'd like the chance to be sitting on the other side of the table for a change, ya know?"

"Yeah, I know."

"Society's slave! That's what I feel like today. . .and for too many days. Feel Sorry for Hattie Day—everybody weep! Don't worry, An-day, I'll probably get over it. I have before often enough."

We carried two full trays of set-ups out to the big porch where all the Harvard men were gathered. They were still dressed in their jeans and hunting togs and boots and were stretched all over the porch, joking with each other and the Doctor. A couple of them stood with one leg up on the stone balustrade studying intently the handsome Mount Desert Island scene that lay before them. Hattie plopped the set-ups down amongst them. They made me nervous, but she spoke easily with them, and with a less bitchy, more fun-loving tone than she had been using in the kitchen.

"Well, here ya are, boys! Don't get too drunk and ruin your dinner!"

"Hattie, this is just wonderful," said Doctor Mountenée. "We thank you very much."

"Don't mention it, Doc. It's just compliments of the house; cocktails should help make the sparkling waters of Frenchman's Bay even more sparkling."

"Yes, I dare say," said the Doctor.

"Well, you are an old daredevil, Doc, as I recall," said Hattie, to the delight of the boys.

As they spoke the usual cocktail party pleasantries, I observed the Harvard men from close up. They were really a handsome, alert, and healthy-looking group. I was envious of them for they seemed so at ease and sure of themselves. They were good-humored and it looked like fun being part of their gang. They delved right into the set-ups, producing a number of pint bottles of expensive booze from their coat pockets and elsewhere. I didn't know my liquor labels all that well even after a summer of handling many bottles; but I knew Johnnie Walker, JB, Black & White, and Seagram's were all good for starters.

The boys talked like all the summer people I had heard all my life, exuding wit, polish, confidence, some sense of humor, and from a few of them, a dash of condescension towards others less fortunate.

One fellow, noticing a pal of his with a bottle of Jack Daniels, said, "Well, I'll be damned, Josh. How long have you been on Tennessee Sippin' Whiskey? Must be that Mountain Man in you. Do you long for the hills of home, with all the moonshine you can swallow?"

"You just haven't acquired the right tastes yet, ole buddy. Scotch is European; bourbon is American. You've got to get with it and progress from the Old Country to the New," replied Josh.

"Well, shist on you!"

"Say, look at those outcroppings!" said one skinny blond fellow as he spied the colorful set-ups. "What minerals do we need to mix with our spirits?"

"Oh, a little quartz here and a little feldspar there," added a little red-haired squat fellow, whom all the other boys seemed to regard with a lot of affectionate humor. He was evidently the Mickey Rooney of the group, expected to be always on, always madcap, mainly, I gathered, because of his short stature, his cherubic face, and red hair.

"The trouble with you, Cornelius the Fourth, is that you don't know your joints from your faults," said a tall, dark-haired lad, lifting his Manhattan to his lips. "And you don't seem to be able to identify your intruding dikes."

"Oh, I been in more joints than I'd care to remember," said

Mickey.

"And you've got more faults than we'd care to list," said the blond fellow, who had a British accent.

"Aw, you guys are too igneous for your own good," little Mickey retorted. "I'd like a little slow-forming sedimentary wit here and there, and not so much of this hot-from-the-volcano stuff."

"Hey, remember, all you geologists, that Doctor Mountenée told us that this part of the coast is rising," the fellow named Josh interrupted.

"Yeah!" exclaimed Mickey. "I just felt us go up right then! Did you feel that little rise, Josh? A little rise in your Levis?"

They all laughed with each other over their geology game as Hattie and I returned to the kitchen.

"Did you get all of that delightful chatter, An-day?" Hattie asked.

"I guess they were making jokes using geology terms, weren't they?"

"How should I know? Summer people and some are not. They get themselves into highsteerics over the damnedest stuff I ever heard of. I guess that's what comes of a Haa-vard education: you learn to talk funny. Let's get back to our pots and pans where we belong."

As was my usual state of being those growing-up summers at the Manor, I felt right then a mixture of confusion and excitement. Hattie's feelings I understood because we shared a common background. She talked the way so many of my relatives and neighbors talked. And it was a relief always to get back to the kitchen where you could fraternize with your own kind. But I was very curious about the Harvard men and how they came to be that way. I was burning to find out what made them so different from the Maine boys I knew. Could I go to college, even though it certainly wouldn't be Harvard, and become like them?

That night at dinner, they requested that we place several of the dining room tables together in the center of the room so they could sit all together at one big table. What most amazed me was to see them dressed for dinner. The summer people at the Manor, and some on Taunton Point, always did this for the evening meal; but I was surprised to see boys without their parents dressing up, too.

They were even noisier and livelier at dinner than they had been with cocktails on the porch. Everything we served them occasioned a joke a witty remark, usually still with some geologic reference. Perhaps, I thought to myself, they are just trying to impress their teacher. The Doctor was the only member of the troupe who seemed to sincerely appreciate Hattie's service and didn't take the good food for granted. He always thanked Hattie and me for our little services rendered.

"Hattie, these biscuits are lighter than a feather, even better than last fall's," he said.

"Why, thank you, Doc," she said. "We prepare them with fairy dough."

"Is that for sale in Summer Harbor?" he asked.

"Oh, no, it's made from our own very secret recipe."

Saturday morning, after the crew had gone to the National Park rock-hunting or dike intruding or whatever, I helped Hattie make up the beds in their rooms. The rooms—and there were six for the boys and one for the doctor—were messed up with clothes, maps, rocks, tools, and books scattered everywhere.

"Boys always tear up beds," Hattie said, "but these Haa-vard men manage to do a good job on the rugs and curtains, too."

She was exaggerating a bit. The rooms were messy, but no more so than those of many other guests we had had; and certainly not as bad as Rosie Talbot's had been. Amongst the discarded dirty socks and underwear, I noticed interesting material that revealed the occupants as several cuts above the average Maine lad: imposing books of a technical and scholarly nature lay atop end tables and bureaus along with geologic tools, trays of bits of rock and stone, and cards and tickets from clubs and places I had never heard of. Several of them smoked pipes. Hattie was more impressed by other findings.

"Here ya go, An-day," she said, tossing me a *Playboy* magazine from one of the boys' beds. "See what nice formations ya find in there!"

I ended up my weekend and my 1959 season at the Manor ten dollars richer and with the wish that I had dared to at least talk a little with one of the Harvard guys, but I didn't. I'm sure none of them even noticed me. Why should they have? I was just the local bus boy in the Maine wilderness. From their talk and the way they carried on, I could tell they considered the Eastern coast of Maine to be one of the last frontiers, largely unexplored territory.

Back in high school for my senior year, I would run into Essie once in a while. I avoided her as much as possible, but in a small high school of less than two hundred students, it's rather hard to avoid anyone. Most of the time, she was pleasant and amusing enough, even when a few of us boys poked fun at her by calling her "Torrid Essie." I let that happen partly in retaliation and in the fear of her making fun of me, shouting out at me when she was in the company of her degenerate friends. That fall, she became engaged to her curly-headed lobsterman, Vaughn Bishop, from Summer Harbor; and by late spring I began to hear the rumor that she was pregnant. She did seem to be living with him and his family already, because instead of riding back and forth on the Taunton school bus, she'd be seen more on the Summer Harbor bus or in Vaughn's suped-up pick-up.

Summer 1960

26

My senior year at Mollusk Memorial High was very successful. I was elected President of my class; and as the student with fourth highest grade average, I was chosen to introduce the graduation speaker. I also served as co-editor of the yearbook, and was a member of a state championship cross country team. I was accepted at the University of Maine for the class of 1964 with two small scholarships. At 18 years old, I was riding high.

The only sour note sounded that June was in a letter I received from Hattie. She had sent me a graduation card just before I was set to return for my second summer at the Manor.

> Dearest Ginn,
>
> I know you'll just turn up your toes and expire, but you'll have to move those damn mattresses all by your lonesome this summer—or get yourself a new Fox.
>
> For I've gone up in the world, across the back parking lot—to the Fitzpatrick estate!
>
> It's a year-round job, you see, with benefits plus, and the Great Movie Writer has even promised me bed-and-board in Hollywood come winter time, and you know, I've

always had stars in my eyes—as well as bats in my belfry.

Stifle your little sobs now; be a man and be happy for me—you're welcome, you know, especially since you're now a high school graduate, to come swing on my garden gate anytime!

Love,
Hattie, the Working Girl

I wrote back to tell her I'd miss her; and as soon as I was settled again in my attic room, I went next door to pay her a visit.

Before we chatted in earnest, Hattie conducted me on a tour of the Fitzpatrick cottage. Beyond the kitchen, the entire downstairs had wall-to-wall deep pile green carpeting and the walls were all painted green, too.

"Green grows my estate," said Hattie.

"The paint must have been a bargain price at the time," I said. "Maybe they're trying to cover up something?"

"Only the beautiful original wood paneling," said Hattie.

The main living room ran half the length of the downstairs, similar to the Manor, and was most comfortable looking with its immense granite fireplace, facing a triple-length couch and a huge highly-polished coffee table made out of an old ship bellows. On either side of the fireplace from floor to ceiling were bookcases filled with hundreds of colorful volumes. Every lamp, piece of furniture, and art object seemed carefully chosen, tasteful, and expensive.

In the windows bordering a circular staircase going upstairs, Mrs. Fitzpatrick had arranged a display of beautiful Italian glass pieces that that morning reflected the sunlight, casting multi-hued patterns on the walls, producing a warm church window effect.

Upstairs there was gray wall-to-wall carpeting. All of the bedrooms were spacious and overlooked the ocean, but the most impressive room to me was Mr. Fitzpatrick's study where he had installed his personal Hollywood memorabilia. For a desk he had an old saloon bar from a Western set, complete with refrigerator and file cabinets. There were glossy pictures expensively framed of various big-name actors and other personalities from Mr. Fitzpatrick's colorful career on the desk, walls, and tables inscribed personally and usually "with love."

Along one wall, on the top shelf of a massive old glass-enclosed bookcase, were arranged his most famous movie scripts, handsomely bound in leather with gold lettering. They were large books, like encyclopedias, much more imposing than I expected scenarios to be; but then the only scripts I had ever known were of the high school variety purchased from Baker's Plays or Samuel French, Inc. The scenarios were illustrated with photographs of scenes from the finished films. I glanced at some of the writing and was surprised to note that a screenwriter, or at least one as successful as Mr. Fitzpatrick, wrote not just the dialogue, but also the directions and camera angles as well.

In one corner of the study, by the window overlooking the sea, was a small bed where Hattie told me he slept when he was working full-time on an important script.

"When he's busy working, he means it when he says don't open this door. He doesn't want to see anyone, including his own children. He also chose this room for his writing because it has the worst view of the bay. He has all the necessities of life built-in right here, sort of an apartment within the house, and it's not unusual for him to stay here for days at a time," Hattie said.

"I'm impressed, Hattie."

"Yeah, well, here the good life IS possible."

"What are they like?" I asked.

"Most of the time these days, he's moody, but he is very sharp and can be a lot of fun; and she's strange, but they're basically both O.K."

"Do you like working here?"

"It's fun to talk to Lawrence Harvey and other stars on the phone. Harvey called the other night about this picture Mr. Fitzpatrick is working on and I answered in my sweetest tone: 'Mistuh Fitzpatrick's residence. May ah help ya?'"

"Do many stars like that call him?"

"Only if they want something, just like everyone else. It can be fun, though, like when you answer the phone, and some dramatic or familiar voice on the other end says, 'Hello, this is Elizabeth Taylor speaking. . .'"

"How are the kids?"

"There are three, and they're spoiled brats, of course, especially the little boy, who's always popping his eyes and pulling on his pecker."

On the third floor of the mansion was a four-room apartment where Hattie now lived.

"You've given up your house?"

"My shack, you mean? I guess probably. I didn't have to deliberate for too many hours on that score, now I'll tell ya. Here I've got running water, a bathroom, and heat, not to mention a view of Frenchman's Bay that's even better than the Fitzes have from their boudoir. That's four up on the old place. This is luxury to me, Andaykins!"

"Did you sell your shack?"

"Nope. I just closed 'er up for the time being. I may have to go back. One never knows, and that shack, that outhouse, and a half-acre is all I've got. Of course, I do have a new sewing machine. . ."

"And Lulabelle, the baby blue Plymouth."

"Yeah, I don't know what I'm going to do with Lula; put 'er up on blocks for the winter while I'm by the pool in Beverly Hills."

After the tour was over, I sat in the kitchen a while longer with Hattie and talked.

"Now, ain't this some kitchen?" Hattie asked.

"Sure is. They've got everything."

"They've got more than everything. Remote control TV, self-defrosting refrigerator, an intercom system, an automatic juicer. It's as good as Cape Canaveral. How about that chopping block on legs? You could chop up just about anything on that, couldn't ya?"

"Sure could. My God, Hattie, what would the folks down on the town dock say?"

"Same as they've always been saying. But just as long as they all get to come in and poke around the place, play with the new toys, they don't begrudge Mr. Fitzpatrick his eighty thousand dollar sprinkler system."

"Weren't Miss Meyer and Mrs. Richmond upset when you left?"

"Sure. But there comes a time, ya know, when a person has to think of herself and nobody else. Besides, I didn't hear them come up with any more attractive alternatives for me."

"I won't know what to do without you, Hattie."

"Sure ya will. I hear tell there's to be a whole flock of young girls your age this year; it took a whole flock to replace me and Caroline. You'll have fun—just remember what I taught ya! Being the only bull in the herd ought to count for something."

27

I was busy re-arranging the glassware in the butler's pantry one sunny afternoon, soon after my visit next door with Hattie, when Miss Meyer stuck her head around the corner from the office to tell me that I had a visitor out in the lobby.

I went to see who it was, and from the back it appeared to be a very well-built, tanned, and tall young lady in a tight white sheath and white high heels. She turned around to greet me, and I could see it was Essie Torrey all dressed up! She had on sunglasses and her hair covered by a white scarf tied around her neck.

"HIYA, COW SHIT! Whaddaya think of this get up? Think I'd pass as a guest in this joint?"

"Ess-ay, you look great, and you're all in white!"

"Yeah, well, I thought I'd surprise ya! I drove right down the front driveway, walked right in the front door, and if ya look out the window, you'll see I came in a white convertible, just like a goddamn fancy person! I drove by here last summer once, but I was too chicken to dare and come in here. Had to wait till I could get the right duds. So, ya gonna show me around? I want to see your room."

I was afraid of that, but I did give her a tour; and we did end up in my attic room.

"So, this is where ya jerk off, huh, An-day?"

"This is my hideout and resting place from the hustle and bustle down below."

She pulled me onto the bed.

"Yeah, well, a shy guy like you needs a hideout for his jerking off; but, look, I have something I want to tell ya. I wanted to tell you personally. . .this isn't the only time this summer I'm gonna be wearing all white."

"You're getting married?"

"Yes, the first of August, to Vaughn, of course. He's the only one I've ever loved besides you, and he wins out because he got me pregnant; and you'd never even have sex with me."

"Oh, Es-say. . ."

"It had to happen. We did try using those rubbers, those French safe things; but Vaughn's cock is so big, and we'd be in such a hurry, he'd only get the safe half on. It was funnier than hell. He'd keep breakin' 'em, too, so, anyway, some of his stuff must have got into me, 'cause I'm on the way. Vaughn's a handsome guy, though, isn't he?"

"Yes, he's very good-looking. I just think he drinks too much and drives too fast."

"Don't he though? He does everything fast. Remember how the coach told him what a great basketball player he'd be if he'd only get some self-control? The way he'd fight for the ball, he'd foul out in the first quarter."

"Similar to your playing," I said.

"Yeah, well, we are wild together, that's for sure. He's as horny as I am. That's what makes it exciting. And Daddy approves of him—how about that? Wouldn't you know I'd end up with a fisherman?"

"It makes sense, but, look, Ess-ay, I've got to get back to work."

She pushed me down on the bed. "Look, Cow Shit! Even though I'm getting hitched, I want you to know that I still want you as a friend. I still want to see ya. Now that I'm pregnant, in fact, we could finally do the dirty deed. You've got nothing to lose, ya know? I'm gonna be down here at Vaughn's grandmother's up in the village, so you'll know where I am. And now I know exactly where you are. There's even a back staircase! We could sneak in and outa here as easy as pie. You took college prep in high school, so you're all prepped for your classes; but I think I could prep ya good in another way! So, expect to be surprised some more!"

She insisted on leaving by the front door, and just as I opened the door for her, she said, loudly: "WELL, THANK YOU, SIR, FOR SHOWING ME YOUR ROOMS. THEY'RE LOVELY, BUT NOT EXACTLY WHAT I HAD IN MIND! GUESS I'LL GO BACK TO THAT MOTEL UP THE ROAD!"

28

Hattie was right. My fun was multiplied four times by the addition to the hotel staff of Cousin Lillie Partridge, Morgan Carlisle, Amanda Guptill, and Allison Blakely.

Except for me, Miss Meyer had to replace the entire staff. Even old Mrs. Spurling retired from her laundry and pastry occupations; she did agree to make a pie or cake every now and then, but nothing regular. Miss Meyer managed to talk me into talking my mother into doing the dining room linen twice a week and supplying good fresh water from our Taunton well for Mrs. Lawson, who didn't like the Granite Neck water, whenever she came and went with the laundry.

Berter Fickett remained, of course, but she didn't count as a regular staff member anyway. Bert was irregular by nature.

It was great having Cousin Lil come to work at the Manor. She had been intrigued by my tales from the summer before and was tired of waitressing at a Taunton diner on Route One which catered to truck drivers, the locals, and some tourists. As a good-looking, brown-eyed, and dark-haired girl, Lil enjoyed the attention she received from all the males who frequented the diner, but the pace was hectic and the tips minimal. She realized that waiting on tables at the Manor was a step up and appreciated not only the more genteel clientele and relaxed pace, but also the pleasant, more intellectually stimulating atmosphere.

Lil, like me, desired to go to college and to escape from working class Downeast, but unlike me, she had also dated more, made out with people. Ever since her freshman year at Mollusk, Lil had dated seniors and boys at the Navy base. Lillie was that wonderful combination of intellectual curiosity and animal sensuality. She was so smart and attractive. With her fine mind and zany sense of humor, I loved being with her more than anyone. One of the delights of my life was to sit for hours with Lillie and swap outrageous stories and observations from our lives. We made love to each other by making each other laugh as hard and as long as possible.

Lil refrained from casual chit chat and the usual gossip. Never did I hear her make a caustic remark about another person. "I don't know him well enough to say," she'd usually remark whenever the rest of us were indulging in the favorite sport of character assassination.

During her two summers at the Manor, Lillie had the romantic habit each night after dinner was served and the rest of us were cleaning up, of running around on the back lawn in the dark. I loved watching her from the back porch or kitchen windows. The light from the hotel caught the whiteness of her uniform and shoes those twilight times.

Julie Lawson, for one, was fascinated by Lillie's early evening romps. "She's like Catherine on the moors from *Wuthering Heights*," she'd say. "I wish she'd go the oval with me. Do you think she might?"

"I don't know. Why don't you ask her?" I said.

Lillie went once, like so many others, but never again.

"Twinkle Toes is too much for me," she said upon her return.

One bright morning in June, Lillie and I were taking a break from house cleaning chores, sipping grape juice in the kitchen when the front door bell rang and Miss Meyer went to the door. I left Lil and my grape juice to go and see who it was; and I shall never forget the sight.

Whirling through the front entrance that I had so timidly exited the year before was this blue-eyed, short-haired brunette clad in a sleeveless, flared white summer dress. She was accompanied by her grandmother, a woman I recalled seeing as a frequent dinner guest. She and Miss Meyer knew each other rather well, and after a few moments of pleasantries, all three walked through the dining room into the kitchen.

"Errr. . .this is where you'll be working most of the time," Miss Meyer told the girl.

"What an impressive spice shelf!" she said.

"Errr. . .Andy and Lillie, I would like you to meet Morgan who'll be helping us out here with the cooking this summer. And I'm sure, Andy, that you remember Mrs. Morgan?"

"Yes, I do."

"So what's her name—Morgan Morgan?" Lil asked me after they had left the room.

It wasn't. Her name was Morgan Carlisle. She was named after her maternal grandparents' surname. She was also only seventeen, which surprised us because she looked and acted several years older.

Hailing from the New Jersey suburbs with Ivy League aspirations, and with a cosmopolitan background that included a Welsh painter from Oregon as grandfather, a Jewish southerner as grandmother, a former dancer turned librarian as mother, and a Columbia journalism professor as father, Morgan provided an interesting, and often abrasive, contrast to Lillie's co-waitress colleague and roommate, Amanda Guptill, a tall, masculine blonde from East Millinocket, north of Bangor.

Amanda was big-boned and athletic, a rough-and-ready type of gal. She had a thick rural Maine accent and a great earthy sense of humor. Both Lillie and I liked her right off.

Amanda was like a lot of the Maine girls we'd grown up with who, by their actions, talk, values, and outlook, are already middle-aged by the time they're out of their teens. The life of the imagination and anything bordering on fantasy is suspiciously regarded if not totally rejected as silly and impractical. Amanda was a happy soul, because she subscribed completely to the lifestyle of her elders; she played the role expertly and fit in. She was quite the antithesis of Lil and me, who dreamed of living a more glamorous and exciting life away from Eastern Maine. Amanda was working on getting married as soon as possible, maybe right after a year of secretarial courses at Husson College in Bangor. She already had her man, was already engaged. He was a handsome French boy off in the Navy and she had his picture on the table by her bed. She was already busy buying stuff for her hope chest and their inevitable life together. She constantly talked of him.

Amanda called everyone "de-ah" and was always poking fun at Morgan because of her sophisticated city upbringing and tastes. For instance, we would be eating lunch prepared by Morgan the way Hattie used to, and Morgan would attempt to elevate the conversation.

"I like the titles of Aldous Huxley's books. That's why I read so many of them. The titles just intrigue me: *Point Counterpoint*, *Eyeless in Gaza*, *Chrome Yellow*, and the one I'm reading now, *Time Must Have a Stop*. They make you stop and think right off. . ."

"They'd make me turn around and go the other way!" said Amanda with a guffaw.

"Oh, but Amanda, I would think that every now and then you'd like to try and improve your little mind a tiny bit. . .or your tiny mind a little bit."

"Lissen, Morgan, de-ah, my mind can take care of itself. Besides, what do INTRIGUING BOOK TITLES have to do with it? Anyone could make up titles like that. How about *Bra-Less in Bangor*? *Aluminum Pink*? *Pound for Pound*? *Time We All Stopped*?"

"I don't think you get my point."

"*Time Must Have a Point*, then!"

"Now, you're being ridiculous!"

"Maybe because I'm hungry. You didn't give me any do-dads!"

"What?"

"DO-DADS! In my vegetable soup, de-ah. All I got was tomato-flavored hot water; and, honey, one does expect some do-dads in her veggies!"

Among us, Allison Blakely, the chambermaid, who had replaced Caroline Cole, made the best referee at these mealtime matches that occurred mainly between Morgan, the New Jersey suburbanite, and Amanda, the Downeast ruffian. Everyone liked Allison. Pretty with light brown hair and blue eyes, Allison carried herself like Audrey Hepburn, whom she resembled. She lived up the peninsula from Granite Neck and commuted, as did Morgan, each day to the Manor. Allison was Downeast royalty from an old Maine family and was well brought up. She could communicate just as well with the lowest class of natives as well as with the highest class of summer people. Allison loved life and people and it showed; and people responded in kind. She had a humorous, wise way of regarding life, and this was revealed in her role as mediator between Morgan and Amanda.

"Truce, girls! Time for dessert," she'd say at a convenient break in the wrangling.

"Aw, Allison, give a girl a break! You always ruin everything. I almost had old Morgan pinned against the wall this time!" said Amanda.

When Mrs. Richmond arrived for her two-week visit in 1960 to see how the season was progressing and to meet the new crew, she was most impressed by Lillie and Allison.

"Why isn't the Blakely girl in the dining room with Lillie, instead of that cow Amanda?" Mrs. Richmond asked right off. "Allison would make a lovely hostess while that cow belongs behind a dishpan! She may be authentic Maine stock, but we must try and preserve our always precarious image of graceful living in the wilds!"

Miss Meyer did arrange to have Allison help out in the dining room evenings when we had big crowds—a big crowd for the Manor being forty or fifty—but she remained chiefly the chambermaid.

However, it was with Morgan that I worked most closely. For two summers we helped cook three meals a day. After a couple of weeks, after she had proven herself capable, Miss Meyer let Morgan and I be in complete charge of breakfast, perhaps the most exasperating meal to serve any place, because there's always such a variation in orders.

We'd have the oatmeal or whatever the hot cereal for the day was simmering in a double boiler on the back of the stove, the coffee would be perked, the bacon and ham cooked, the stewed prunes and apricots ready, the juice supply replenished, the bread for toast and the jams and jellies all set, the batter for the pancakes mixed, the fresh berries picked over and washed; but no matter how ready we were, if the guests were all in the dining room at once, as they usually were on nice sunny mornings, it was wild working in the kitchen.

In would come the aggravating egg orders in quick succession.

"One order of three-minute boiled! Two orders of fried, one over and one up! Two orders of scrambled! One order of poached! Two four-minute boiled!"

"Doesn't anyone want pancakes?"

"Not yet!"

"Push them, will ya?"

"I'll do my best!"

"Are there any more fresh blueberries out back?"

"Nope. They're all in the pancake batter by now."

"Damn. Is there any honeydew melon?"

"Nope. Only cantaloupe."

"I need some more of Mrs. Billings' fresh homemade frozen doughnuts!" said Amanda. "Can you sugar 'em for me, An-day?"

"Yes," I said, pulling the doughnut tray out of the oven, throwing half a dozen in the brown paper bag filled with powdered sugar and shaking the bag like a wild man.

"Andy," Morgan asked, "can you do the boiled and poached while I'm preparing the fried and scrambled?"

"Why not, Morgan, honey? I'd love to, seeing that they are the hardest to do."

"What do you mean? It's not exactly easy to keep the scrambled from getting burned or the fried yolks from breaking!"

"Two orders of three-minute boiled!"

"What else would they expect them to be in three minutes?" I asked.

"Maybe they got the word that we do all boiled eggs for five minutes regardless of order," said Morgan.

"You know that's not true! We try to be accurate and please our hungry customers who tip us so well."

"Yeah, sure. . .Oh, damn! The yolk broke! Hand me another egg quick!"

"Two orders of blueberry pancakes with ham!"

"Want me to do the pancakes, too?" I asked.

"Please!" said Morgan. "Now, the scrambled is burning!"

Miss Meyer had carefully and painstakingly taught both of us how she wanted the breakfast cooked. The rules included no burnt-on scrambled eggs or broken yolks. Nothing must look or taste greasy. Paprika, unless the guest instructed otherwise, was to be sprinkled lightly on top of all egg orders to make them look more appetizing. As much as possible, no boiled eggs were to be broken, but peeled whole and placed in egg cups, so the shelling of very hot soft eggs was always an ordeal. I learned to shell them fast under hot running water in the sink.

Doing the pancakes was most fun, but one morning, Morgan and I had a disagreement about their preparation.

"You use too much grease," she said. "After the first or second greasing, you don't need to apply more. The griddle should be hot enough."

"What a wild, unfounded theory," I said.

"It's not unfounded. It's founded. I found out and now you will. You don't need grease. Pay attention! Here, let me show you."

"All right, Miss New Jersey; but if they stick on, you'll have to do the scraping off!"

"Oh, no! You're the kitchen boy; I'm the assistant chef. You have to clean up my mess. Know your place, peasant!"

Morgan was right. The pancakes didn't stick and tasted better and were much lighter the way she did them. I apologized and told her how impressed I was by her culinary knowledge. She did love cooking.

We'd argue over matters other than food, too. One morning we were practically screaming at each other over whether it was "better to be red than dead," when the milkman with his racks of bottles entered the kitchen. He stood there for a minute listening to us debate communism vs. capitalism; and then simply asked: "Well, what are you gonna do about it?"

He had us there.

One old lady, a Mrs. Kincaid, who once told me that she was so rich she owned a whole town in Connecticut, loved our breakfasts so much that she often asked permission from Miss Meyer to eat in the kitchen where she could be "as close as possible to the preparations" and "drink in the wonderful smells." She also invited friends from neighboring summer colonies to join her at the Manor for breakfast.

"How ever do you prepare such wonderful coffee?" she once asked Miss Meyer.

"Errr. . .we blend S.S. Pierce with an Italian brand."

"And those exquisite doughnuts; whose are they?"

"Errr. . .Mrs. Billings from nearby Cold Bay."

"Marvelous!"

"And we make our own magnificent omelets by breaking some eggs," Morgan whispered in my ear.

Morgan read all the time. It was one of the joys of my young life to lie beside her down on the rocks or sit beside her in the back dining room, or up in our attic rooms (I was at one end and Lillie and Amanda were at the other end), or under some trees on the back lawn reading and discussing books. Besides Aldous Huxley, she introduced me to Ogden Nash, Willa Cather, Tagore, and most important of all,

Thomas Wolfe, the first major artist beyond Chester Gould, creator of Dick Tracy, and Max Shulman, to make such a difference in my life. Up to Wolfe, I had trafficked haphazardly upon the recommendations of my mother, teachers, and church group leaders in the melodramatic excesses of Lloyd C. Douglas, A. J. Cronin, and Thomas B. Costain; through B-picture tales of Zane Grey and men's adventure stories; the comedies of Betty MacDonald, Clarence Day, the Galbraiths, and Edward Streeter; the soap operas of Faith Baldwin and Grace Livingston Hill; the mysteries of Sir Arthur Conan Doyle and Agatha Christie; and the Maine books of Mary Ellen Chase, Edmund Ware Smith, Kenneth Roberts, Elisabeth Ogilvie, Ruth Moore, and John Gould. But, even though Ruth Moore came close, none of them made the impact of Thomas Wolfe.

With the reading of *Look Homeward, Angel*, it was as though my search for guidance and meaning for my life was ended. I had found a great man to guide me, someone to tell me about myself, about my feelings and needs. How I loved his lyricism of language, the way he plunged heart, body, and soul into life and out of this life made literature. The beauty, power, and flow of his words thrilled me. His cry of "O Lost!" His trains racing in the night through towns and cities across America. His bigness. His vision. His spirit. His loneliness. I lay in my attic bed with Tchaikovsky or Strauss or Wagner blaring, laughing and crying, exciting myself almost to death over this great artist's tales and descriptions of Eliza, Ben, Helen, and W.O. Gant, his family, and all the other people from his Asheville and Chapel Hill, North Carolina world.

Wolfe's autobiographical creation of Eugene Gant was me. I knew with Wolfe that I had found my calling. There could be no greater role for me to try and play than writer. I longed to see my name on books.

Morgan was the first summer girl I was to get to know well. I was acquainted with a few on Taunton Point, but I never knew them. Through Morgan, I was learning so much. She had gone to private school in Manhattan; she had rich relatives in Atlanta. She had lived her life among artists, professors, business and professional people, the doctors and lawyers of the New Jersey suburbs. Morgan was planning on going to an Ivy League college.

29

With Hattie and her Plymouth now servicing next door, I assumed the duties of chauffeur/errand boy the summer of 1960. Since Berter Fickett retained the old Chevy beach wagon for her own use, Mrs. Richmond, as promised, volunteered her 1957 Oldsmobile 98.

She drove up from Greenwich one early July weekend and had me drive her around the National Park so that she could satisfy herself that I could manage her car.

I drove very carefully and slowly, so slowly, in fact, that my portly co-boss was prompted to exclaim, "My God, Andy! If you continue proceeding at this breakneck speed, we'll be lucky to get home before Christmas! Either pick it up or let me at the wheel!"

"The speed limit is only thirty-five in this park," I said.

"Not when no one's looking! It's impressive how careful and law-abiding you are, Andy, but careful people don't go very far very fast. In fact, on today's speedways, Grandma Duck would by peddling along in her electric car creating a menace. There are minimum speeds as well as maximum, ya know."

I passed the Richmond Test and as soon as she went back to Connecticut and her part-time job as a hospital administrator, I became the full-time daily driver for the Manor.

I liked the new job very much because I could get away from the hotel and enjoy a certain amount of prestige and envy among my female co-workers as the man with wheels.

Miss Meyer had me on the run all over the countryside in search of specialties for the house. I drove to an old German immigrant lady's for gladiolus and to a farm up the peninsula for homegrown herbs and vegetables. In town there was an old couple who grew wonderful raspberries and a lobsterman's wife who prepared upon request a delicious cold lobster salad. I had to drive seven miles away to Cold Harbor, a tiny fishing village, for the homemade doughnuts manufactured by Mrs. Helen Billings.

Helen lived in a simple white frame house with a huge tree in the front yard with a spare tire swing suspended from one limb and nailed to the same tree was a sign that simply read DONUTS.

Helen Billings looked the part of the doughnut woman. She was short, round, and dumpy, her hair in a hairnet, bifocals halfway down her nose, puttering around her kitchen in an apron she made herself. The kitchen was a bubbling factory out of a fairy tale with cauldrons of boiling grease on the old oil stove and racks of doughnuts all over the place.

She had an apprentice in her middle-aged, half-witted son whom she called "Child."

The tree swing was Child's and he had other toys scattered around the house and porch. He was as rotund as his mother, both evidently prone to sampling their wares. He bounced about the kitchen, fetching things at his mother's command. Child would giggle, laugh, and clap his hands at anything Mrs. Billings or I said that hinted of friendliness and good times; but when she scolded him, which was rather frequent in my presence, he'd clasp his hands together and bow his head, like a sad dumb animal.

"CHILD!" Mrs. Billings would yell. "Bring me that pan NOW!"

"CHILD! If you don't cut out biting your fingers you won't be able to swing on the tire today, and I don't mean mebbe!"

"CHILD! Stop yer foolin' around and bring me the molasses!"

And to me, "Here, how many would you like this trip—three dozen? A nice mix, huh? Some plain, some chocolate, some molasses?"

For other desserts, I drove to a place just outside the village of Summer Harbor called Apple Pie Heaven, a small jerry-built truck-stop run by a big, tough, good-looking blonde named Ramona Snook. Mrs. Richmond liked to say that Ramona made "pies conceived in Heaven."

"What'll it be, bub?" Ramona would always ask me.

"What have you got?"

"You're in luck today, hon. Just take a gander at this handsome strawberry rhubarb number hot from the oven. Ain't she a beaut? Came out quite nice--a real taste-tempter, I'd say. That's in my expert opinion, of course!"

Beyond picking up specialties, I made daily excursions to the institutions that govern our existence: the bank, the post office, the gas station, and the grocery store.

While business at the bank, the gas station, and post office was cut and dried, shopping at the grocery store was another matter.

The proprietor of W. A. Guilford and Son was the son, Wyman Guilford, a tall, white-haired, bespectacled, and handsome gentleman who always looked as if he had just witnessed an unspeakable horror, and thus had been rendered vacant in expression and memory. He acted absent-minded and forever distracted, especially if one were speaking directly to him.

"Wyman, darling, do you have some lovely fresh pork chops?" I once heard the Admiral's wife from Granite Neck ask Mr. Guilford one day.

"Ah, why, uh. . .maybe. . .let's see. . .lamb chops? Uh, no, yes, perhaps. . .let's see. . ."

Wyman's eyes would search the store, looking for an escape hatch maybe, anything but look her in the face.

"I said PORK CHOPS, darling!"

"Oh, yes. . .sure, uh. . . let's see. . ."

Rumor had it that Wyman had wanted to be an engineer when he was young, but his father, along with the Depression, had forced him into butchering meat and ultimately taking over the store; and, thus, he had always hated the store. However true this was, everyone, summer person and native alike, liked Wyman. Personally, I always found him a bit strange and hard to talk with, but this might have been because he was so very shy and awkward with people. Or maybe it was because he despised the role he had to play.

Certainly, he must have found orders from the Manor bothersome. Miss Meyer and Mrs. Richmond both were always having to add to the daily order phoned in each morning. Rush trips between Guilford's and the hotel were not uncommon at all hours, way after the store was closed for the day or weekend. It seemed as if an emergency was forever arising in the midst of meal preparations. One night Mr. Guilford, summoned from his bed, met me in his pajamas and overcoat at the back door of the store with a package of meat.

I was always being torn from my dishpan with cries like the following:

"Oh, my God! We're out of cream! An-day, rush to the store!"

"Err. . .Andy, take your apron off and run up to Guilford's quickly and get two quarts of harlequin ice cream and a dozen fresh peaches."

"Jay-sus Christ! There's no orange juice left for morning, and Mrs. Lawson must have her juice! An-day!"

When Miss Meyer, propped up against the kitchen sideboard, the phone in her right hand and the usual cigarette in her left, phoned in the grocery order every morning after breakfast, she'd say, "Errr. . .hello, this is Miss Meyer at Frenchman's Bay Manor. I'd like to. . .what's that? Pardon me? Oh, yes, I'll wait. . .errr. . .O.K., now, I'd like a dozen tomatoes, two bunches of celery, a dozen Florida oranges, a box of SOS pads, a package of Diamond walnuts, a leg of lamb, and two six packs of Miller's High Life."

No matter what else was on the order, she'd always add on a six pack or two of Miller's, her favorite brew.

Every so often, Miss Meyer would order a large platter of lobster salad from Vaughn's grandmother; and that summer of 1960, I'd often see Essie with Vaughn, his grandmother, and other relatives. One time, I caught a glimpse of Essie in a white bikini playing croquet on the back lawn with Vaughn in his swim trunks. They were smoking, swigging beer, swinging their mallets, whacking their balls, and laughing hysterically.

By my last year at the Manor, I was over twenty-one and could legally buy liquor, so "mercy missions" to the Milbridge or Ellsworth liquor stores became added to my other errand trips. "Thank God, you're finally twenty-one," said Miss Meyer, "now you'll really earn your keep."

What I enjoyed most about chauffeuring was not the running of daily errands, but the picking up and delivering of guests.

My first trip to Union Station in Bangor was to pick up the Violet Sisters, a couple of red-haired, middle-aged, overly plump old maid sisters from New York. When I arrived at the station, afraid I was too late for the train, I met my uncle Eugene Crowley from Taunton Point out on the platform all by his lonesome. Uncle Gene had always been one of my favorite relatives because of his practical jokes, his wild sense of humor, his love of people, and his relaxed way of life, seen mostly from the viewpoint of butler, gardener, handyman, and chauffeur. He used to work on the Maine Central steamboats with my father; but since the boats stopped running, he had spent most of his adult life working for the summer people, a servant to the rich. He was a handsome man of regal bearing and with a love of liquor, which lent a comic slur to his speech which was always peppered with amusing observations and yarns. He was standing there that day with his back to me, his left hand in his pants pocket, a cigarette poised in his right, his hat situated jauntily on his head, as usual, humming his theme song, "Linda."

"Hi, Uncle Gene."

He smiled. "Well, my soul and body, what have we here? You planning a big trip or running away from home?"

"I've just been promoted to chauffeur."

"It couldn't have happened to a nicer boy. Make sure now that you get a good tip and don't run over any skunks."

"Is the *Bar Harbor Express* in yet?"

"You mean the *Bangor Express* nowadays, don'tcha?. . .No, that old choo-choo gets later and later every trip. Pretty soon it won't come at all; then I can retire."

I didn't reckon on the train's having so many people on it, nor half as many red-haired women who all seemed to be traveling in pairs. All I could do was wait and see who was left standing there after the crowd had largely dispersed, which I did, and almost simultaneously, it seemed, the Violet girls and I discovered each other, and made our way, chatting amicably enough, with my answering all the questions they fielded, and pointing out what noteworthy or historical aspects of the roadside scene I knew as a young man of eighteen.

For instance, traveling through Lucerne-in-Maine, from Bangor to Ellsworth, I showed the ladies where Log Lodge, advertised as "the largest log cabin in the world," used to be before it burned down.

"My father said it was because the insurance got hot," I explained.

"Why, young man, whatever do you mean by that?" one of the redheads asked.

"It means that the guy who owned it burned it down for the insurance."

As we drove by another spot, I told them what my father had told me.

"During the 1930s, a whole family of people was killed right here. They were riding in a truck filled with dynamite. Some of the kids were sitting on kegs of dynamite licking ice cream cones when a cigarette touched off one of the kegs. Parts of their bodies were scattered everywhere, all over the place. They even found an arm dangling from a telephone wire."

"Why, young man, that's terrible."

Miss Meyer later told me that I had been a great hit with the Violet gals. They had greatly enjoyed their tour with me along the Bangor Road and Route One.

One other time, at the Bar Harbor Airport, I had to pick up a rich lady from Park Avenue named Mrs. Chittendon, whom Miss Meyer had warned me to treat very well, to go easy on my story-telling, and not to argue with her since she was a woman of strong opinions. While waiting for her plane, I chatted with another uncle of mine, Rupert Haskell, who worked as a ticket clerk during his summers away from his school teaching job.

Mrs. Chittendon was a middle-aged widow of aristocratic bearing. She wore tinted sunglasses, a wide-brimmed hat, a beige summer suit, and carried an expensive-looking handbag. She carried herself erect and spoke with an imperious tone of authority. Her suitcases, however, were ancient, tattered, roped together, and falling apart.

"Those bags have been around the world with me," she said.

On our way to the hotel, Mrs. Chittendon made me keep stopping at a dozen or more little drive-in places, so she could see "what all the quaint little people had with which to barter their existence."

She also started talking politics.

"I shall never survive if Kennedy wins in November," she declared.

"Why not?" I had to ask.

"Because that boy, Jack, is the son of an out-and-out scoundrel! I don't know the boy, but I knew his father, and Joe Kennedy, take it from me, is an awful man! And an apple doesn't fall far from the tree."

I never learned what she meant was so awful, because I did as my boss had suggested and asked few questions, replying most of the time with an agreeable "yes, ma'am."

"There used to be a wonderful old woman who lived in a shack down on Mount Desert who baked the most delicious blueberry pies I've ever eaten. I don't suppose we could try and find her?"

"We're on the mainland, ma'am," I said. "It would take quite a bit of time to double back to the Island, and I've got to be back at the Manor."

"Oh, all right. Maybe I can find out from Jean about the name of that woman."

During these chauffeuring jobs, I had to forgo my usual outfits of jeans and cotton shirts and dress more formally in white shirts and black or gray slacks.

One couple I had to drive all over the county was Professor and Mrs. Economy. He taught in the business school at Cornell and nurtured a keen side interest in rural sociology. He made me drive them through and around all the little fishing villages in Hancock and Washington counties, at least every other afternoon of their two-week stay. He likened the villages dominated by a large sardine factory, lobster pound, or blueberry cannery to feudal colonies from the Middle Ages.

"Fascinating," he'd keep saying.

On the way back to the Bangor Airport, we were late, but Dr. Economy just had to have both his *New York Times* and *Herald Tribune*, which was his usual daily habit. He couldn't exist without them. It was early in the morning, but I knew enough about Bangor to know there was one rather large downtown magazine and newspaper store on Center Street called Mr. Paperback where I might be able to purchase both publications. In my rush to get there, however, I went down Center Street, which is one-way, the wrong way, causing a number of on-coming cars and trucks to honk and toot and one loud-mouthed woman to scream at me out of her car window, "WRONG WAY, SHITHEAD!"

I was embarrassed and backed up as fast as possible, apologizing to the Economys in the back seat; but they seemed unperturbed by the incident and much more concerned about the newspapers. "Can we still get the *Times*? The *Times*, at least, I MUST HAVE!"

"Yes, I'm trying."

Rounding the block, I saw that the store was open; the *Times* and *Tribune* both were for sale and purchased; and we made it to the airport just in time for their Northeast Airlines flight to New York.

Relieved that we had made it, when I really didn't think we would, I stopped on my way back to the Manor and treated myself to a banana split and coffee milk shake.

30

Most afternoons, the girls and I would splash about and frolic in the freezing waters of Frenchman's Bay, afterwards soaking up the sun on the granite ledges, reading, talking, and joking with each other. I would try to impress my female companions with the number of push- ups or sit-ups I could do in succession and they would play the portable radio, tuned exclusively in those days to WMEX-AM in Boston, a popular rock-'n-roll station. The girls would let down their bra straps, roll their hips, and do other weight-reducing exercises. It was very pleasant those sunny afternoons lying nearly naked on the rocks with these bright, good-natured females; and our privacy was hardly ever invaded save for an occasional sea gull or one of the hardier summer people hiking the rough route about the cliffs and rock beaches of the Neck.

One time, though, a wild bunch of young men from the Three R's Remedial School for Rich Boys came upon us from the bushes behind the rocks, wielding machetes and sticks and yelling at the tops of their illiterate lungs. They were naked except for their cut-off jeans and bathing trunks and obviously they had hoped to scare the hell out of us. They succeeded, initially; but after a few moments, when they had laid down their arms and began to assume more of a civilized posture, we conversed and joked amicably enough. The girls, in fact, greatly enjoyed the company of all these handsome, well-tanned, athletic young males from wealthy families.

I tried proving my superiority to them by plunging head first into the freezing ocean from one of the ledges, an act which did impress these non-reading rich jocks for its brave recklessness. They had all stuck their toes in Maine waters, and probably tossed a few of their buddies in the brine for fun; but preferred to immerse their total bodies in their own exclusive warm salt water pool, down the street, and off limits to the likes of us.

On another afternoon on the ledges, we came upon a rich summer girl named Dianne Winthrop, lying languidly prostrate upon the rocks, tanning her shapely, bikini-clad body in the sun while perusing James Michener's *Hawaii.* Dianne was genuinely glad to make our working class acquaintance.

"I'm so terribly bored at Uncle's *soirées* these days. This whole lifestyle of Philadelphia on-the-rocks serves no sensible, satisfying purpose for me!" she wailed.

"No one gets up before noon, except me. Everyone goes to the pool, golf course, or sailing in the afternoons. Everyone has cocktails with the same people at the same yacht club. Dinner is served at nine or so. It's such a silly, lazy routine. I'm being a real rebel, you see, getting up early and coming down here to the rocks by myself, not associating with them."

"And talking with us peons!" Amanda said.

"Oh, but I want to so much! I wanted a summer job this year, as you have! Something REAL, something WITH MEANING. And PURPOSE. I want dirt on my hands for once. My life is so secure, routine, and boring. I can hardly wait to get to Bryn Mawr in September just to get on my own and start my life. May I come and visit you at work some day?"

"Sure," I said. "Why not?"

Dianne did visit, the first rainy day, but at an awkward hour, since we were just starting to serve dinner and the girls couldn't or wouldn't talk with her; so I was commissioned to give her a brief guided tour of the Manor and our attic digs.

She wore a huge, bulky-knit orange sweater for the occasion over what looked like nothing else, and dark glasses. She was most impressed with Lillie's and Amanda's room at the end of the attic. "You five must have a lot of fun," she said, upon her departure. "Thank you, Andy, for showing me." She left and we never saw her again.

The girls began to make fun of Dianne, and she became a popular reference and joke during many of our conversations for the rest of the summer.

"I'm so terribly, terribly bored with being rich!" Amanda would mimic. "I just can't bear the sight of another yacht! Tell me, what do you DELIGHTFUL HICKS do with all that DIRT on your hands? Do you lick it off and call it lunch? Excuse me, BRUNCH! We rich people never eat LUNCH."

"Hello, this is Dianne Winthrop speaking, you know, the RICH BITCH ON THE ROCKS? I would like to be poor for the summer; could you please let me know how I should manage this? Please hurry because my limousine is waiting to take me to Radcliffe to begin my new life of toil and hardship! It's going to help mold my character, you see. I'm majoring, after all, in LIFE'S REALITIES!"

One afternoon, the girls almost succeeded in drowning me. We were at Allison's family camp on Smith Pond up the peninsula, a retreat for the working-class natives of the area and a place where we could really go swimming. The girls had rowed out to a float a few hundred feet off shore, and I, being the only male, decided to play Buster Crabbe, shunning the boat and swimming the distance. It was tiring, however, since I wasn't a long-distance swimmer, and when I reached the float and tried to mount it, the girls, with the sole exception of Cousin Lil, started beating at my hands and arms, not letting me climb aboard. They were laughing gaily, hitting me all the while, like a bunch of horrid Bacchantes, while my treading in the twenty feet or so of water became rather desperate. The more I hollered at them, the more they beat at me. Finally, and just in time, it seemed to drowning me, they let me join them, where as soon as I regained my strength, I began to toss them all off into the drink.

Another sunny afternoon, we went swimming off the town dock which was nestled in a cove where supposedly the water was warmer than down off the Neck, probably because of all the harbor pollution, but the degree of difference was imperceptible to our skins. Allison had planned this particular outing, because her best friend, Lizzie Guilford, daughter of Wyman, lived nearby in a big sea captain's old mansion overlooking the harbor. After our quick dip, Lizzie invited us all to have tea and Nabisco sugar wafers with her and her mother.

The Guilfords, being Downeast royalty, prominent landowners and pillars of the Catholic Church with generational ties to the community, expected visitors to their house to be properly reverent in regard to the unstated, subtle rules of decorum. Both Mrs. Guilford and Lizzie spoke as if assured of their place in society, if not history. I liked them, because they were very nice and thoughtful, but I always felt vaguely uncomfortable with them, as if they were judging me as being a bit too crude and rude, too effusive and lively, not reserved enough in my actions and too open with my off-the-cuff remarks.

I remember Mrs. Guilford speaking calmly but pointedly about the traditions and customs of HER MAINE.

"You see," she said, "Maine coastal people, who once ruled the seas of this planet, are a breed apart in at least one important and significant way. They are always most cognizant of the elements, of nature, and wisely adhere to that power that created us all. Maine folk take their weather reports seriously. Any one of the men down on the dock knows he'd be a fool to go out hauling traps if the fog was coming in. There's a good reason for all the superstitions you hear Maine people spout. Next to the ocean, man is a pitiable creature, weak and frail. Maine people here in villages like Summer Harbor know they are here by God's grace, that the ocean is far mightier than they, and deserves always our utmost respect."

It was easy to understand why Mrs. Guilford enjoyed teaching Sunday school as she did.

Nights, the girls and I played jokes on each other. Once I unscrewed all the light bulbs that led to and down the attic hall to their room, placing obstacles such as pieces of furniture, boxes, and chamber pots in their way so that they would stumble and bump into them in the dark, and hopefully raise a fit and scream, which they did, making me chuckle like a madman from the confines of my room, listening to them behind my closed door. Morgan had been saving orange peels for days in the back pantry with which to make candy when it occurred to my teenage mind to place a bunch of the soggy citrus at the foot of her bed one night. This scheme backfired right into my face; but it was worth it because it was a pleasant sight to see Miss New Jersey so angry and pretty standing there in her nightie in my doorway, throwing handfuls of the peels at me.

Even Amanda the Cow had to admit that Miss New Jersey was getting more and more human.

We took our little games outside the Manor as well. We used to peek in the windows of many of the summer mansions when a party was in session and then run as fast as we could, once straight through a bed of imported roses, whenever somebody almost detected our uninvited presence behind a hedge or beneath a tree. We'd always check out Mr. Fitzpatrick's to see if any big name stars were there; but there were usually only the same old summer people. One night we managed to crawl up on the roof of the yacht club from where we had a fine view of the upper crust goings-on down on the large open porch that faced the water.

We traipsed all over the Neck, usually ending up late at night at the children's playground where we'd teeter totter, slide and swing in the streetlight shadow of the rusty, yellow, narrow old standpipe or water tower.

Once in a while some of my male friends like Lester Moon would join me in heckling the girls. "Gawd, An-day, here you are down here with all these girls!" he'd say. There was this lighted path through the woods leading from the playground and tennis courts down to the yacht club and dock, and sometimes when the girls would be walking on this path, Lester and I would run ahead and hide in the bushes, jumping out and screaming at the girls when they came by us. On the swing set cross bar, we'd compete with each other to see who could do the most chin-ups in front of our female companions. One night, especially to Morgan's great amusement, I crunched my balls on the cross bar while executing some gymnastics. I yelled while she laughed. Morgan seemed to enjoy seeing males in pain.

Partly out of resentment from being excluded during the daytime, and partly because it was a sneaky, amusing thing to do, we started going to the summer people's salt water swimming pool after work in the evenings.

Dickie Joy, a handsome blonde muscleboy, one of Lillie's, Allison's and my classmates at Mollusk Memorial, filled out the lifeguard's trunks during the daytime at the summer folks' pool, and one afternoon, I stopped by to learn all about his job, especially how he could tell the next day if someone had been swimming in the pool the night before. Willing to please, Dickie showed me the skimmers which he set in position at night, and which, if turned upside down in the water in the morning, would indicate that someone or something had disturbed the waters. I remembered this fact and how the skimmers were screwed on and off; and then I returned to the hotel where the girls and I made plans for our clandestine dip that very night. We wore our swimsuits under our regular clothes and carried our towels wrapped up in light summer jackets or sweaters. No doubt, we looked like such an innocent troupe of late-night hikers creeping along the darkened walks and roads which led to the pool.

Once there, we undressed quickly, and silently, me in my own little corner, the girls in theirs. We left our street clothes in piles near the end of the pool that bordered the bushes and underbrush through which we planned our after-swim leave-taking.

We slipped into the shallow end of the pool and paddled to the middle where we floated about. It was delicious to lie there on one's back in the water still warm from the day, gazing up at the stars. This was the first swimming pool I had ever been in, outside or inside. We had to be as quiet as we could because there were two summer cottages nearby; and in a summer night on a secluded peninsula, the slightest sound carried for a great distance.

But everyone wanted to use the diving board! So we planned for the grand finale, lining up and diving one after the other, so that the noise occurred almost simultaneously. We swam to the shallow end of the pool, hurriedly dried and dressed ourselves, hastily exiting the scene, ending up in our warm attic bedrooms where we congratulated ourselves on our clever escapade and toasting our derring-do with cups of cocoa and marshmallow.

Beyond the sneaky dips in the pool, which, after a time, became almost a weekly routine, probably the most special adventure the girls and I shared together that summer was the overnight at Morgan's grandparents' cottage in the company of a well-known Maine authoress, her son, and dog.

Morgan's grandparents had gone on a European tour and Viola Richardson Cash, the authoress and family friend, had been engaged to stay with Morgan in their absence. Morgan's grandfather had done the sketches for one of Mrs. Cash's popular books about the Peninsula where Summer Harbor and Granite Neck were located. Morgan's grandparents owned two-thirds of what was called Cranberry Island, which was actually more of a peninsula connected to the mainland and the tiny fishing village of Cold Harbor.

That night at the Manor, we rushed around finishing up our work so that we could get to Morgan's before it was too dark to explore the island. We could always finish earlier nights if we stopped some of our joking around and talking as much as we usually did in the course of a dinner's serving. We were done by eight p.m. that night, and as we went merrily out the door, Miss Meyer told us she'd miss our company.

"It's only for one night," I said.

"Errr. . .I know, Andy, but let's say, I've grown accustomed to all your faces," she said, grinning after us, and reaching for another sip from her beer glass.

"For a minute there, I thought she was going to sing," I said.

"She makes me so sad sometimes," Amanda said, getting into Morgan's car.

"She's really a very lovely person," Morgan said. "Kind, decent. . .and lonely."

"She can be a bitch, too," I said.

"That's not fair, An-day," Allison said. "She's trying to make a go of this old place without much help."

"Who knows what tragedies she's seen?" Lillie asked in a comic way, making us all laugh.

"And at least she didn't say she had grown accustomed to our *feces*!" I said.

"No, that's you, toilet boy!" exclaimed Amanda. "You get to see everyone's feces, especially Mrs. Talbot's!"

"Now, Amanda," corrected Allison, "I, as chamberlady, get to see my share, too."

We soon put Miss Meyer and our toilet cleaning in the back of our minds with the ubiquitous rock-'n'-roll music blaring from WMEX as Morgan manipulated the Olds 98, a darker twin to Mrs. Richmond's and owned by Morgan's grandparents, about the twisting, narrow roads through Summer Harbor, the various other little harbors and hamlets, and the sea marsh areas at speeds always exceeding the posted limits. As we drove, Amanda commented on the songs on the radio. After Connie Stevens had finished crooning her "Sixteen Reasons," for instance, Amanda said, "I can sure think of better reasons than those for loving a man!"

"Eastward," the Morgans' place, was perfectly situated. The little gray-and-white cottage, like Frenchman's Bay Manor, seemed a natural part of the landscape, as if it grew there with its weathered shingles, its heavy red-painted front door and plain frame windows facing the drama of the sea on two sides and the serenity of the island woods on the opposite sides.

Before we went in the house for the night, Morgan took us on a hasty tour. There was still a little light, so we scrambled along an improvised path by the sea, over ledges and sandless beaches strewn with rocks, similar to the ones on Granite Neck, and ultimately up along the woods that bordered the shore. Morgan chattered along the trek, letting us in on her past as a child summering here, on her knowledge of the other offshore islands, of the history and science and lore of the place, and in on her love of these beautiful acres. I was so impressed with her comments, which I thought ranked among the most witty and intelligent I had ever heard from someone my own age.

"Hasten, fellow Manorites!" she yelled, "to where I now stand in order that I might direct you further along in our quest of island flora and fauna. Gather round me now that I might recount the wondrous plans for the final leg of our nocturnal journey."

She could speak so well and so confidently, I thought, even when mimicking some tour lecturer as she was doing now. How impressive she could be with her bearing and vocabulary! I was thrilled watching her there in the fading Downeast twilight, her brown hair blowing about her beautiful, intelligent face, while a breeze stirred the evergreens behind her and the ocean lapped at the ledges where we stood.

Just as it became dark, we visited a little old lighthouse renovated as the summer home of a Mrs. Pott, a tiny, wizened old lady, the very person to be found occupying such a charming, cramped, and narrow a dwelling. She looked and acted like a character out of some fairy tale; and she was evidently obsessed with her grandson Henry about whom she talked incessantly, insisting that Morgan be sure to come visit him when he was up from New York.

"He'll be there for sure come August, Morgan dear. You must come over. Henry's the handsome one, remember? So good looking. . .and he really liked you. Don't forget now. . ."

Every time we tried to talk with Mrs. Pott about the novelty of living in a lighthouse and living by the ocean on an island, she'd make a few perfunctory and cliché remarks and always return as soon as possible to the subject of her beloved grandson.

"Henry's going to be an engineer. He's studying hard and he'll do well. He'll be here in August. . .just you see. And you'll have to come over, Morgan dear. Remember how Henry liked you when you were just a tyke? He'd adore seeing you now, so grown up. . ."

Morgan promised Mrs. Pott that she would run right over to the lighthouse the very moment she received word about handsome Henry's arrival. On the way back to Eastward, however, she confided to us, "Henry's queer and ugly as sin! He has this high scratchy voice, and when Mrs. Pott dies, along with her mind, Henry'll probably inherit the lighthouse, and we'll have to put up a fence!"

Back at the Morgans', we met with our bespectacled, heavy-set, and schoolmarmish baby sitter, Mrs. Cash, and her giant St. Bernard named Randy. Mrs. Cash was seated on a cushioned deacon's bench across from a handsome granite fireplace which provided the central focal point for the rest of the downstairs which was really one large open room, in one corner of which was situated Mr. Morgan's easel and artist's materials. Paintings, wood carvings, and other fascinating art objects were all over the place. It was a very cozy and warm atmosphere.

"I'm having sardines and beer. Won't you join me?" Mrs. Cash asked with a welcoming smile.

"I don't want any," Morgan said, "but if any of the rest of you do, go ahead."

Right after we brought in our overnight stuff, took off our jackets, and arranged ourselves around the fireplace, the rest of us did join Mrs. Cash.

The lady was a well-known writer of books about Maine, a couple of which had been national best-sellers; and I was thrilled to be in her presence, waiting anxiously upon her every utterance.

"Burrrrp!" she erupted. "Excuse me, I just adore these hot-peppered sardines. They are hard to get around here even though the local factory prepares them. They send them to Mexico. They are so delicious that someone better take this case away from me before I devour them all."

"I read one of your books one time," said Amanda.

"Poor dear. . .did you recover?" asked Mrs. Cash, with a laugh. "Seriously, which one?"

"*They Traversed Through The Timbers*, I think it was called. It was all about your experiences with your husband, the game warden, up in the Maine woods some place. I thought it was pretty funny, and educational, too."

"Yes, I dare say. I guess it was pretty funny. Well, I'm glad you enjoyed it. That makes the effort worth it," Mrs. Cash said.

"Yeah. I made a book report out of it."

"I wish more students would do the same. Then, maybe, I could pay my bills."

Amanda's talk broke the ice and we all began to question the famous authoress about her writing, but she said she really didn't want to talk about it.

"It's mainly because in the summer especially, I get these awful people all the time from New Rochelle or wherever who seek me out to tell me how they simply love all my books. When I hear them knocking, I usually take refuge under the kitchen table or tell them that Mrs. Cash isn't around."

Later in the evening, while gathered about the fireplace telling jokes and stories, we suddenly heard the loud roar of an engine coming down the island's dirt road from the causeway towards the cottage. The noise finally subsided right outside the front door.

"Sounds like a Whirlybird jes' landed," Amanda said.

"That's only Carlton," said Mrs. Cash. "He's got a new motorcycle."

"Carlton's Mrs. Cash's son," Morgan said.

Carlton was big, too. He stood over six feet in the doorway and looked to weigh well over two hundred pounds with a mop of unruly black hair. He had on a black leather jacket and heavy boots.

"Just in time for the party, I see!" he boomed.

Morgan jumped up from the hearth rug to greet him and introduce everybody.

"Carlton, this is Andy."

"My competition, huh?" Nice to meet ya, An-day." He shook my hand.

"This is Amanda."

"How-day, Carlton!" Amanda boomed back in her inimitable way.

"How-day, yaself, there, hon-ay!"

"And this is Allison and Lillie."

"Well, now, Morgan, I used to think you were the prettiest gal around these parts, especially in the summer, but now I don't know about that. . ." He grinned at Allison and Lillie. "You're both great-looking gals."

"Hey, what about me, Carlton?" asked Amanda.

"I'd say you're a very spunky little gal, Amander," he said.

"Is spunky as good as pretty?" Amanda asked.

"In your case, I'd say most definitely," he said.

"Look, Carlton, can I get you a beer?" asked Morgan.

"Hon-ay, you can git me a whole case if you're a mind to, 'cause I'm gonna have some fun with you kids here tonight."

"Well, will you consider starting with one?" Morgan asked.

"Most definitely, de-ah."

"You don't have to wait upon Carlton," Mrs. Cash said. "He knows where the beer is, even if he doesn't know anything else."

"Now, would ya look at Ma over there with her dog," said Carlton, "putting away some of them hot-tasting Mexican fish and some beer. Written any good yarns for the ladies today, de-ah?"

"No, but I've been making plenty of good observations," Mrs. Cash said.

Needless to say, Carlton ruined the rest of the evening, for the ladies present anyway. I kind of enjoyed his earthy humor; but Morgan became very short with him and finally forced him to leave after a few beers. He roared away like he came into the night on his cycle, and we all went to bed. The girls and Mrs. Cash were to sleep upstairs sharing three bedrooms, while I bedded down on a cot in the corner of the downstairs living room. In the morning we were all awakened by Mrs. Cash who served us a delicious eggs-bacon-and-toast breakfast cooked by the authoress herself.

"Have a good day," she said, as we started to leave for work, "and give my fond regards to Miss Meyer. Tell her I don't know how she puts up with such a crew!"

31

The regular luncheon and dinner guests to the Manor included several outstanding figures of human and superhuman interest.

For instance, there was a tall, handsome, and white-haired lady named Belle Kane who lived on the Neck in one of the less imposing shingle-style cottages and who came for lunch every Wednesday on her cook's day off. Where she went for dinner on Wednesday nights we never found out. Anyway, Belle's regal bearing and stature stamped her as a qualified member of America's East Coast Aristocracy, or so she acted. Despite her crusty appearance and her curt, crisp way of talking, Mrs. Kane could be quite affable.

"What's for luncheon, Jean?" she'd ask Miss Meyer upon entering the hotel. "Creamed chicken and fresh peas on patty shells, I hope?"

Belle invariably asked the same question every Wednesday because this meal was her favorite, and even if we weren't serving creamed chicken that day, we'd prepare some especially for her. "It's light and yet filling," Belle would say, "just the right thing for midday."

After luncheon, Belle would expand her visit to the kitchen where she would gossip for an hour or so with Miss Meyer before strutting in military fashion back to her house across the Neck.

"From the way she parades around, you'd think she had a good-sized broom stuck up her ass," Bert Fickett once said.

Every other week, we'd receive the Pettengills for dinner. They drove an old 1952 black DeSoto with newspapers covering the windows on the passenger's side. These papers, we learned, protected the delicate face of Mrs. Pettengill who was rumored to have undergone at least five face lifts.

The result was ghostly. Her face was like a painted porcelain doll's with very smooth, almost shiny white skin offset by bright red lips and heavily-mascara'ed eyes. Her hair was dyed bright orange and at a distance across the dining room at candlelight at night she looked rather young and pretty; but close-up, she resembled a clownish hag, her wrinkled neck and hands revealing her real age.

"Her face resembles raw chicken breast once the skin has been removed," Mrs. Richmond once commented.

Mrs. Pettengill's husband, George, who drove the DeSoto, looked more his age. He had snow white hair and was bent and stooped. It was fun for us to watch out the kitchen windows whenever their car pulled up to see Mr. Pettengill scurry as fast as his septuagenarian legs would carry him to hustle the Missus under hooded veil from her side of the car to the protective confines of the lobby without a single ray of dreaded sunshine striking her creamy skin.

She spoke in a teeny little voice, her red Cupid's bow lips—or were they bee-stung lips?—barely moving. "Dear," she would address one of the waitresses, "Might you have a little more heavy cream for my berries? All I need is a smidgen."

Nearly every summer weekend the dining room would be graced and rocked by the affable presence of our most frequent, and one of the loudest and richest of the native feudal lords, Mr. Erastus Bull, president and boss of Bull's Blueberry Cannery. A graduate of Harvard, he dressed like a cowboy and was usually accompanied on either arm by at least two, and sometimes several, fat old Maine gals all a-twitter in their flimsy floral prints and white pumps. Their hair would be blue, their arms and ears a-jangle with expensive but gaudy baubles, their eyes looking at the world through double lenses. Mr. Bull would be pinching, kissing, and hugging the ladies, keeping them all chuckling and happy. His wife had died several years before I knew him.

"Wha'd you like for your little shore dinner, honeybun?" he'd ask one and then to another, "Don't you whisper now, Carrie. You speak right up and tell the Blueberry King. We'll have anything that's on or off the menu!"

Another such guest was Mr. Jesse Weinstein, a New Yorker who was trying to get the U.S. Navy, which was planning on building more housing in Summer Harbor for its married personnel and their families, to buy up all of his land holdings adjoining the National Park. Right near the entrance, off the main drag, he had even built a sample modern house which within a year's time became warped and rotten and finally collapsed, but not before his whole deal with the government fell through.

Before this economic catastrophe, however, Mr. Weinstein used to dine in great vulgar style at the Manor.

One night he arrived in his baby blue Cadillac with his beautiful daughter on his arm. After welcoming them and ushering them into the living room to await their meal, Mrs. Richmond announced to the kitchen staff, "The eyes of Israel are upon us!"

Because none of the hotel guests would speak with Mr. Weinstein, he talked to me while I was trying to get a fire started in the fireplace.

"Ya know how many bathrooms I got in my place in Westchester?" he asked.

"No. How many?"

"Twenty-nine. Yeah, twenty-nine bathrooms. Ain't that sump'n, huh?"

"Yeah. That's a lot of bathrooms."

"Well, it's a regular estate—bigger than this place."

"We have only ten bathrooms here."

"Yeah, yeah, this is so. This place ain't that hot, except it's old and got a great view; but this place ain't that hot."

"Yeah, and it will be less so if I don't get this fire going."

One Friday night, which was always lobster night, Mr. Weinstein ordered a lobster bigger than those we usually served which were one-and-a-half or two pounders.

"Gimme a five pounder!" he said.

"That's against the law," the waitress tried to explain, realizing the Maine law about illegal lobster size. "You can't have one larger than three pounds."

"Then gimme that, just as long as it's the biggest."

We had to place a special rush order with Hick Young, the local lobsterman, for the oversize crustacean, which did not arrive until half an hour later; and since it took another twenty minutes to boil it, Mr. Weinstein and his beautiful daughter had their dinner served an hour late, by which time, the dining room had nearly emptied. Mr. Weinstein didn't even eat the lobster after it was served him.

We kids ate it instead, which was typical after cleaning up the dining room. We'd eat some of the good stuff the guests left.

Once in a while, we received surprise guests like the young yacht club set, who one foggy night had to tie up their craft while cruising the coast at the yacht club until the soup lifted. It was after dinner, and after all the other restaurants in the area had closed, when they called to see if we could feed them anything. Miss Meyer, forever cognizant of unpaid bills and always willing to fill up her dining room at most hours, agreed to have me go down and pick them up at the club in Mrs. Richmond's car.

They were three young men and two ladies, healthy-looking in their boating togs, and no doubt well-heeled, and certainly out for fun. They had secured some liquor from their yacht or the club, and were in a jolly adventuresome mood. Two of the guys and one girl piled in back while the other guy and girl sat up from with me.

The highlight of their visit was the impromptu after-dinner dance they threw in the living room in the company of Julie Lawson, who was the only hotel guest still downstairs, quietly curled up in a big chair near the fireplace, her usual position at nightfall.

"You're all so young, athletic, and beautiful!" she told them; and one of the young swains responded by swinging Julie around the room to some music by Lester Lanin. Mrs. Lawson was a good dancer which surprised and thrilled the girls and me who peeked at the proceedings through the screen which cordoned off the entrance between the living and dining rooms when the dining room was closed.

"Wowzie wow!" said Amanda. "Look at old Twinkle Toes go! She can cha cha cha as well as tippy toe!"

Probably our most locally prominent luncheon guest who visited the Manor only once, as far as I know, and that time without paying, was long-time summer resident Mrs. Agatha Bradley, multi-millionairess and philanthropist, whose reputation, like that of any exceedingly wealthy person, preceded and overwhelmed her.

Mrs. Bradley was the heiress to a Baltimore fortune founded on transportation. The Bradleys were fairly famous American millionaires who had given a building or two to Harvard, owned a professional basketball team, and had established a well-known and well-endowed foundation for the arts and sciences. For at least three generations, they had summered on Granite Neck in the grand style, occupying several estates complete with chauffeur-driven Rolls Royces and Bentleys, at least one huge yacht, and large, fancy flower and vegetable gardens. They employed a number of local people year-round.

Mrs. Bradley's parents, who had sailed to Paris to purchase her wedding trousseau, had gone down on the *Titanic* in 1912, along with all the new clothes. After her marriage to Mr. Bradley, which lasted long enough for her to give birth to two children, she had remodeled the main house on the Neck, filling it with all manner of rich booty from the worlds of fine art and craftsmanship. It was said to have been the grandest show place on the Neck at the time, and rivaled and even surpassed most of the cottages across the bay on Mount Desert Island. But right after Mr. Bradley left her, an agreement which the local gossips claimed had cost her three million dollars, she had the house razed to the ground; and took up her summer residence at one of the other less-imposing mansions down the street from the Manor.

By 1960, the summer she came to tea, Mrs. Bradley was having another cottage built upon the site of the razed one. Rumor had it that she kept changing her mind, and the carpenters had to keep tearing down what they had just constructed. One of the women who worked for Mrs. Bradley told me that the sideboards, sinks, and kitchen appliances were all rubberized so that there would be a minimum of noise emanating from those quarters when Mrs. Bradley was trying to nap. The lady must have been very particular and precise when it came to the time for meals and the details for her dining. I was told that on her own table, there were outlines drawn for all the dishes and silverware so that a novice waitress would know exactly where to place everything.

That day she came to the Manor, we didn't take time to draw such outlines, but Miss Meyer certainly did caution us to take careful pains to see that the multi-millionairess enjoyed her little meal with us.

As her chauffeur drove the Rolls under the *porte-cochère*, the girls and I leaned out of the kitchen windows to get a good look at the fabled rich lady. It was like a Royal Visit, and we were very excited.

"Errr. . .be extra nice and efficient," Miss Meyer said. "Give her anything she wants. She might enjoy it enough to come back, or at least send us business."

But what a disappointment Mrs. Bradley was. She looked like a dried-up little bird of a woman, dressed very conservatively. She simply joined her cousin, a guest at the hotel who had invited her, evidently talked little, never smiled, picked at her lunch, and left as quickly as she had arrived.

"She sure ain't my idea of no millionaire!" said Amanda.

"Maybe she's all worn out from spending her money," I said. "Lived too hard and played too hard."

"Errr. . .did she enjoy her meal?" asked Miss Meyer.

"She had two rounds of tea," said Lil, "if that's any indication."

32

In my heart of hearts, I longed to go to college at one of Maine's most prestigious colleges: Bowdoin, Bates, or Colby; but I didn't even try applying. No one steered me in that direction, even though two of my adult mentors, my high school history teacher and my dentist, had both gone to Bowdoin. Guess I didn't seem like the Bowdoin type to them. There was no guidance department at Mollusk Memorial in 1960 and my parents had told me they couldn't give me a cent. So, my choice came down to Washington State Teachers College in Machias or the University of Maine at Orono. Luckily, I got into Maine.

I received a letter from my roommate-to-be, Tom Haskell from a Portland suburb, and a handsome picture of himself. The girls were delighted.

"Lemme take a looksee at that hunk o' man, An-day!" Amanda said. "Wow! How's about if I enroll in your place? They might discover the error by morning, but what a night I'd have—in a boys' dorm with the likes of that Tom!"

"He certainly is attractive from his school picture," said Allison.

"And in his letter, it says he's an athlete of major proportions," added Lil. "I just wonder how major?"

"And what proportions?" asked Morgan.

"Why don'tcha invite him down here so's you two can git acquainted before you have to live together?" asked Amanda.

"He says he has a summer job, too," I said.

"Well, maybe he needs a vacation!" Amanda said. "Poor boy'll be all tired out before he has to start his studies."

"If he comes down here, and meets you conniving females, he would really get worn out," I said.

"If he looks half as cute as his senior photo, ya could bet on it!" Amanda said.

Like everything else we did, the girls and I made a big production out of taking a picture of me to send back to Tom.

"We've got to make you look like a potential Big Man on Campus, An-day, so let's pose ya with all of us gals huggin' and kissin' ya as if you were a war hero!" Amanda said.

After work, one night, before the season was officially over and Morgan had gone home to New Jersey, Amanda back to the North Country, Allison onto school at Katherine Gibbs fancy secretarial school in Boston, Lil back for her senior year at Mollusk Memorial, Miss Meyer and the girls threw me a little party in the servants' back dining room. Hattie Pinkham was invited over from next door, and Berter Fickett even stopped by. She kept slapping me on the back, exclaiming, "College boy!"

To join in the festivities, Mrs. Richmond sent me the first of many letters she wrote to me over the years. It read:

> Dearest Andy,
>
> Jean informed me via the telephone of the party given in your honor the other night. I wish to add my very best wishes to theirs.
>
> You know, college can be such an invigorating and inspiring challenge for a young, developing person such as yourself. How I wish I could have gone as a girl! But it wasn't in the cards, or the crystal ball either; and because I didn't get to go, I value a college education more than most graduates do.
>
> Be selfish, Andy! Drink it all in! For the next four years, take advantage of all the opportunities of such a wonderful place. Don't let anything slip by you. Use the

University of Maine to your best advantage! Meet and talk with and get to know all types of people. See how you look standing beside them! And don't be afraid. Get confidence in yourself! Pursue whatever looks worth pursuing or interesting. Sit up all night talking. Don't be afraid of taking risks. Use your senses—try things—experiment! Don't study all the time and don't shy away from the strange or different. Try yourself, begin to find out who you are and what you can do, how much you can take and give, what you want out of life. Oh, and READ, READ, READ! Street knowledge, which is most important, is doubly enriched by book larnin'!

As charming a young man as you are, you must lose your innocence—sad but necessary. Innocence may be cute in a baby, but in a man, it's dangerous and stupid as hell.

I envy you—oh, you don't know how much!—at this exciting time in your young life. My thoughts go with you. Do keep in touch. Collect some good stories to share. My lecture—*fini*! For now. . .

See you next summer!
Fondly,
Madella Richmond

The guests even got into the act, asking me what I was going to major in, giving me suggestions about what subjects to pursue, and reminiscing about their own past college experience.

"I was in philosophy," said Julie Lawson, "and how we phil. majors used to amuse ourselves with Doctor Pedagogue's lovely lectures. . .he'd wander and we'd wander with him. . .I do hope you read some philosophy, Andy. . .it's the basis of everything, you know. . ."

"I want to, Mrs. Lawson," I said.

"Pssst, An-day," Amanda said, "If you start wandering the way Twinkle Toes does, you'll get lost!"

"Errr. . .I'm alarmed that you'll get so learned that you will have outgrown working at the Manor," said Miss Meyer. "I'm afraid you won't come back next summer."

"Oh, I'll be back, Miss Meyer," I said. "This is home now."

"Yeah, An-day," said Amanda, "but YOU CAN'T GO HOME

AGAIN! Remember what your hero Wolfe said?"

"But he meant home in the psychological sense more than the physical sense, Amanda," I said.

"Huh?" Amanda asked. "You're getting to sound more and more like Morgan!"

"Is that so bad?" asked Morgan.

"Not if you're hankerin' to go to college and become one of them there intellectuals like you, Morgan!" said Amanda.

"College changes one. . ." Mrs. Lawson said.

"How?" I asked.

"Imperceptibly. . .slowly. . .but definitely, deeply, and irrevocably. . ."

"Huh again?" asked Amanda.

"You begin to perceive. . ." said Mrs. Lawson.

"Oh yeah! Now, I get it!" exclaimed Amanda. "Thanks for the explanation, Mrs. Lawson. I think it's really worth a few thousand bucks to learn how to perceive!"

"It is," said Mrs. Lawson. "You, too, should go to college, Amanda. Then, you can begin. . ."

"Right! Right! *Begin the Beguine*!" said Amanda.

"Errr. . .good luck, Andy," said Miss Meyer. "Study hard!"

Just before leaving the Manor for the University of Maine, I was paid a visit by Essie Torrey, whose surname was now Bishop. I knew Miss Meyer had ordered a lobster salad that day for the evening meal; but that afternoon before I had time in which to drive up to the village to get it, it arrived via Essie. I looked up from my dishpan, and there she was a-knocking at the kitchen door.

"Yoo-hoo! The lobster salad gal is here!"

Essie the mermaid surfaced once again; and I couldn't believe she'd click into the Manor in her white bikini with only a flimsy towel thrown over her shoulders. To both Miss Meyer, who was seated at the folding table puffing on her cigarette, and to me, Essie explained, "Do forgive my appearance, but I was headed out the door to go for a swim, when Grammie Bishop asked me to drop off this salad, so here it is!"

Then Essie turned to me: "How are ya doin', An-day?"

"Oh, I'm great, Ess-ay. Have you ever officially met my boss, Miss Meyer?"

"Well, yes, we did meet at the beginning of this summer when

I came in to see you, An-day. Put 'er there, Miss Meyer!"

As Essie bent over to shake Miss Meyer's hand, the towel slid off her shoulders to the floor.

"Oh, shit!" said Essie, with a laugh. "Will ya look at me!"

And who could help not looking. Essie's incredible body, even though she was two or three months pregnant, was a sight to behold. I'll never forget the look on Miss Meyer's face as Essie stuck out her fabulous bosom in greeting to her. While Essie had placed the salad on the folding table, she picked it up again, and came toward me, asking, "I assume, An-day, that you know where to put this?" I looked down upon her nearly exposed breasts, which seemed to be part of the lobster salad. I pictured her breasts smeared with the lettuce, the bits of succulent meat, the deviled eggs, tomato slices, olives, and tangy dressing and with my tongue licking them clean.

"Here, I'll take it out to the back refrigerator," I said, placing my hands under the platter; and for a brief moment, there we both were with our hands holding the platter together.

"Easy now, don't drop it, you foolish thing," she said. "I worked all morning making the best salad I could, following Grammie Bishop's famous recipe to a T. I learned how to marinate the meat with the Russian dressing and how much mayonnaise to add and what spices to mix in."

"It looks great, Ess-ay," I said.

In front of Miss Meyer, Essie invited me to go swimming with her; but in actuality, we snuck upstairs to my room. Lillie and Amanda had gone off with Morgan; but I still closed my door in case they came back early.

Essie wasted no time. She had my pants off as fast as when we were down in the woods behind the Taunton Ferry School.

"I don't know whose cock is bigger—yours or Vaughn's? Of course, he's uncut, and you're cut, so that makes a difference."

"What do you mean?"

"Oh, Cow Shit! You brilliant college prep boy, you! You're *circumcised* while Vaughn isn't. He was born at home and still has his *foreskin*."

As unbelievable as this may seem, I didn't know what she meant. I knew, because we had been in phys. ed. classes and basketball together, that Vaughn's and Victor's penises looked different from mine, but I had never discussed this difference with anyone up until then.

"You know so much about books," said Essie, "but you don't know about the important stuff in life."

I had expected Essie to be rough and wild with me in lovemaking, but she was really very nice, warm, patient, and helpful.

"Go slow and easy. Take your time, even though we haven't got much," she said. "Remember, you're not dribbling a basketball down the court and trying to make a basket before the buzzer goes off!"

Just like the rest of her body, her hands were incredible. She helped me to adjust by body to hers and helped guide me into her, when she felt she was ready, all the time cooing in my ears, "Easy, go easy now, easy. . ."

She made this little gasp when I entered her, almost a wince, and I worried that I was hurting her.

"Are you O.K.?" I asked.

"Yes, go ahead."

And so we did the dirty deed in my summer bed; and upon completion and withdrawal, I asked her if she had an orgasm.

"No," she said, "but you did, didn't ya?"

"Yep!"

"Did you enjoy yourself?"

"Yes, very much. But I'm sorry I wasn't good enough for you to get something out of it."

"You talk too much, Cow Shit! You shouldn't talk when you're fucking. It's kinda hard to carry on a decent conversation, ya know."

"I'll try and quiet down and concentrate the next time," I said.

"Yeah, " she said, patting my hair, "well, now ya know."

Summer 1961

33

My freshman year in college began traumatically but ended triumphantly. While my teachers had done a decent job in preparing me academically, I was not prepared for college socially, psychologically, or emotionally. My roommate Tom Haskell had gone to prep school, as had a number of other boys on my floor, and he and his pals talked a different language than I. Tom told me right at the outset that whenever his friends came into our room, I'd have to leave; and most of the time, I did. I didn't know a thing about fraternities, which, in 1960, controlled the social life of the University of Maine. I wasn't rushed for a single fraternity, but Tom, being a talented jock, was rushed by several of the "best" ones. I knew I'd have to spend my four years living in a dorm and never going to a frat party. All boys who could breathe were inducted into the Reserve Officers Training Corps, so four times a week I was in the U.S. Army preparing for second lieutenanthood. I tried hard, but I wasn't much of a soldier. Academically, I almost flunked geology. I got my first "D" in any course in my life the first semester. I was afraid I'd lose my scholarships and have to leave; but I studied hard second semester, and got on the Dean's List. By then, too, I had made a few friends, and learned how to survive in Orono. I had gone in one year from being President of my high school class and co-editor of the yearbook in a small rural school of 120 to a college class of 1,200 where I was a nobody both academically and socially; and felt, and no doubt acted, like a total freak.

However, I returned to Frenchman's Bay Manor for the summer of 1961 in hopeful and even ebullient spirits. For one thing, Mrs. Richmond was to be in charge for the whole summer, with Miss Meyer remaining in New York City at her other job as executive secretary to one of the big wigs who ran the Waldorf-Astoria Hotel.

Early in June, Cousin Lillie, who had returned for her second summer, and I were summoned to help out Mrs. Richmond, who had just arrived with her grand-nephew Ronald, and start cleaning up and getting the hotel ready for the new season; and right off, there was a scene with Ronald, who was a sensitive twelve-year-old boy who wanted to take a bath, but not under the circumstances his great aunt had arranged for him.

There was no heat nor hot water in the upstairs bathrooms, so our portly bosslady suggested that Ronald take his bath in an old metal tub in the middle of the kitchen floor. I was instructed to heat up the water for him on the big gas stove. While I proceeded to do so, Ronald started timidly undressing. Mrs. Richmond returned to her newspaper, and Lil continued washing the dining room glassware in the pantry. Ronald was half-undressed when he started pulling down the kitchen window shades.

As the shadow crept across her *New York Times Book Review*, Mrs. Richmond erupted. "Ronald! What in hell do you think you're doing? Now, who beside the little birdies do you expect is going to be peeking in at you? Honey, no one gives a tinker's damn what a twelve-year old boy's body looks like!"

Ronald wasn't so sure and looked as if he were going to start crying. Cousin Lil, always very discreet at such moments, said that she would be leaving the glassware and working on the upstairs bedrooms while Ronald was taking his bath.

"Oh, God, all right!" said Mrs. Richmond. "We'll all busy ourselves elsewhere whilst the lad is scrubbing behind his ears!" She extricated herself from her armchair and waddled down the hall to her office while I poured the steaming hot water from the kettles and pans on the stove into the tub, and a greatly relieved Ronald, with all the females gone, quickly finished undressing and stepped into his bath.

At lunch that day, served in the kitchen on top of the old zinc-topped table and midst all the smells of soaps and cleaning chemicals, Mrs. Richmond had us all a-twitter over her storytelling.

"Say, have I recounted to you galley slaves the sad-but-true tale of the rich Armenian lady from Greenwich?"

"No, you haven't," I said.

"Well, crew, lend me your ears, and listen to this. I was at my position as Grand Executrix of Blue Cross at the Greenwich Hospital when I learned of this incident. It seems that this beautifully coiffured, tailored, and handsome woman came in to see a doctor about her husband's recent ailment. She sat across from his desk, calmly composed, looking for all the world like a million dollars. The doctor, who was obviously very impressed with her, proceeded to inform the lady of the nature of her husband's distress in all manner of technical medical terminology. After he had concluded his spiel, he asked the lady if there were any more questions, to which she replied, "Quit kiddin', Doc!"

"Obviously, the poor thing was some war bride who had picked up what English she knew from American sailors or the movies. She hadn't the faintest idea what the doctor was telling her. Uh. . .Lil, honey, pass me that peanut butter, would ya? I craves to dab a leetle bit on ma braid."

When we had finished eating, Mrs. Richmond said, "Clear the decks! You two plus Ronald must now return to cleansing the Augean Stables whilst I hie meeself to the cloisters to see if I can balance the books. Ya know, it costs us three thousand smackeroos—which we pay the State of Maine—before I can even turn the key in the door."

Her favorite story of that summer, which she told and re-told to every guest who would listen, was the famous one about the man from Texas who had become an oil millionaire but who was uneducated in the ways of society and had to put on a wedding for his beloved daughter. He wanted it just right, so he asked one of his friends, "What am I to do?" The friend suggested he look in a copy of the Sunday *New York Times* where they often describe a whole wedding ceremony and then copy one for his daughter. The man does so, and the wedding and the reception are a huge success. At the end of the affair, his friend comes up to him to tell him how marvelous the whole event was, but also to ask a question. "There's only one thing that bothered me," he said. "What was that little man up to running around among all the guests pinching all the ladies' breasts?" "Oh," said the millionaire, "in *The New York Times*, it said that 'a titter ran through the crowd'!"

No matter how many times Mrs. Richmond told this, she would laugh her head off, she loved it so. One night after dinner, while I was at my dishpan at the end of the kitchen, she was in her usual armchair at the other end entertaining Reggie Hillock, Dolly's husband, and a great pal of Madella's. She was telling him the joke, but they were both so tight and laughing so hard that neither of them could pour the whiskey into their glasses without slopping it all over the table and floor. At one point, I rushed over to help. "You're pouring it on the floor, Mrs. Richmond!" I said. "Well, then, for God's sake! Get down there on your hands and knees and lap it up! That scotch cost me a bundle!"

Unlike Miss Meyer who very infrequently ventured into the living room after dinner where some of the guests would congregate for talks and drinks around the fireplace, Mrs. Richmond was in there frequently, holding forth, and usually the center of attraction. When the conversation was too dull for her, she'd tell us, "We've got to get busy and round up some new guests. These people here now are boring beyond redemption! All they know is what they read in *Time* magazine! They must have spent the greater part of their lives inhabiting dank caves! Hand me ma address book!"

And she'd actually call up or write her many friends around the country, insisting they spend part of their summer vacations Downeast; and in a sizable number of cases, they'd show up. She'd give some of them bargain rates. One man I recall was Tex Blowhard, a gentleman from the Lone Star State, who arrived, thanks to his company's generous expense account, a fact he freely admitted, via a shiny new black Chrysler Imperial, with all the extras. Accompanying Tex was his lovely, raven-haired, young child-bride; and a fistful of dollars. Tex and Mrs. Richmond had evidently known each other over the years, and had shared many good times in Manhattan together with mutual friends.

"Member, 'Della," he asked her, "that time you and me and the Clemsons were on our way from dinner in some fancy watering hole, to a Broadway thee-a-ter and you stepped off the curb in your flowing gown right into a pile of horse shit?"

"Omigod, yes, Tex! We certainly did have us a guffaw over that. What did you say to me?"

"I told ya that you might think of yourself as some sophisticated New Yorker, but that you kept running into your heritage!"

They laughed, and Tex would turn around and wink at us, the kitchen help. He certainly was a stereotyped Texan in his fancy boots, Stetson hat, and string tie. He shouted in preference to talking, slapped people on the back all the time, and laughed loudly and frequently. He also granted the help the most generous tips of the season.

"Here ya go, son," he said, handing me a ten dollar bill one afternoon. "That's from Goodyear, remember! I represent my company well!"

Tex, though, was completely different from most of Mrs. Richmond's friends who came to visit. Most of them were old ladies who had either been Christian Scientists like Mrs. Richmond and Miss Meyer or were early feminist leaders, now practicing some new religion or philosophy. They'd come and stay for weeks, some at Mrs. Richmond's expense, and they'd sit around for hours talking and arguing about this or that belief. They made tapes, both in English and German, to trade with each other. Morgan's grandmother, even though she was born Jewish in Atlanta, was a Christian Scientist, too.

One afternoon, Mrs. Richmond yelled across the kitchen to me, "Andy! We've got to go get Kitty! She's holed up in some seedy establishment over in Castine, for God's sake! Finish walloping those pans and then go bring the car around. We must rescue her!"

The seedy establishment was an old boarding house called The Catamaran Club that was situated on one of the pretty tree-lined streets leading down to Castine's harbor. I parked the car and we went in. "My God, they've even got oilcloth on the tables," Mrs. Richmond whispered to me in disgust as we walked through the lobby. I didn't see that the place was all that bad. It wasn't as fancy as the Manor, but pretty typical of a summer Maine boarding house of that time. It was rustically quaint, like some kind of sailor's lair right out of *Moby Dick*, the perfect hangout for a merchant marine town like Castine. I expected Queequeg to materialize at any moment. Instead, we met Kitty.

Kitty was over seventy years old, and what Mrs. Richmond saw in her was hard to deduce. She was pleasant enough, I suppose, but awfully vacant-looking.

"Andy, I'd like you to meet Kitty. She befriended me and helped me out when I was a simple farm girl lost in Manhattan; and now, I'd like to try and return the favor."

Mrs. Richmond later told me that she thought Kitty probably was suffering from some kind of dementia brought on by all the booze she had swilled when striving for women's rights.

Kitty was joined at the Manor by another old cronie named Birdie.

"Doggie must be next!" said Lil.

Birdie was much more interesting to me than Kitty, who spoke nary a word. Birdie was sharp-tongued, funny, and very opinionated. Even though in her late eighties, she still drove her own car and kept up on things. One of her sons was in the U.S. State Department and another was the publisher of a glossy landscape magazine. Birdie was always urging me to improve my mind through reading these intellectual journals like *Manas*, a subscription to which she sent me during my sophomore year in college. One day when I was rushing through the living room, I spotted Birdie perched on one of the couches reading *The Agony and The Ecstasy*, the novel about Michelangelo. I asked her how she liked it. "It's too heavy," she said. "I won't be able to finish it unless it comes out in paperback. My wrists can only bear so much weight."

Mrs. Richmond always attempted to bring some discipline to her manager's duties, and formulate some set routine for all of us to follow; but she simply loved talking and reading too much. There was never enough time in one day for her. Everything, thus, ended up half-done, hurried, and hastily thrown together. Miss Meyer ran a much tighter ship than Mrs. Richmond. They talked daily on the phone to each other, Miss Meyer no doubt very worried that the ship was sinking.

For instance, we'd just get started on dinner preparations, and she'd gather us kids around her for a lecture on some philosophic point which she wanted to make at the moment. She should have been a teacher.

"C'mon, ye little chillun!" she'd say. "Lemme tell ya all about Saint Francis of Assisi! Now, he was a grand character!"

We'd often end up sitting for hours entranced, listening to this huge woman, who loved life and learning, amuse and enthrall us with her tales and theories. When we could get a chance, we'd even ask her questions. One late afternoon, she was discussing her theory about how suicide would have to become more frequent and accepted in the future, when suddenly a billow of black smoke emanated from the oven of the kitchen's gas stove.

"My God, WHAT *WAS* COOKIN?" our boss roared, struggling to extricate her immense body from the armchair, finally clomping hurriedly as she could across the room to the stove where she took out the remains of the expensive roast beef, which she had just purchased that morning from a butcher in Bangor. The meat was now charred coal black.

"This has been done these many years!" she said. "But there's no sense in crying over a charred corpse. . .Andy, hurry dear, and see what edible viands we have stored in the freezer for just such an emergency! Girls, dinner may be a few minutes late this evening. Kindly post a notice and tell 'em it'll be worth waiting for!"

And it was, as always, for Mrs. Richmond loved preparing delicious and expensive meals.

"Remember, people go to Paris for the great food, not the Eiffel Tower!" she'd say. "You start baking bread and people smell it, they'll leave the Louvre like a pack of wild dogs and come a-running."

Another afternoon, we were all sitting around our portly employer, as usual, laughing and enjoying her company and yarns, when she got up to check the stove, forgetting that she had turned the gas on without lighting it, and having her lit cigarette in her hand. She just reached the stove, when. . .KA-BOOM! She was blown across the kitchen against the wall of pans and utensils which came crashing down on her and around her. She landed on the floor; and we kids sat there at first stunned and horrified over one of the funniest sights we had ever seen.

"CHRIST, I'VE BEEN BLOWN UP!" she hollered. "Am I dead? Come help me, kids!"

We rushed over to her and discovered that despite her hair being singed all around her face, which was covered with black soot, she was just stunned. After the shock had subsided, and then limping around for a few days, she had a good laugh over her explosion, and told the story over and over.

"Say, did I ever tell you about the time I got blown up in my own kitchen?" she'd begin. "It was a lovely afternoon. . ."

Another time, Mrs. Richmond told us about the opera. "You see, my dears, when I arrived in New York City, as rude a bumpkin to ever come down the pike, in the early twenties, there were over two hundred new shows on Broadway in a year. World War I was over and there was excitement in the air! It was such a lovely, promising time, and I was young and ready to join in. I was desirous to put Kansas way behind me and learn and get to know everything about New York, which I equated with life itself. And one night, I was taken to the opera at the Met; and, my darling dears, I was simply overwhelmed with it all. Such beauty! I just never expected to be so thrilled. I became a rabid opera fan overnight. I went all the time after that, and even got to know some of the singers.

"But later, when I journeyed to London for the first time, I found the opera at Covent Garden even better than New York's; and as I made my way across Europe, the story was repeated. The Paris Opera surpassed London's; and then, when I finally arrived in Rome, it was New York all over again. My God! The excitement—*the grandest show of all*! Rome's opera was the best, of course. I never did travel beyond Rome. Perhaps Vienna had something even finer, but I doubt it."

One day our inimitable boss discovered that one of the lawn chairs had been so poorly re-upholstered as to be dangerous; and she was outraged. A generous person, she detested being cheated by anyone. She ordered me to put the chair in the car; and off we drove to Ellsworth, where, bursting through the front door of the upholstery shop, she bellowed to the proprietor and any customers present, "WHAT KIND OF JOINT ARE YA RUNNIN' HERE?"

She'd frequently run out of money shopping and would either cajole the manager into accepting her I.O.U. or would snag a passing friend or client to foot the bill. For instance, once I was with her in the IGA Foodliner in Ellsworth, our cart was full to overflowing, and we were at the check-out counter when she discovered she had too many goods and not enough cash.

"Say, Andy, have ya got a ten spot on ya?"

"No, only a couple of dollars," I said.

"Well, we may need it. Seems like me eyeballs are bigger than me cash reserves. Say, is that Reggie Hillock passing down the aisle?"

It was, and she hailed him over the heads and to the surprise of all the other customers in the store. "Say, Reggie! How would you and Dolly like to come for dinner and drinks Sunday night for ten bucks?"

"Madella, that would indeed be a bargain," Mr. Hillock said, smiling back at her.

"There's a catch, Reggie. I need the ten now—in advance—so we can pay for all these foodstuffs."

They both laughed at her plight as Reggie dug into his pants pocket.

Mrs. Richmond told Morgan, Lil, and I to read, read, read, all the time. We were forever discussing books. One topic of conversation would lead to another and suddenly Mrs. Richmond was recommending yet another book that WE MUST READ.

"Here, Andy, read this new selection from the Literary Guild by Paul de Kruif and then we'll talk about him. I heard him speak once. He was connected to the same foundation, you know, as one of our more prominent guests."

"What, you kids never heard of Willa Cather? Your teachers have been remiss. This is outrageous and shameful. She's one of our most important writers. Drop your sponge mops and hie yourself into the library and search the shelves for *My Antonia* or *Death Comes for the Archbishop*. I know we have those two, and there's probably more."

"Say, Andy, how did you like Errol Flynn's *My Wicked, Wicked Ways*? Fun, wasn't it? Sort of a companion piece to Mae West's *Goodness Had Nothing to Do With It*. I enjoyed it except for the very last part where old Errol starts feeling sorry for himself. Up till then, it's a grand yarn."

And most important to my later life, she was the first to tell me about Flannery O'Connor. "Get yourself upstairs right now to the back hall bookcase—where my favorite books are near at hand—and look for a book called *A Good Man Is Hard to Find*. God, it's good. So much so that I have to keep replacing it. People either wear it out from passing it around or walk off with it in their bags."

Like so many essentially good-natured and jolly people, when Mrs. Richmond became serious, it was always a sudden shock. She turned to us one night when we were talking about Hitler, and spoke to us in grave, sinister tones. "Listen, there's a chilling book upstairs which all of you must read. It's called *The Devil's Chemists* and it's written by one of the American lawyers at Nuremberg and is concerned especially with this huge German company called I. G. Farben which was responsible for some very evil doings during Hitler's reign."

Born around 1900, Mrs. Richmond liked to say that she was "as old as the twentieth century and just as bustling."

34

I was busy polishing brass in the kitchen the last week in June, 1961 when Morgan Carlisle re-entered my life, accompanied this time by a tall, dark, handsome, and muscular young Greek-American named Orpheo Arion. He was a member of her high school graduating class in New Jersey and evidently her constant companion. She had promised him this trip to Maine for his graduation present. I envied him and wished him gone, because I felt very inferior in his self assured presence, but he was to stay with Morgan at Eastward for a couple of weeks before spending the rest of the summer working on some Pennsylvania farm.

For openers, he said, "I'm surprised you have phones here."

"Oh, yes, and electric lights, too!" I said.

Morgan laughed, thank God, and rushed about the kitchen, her usual energetic self, looking, if anything, more lovely than I had remembered her.

"Orpheo just can't get over the progress being made here along the primitive Maine coast," she said.

"What kind of name is Orpheo?" I asked.

"Greek," he said. "I am one hundred percent Greek and I have devoted my life to the ideals of ancient Greece, the Golden Age."

"He's even on the wrestling team," Morgan said.

"And a state champ," he said, "at the 181 pound weight." He flexed his muscles.

"Is that why you're going to work on a farm this summer—to get back to the simple life?" I asked.

"Life in Athens was hardly simple," he said.

"Did they have phones?" I asked.

"They didn't need them," he said.

"Now, boys," said Morgan, "I've got to run. Many errands to do. We just got here, but I did want to check with Mrs. Richmond to let her know that I have arrived and will be at her beck and call."

"She's out, but I will tell her," I said.

"Would you, Andy? That'll be O.K. I hope to start soon since I am broke and Smith is already costing plenty."

"Morgan! You got into Smith? You didn't tell me!"

"I thought I wrote you. Probably forgot. I was so delirious about the whole thing."

"That's great. Where will you be going, Orpheo? Mount Olympus?"

"Antioch."

"Where's that?"

"Yellow Springs, Ohio."

"What's it noted for?" I asked. "I've never heard of it."

"Having a Greek name. No, I'm not sure. It's really very experimental, very free. You work for three months and then go to classes for three months. The arrangement appeals to me."

"Orpheo," Morgan said, "we must be off. Andy, get all that brass polished before I get here. And do come over to Eastward if you get the chance. Ask the Great Dame for the car."

"I will. Nice to meet you. Probably see you again when Morgan starts work here."

And so we did. Morgan began work the first of July and Orpheo was there at the Manor nearly every day, having lunch and dinner with us, doing his laundry, exercising his wrestler's body about the grounds, going swimming and down to the rocks with us, lying upstairs in the attic on my bed, reading my books.

"Hey," he said, "you've got the whole *Studs Lonigan*. I missed part of it."

"Be my guest," I said. But I didn't expect Orpheo would then lie right down on my bed and stay there until he finished reading the part that he missed; but then, Orpheo was like that. He took things—and other people—for granted.

After his two-week stay and Orpheo had departed for his Pennsylvania muscle-building farm experience, Morgan confided in us the story of their first date. "We climbed up on top of the high school and ran around on the roof," she said. "At that moment, I knew he wasn't like other boys."

He certainly wasn't; in fact, it seemed to me as if Orpheo tried to be different on purpose from everyone else. For instance, there was the business with the recorder.

In trying to convert Morgan to his Greek ways, Orpheo had somehow convinced her that she should learn to play the recorder. Orpheo was a hippie before his time, a flower child of the early sixties. Anyway, at first we were all amused by Morgan's attempts to make music with her tin ear, but as she practiced so diligently, day after day, the novelty wore off considerably and her practicing became monotonous and annoying for those sitting around trying to relax on the back lawn and even down on the rocks. Finally, one of the guests, Julie Lawson, complained.

"What is all this peeping and tooting about the grounds while I'm at nap?" she asked Mrs. Richmond. "It must somehow be stifled."

It was. For the rest of the summer for a portion of every afternoon off, Morgan would hie herself with her recorder to the grocery storage room in the Manor's cellar, where, behind closed doors, she could practice as long as she wished and no one would hear her.

Missing my repartee and jokes with her, I tried most unsuccessfully to get her to stop playing altogether with a series of practical jokes. Since the light switch for the storage room was upstairs in the kitchen, I'd wait until Morgan was seated with her recorder in the room and then I'd quietly lock the door behind her, sneak up the cellar stairs and throw the switch, plunging my musician friend into total darkness. Such jokes didn't work, though, since Morgan was big on retaliation. That night, as I was putting the garbage under the back porch, so that the raccoons wouldn't get it, a hand suddenly appeared, slamming the lattice gate and locking it behind me. I turned around to see Morgan bent over in glee, laughing her head off at my trapped predicament.

I used to steal a look at the letters Orpheo would send Morgan from his farm and at the ones she would be writing him. I liked the way they corresponded with each other, calling each other "O" and "M." That seemed pretty sophisticated to unsophisticated me. I also liked the way they put things. They seemed so clever with their wording.

For instance, one time Morgan was writing to her Orpheo about a visit she, Lillie, and I had made the night before on the enclosed porch with Cecily, a well-to-do, well-traveled, and beautiful young guest our age from California who was touring the Maine Coast with her father and his glamorous mistress in a fancy Lincoln convertible.

Morgan wrote:

> Dear O.,
>
> Such mad adventures we share here! Why just last night, as I was dusting off the lamb chops that had fallen on the floor behind the stove in preparation for dinner, there came this invitation to join with partners Lillie and Andrew for an after-dinner tête-à-tête with 17-year old cosmopolitan/debutante Lady Cecily Cavanaugh from California who would be receiving us from her royal swing on the back porch. Needless to say, we-all could hardly wait for such a chance to chat with someone who had been everywhere, seen and done everything. We hurried through dinner, scrubbing the kitchen grease off our faces, trying to look as presentable as possible. And then, at the appointed hour, finally trooping in single file into the guest section, yours truly leading the way.
>
> We took S.S. Pierce mixed nuts as our offering. We proceeded to arrange ourselves about her gilded sandals while she instructed us in the ways of the wicked world. Oh, my, how she had tasted, seen, felt, heard, and smelled! And ALL, my dear, believe me, ALL IS ROT. ALL IS DECADENT, and, really, darlings, none of you happy innocents should even bother leaving your happy little kitchen state; for there's NOTHING OUT THERE worth pursuing. It's all so DREADFULLY ROTTEN! You may think the Louvre is wonderful, but it really isn't. It's the same as the British Museum, Palm Beach, Beverly Hills, and the Grand Canyon; EVERYTHING IS SO DRAB

AND ROTTEN. LIFE HAS NO MEANING! WE ARE BORN TO DIE!

In sum, Cecily Cavanaugh was a dreadfully spoiled and ROTTEN BOOR; and I felt dreadfully sorry for her in her jaded loneliness at the advanced age of 17. Too much or too little too soon or too late, I'm not quite sure.

Do write me soon of your haying and milking adventures.

Love,
"M"

After studying such letters I'd race upstairs to my room and practice writing the same way to my relatives and friends.

Dearest Mother,

I know I will see you soon since you will be delivering, right on time as usual, the Manor's linen and fresh spring water to us holed up here in the summer hostelry; but even so, I just had to script you a few notes, so oft are you in my mind, along with the usual mass of cobwebs.

You know they love how magnificently you wash, iron, and fold the napkins and table cloths here. I explain simply that it's your aristocratic upbringing that's mainly responsible; for until our fall from grace (Grace pushed us!), we were such a rich and proud old Maine family. You were simply used to linen done up in a nice way, weren't you, Mom?

And even though you and Pater can no longer afford to board me at an exclusive summer camp, it was certainly smart of you to let me work here at the Manor where I can at least learn secondhand the way of life that I should be preparing for.

I'll gladly suffer the scourge of dishwater hands for the ultimate realization of my beloved dream—to be able to assume, once again, my natural place in the ranks of Downeast nobility!

Thus, until we meet again (Tuesday?), I remain, your son, more than anyone else's. . .

Love,
"A"

When I did see my mother, after she had received the above, she inquired, "Are you all right?"

Orpheo finished his farming before the season was over at the hotel, so he rejoined us at the end of August; and, once again, Morgan spent most of her off-duty time in his company, away from Lillie and me. While Morgan was working, Orpheo would sleep late and hang around Eastward and Cold Harbor fishing village where he tried to make conversation with the fishermen and their families, people whom both he and Morgan revered as being closer-to-nature and thus wiser and more noble than regular folk. In the afternoons, he'd hitchhike over to Granite Neck where he'd wash his clothes in the Manor's laundry and eat supper with us in the back dining room. After a while, Mrs. Richmond put a stop to his washing, telling Morgan, "My dear, I can surely understand your enthusiasm for this young Greek god, but our waitress uniforms must come before his B.V.D.s."

For reparations, Orpheo planned us all dinner. Even our boss was invited but she declined to attend.

That suppertime we waited in feverish anticipation for Orpheo's meal. He arrived late with a grocery bag; and Morgan, Lil, and I gathered about the dining room table as our host emptied the contents of his bag. There was a bottle of imported Greek wine, a loaf of black bread, and a slab of cheese.

"Why, it's a true Greek meal!" I said.

"Dig in," Orpheo said, busily caving off bits of cheese and slicing the bread with one of the Manor's knives.

"I think I'm going to warm up a little soup, if you don't mind," said Lil, who wasn't very excited over her supper prospects.

"Soup! All one needs is bread, wine, and cheese for sustenance and good health!" said Orpheo.

"Well, Orpheo," Lil said, "at the risk of being unpoetic or anti-Greek, I'm afraid my stomach craves more than sustenance."

One night, Orpheo accompanied us on one of our midnight pool swims. He was a good swimmer, and because of this and because it was against his very nature, he couldn't paddle about the pool quietly as we had been doing. He made too many noisy splashes, and Lil and I became frightened that we would be caught and our tradition of clandestine dips ended. We left the pool earlier than usual that evening with Orpheo and Morgan following behind us.

Lil was dating a boy about two years younger than herself that summer; but he had a car and could take her places, certainly an important consideration in his favor. Most weekend nights, she'd be out with him; and when Orpheo was visiting, he and Morgan would be together, and I'd be alone. One night, when they were all out, and I didn't feel like reading or playing records, I became rather depressed and feeling sorry for myself, and decided to get drunk for the first time in my life.

I searched the shelves and closets of the kitchen and pantry and found some cooking sherry, some other kind of wine, and a half bottle of whiskey. In my foolish state, I decided to mix them all together. The mixture was a sickish one, but because I wanted so badly to be drunk, I drank quite a bit of it; but nothing happened. It was a great disappointment, for I expected to be transported to a more euphoric state where being left alone didn't matter; but I just felt stupid and sick to my stomach. I put the bottles back, rinsed out my glass, and went to bed.

Before Orpheo had returned to Maine, there had been one date with Morgan together with Lil and her boyfriend Morton. One night we had gone to the Bangor State Fair. We didn't get there until 9:30 p.m. or so, and many of the exhibits and rides were already closed down when we arrived.

We did go on this one ride called "The Bump," whereby all four of us were squeezed tightly together side-by-side in this cart which ran around in a circle at a fast clip until it came to this drop-off place, causing one's stomach to fall along with the cart. It was a simple but hilarious sensation and we were all laughing very hard until I realized that I had placed my eyeglasses in the shirt pocket side against which Morgan's body was pressing very tightly.

"Morgan!" I yelled in her ear, "I think my glasses are going to get crushed!"

"Well, I'm not about to get up!" she yelled back.

On the way back to the Manor that night, we sang along with the music on the radio. There was this one tune, popular at the time, which Morgan loved, called "Michael Rowed the Boat Ashore." When that came on, Morgan and Lil harmonized while Morton kept his eyes on the road and I hummed. Morgan and I were in the back seat, and around midnight or so, our usually sprightly and animated conversation wound down and I watched her nod off; and, suddenly, as we were rounding a sharp curve, she fell off the seat onto the floor.

"For God's sake, Andy! Why didn't you stop me from falling?" she asked.

"I don't know," I told her; and I didn't.

Morgan didn't care for the movies the way I did, but I did get her to go to one: *A Raisin in the Sun* with Sidney Poitier. There was a matinee at the Grand in Ellsworth one afternoon; and she, Lil, and I loved it. On the way back to the hotel, Morgan talked about her black classmate in New Jersey named David in relation to Poitier's portrayal of the frustrated young black guy in the movie. She and Orpheo had discussed David previously. The poor fellow was evidently one of the very few black students at their school, and it was weird to hear privileged whites talk about him like he was supposed to be a certain way to fit their stereotypes. We also talked about the American racial situation in general.

"Andy," Morgan said, "I know you adore my grandmother Morgan, but she's racist."

"Maybe she can't help it, having grown up down south?" I asked.

"There are just as many racists up north," said Morgan. "And Gram should know better. I'm trying to make her see the light."

I couldn't argue with her there at that point; the only blacks I had seen in real life were the Harlem Globetrotters when they played an exhibition game at Ellsworth High School once, the porters on the *Bar Harbor Express* train, and some of the summer servants on Taunton Point and Granite Neck. At the University of Maine, there was one black professor and a few black students, but mostly from Africa. I had never really had a real conversation with a black person.

35

The backstage cast of 1961 also included another waitress who worked with Lillie named Jenny Sue; and Mrs. Richmond's younger sister named Grace, taking the place of Allison Blakely, was to act as chambermaid. There couldn't have been an odder couple than Jenny Sue and Grace.

Mrs. Richmond's sister, for instance, was a nearly sixty-year-old grandmother, garrulous, and slow-moving; while Jenny Sue was fast enough on her feet, but dim-witted. While Grace was basically kind and motherly, Jenny Sue was bad-mouthed and stubborn. Both lacked a sense of humor about themselves, and together they added up to a cranky bother for all of us. Often we others, including Mrs. Richmond, ended up doing their work for them. With Grace, at her age in a hard job, it was understandable, for she quite naturally tired easily; but with Jenny Sue, it was inexcusable, and Jenny Sue loved to make excuses.

"It's Jack, my husband," she'd say. "I'm late this morning because of him. I was getting ready for work, getting my uniform on and everything, and wouldn't you know he'd start in hollering! I told him I had to be at work and couldn't wait on him, but you know what a temper he has. He yelled and cursed so that I was afraid we'd be evicted from that beautiful dump we live in. Anyway, he works awful long hours at the base sometimes (Jack was in the Navy), and when he comes home, he wants me to be with him. I hope you understand. That's why I'm late today."

Jack did have a temper. He was very jealous of her and kept a close watch of her comings and goings. One night when we had a large number of dinner guests and Jenny Sue was late in getting home, he showed up in the kitchen doorway in a mad fury.

"WHERE'S MA WIFE?" he yelled.

"Who are you?" I asked, since I had never met Jack in the flesh.

"I'm Jack. I wanna know where Jenny Sue is."

"Oh, she's in the dining room. We had a lot of guests this evening with two settings. We're just finishing up. Would you like a cup of coffee while you're waiting?"

"NO! I AIN'T WAITIN'! BY JESUS, I WANT MY WIFE HOME RIGHT NOW!"

"Well, it'll probably be a few minutes yet. . ."

Jack barged right by me and went into the waitresses' pantry, yelling, "JENNY SUE! JENNY SUE!"

"Hey, what's all the commotion out here?" asked Mrs. Richmond, suddenly emerging from her office.

"I WANT MA WIFE!" Jack said to her.

"You do? Well, now just who might your wife be?" asked the boss.

"Jenny Sue Craddock, that's who," Jack said.

"Well, my dear young man, if you'd be so kind as to wait out in the kitchen, I'll see that Jenny Sue joins you momentarily."

"Awright, but it'd better be soon," he growled.

After Jack and his wife had left the premises that night, Mrs. Richmond was a bit miffed about the incident.

"Well, we certainly can't have this type of thing occurring again. I feel sorry for Jenny Sue having to put up with that berserk sailor; but from now on, we will have to make do with less of Jenny Sue's services. They've been getting less and less anyhow."

For the rest of the summer, in fact, Jenny Sue was laid off except for whenever we had a big crowd. Morgan was either promoted or demoted from the kitchen helper job to waitressing with Lil; and whenever we did need Jenny Sue, I would have to take the car and drive up to the village where they rented an apartment in the rear of this old farmhouse.

One morning I was greeted by Happy Jack.

"What the hell do you want?" he asked, standing in the doorway in his underwear.

"Mrs. Richmond would like Jenny Sue to come down to work today since we have a lot of people coming tonight."

"Well, she might not be able to make it," he said.

"Why not?"

"She's got plenty of things to do around here."

"I see. Well, please let her know that Mrs. Richmond would like her to come down if she can."

"Yeah, I'll be sure to do that." As he was talking, I noticed Jenny Sue behind him in her slip giving me hand signals that seemed to suggest that she'd be down at work as soon as she could.

I don't think up to that time that I had ever met such an angry young man with the ornery disposition that Jack had. He seemed to hate the whole world. One afternoon, when Hattie Pinkham was visiting from next door with Mrs. Richmond, I asked her what she had heard about the Craddocks.

"Up town they call her 'Miss Personality' and him they call 'Personality Plus,'" Hattie said. "Cute couple, aren't they? He looks like he's about sixteen but acts about twelve."

Jenny Sue did show up that day when I had driven up to get her; and at lunch she talked, as usual, about her husband and sex, her two favorite topics.

"Everyone at Ellsworth High School thought I was pregnant when I left school to marry Jack, but I wasn't," she said. "I just couldn't stand it in that snob joint any more. I had learned all I was going to learn, and I'm glad I made my decision to quit. But, even now, after a whole year, whenever I go to Ellsworth and see all my old friends, if you could call them friends, they all wanna know if I lost my baby or not! Honest to God! And even when I tell 'em there was no baby to lose, they don't believe it!"

Jenny Sue turned to me. "You know, An-day, the same type of thing was true about your friend Ess-ay."

"What do you mean?" I asked, not realizing that Jenny Sue knew Essie.

"All the rumors they always had about her before she married Vaughn Bishop. They had her pregnant months before she really was."

I wondered how much Jenny Sue knew about my relationship with Essie, if Essie had talked to others about me. Were there rumors about me, too? I made a mental note to try and talk to Jenny Sue alone sometime.

As for Grace, she was always muddled over something and mumbling about it. I can see her now bent over the zinc-topped table with her white hair, white uniform, and white shoes, talking to herself.

"Now, where did I put the mop? I had it right where I could put my hands on it, and now it's gone."

One would never know that Grace was Madella's sister, for the physical and mental differences between them were considerable. Where Madella was portly and gregarious, Grace was thin and quiet; and while Madella was quick-witted and fun to be with, her sister was dull and largely devoid of wit. The younger sister seemed much older.

Grace would stand in the kitchen with her cleaning equipment every morning and moan, "God knows I'm no stranger to work. I've worked all my life and Madella needs me now. She doesn't have to pay me much beyond room and board, so it makes a good deal. And I'm just glad to get out of Yonkers for the summer and be up here in Maine, even if I have to scrub out toilets. . .God knows, it makes a good change of scenery."

It was infrequent that Grace would join us or Madella with the guests in the afternoons or evenings for talks and laughs. She usually went off some place by herself, rummaging around, mumbling, and reminiscing. She lived mostly in the past and would often talk about hers and Madella's childhoods out on the Kansas plains and then about the days when they both had married and migrated to New York. It was hard to tell if Grace had ever been very happy or alive, even from her storytelling, which might be described as matter-of-fact monotone.

"Grace can be such a sad sack," said Mrs. Richmond one time, "but having a bum for a husband and two boys to raise practically on her own, she's always had to struggle. She's accident-prone, too. When she was a child, she fell down a well. I suppose if you begin life by falling down a well, you do look at life a little differently."

When she mentioned about Grace's having two boys to raise, I thought of Essie, since she had given birth to twin sons in February of 1961. My mother had sent me the newspaper clipping to Orono. I'd seen Essie several times around town with her babies. She looked good, almost back in shape after her pregnancy; but while she was always all smiles when she saw me, she was too busy with her boys and her husband to come visit.

I did see her one day in the middle of Summer Harbor when I was going to pick up my grocery order.

Essie hollered from the backseat of this Chevy sedan, "HEY, COW SHIT! GET YOUR TIGHT ASS OVER HERE!"

I went over and there was Essie the Earth Mother spread over the backseat nursing both of her boys at the same time. "I feel just like a goddamn circus queen!" she said. "You wanna suck on me after they're done, An-day? Right here in the middle of town? Maybe this is just what I'm meant to do. Sit here and anyone who wants to can climb in here with me in the backseat!"

"For both pleasure and nourishment," I said, grinning at her.

"Yeah, that's right. I've got plenty of both to give."

"And you once said you wanted to run a whorehouse," I reminded her.

"Yes, but *indoors*! Not out in the daylight. Even I have my standards!"

36

We were used to demanding guests at the Manor, but Mrs. P. Canfield Gay out-demanded all of the others. She usually arrived for her little sojourns on and off throughout the summer in the middle of the night without warning. Mrs. Gay didn't believe in making reservations; and she always traveled with an entourage of characters and a lot of commotion.

In 1961, her traveling companions included her handsome and mustachioed brother Vance, her black chauffeur Carlton, some dumpy little lady friend who giggled all the time, and a young couple who hadn't been married very long and whose connection to Mrs. Gay was never made entirely clear. They arrived that time around ten p.m. honking the horn of their salmon colored 1959 Cadillac limousine. And as soon as she alighted, Mrs. Gay demanded service.

"We are famished, Madella, darling. We need nourishment. We crave foodstuffs. We had planned to grab a bite along the road, but somehow, we forgot; and then it got to be too late. Maine closes down so early even in the summer. Sandwiches and wine will do, but we must have something before we all faint. . .and it's only the shank of the evening!"

"Juiced up and crazy as ever," Mrs. Richmond informed the girls and me in the kitchen to which we had been hastily summoned. "See what ya can find in the pantry refrigerator that we can slap between some slices of bread. I'll heat up some soup."

After they had all eaten and drunk, and Mrs. Gay and Company had gone upstairs to their rooms, Carlton the chauffeur confided in Mrs. Richmond that he wasn't sure of a place where he could stay in Summer Harbor.

"Well, Carlton, there are two other places in town: the Seaside Inn which is in the village and the Lookout Motel at the entrance to the National Park road. I'll call them both for you to see if there's a room." She did and informed him that they would hold a room at the Lookout.

In about a half hour afterwards, near eleven o'clock, Carlton called back to say that there wasn't a room at either the Lookout or the Seaside.

"Jesus Christ!" said Mrs. Richmond. "Don't tell me those two seedy joints had the nerve to refuse you! As if they could afford to be racially prejudiced! Come on back here, Carlton, you can stay here."

I was surprised, or at least somewhat confused, at my boss' generosity and camaraderie with Carlton, since she was always telling Negro jokes and talking like "Beulah" of radio fame. Once when she had finished talking to a prospective guest on the phone, she said, "Gawd, I always think that might be a nigger I just booked! They're getting educated, ya know; and sometimes they can sound white on the phone." Another time she hailed me from across the kitchen, asking, "Say, Andy! What was the headline in the *New York Daily News* the day the first Negro astronaut was sent aloft?" "I don't know," I answered. "THE JIG IS UP!" she exclaimed in glee. She also used to like to mimic the way her black maid in Greenwich used to talk, saying "braid" for bread and so on. But when Carlton returned, she was very nice to him. She told him to park Mrs. Gay's Caddy out back where she wouldn't be likely to see it, and even showed him to one of the guest rooms off the back hall where he could stay, sharing the servants' bathroom and back dining room. Carlton was pleased and relieved that he didn't have to spend the night in the car.

For the few days the Gay entourage was in residence, it was great fun for us being with Carlton. He was the first black American I got to know and I loved his stories about growing up in Philadelphia and then working for someone as eccentric as Mrs. Gay.

One misty morning after Mrs. Gay's arrival, I was busy polishing the carriage lamps and sweeping off the steps of the front entrance, when I was interrupted by the dramatic, haughty toned voice of Mrs. Gay who had risen early for a stroll around the grounds before breakfast.

"Boy!" she called. "Come brush my feet!"

The lawn had been recently mowed and her pumps were covered with bits of grass. She stood on the first step of the entrance with one of her feet stuck up in the air for my sweeping. I took the broom which I used on the steps and began carefully to do as she asked.

"Thank you, boy," she said, when I had finished, and turned to regally ascend the steps to the lobby. I couldn't help but notice the way she was dressed. She always wore clothes that were several sizes too small for her voluptuous figure and dresses that always showed a lot of cleavage. She sported a great deal of jewelry and wore wigs of various shapes and colors. The girls kept confusing her in the dining room because of her different wigs. One meal she would appear as a redhead, at the next as a champagne blonde, and one dinner even in a pink-colored wig that reminded one of pictures of Martha Washington.

Once when Mrs. Gay was visiting the kitchen, we dared ask her what the "P" in P. Canfield Gay stood for.

"Penelope," she said. "My grandmother. . .but don't you dare call me Penny! I am no kind of Penny!"

When Mrs. Gay was drinking, which was most of the time, she could be outrageous: laughing too loudly, flitting from table to table in the dining room, telling bawdy stories, and racing throughout the hotel. One night she came out into the kitchen and plopped herself down in one of the big armchairs to have a nip with Mrs. Richmond. As she drank, she told us all about her beloved dead husband who had been a very successful Wall Street broker. Since he had passed away, she had become a "wanderer and a wayfarer," as she put it, traveling all over the world at a moment's notice in search of a happiness she could never find.

"I can never be alone. I must always have people around me to help stem the grief," she said. "And I am always bored. There's never enough excitement to make me happy. No one can ever replace my husband, but I keep searching anyway. What else can I do?"

After she had left us that night to stumble upstairs to bed, Mrs. Richmond said, "She's a goddamn spoiled brat, kids, that's what she is. There's no excuse for being bored in a world as interesting as this one is. There's plenty she could be out doing for others with her money. She gets carrying on like tonight and I just want to slap her."

One morning Mrs. P. Canfield Gay came downstairs in her scanty, silky slip with nothing else on and sat there in the living room without moving. The girls, Carlton, and Mrs. Richmond all tried to get her to go back to her room or at least put on a robe, but she wouldn't hear of it.

"I have a beautiful body," she said, "and the sight of it shouldn't disturb anyone."

It took her debonair brother Vance, who looked as if he also wore a wig, to finally remove his pouty and stubborn sister from the couch by which all the other guests had to pass on their way to the dining room for breakfast.

"At least we got to see what she looked like without a wig!" said Lil, commenting afterwards.

37

One afternoon Mrs. Richmond received a call from a Mr. Jarvis-Brigham who said he was in Mount Desert, had been there for years, and would like to see the view from the other side of the Bay. Would there be a room he could let for a few days? Mrs. Richmond told him of course and that we would be expecting him.

He arrived just before dinner in a conservative blue Ford sedan, parked his own car, and carried his own bag. Mrs. Richmond showed him to his room and then returned to the kitchen, her face aglow with good humor.

"That ain't no man!" she said to us.

"What do you mean, Mrs. Richmond?" I asked. "Wasn't that Mr. Jarvis-Brigham whom we were expecting?"

"That's right, Andy, but turns out he ain't no man. He's, shall we say, of the lavender crowd? The limp-wristed set? You know what I mean?

"I guess so," I said, not really getting the drift. Even though I had been to college for a year, and heard the jokes about Liberace and other effeminate males, I didn't know much about homosexuals.

"I must talk to you about this at a later date," she said, "as part of your education."

It was after I had been down to the rocks the next afternoon and had been visited by Mr. Jarvis-Brigham that she did talk to me. I stood there in the kitchen in my damp swim trunks and tee-shirt, while she interrogated me.

"Did you go for a swim alone?" she asked.

"The girls didn't go down today, but Mr. Jarvis-Brigham came down."

"Oh, no," she said. "Tell me, Andy, just what did he say to you?"

"Not much. I guess he came down for a swim, too, but it was low tide, so all he did was take his clothes off and go down by the water and splash some all over himself, yelling, 'MAGNIFICENT!' I thought that was pretty funny, even for this place."

"Was he nude?"

"Yes; and that kind of surprised me for I had never seen an older guy naked before. . .and someone could have seen him down there, but he didn't seem to care."

"What did he say to you?"

"He came up beside me where I was reading and asked me what I was planning to do with my future. I told him I was working my way through college and he kept on exclaiming and shrieking how magnificent and wonderful that was."

"He didn't touch you, did he?"

"No, but he did sit very close to me while he was drying himself. He told me how 'simply exhilarating' the Maine ocean waters were and so on and how he had to come here every summer to exult in it."

"God, he is an exhilarating exulter, all right, but at least he let you alone. No harm done."

"What do you mean?"

"Oh, Andy, dear, he's one of those types of men who likes young men like yourself. Don't you know about them? Homosexuals? Gay fellows? They're even around here in Maine, just as in the cities. He probably wouldn't hurt you or a fly; but I wouldn't want him confusing you with his needs and demands. I'm relieved that nothing happened. He's no doubt a very fine and sensitive person, but while he's here, don't go down to the rocks alone, O.K.?"

"O.K.," I said. "He told me he went to Harvard with President Kennedy and that he came from a very prominent family in Boston."

"That's probably very true with his name, and he looks to be about the same age as Kennedy. He's also got the class and style; but then, maybe he was just bragging to you, trying to interest you, or trying his luck by comparing himself to our virile young President. In that case, what a come-on!" And she laughed.

I never did get the chance to talk again with Mr. Jarvis-Brigham during the remainder of his short stay; but when he left, he dropped by the kitchen to give me a ten dollar tip and wish me well.

Another surprise guest that summer claimed Kennedy connections as well. He came with his wife to stay only one night, and ended up so enchanted with the Manor that they stayed several. Upon his arrival, he happened to mention to Mrs. Richmond that he was the Undersecretary of Defense in the Kennedy cabinet. Mrs. Richmond told us this information as soon as she came back to the kitchen.

"I want to check this one out just for fun," she said. "We seem to be getting a number of notables without reservations. Let's find out if he's for real or just a poseur. I don't know why he would tell me about his position, unless he thought I'd be impressed and give him special service, or maybe he was feeling insecure."

She made some calls and come to find out there was indeed an Undersecretary of Defense by the same name, so we had to assume he was who he said he was. We gave him and his wife the lavish treatment with extra helpings and all; but it wasn't worth it from the help's standpoint, for when he left, the tips were minimal.

"Give me a Philadelphia lawyer any time over any old Cabinet members," said Lil, ever conscious of her savings for college.

38

Mrs. Richmond had her troubles with Julie Lawson, the tip-toeing Belle of Tampa. One morning she opened the refrigerator in preparation for breakfast only to discover the orange juice supply, replenished the night before, half-gone.

"O.K., kids, where the hell hath the orange juice evaporated to?" she asked.

"I don't know," I said. "We made up a full jug just last night."

"Well, my God, this has happened too frequently this summer for my peace. I must have retribution. We shall set a trap for this thief-by-night. You, Andy, are appointed first watchdog this very eve in charge of refrigerator one."

"O.K."

I knew who it must be even before beginning my first watch. Who else around the Manor would have to have fresh orange juice in the middle of the night, except for some health fanatic like Mrs. Lawson?

To make our juice, we used frozen concentrate, but added fresh juice from a few oranges to each jug. We usually made up two or three jugs a night.

Sitting there in the dark of the kitchen, I was a bit startled to hear the giggling and the sound of two people sneaking through the butler's pantry. But I kept calm, and when the chuckling thieves opened the refrigerator and its light bathed us all in an eerie glow, I was not surprised to see Mrs. Lawson and her teenage son Parker revealed as the capering culprits; and neither were they especially surprised to see me.

"Oh, why, Andy. . .ah you a spy?" she asked with a giggle.

"Yes, Mrs. Lawson, I'm afraid so. Mrs. Richmond is quite upset over the missing juice."

"Oh, but this orange juice is so delicious and good for you at night before retiring after an active day. Why, Parker and I need it for our muscle tone and general good health. Being from Tampa, you know, why there's always such delicious fresh fruit all year long. We're simply used to having it whenever and wherever we want. . .won't you join us?"

"No, but I don't see why you can't request that you have your own extra juice," I said.

She giggled some more and Parker grinned.

"It's fun," she said, "doing it this way."

The Lawsons played other little games also, like the time they set my bed on fire. Parker had brought some firecrackers with him to the Manor from the camp he attended every summer; and he and his mother, in one of their jolly after-dinner moods, had run up the attic stairs to my room and planted the firecrackers under my bed while I was washing the evening pots and pans. I finished my work just in time, for when I reached my room, I found the box spring smoldering and the room filled with smoke. A quick dosage from an ancient copper fire extinguisher on the stairwell saved my bed and put the fire out, but when asked about the matter by Mrs. Richmond, Julie just giggled and attributed the whole incident to just "Parker's need to play some joke on Andy."

It was that summer of 1961 that Julie became highly disenchanted with taking her meals with the other guests in the main dining room. Mrs. Richmond arranged to have a special private table for her and Parker in the servants' back dining room off the kitchen; and so that the waitresses would know when she wanted something, she was provided with a little silver bell to ring. However, in the rush of serving the other guests, and because Mrs. Lawson and son came and went when they felt like it, this constant bell-ringing could prove very annoying.

One busy, hot night, when Mrs. Richmond was cooking, the bell kept ringing; and Mrs. Richmond, her hair hanging in her sweaty face, told all of us to ignore it.

"Let her ring her goddamn southern belle arm off!" our boss said. "She probably wants to know if it's going to rain or she needs some more Kellogg's Concentrate or some other bird feed, sprinkled on top of her sassafras! I regret the hour I ever handed her that damn bell!"

"Well, just be thankful you didn't give her a gong!" I said.

"Or a gun!" she added.

For her afternoon exercises, which she practiced religiously every afternoon after her nap, Julie had to forsake her own small room for a larger one, and usually she did this without consultation of the staff, but she generally knew which rooms were occupied.

However, one time Mrs. Richmond was showing prospective guests, a New York doctor and his wife, to the Round Room, one of the most beautifully appointed in the hotel.

"Now, here's what we call the Round Room," Mrs. Richmond was saying, "for it is located in the tower of the building with a lovely semi-circular view of the bay. As you will presently see, it's a most handsome setting."

Swinging wide the door, however, Mrs. Richmond and the potential guests were greeted by more than a pretty view of the bay, for there, nude, in a yoga position on top of one of the beds, squatted Julie Lawson.

"JULIE!" Mrs. Richmond exclaimed. "THIS IS OUTRAGEOUS!"

Julie giggled, and hastily wrapping a towel about herself, apologized.

"I'm sorry, Madella, but my little room is so impossible for my movements. . .one needs open space and air to breathe."

Julie tip-toed past them and down the hall, while Mrs. Richmond turned to the startled couple to futilely ask, "Could I show you another room?"

"No, I'm afraid not," said the doctor, glancing at his wife as if to say, "This is quite a weird place we've stumbled upon, isn't it?"

Mrs. Richmond returned to the kitchen in a rage.

"This is the last straw! Now that dizzy dame is costing me money! Next, she'll probably start disrobing and doing Egyptian handstands in the lobby! I've got to lay into her, I guess. I know those people were sold on the place if they just hadn't caught sight of Twinkle Toes in the buff making like some kind of Buddhist offering on top of my bedsheets. After that, they could hardly wait to vacate this loony bin, and who could blame them? The big excuse for putting up with Miss Julie Lawson and her shenanigans has always been the money, but now I'm not so sure."

Later, after she had calmed down, had a cocktail or two, and regained her sense of humor, Mrs. Richmond relished the scene with Julie and the doctor, spoke of it over and over, embellishing it, ultimately forgiving Julie and even changing her opinion of the prospective guests.

"What a couple of unadventurous boors they were! Why, at no extra charge, they could have stayed here and had their own private nude yoga sessions while eating high off the hog! Now, what other enterprising hostelry on the Maine Coast offers such novelty? I hope they enjoyed their scenic post card vacation at the Knotty-Pine-Tru-Vu Motel where nothing fun ever disturbed their bourgeois dreams! At least, they can thrill their friends forever back in Scarsdale with the shocking tale of The Naked Woman in the Round Room!"

Julie Lawson consumed quarts of "fresh spring water," which my mother brought down to the Manor two or three times a week with the clean laundry. The water came from our drilled well and tap, but Julie preferred to refer to it as fresh spring water. My mother transported the health-giving fluid in old fruit juice jugs and bottles, and at the height of Julie's summer stays, dozens of such containers were in use and scattered all over the back porch, up in Julie's room, and wherever the athletic Mrs. Lawson might be wandering.

One afternoon, while Morgan, Lil, and I were lounging in the sun out by the garage and back driveway, where Julie parked her car, we noticed that she had just finished sipping from one of the water bottles and had placed it in a most precarious position on top of her car. She had forgotten about it, too, for she was in the driver's seat, turning the ignition, about to go out for a drive. We all began to chuckle as the car started up the drive with the bottle wobbling but still balanced on top.

"How far do you think she'll get?" asked Morgan.

"It depends upon the staying power of that bottle," said Lil.

The answer was not long in coming, for just as Julie stepped on the gas to pull her car up onto the main road, and just as she was shifting from first gear into second, there came the awaited tinkle-crash as the bottle hit the pavement.

True to her fashion, Mrs. Lawson failed to be bothered with the sound of breaking glass, shifted into high gear, and drove away, while Morgan, Lil, and I raced laughing up the driveway to pick up the broken pieces.

39

It was a family tradition that as many members of the Danzer clan who could make it would congregate at the end of August every summer at Frenchman's Bay Manor for a week or so of watercolor painting, outdoor hiking, and family frivolity.

There were nine of them who usually came: Professor Danzer, who was in the architecture school at M.I.T.; his wife Florrie, a chemical firm heiress; their eldest daughter Kippy, a grad student in architecture at Yale; their prettiest daughter Kristin, majoring in silversmithing at the University of Iowa; and Dietrich, their son and youngest child, still in prep school in 1961, but destined for study at Cal Tech. There was also Uncle Karl Shoppe, the Danzers' businessman brother-in-law; his wife Josie, Mrs. Danzer's look-alike sister; their son Karl, Jr. and Karl Junior's wife Gaye, who were both teachers.

They arrived in three or four small, beat-up, and road-weary Volkswagens; and they would be dressed very casually and would always be in high spirits, joking with each other, greatly enjoying each other's company. They carried their own bags and preferred to be more self-sufficient than our usual guests; and in the summers I waited upon them, I never received a tip.

Since they occupied half of the rooms in the hotel, the Manor during their stay seemed literally their home, as if the name had been changed to Danzer Manor. They were everywhere and always busy doing something industrious, creative, or crafty. When the hotel was crowded, they only too obligingly pitched in and helped out, making beds, washing dishes, and helping to wait upon their fellow guests. All of these activities the Danzers participated in were never referred to as chores or work. It was fun, accompanied by much humor and gusto by the whole clan and with much appreciation by the management and staff, with the possible exception of me.

I don't know why, but I know I didn't like the way they'd do this. Their attitude seemed condescending to me, as if they were showing us, who worked hard at our menial jobs because we needed the money, that anyone could do what we were doing. In their view of the world, I suppose, they were illustrating that guests and servants were one in the same; but this wasn't so. *The guests could leave.* I saw their whole attitude as a way of cheating us out of our tips. Also, their coming and going from our quarters disturbed our comfort and limited our freedom. We couldn't be ourselves, or talk and joke the way we usually did with each other.

In all the summers I waited upon them, I never shared a real conversation with any of the Danzers, as I had with so many of the other regular guests who acted as guests. Only Mrs. Danzer and her daughter Kristin spoke with me. During my last summer at the Manor, when Mrs. Danzer found out I was to become a teacher, she advised me, "Don't give your students homework." I never asked her why, because I never questioned the summer people to their faces. They knew best; and I had to puzzle out what they meant afterward.

Kristin once shocked me by telling me that I was the main reason she kept coming back with her family each summer, a startling statement which I wanted to believe—for Kristin was very beautiful and sophisticated—but which I immediately dismissed as a cruel joke, made at my expense, for her momentary amusement, and maybe for her entire family's. At that point in my life, I saw myself as a Downeast goon, good for a laugh, and a dependable slave; but not someone a pretty girl like her would fall for. The only "date" we ever went on was during the summer of 1962 when we went with her brother and sister to Ellsworth to see the movie *Hemingway's Adventures of a Young Man.* I loved the movie, but I didn't dare say so, because right away, Kristin, her brother and sister, all started making fun of the film and especially the acting of Richard Beymer, who played the young Hemingway.

Every morning, unless the weather was very bad, all of the Danzer family members, except Mrs. Danzer and Mrs. Schoppe, who both preferred needlework to painting, would go off to the National Park and environs painting their watercolors. After a week or so of this, they would amass great numbers of paintings and sketches and hold a mock exhibition of them in the living room and library to which all the other guests and the help would be invited. It was fun trying to guess who painted what, for much of the work was unsigned. The paintings would be arranged about the rooms, and one would overhear such amiable chatter as:

"Have you seen Daddy's version of the sea gulls competing for bread crumbs?" asked Kristin.

"No," answered Mrs. Danzer, "but how about Karl's purple rocks? What's the matter, Karl? Don't you know how to mix pink?"

"I prefer, you should know by now, to be regarded as a totally unrealistic interpreter of nature's scene," said Karl Senior. "I am a dilettante impressionist!"

"And not just in your painting," said Mrs. Schoppe.

"Let's see, what ever could this be?" asked Mrs. Danzer. "It seems to be a tree—King Spruce against an ominous sky?"

Dietrich laughed. "Hardly, Mother. Those are my black thoughts on a bright Maine day."

"You're such a deep boy," said Aunt Josie.

Professor Danzer said, "Here is my masterpiece of the summer of '61: 'An Angry Ocean Stilled.'"

"How haunting," said Kippy.

"How Daddy!" said Kristin. "You should really stick to your little scenes of villages nestled by the sea."

"You want me stagnant or happy?" asked Daddy.

We servants in the crowd, except for Morgan, never dared say anything to the Danzers and Schoppes about their art works, unless they asked us to make a comment, which I don't believe they ever did.

The highlight of the clan's stay every summer was the birthday party thrown for Big Karl, as Mr. Schoppe Senior was called; and it was always a rollicking bash involving much extra attention and work from the staff. From the beginning of their stay, the Danzer-Schoppes spent many hours planning their little joke-gifts and writing their testimonials, many of which involved the memory of one of Big Karl's long lost loves, a French-Canadian woman from Prince Edward Island called Mag.

There would be such gifts as a bundle of Mag's old love letters to Karl, and each of them would be dramatically read in turn to Karl by every member of the family seated around three of the tables pushed together in the middle of the dining room. There would be gifts like one of the oars that Karl had used to help row Mag across the Bay of Fundy in one of their mythical escapades. One time, Karl opened a fancy package to find a pair of Mag's old panties, which, to the delight of the family, he boldly tucked into the top of his shirt to use as a bib.

At the end of the summer of 1961, the Danzers became Cousin Lillie Partridge's benefactors, for it so happened they were returning to Boston on Labor Day weekend at the same time Lil needed a lift to where she had enrolled in a medical technology school for the fall. With little guidance from her family or her school, Lil had given up Mount Holyoke College for a two-year tech school. The Danzers were only too pleased to give Lil a ride into her future. She even got to stay overnight in their impressive house in Cambridge which had been designed by the architecture professor himself.

Summer 1962

40

After her freshman year at Smith, Morgan wrote to tell me that she wouldn't be returning to the Manor for the summer of 1962, that instead she would be working in some student intern position at the McGraw-Hill Publishing Company in midtown Manhattan. Cousin Lillie, too, after her year in Boston, was already working at a suburban Beantown hospital, and wouldn't be back.

When she learned of these developments, Miss Meyer called me to see if I knew of some girls "of equal caliber" to Morgan and Lil for possible replacements; and as luck would have it, I did. Our family friends, the Barclays of Bangor, had a daughter Ellen, four years my junior, who had just completed her sophomore year at Bangor High and was looking for a summer job. Her brother Russell, my age and a lifelong pal, had copied me by getting a hotel job at Pemaquid Point; and Ellen longed to join either Russell or me at a coastal resort.

"I don't want to be scooping ice cream all summer in Bangor," she moaned.

Tall and slender with light brown hair and brown eyes, Ellen tanned easily and looked athletic. When she smiled her great smile, she squinted. She had a great sense of humor and we looked at the world the same way. I had always adored her.

Ellen had a best friend named Sally French, who was also looking for a summer job away from Bangor; so I told Miss Meyer about the girls. As soon as school was out, they came down for their interview, and Miss Meyer hired them on the spot.

"Errr. . .Andy, you couldn't have suggested better or lovelier girls. They are smart and full of energy. I think they'll be wonderful."

The girls were engaged as waitresses and they were to stay in the attic bedroom which Lil and Amanda and Morgan had occupied down the hall from me.

In marked contrast to Ellen and Sally, the all-American teenagers, were the German War Brides: Mia Jones and Hedy Smith, thirty-year-old German women-of-the-world who had both married American sailors and ended up at the Summer Harbor base. Mia was hired as chambermaid and Hedy was to be a kitchen helper and assistant cook, similar to Morgan.

Suddenly, I had become at the age of twenty, the veteran employee to whom all the girls and women looked for advice and expertise. I was treated as a sort of assistant manager who knew how Miss Meyer and Mrs. Richmond expected the hotel to be run. Since I was also on the same level, they could also confide in me. So, I instructed the four new staff members, and gradually we became an efficient and convivial team.

In the afternoons when Mia and Hedy went home to their husbands and children, the girls and I went down to the rocks, as usual, to swim, read, listen to the transistor radio and rock-'n'-roll music, and lie in the sun. When it was stormy, we'd stay upstairs in the attic and listen to music, read, and joke around. Always, the girls would make fun of Miss Meyer, the guests, and especially Hedy with her heavy German accent. Sally, who was a pretty good mimic, would usually do Mrs. Smith.

"Zay, girls, deed I tell you about zee time ven I vas a prostitute in 'Amburg? I even had a card vith my peecture on eet. I made lots of money. Ees hard being a prostitute in Summer Harbor!"

Ellen specialized in Miss Meyer ordering groceries over the phone: "Errr. . .Fred? Joe? Oh, Bill. . .this is Miss Meyer over at Frenchman's Bay Manor. . .Errr. . .fine, and you? . . .Errr. . .I would like to order some things which Andy will pick up later this morning. Errr. . .one bag of Maine potatoes, eyeless. . .a half gallon of Neapolitan ice cream, two jars of tomato paste, two packages of Pepperidge Farm patty shells, two honey dew melons, a pound of salt, a keg of nails, and two six packs of Miller High Life. . .Errr. . .make that *three* packs. . . Errr. . .ya got that, Bill? George? Fred? Errr. . ."

Ellen and Sally also loved the names of the different foods and specialties served at the hotel.

"What's on the menu for tonight, Miss M?" Sally would ask. "Lettuce, turnip, and pea on patty shells with roast tripe soufflé?"

"Errr. . .there's a choice of soups: clam bisque or mock turtle; roast beef with mashed potato and creamed cauliflower. For dessert, there's a choice between fresh fruit compote with raspberry sherbet or maple parfait."

"Love that *bisque*!" Sally exclaimed. "C'mon, Ellen Baby, git out the parfait glasses, while I go mock the turtle!"

Miss Meyer was at the Manor for the whole summer of 1962, while Mrs. Richmond came and went, joining us for two full weeks in August; and with her arrival, the girls gained another addition to their Manor mimicry repertoire. The first day Mrs. Richmond saw Sally, who tended to be a bit sloppy in both dress and demeanor, she said, "Ya better slick up, kid!" That remark sent the girls running into the pantry in high-steerics. They loved the way Mrs. Richmond phrased everything with her Sophie Tucker delivery.

"Roast chick for sup, gang," Mrs. Richmond said one afternoon. "And ya know what that means."

"What *does* that mean?" Ellen asked.

"Ya gotta count out the frozen peas, mash the taters, chill the cranberry preserves straight from the can, and locate some yallar vegetables, ya know: The Roast Chick Plan. Someone's gotta stuff the birds, too."

"Hey, Andy!" Sally would yell. "Wanna come help stuff some birds?"

One night we were serving roast lamb and Miss Meyer and Mrs. Richmond were both a little high on Old-Fashioneds when an argument ensued between them over which side of the plate the meat should be on. They both had forks in their hands. Miss Meyer would slap a piece of lamb down on a plate and then Mrs. Richmond would pick it up with her fork and slap it down on the other side. "For God's sake, Jean! Didn't you learn anything from the time you spent at Schraft's? The meat goes on the right side!" The girls and I stood there most amused but not daring to mention the fact that the plate was round.

Another night after dinner, Mrs. Richmond and Miss Meyer were instructing us on the preparation of after-dinner drinks. That night it was Kahlua. "Get a silver spoon!" Mrs. Richmond commanded, "and a pint of whipping cream and bring some of them fancy little liqueur glasses with the Kahlua. Now, here's whatcha do. Take the spoon, hold it at the right angle, so that the cream runs down it so it doesn't mix with the liqueur. You should have a head of heavy cream on top of each one; and then when ya sip it, try to sip the liqueur through the cream. Now, easy does it. . .isn't that a taste sensation? Just the thing to top off a good meal of ten thousand calories! If we could slip a little of this Kahlua-and-cream into Julie Lawson's cereal bowl, she might throw away her orange juice bottle!"

Mia and Hedy, despite their common heritage, language, and history, were almost direct opposites of each other. While Mia was petite, beautiful, well-proportioned, feminine, and stylish with an appreciation of the arts and the finer things in life, Hedy was big-boned, mannish, crude, and low-class. Mia told us on the sly one time that if they had been back in Germany together, she would never have associated with the likes of Hedy. But in Summer Harbor with both of their husbands stationed at the Navy base, their sons attending the same grammar school, and both of them working at the same place, she had no choice. Hedy drove and Mia didn't, so Hedy forced herself upon Mia.

Both of their sons were born of previous husbands. Mia's boy, Hans, was a handsome, sensitive child with a beautiful, quick smile; while Hedy's boy, Rudolf, was a shy, sullen child used to Hedy's terrible rages and harsh punishments. Mia's husband, Joe, was a tall, lanky, all American fellow who very much adored his wife. In contrast, Hedy's husband Herman was shorter than she, bespectacled, shy, and obviously hen-pecked. Hedy wore the pants in her marriage while Mia and Joe seemed very happy and to go well together, always joking with each other.

The girls took to calling Hedy "The Nazi," which she didn't seem to mind. As she said, "My farser vas a Nazi! And ve vere very proud of heem."

It seemed as if every lunch time revolved around the storytelling of Hedy and Mia and their comparison between life in Germany and in the United States.

"Eet ees so boring here," Hedy would lament. "Vy, back een 'Amburg, zere vas alvays somesing going on, some place to go, vile here you haf to drive so far to just see a movie or go for a dreenk."

"Don't judge the whole United States by Summer Harbor," I said, even though I had hardly been much beyond Bangor myself.

"Thees ees true," Hedy said. "I can hardly vait until Herman's time ees up so that ve can moof avay to New York or some place vere there's more people and sings going on."

Mia's life had been very dramatic and romantic to us and even though she didn't like to talk about it very often, she did tell us a few things.

"When I was a little girl, and we'd go down to the candy store after school, we'd raise our arms and salute each other with 'Heil, Hitler!'" Mia said. "We made a game out of it, for that's what it seemed to us as small children. We saw Hitler as funny."

"Too bad Hitler didn't have a sense of humor himself," I said.

"He probably thought he did," said Mia, who continued: "The worst time of my life was when the allies began the bombing of our city. I lived in Bremerhaven which was entirely destroyed by the bombers. We ended up living in the cellar of our house: my mother, brother, and me. One awful night, I remember seeing my mother getting raped by a Russian soldier. When the British and Americans came, we expected more of the same, but they were much nicer. Russians were animals, just let loose to rape the German women. I never learned what happened to my father."

"And your brother?"

"He is still living in Bremerhaven. He is married now and has his own family."

Unlike Hedy, Mia spoke good English, as well as French. After her mother's death, and soon after the war, Mia married for the first time an American, Hans' father, and they went to live in Paris, years that Mia termed her happiest. She loved Paris and the French. Her first husband was a very sensitive, good-looking man who wrote poetry, was trying to become an artist. They had a circle of artist friends. Mia learned French, and her baby was only a couple of years old when her young husband committed suicide. She moved back to Germany, worked at various jobs, trying to bring up Hans alone, when she met Joe, who was stationed in Germany, married him, and moved to America.

Hedy's life story was much different. She had grown up in the German countryside, been a farm girl, who had moved after a few years of schooling to the streets of Hamburg where she became a prostitute specializing in American servicemen, including radio technicians like her little Herman.

Hedy was always making huge German cream cakes dripping with all kinds of pieces of fruit. Her cooking was good, but on the rich and heavy side. But the worst thing about Hedy was her lack of a sense of humor. She'd frequently snap at us and Mia whenever we'd be making jokes about Germany or the Nazis.

"Eet ees not funny! Hitler vaz simply zee man Germany needed at zee time. He vasn't all bad. Zee Nazi movement had eets gout points."

Mia would get giggling when Hedy started talking like this. She'd tell us afterwards, "Hedy probably even has her father's uniform in her closet and likes to try it on and strut around. She has the same sense of humor Hitler had, you see."

41

It was an early August morning when I had just finished with my kitchen chores and was on my way through the living room to go and get some bags of guests who were leaving, when Mia, who was dusting around the fireplace, asked me in a very sad tone of voice if I had heard the awful news.

"What news?" I asked.

"The blonde actress, Monroe. . .she's dead. They think she committed suicide."

"Marilyn Monroe? Are you sure? When did it happen?"

"Sometime last night in Hollywood. An overdose of pills."

I was shocked by her words and didn't believe her. I wanted to see the newspapers and listen to the radio to have it confirmed and learn all the details. Like so many others, I had loved Marilyn ever since first seeing her on the screen. *Bus Stop*, *The Seven Year Itch*, and especially *Some Like It Hot*, were three of my favorite movies. For reasons I hadn't then begun to define, she meant a great deal to my emotional self and I had devoured many magazine articles on her. She had excited my youthful imagination more than most other actors or artists of the time. Along with Elvis Presley, Marlon Brando, James Dean, *MAD* magazine, Hugh Hefner and *Playboy*, the

Kennedys, and rock-'n'-roll, Marilyn was of major cultural importance during my growing-up years. Just then, however, I couldn't stay and talk longer with Mia. I had to get upstairs to old lady Stubbs, the guest who was leaving that morning, and who was calling for me from her room upstairs.

"Louie! Louie!" she called.

"Coming, Miss Stubbs!" I yelled back.

Mia suddenly was laughing.

"What are you laughing about?"

"She called you Louie. Do you know what that sounds like to a European like me?"

"No, never having been to Europe, how could I? I suppose she calls me Louie, because, even after four summers of carrying her bags and tending to her needs, she still doesn't know my real name, and Louie is as good as any other."

"In France, if one hears an older woman calling a young man like you 'Louie,' it means, Andy, that she wishes your services, and not just to carry her bag."

"Oh, Mia! You see sex in everything!"

"And why not, if it's there?"

Miss Stubbs called again, now from the top of the stairs. "Louie! Come get my bags!"

"Be right up, Miss Stubbs. Mia, I have to go, but I want to talk more about Marilyn. Did you love her, too?"

"Of course. Anyone who loves life, who is sensitive and alive, must have loved her. She was so beautiful and warm. You just wanted to hug her, be with her. I feel very sad."

When I got to Miss Stubbs' room, her secretary-companion, Miss Coverly, was rushing about checking and double-checking everything; and the little lady, who claimed to be a multi-millionaire, stood there surveying our work. At one point she pressed a bumpy finger to her forehead, saying, "I've got an egg on my head and some advice for Miss Meyer!"

"What happened?" I asked.

"This morning, when I was making preparations to leave, I tried to open a drawer in that large bureau to get my clothes, and the drawer was stuck, so I pulled, and succeeded in pulling the bureau down on top of me! I could have been seriously injured if not for the quick actions of Miss Coverly here."

"Yes, Andy," said Miss Coverly, "you should tell Miss Meyer to have some blocks of wood or some kind of braces placed under the front legs of that chiffonier. This morning I caught it just in time; it could have fallen on top of both of us!"

"It DID fall on top of me!" Miss Stubbs exclaimed. "It bumped my head and caused this swelling and pain. A terrible way to end my vacation!"

"I'm sorry," I said. "I will report this to Miss Meyer."

After taking down all their bags, packing them in the car, and seeing them off, along with both Miss Meyer and Mrs. Richmond, who assured Miss Stubbs that such a terrible accident would never happen again, I hastened to the village in the car to do the morning errands, and especially to get the papers to read about Monroe's death. In the drugstore, I bought the *Boston Globe* along with picking up the hotel's copies of the *Bangor Daily News* and *The New York Times*, the latter being no good since it was a day late. But both the *News* and the *Globe* carried the story on the front page with pictures and I took the extra time to sit in the car and read the stories, letting the grocery shopping go for a few minutes.

I still couldn't believe it, but it was true. Why was I so shocked and bothered by her death when I was twenty? Hemingway's suicide and Faulkner's death had interested me, since I had read them and liked them. James Dean's death had shocked me, but not as much as Monroe's. She was important to me and my dreams; her movie career had paralleled my growing-up. She had made me laugh and feel good. She had been poor and had become rich and famous. I felt as if a part of me had died too soon.

I talked about Monroe's death all day with my bosses, the girls, Mia, and Hedy. Mia and Mrs. Richmond seemed as affected as I was, while the others said little or remained unmoved.

"I once asked my doctor in Greenwich," Mrs. Richmond said, "what it was about Monroe, beyond her obvious physical endowments, that excited men so. And he said it was her innocence and vulnerability combined with her humor and her love of sex. She seemed strangely innocent and sweet and yet very earthy. Certainly, she was special; and she excited women as much as men. I know I adored her, poor thing."

Mia was like Marilyn. Not only was she blonde, beautiful, and sexy, but she, too, exuded warmth, fun, humor, and earthiness. I liked the way Mia laughed from deep down, the way she could always laugh at herself and the situation, the human way she regarded life in general.

She was always trying to get me to loosen up and not be so stiff with her. One night at the end of the summer she took me to a dance at Summer Harbor Town Hall, and out of her Manor uniform and work shoes and into her party dress and high heels, she was perhaps the prettiest and sexiest woman off the movie screen I'd ever seen up till then. It thrilled me the way she took my arm and giggled as we walked along Main Street.

Just before we reached the hall, Joe Jones, her husband, drove by with some other sailors on their way to the night shift at the Navy Base. Mia called to Joe, "Hey, Joe! Look here! I've got a new lover!" She hugged me close to her, and I must have blushed. Her husband, just then, reminded me of Joe DiMaggio, Marilyn's husband. He was tall, lanky, and black-haired. A nice guy who even pitched for the Base team.

At the dance we sat on the sidelines and drank booze from the community pop bottles being passed around. I didn't drink much, because I didn't like whiskey mixed with ginger ale and also didn't like the idea of drinking from the same bottle as several other people. Mia ribbed me for my abstention. She also tried to teach me the way to dance with a woman like her.

"You're so stiff, Andy! Here, let me show you where to place your hands. Don't be so afraid of me or to hold me tight. That's what you should do. C'mon, boy! C'mon, Louie! Let yourself go with the music. Enjoy our closeness."

Certainly, that was one of the best dances I ever had, thanks to my own German version of Marilyn Monroe.

42

Mrs. Richmond's summer vacation in August 1962 happily coincided with the season's most gala event: the pre-wedding party for Alice Anderson, the youngest daughter of a noted Boston doctor from one of the most prominent and respected families from my hometown of Taunton. The Andersons had summered on Taunton Point for generations; and their family tree read like a *Who's Who* of American history and culture. Alice's older sister, for instance, was then married to one of the country's most famous Broadway composers and she frequently appeared in nationally syndicated gossip columns. The older sister Anne was to be at the party along with her husband and about fifty other guests who would really fill up the Manor's main dining room; and it seemed as if we were busy planning for the event for the better part of the summer.

To help out, Bert Fickett was re-employed as assistant to Miss Meyer and Mrs. Richmond. My mother, Sid, and my aunt Bunny Crowley, were imported from Taunton, not just because they had known the Anderson family for years and had worked for them; but because they were veterans of decades of such summer parties and could help supervise the dining room. Mia and Hedy were to help wait on the people along with Ellen and Sally, while I was in charge, even though I was under-age, of serving the champagne. Cliff and Alvina Masters were to serve, once again, as bartenders.

Dr. Mans Anderson, Alice's father, came to the Manor a week before the party to make final arrangements. He also brought with him several cases of imported French champagne, which I helped him unload from his car, and which he told me should be placed into tubs of ice the morning of the big day. I was given a heavy duty corkscrew and told to keep re-filling the guests' champagne cups whenever they were emptied. "Keep it flowing as long as it lasts!" said the good Doctor.

The regular hotel guests that night were to be served dinner a half-hour earlier than usual, so that they would be done eating at least an hour or so before the Anderson party started arriving.

It turned out, of course, to be a mad evening with all kinds of rushing to and fro, here and there, hither and thither.

Before the dinner actually got underway, Mrs. Richmond, Miss Meyer, Berter, and the Masters were all pretty well oiled, making what they thought were hilarious jokes with each other and stumbling about the kitchen and pantries giving the rest of us orders. Luckily, everything was just about ready to go anyway, and we all knew approximately what had to be done when and how.

The black bean soup was the first course and the girls, my mother, and Aunt Bunny were busy dropping lemon slices in the center of each plate to be served.

"Don't sink the slices, for God's sake!" Mrs. Richmond admonished. "And don't slop the soup. They must each look like goddamn illustrations out of Fanny Farmer!"

Berter and Aunt Bunny were ladling out the soup from the big stove, when Ellen asked for four more, and Berter said, "There ain't no more! I thought your last order was the end! All we've got left at most is a cup!"

"Errr. . .how could this be?" asked Miss Meyer, scurrying across the kitchen with her underwear straps fallen down on her arms, her hair a mess, and her cigarette ashes grown to a precarious inch or more.

"We didn't count right, I guess!" said Berter.

"Omigod, this is outrageous!" said Mrs. Richmond. "Is there another can of Campbell's down in the cellar?"

"I'll go and check," I said; and there was exactly one can left.

"Add lots of water and sherry to it. We'll stretch 'er out," said

Berter.

"We could even throw in a few more lemon slices," said Sally.

I had to wear my white waiter's jacket as well as a black bow tie for the occasion. Miss Meyer showed me how to wrap each bottle of champagne in a white dinner napkin and how to hold the bottle as I was pouring. At first, I thought I had one of the easiest jobs, but people seemed to drink up the bubbly as soon as I filled up their glasses; and they seemed to have toast after toast. Before I knew it, one tub was all gone and I was well into the second one.

Throughout the evening, we in the kitchen sipped a lot of the champagne, too; and the girls smuggled a bottle up to their room as I did. Two of the guests who drank a number of glasses were a husband and wife team who ran the local art gallery in Summer Harbor village. After a while I thought he especially shouldn't be drinking any more, but when I asked Mrs. Richmond about it, she told me to keep serving him and the wine until it was all gone.

"But some people aren't even eating anything. They're just drinking," I said.

"That's what I call being sensible!" my portly boss explained. "Then they won't notice whether the food is any good or not."

The crabmeat salad was the second course and it went well; we even had enough to go around.

That night the dining room never looked more beautiful and glittering and everyone there seemed to be enjoying themselves immensely, especially the pretty and animated bride-to-be and her handsome fiancé, who was in medical school, destined to become a doctor like his father and Alice's father.

There was but one casualty: one lovely socialite drank too much and passed out at the table, her face falling flat in her food. She was carried out of the dining room and dumped onto one of the living room couches.

The main course was roast beef, and at one point, I heard my Aunt Bunny tell my mother, "We shouldn't be serving the meat like this. It's practically raw and not even cooked through!"

But Mrs. Richmond didn't agree. "Send it right in!" she said. "It's just right!"

I had to keep the fires in both the dining and living rooms going all evening, too, and towards the end of the party, as I stepped into the living room to see how that blaze was doing, I ran into Mr. Art

Gallery, who had evidently just puked into his hand. I rushed to get him a napkin, which he took, muttering, "My God, that cheap wine."

By midnight or thereabouts, the party was over, and Dr. Anderson came out to the kitchen to thank us all for "a splendid feast," and the dishes were mostly all washed and put away.

Mrs. Anderson was saying good night to my mother when she spotted me.

"Well, I must say, Andy, that you certainly look much more handsome in a white dinner jacket serving champagne than you do when delivering laundry on Taunton Point!"

43

I was always a bit unnerved by the local garbagemen who serviced the Manor for the summers I worked there. They might come any time to collect the garbage, but usually it was at night in an old, open-backed truck, and there were four of them: the father, Alvie Robinson, and three of his sons. They were clamdiggers or common laborers by day; and they were always unshaven and grungy in appearance. At first glance, the only way one could tell the difference between generations was in noticing that the old man usually wore a hat and had no teeth. They were all native Downeasters like me, but I had trouble communicating with them. I didn't trust them. They seemed like co-conspirators in some dark and dastardly plot; I didn't turn my back in their presence. They'd as soon kill me as anyone, I reasoned.

When I divulged my fears to Mrs. Richmond, she said, "Oh, Alvie and the boys are just poor, uneducated, and rather dim-witted, Andy. They probably suffer from some sort of brain damage aggravated by syphilis, rot gut drink, and inferior genes. They might look evil in the night, but in the light of day, they are just pathetic, poor, hangdog creatures, probably in need of vitamins and a good dusting of lice. Don't judge a man by his unfortunate appearance."

I wasn't so sure. The way that Alvie and the boys looked at me standing up in the back of their truck against the black of night while I handed them our garbage. They looked like wild-eyed beasts ready to lunge for my good boy's throat.

I tried always to be my chipper self anyhow, gaily lugging out the trash into the dreaded shadows of the garage. Alvie and the boys would be there lurking around in the dark.

"Here ya go, Alvie—with my compliments!"

Maybe that was it: my little wise-ass comments that I loved to tack on. I was just beginning to realize that many people didn't always appreciate my sense of humor.

Alvie, most often, wouldn't say anything. One of the boys would spit and usually in my direction. There was a conspiracy of silence and I did all the talking. My chattering to myself was like whistling in the dark.

"Here's an awful soggy bag, Alvie. Watch the bottom."

One of the boys would snort or grunt. They'd all usually be chewing something, or smoking. They wouldn't extend much of a hand. I'd have to do all the hoisting and most of the reaching up onto the truck.

Mrs. Richmond would like to know if you'll be back by Thursday? We've a full house all week and the garbage really piles up."

"Mebbe," said Alvie. Sometimes you could get an "ayuh" out of him, but usually it was only a "mebbe."

That might have been the week Alvie didn't come at all, and because he had no phone, Mrs. Richmond asked me, to my horror, to take the car and go find out where he and the boys were. She gave me his address which turned out to be an old, unpainted, double-story frame house near the center of the village. The yard was as littered as one might expect of a garbageman. When I arrived, I didn't see the truck, but I went to the door and knocked anyway. No one answered, so I opened it and peeked in.

"Anybody home?" I asked.

No one answered.

Then I saw Alvie. He was lying across three straight back kitchen chairs in front of an oil stove.

"Alvie?" I called.

"Yeah?" he finally responded, raising his toothless head a bit from the chair.

"I'm sorry to bother you, but Mrs. Richmond down at the Manor wanted to know what happened to you."

"Be down tonight," he said.

"You will?"

"Been sick."

"I'm sorry."

"O.K., be down tonight."

"Good. I'll have the garbage all ready."

"You do that."

That was the longest conversation I ever had with Alvie Robinson.

44

Some suppertimes when the leftover supply had dwindled or Miss Meyer just wanted to treat us, she would give me five dollars and tell me to take Ellen and Sally up to Apple Pie Heaven in Summer Harbor for our evening meal.

Apple Pie Heaven, owned and managed by Ramona Snook, got its name, of course, from its specialty: fresh, hot Maine apple pie made with Maine apples that were picked by Maine natives. That's how it was advertised on the menu; and Ramona would always add, "And my crust ain't from no Flako package!"

She also served hot dogs dressed up in all manner of clever disguises. "Everything You Can Do to a Dog, We Do," one sign out front proclaimed; and inside were hand-stenciled, colorful signs all over the place: TRY THE DOG OF THE DAY, A DOG IS MAN'S BEST MEAL, THE DOG DAYS OF SUMMER ARE HERE YEAR ROUND, and HOW MUCH IS THAT DOGGIE IN THE WINDOW? ASK YOUR WAITRESS!

As Ramona Snook would say, "My dogs is all-American and all meat, no matter how we dress 'em up. There's nothing Grade D served in this establishment, not while I'm tendin' grill."

There was always a colorful list of dog dishes on the menu: Kraut

Dogs, Franks à la King, Spaghetti Dogs, Mexicali Rose dogs, French Fried Frankfurters, Dog Biscuits, Downeast Dogs, and the like. Mrs. Snook thought of herself as quite the witty wag.

"My son Chip helps me with the specials," Ramona would always say, referring to her teenage, overweight, and effeminate boy who called her "Mummer" and whined a lot. He advertised his coin collection on little printed cards displayed on every table top in the Heaven. "Chip Snook, Numismatist, Coins Bought and Sold. Inquire Within."

"Inquire within where?" we once asked Ramona.

"In the kitchen. Chip's on the grill and he's getting to be a damn good *shot awdah* cook."

Anyway, the girls and I would go there for supper, play the jukebox, order our hot dog specials and apple pie, laugh and talk with Ramona, Chip, and the other customers.

Ramona was an attractive, buxom blonde in her mid-forties and always had her share of active suitors hanging around the Heaven, like Sherwood, the Coca Cola truck driver, who would sometimes let his battle of wits with Ramona go too far.

One time just as the girls and I had finished placing our orders and were playing some of the hits of the time: Claude King's "Wolverton Mountain," Eddie Hodges' "Bandit of My Dreams," and Ray Stevens' "Ahab the A-Rab" on the jukebox, Sherwood entered, at the end of his day's run, and it wasn't Coca Cola that he ordered over Ramona's counter.

"Say, Mona! You missed a good trip down to Jonesport with me today."

"Yeah? What was happenin' down there—bottom fall out of a bait barrel? Big herring catch? Lobster smack run ashore? Tide go out?"

"Nope, nothing that eventful. It was just a goddamn beautiful day, a glad-to-be-alive day, just made for you and me."

"Look, Sherwood, I'm awful busy here tonight. I'm one girl short, so I have to be on the grill with Chip."

"Jesus! You and Fairy Face on the grill together! What a cute picture that is! Do you think he'll be able to stand it with all that awful animal grease splattering?"

"Would you please refrain from talking so loud and referring to my son that way. He's a numatist, numismatist, you know. . .what's that word for coin collector?"

"Stupid!" said Sherwood. "Don't he know that it's better to spend coins than collect 'em?"

"God, Sherwood! Don't you have a hurry-up order of Coke to deliver over in New Brunswick some place?"

"Hey, you're all the time praising that Chippy boy of yours. He ain't no real coin collector. He's jes' an amateur with a couple of Indian Head pennies, a silver dollar worth a dollar ten, and some foreign coins that the sailors down to the Base give him for sweet favors!"

"That's it, Sherwood! You ain't being funny tonight. You're getting real narsty. Pay your bill and hit the road. I've had it with that type of talk from the likes of you!"

The girls and I looked at each other with amusement as did two sailors sitting at a table opposite.

"Yeah," said Sherwood, "you might have, but I haven't. I wanted you to go Downeast on the Coke truck with me today, but, no; you can't ever tear yourself away from your goddamn hot dogs and fuckin' flaky pies!"

"You had plenty to drink before you even come in here, didn't ya?" asked Ramona.

"Lissen, Mona. I'm gonna punch out Fairy Face and rob his coins, if you don't start payin' attention to me; and I don't care who knows it."

"You don't have to announce your intentions to the world, Sherwood. Your very appearance reveals your station in life: the last stop on the line—before crossing the border into Nowhere! Why don't you make it easier on all of us, and beat it!"

At this point, a traveling tourist entered the Heaven and asked the proprietress, "Pardon me, Miss. Is this the way to the National Park?"

"Ayuh! Go on down there and see the pine trees and caves. On a clear day, you might even see a walrus at play!"

"Thank you!"

"Don't mention it! That happens a dozen times a day. They just stick their heads in the door and never come in and buy. It's like they think I'm running an information booth."

Chip entered from the kitchen and immediately Sherwood threw one of Chip's cards off the counter into his face. "Get your christled coin cards out of my face, Chippy Boy!"

"Sherwood, I told ya to beat it, and I mean it!" Ramona hollered.

"Ah, but you don't really mean it, do ya honey? Ya know I'm jes' kiddin'."

"YOU'RE NOT KIDDIN' AND NEITHER AM I! You've put on enough of a show this afternoon. These people didn't come here to listen to you drown out the jukebox and ruin their meals with your crazy talk."

"Now, Mona, lemme jes test the validity of your hypothesis," Sherwood turned around on his counter stool to face the two young sailors and to one of them he called, "Hey, Specialist Fourth Class!"

"What do you want?" asked one of the young men.

"Were Mona and me in our discussion bothering you and your pal?"

"Nope. We could see you-all was nuts right off."

"YOU-ALL!? Texas boys, huh? Now I got it, Mona. You like these Texas boys comin' in here with those drawlin' accents."

"There's more to the competition than just an accent, Sherwood. And now it's time for you to say good-night to everybody."

Ramona came around the counter and took Sherwood forcibly by the arm and dragged him across the restaurant to the door.

"Hey, Mona! C'mon! I don't want to go yet. I wanna talk to the Texas boys!"

"You can come back when you've sobered up," she said, pushing him out the door.

"I'm sorry, kids," Ramona said to us. "I hope he didn't upset you. He gets this way when he's been drinking too much of his Coke. I hope to hell he goes right home to bed. Luckily, he lives close by. Say, can I get you some fresh-baked pie?"

"Yes, you certainly can," I said, relieved that Sherwood had finally driven away. "We also have to pick up some pies Miss Meyer ordered for the Manor."

"Oh, that's right," Ramona said. "You know, I used to bake pies and pastries for the Manor before they hired that old Mrs. Spurling, known all over for her flaky crust! Tell me, does she still wear that old beach towel over her head when in the process of bakin' biscuits? Jesus, I heard she'd have a regular shit fit if her popovers ever fell! Anyway, I notice the Manor still orders my pies every now and then."

"Your pies are delicious," I said.

"You're damn right!" Ramona said.

45

I enjoyed the daily run with the car as much as I enjoyed washing and waxing it, pretending it was mine. Actually, for the first three summers I drove it, *it was mine* in a real sense. No one else drove it or had the care of it; and that Olds 98 had excellent care in my hands. Except for the accidents.

One afternoon I had to drive Miss Meyer and a prominent guest, Mrs. Chittendon of New York City, to Mount Desert to have their hair done. While waiting for the ladies, who were in downtown Bar Harbor, I was to drive to this place the other side of town that made homemade pies, which I never thought were half as good as Ramona Snook's, but which Miss Meyer wanted to keep trying. On my way there, I made the mistake of proceeding down a very narrow one-way street the wrong way; and by the time I realized my error, a big square delivery van came barreling right for me with no sign of either slowing down or allowing me room, so I had to take the Olds up onto the sidewalk. The subsequent loud crunch and scrape was awful; and when I got out to survey the damage, I realized that the whole rocker panel on the passenger's side was bent under the car! My nerves at that point were all shot, I was scared; and in my suddenly panicked state, I backed the car hurriedly out onto the street, headed in the opposite direction; but as I did so, the same thing happened to the rocker panel on the driver's side!

I couldn't believe it; a skilled engineer couldn't have evened them up any better than I did. I was completely unnerved by this incident, for I had always been extremely careful with the car and proud of my unblemished driving record. I calmed down as best I could and drove slowly on to the pie place, where I picked up Miss Meyer's order, and went back to the hair dressing salon. Miss Meyer never paid any attention to the car, so I knew she wouldn't see anything wrong with the Olds. I knew, too, though, that I couldn't keep the accident a secret for long, because I had to take the car for service to Houston King's Esso station in Summer Harbor, and Mr. King would see the damage right off.

Soon after this first scrape, during Mrs. Richmond's August visit, I was told to get the car cleaned and ready for my other boss to drive to Bangor where she was planning to pick up by herself a close friend who was coming to stay at the Manor.

I cleaned the car inside and out, praying that Mrs. Richmond wouldn't look down and notice the missing rocker panels. But when I got in the car to back it out of the garage, I neglected to close the rear door on the driver's side tightly; and in backing up, I didn't bother to look over my shoulder, since I had done this so many times. I had the radio blaring with rock-'n'-roll music, being Mr. Cool, when, for some dumb reason, I must have thought I was already out of the garage, because I started turning the wheel. Suddenly, the door that was slightly ajar caught on the side of the garage and was ripped open. When I saw and heard what was happening, I reacted immediately. But instead of slamming on the brakes, I pushed down hard on the accelerator! There was a great wrenching of metal and a ripping of wood, as the car shot out through the garage door all right, but the rear car door was now flush with the front one and part of the garage door was wrecked.

Mrs. Richmond had just finished her bath and was upstairs in her room right over the garage getting ready for her trip when she heard the horrible noise from below. She clomped downstairs as fast as her three hundred pounds could carry her and stood there, in the back porch doorway, *stark naked*, holding her slip in front of her.

"MY GOD, ANDY! WAS THERE AN EARTHQUAKE? WHAT MADE THAT GODAWFUL NOISE? WHY, THE VERY FOUNDA-

TION OF THE HOUSE HAS BEEN SHAKEN!"

I was practically in tears and blubbering as I faced my nude boss. "I caught the car door on the side of the garage when I was backing out!" I wailed. I thought I was going to break down completely in front of her, I was so upset and ashamed.

"OH, MY GOD! OH, MY GOD!" she kept exclaiming, while clutching and re-clutching her slip about her. "Well, of course, this will have to be reported. I'll call Houston immediately. And, Andy, you'll have to pay for this!"

Mr. King arrived right away and pried the front door open, so that the car could be driven. The sight of the crushed rear door on top of the bent-in rocker panels sickened me.

"Ya shouldn't have closed the rear door like ya did," Houston told me. "'Cause when ya did, ya snapped the hinges. Now, the whole door will probably have to be replaced."

I felt awful for the rest of the day, but even though Mrs. Richmond threatened to dock my pay, my pay check never showed it.

As it turned out, I wasn't the only one who had accidents with the Olds that summer. One night we ran out of rainbow sherbet right in the middle of dinner and Miss Meyer sent Ellen on a rush excursion up to Guilford's Store. In her hurry, trying to navigate the winding narrow drive along the shore at an unsafe speed, she swerved to avoid a pick-up truck coming around a sharp corner right in the middle of the road.

On her way into the kitchen after the trip, Ellen paused nervously by my dishpan to say, "Andy, when you get a chance, go take a look at the car out back and then you'll see why I'm still shaking and so late."

Intrigued, I did so right away; and there back of the garage was the beautiful silver Olds with its rocker panels bent under, a broken rear door with a scrape along the side, and now with the rear fender on the passenger's side completely smashed in.

"What happened?" I asked Ellen once I got the chance.

"Oh, I bounced off a couple of trees alongside the road. There was nothing I could do to avoid a head-on collision with this stupid pick-up. But what am I going to tell Mrs. Richmond? I don't dare face her."

Ellen was lucky that night. Mrs. Richmond was well into her cups by then and in wonderful high spirits. When told of the latest accident, she laughed it off, saying, "My God, you kids and driving machines were never meant to be! We'll see about this latest crack-up come the dawn. Don't cry, Ellen, dear. We got the sherbet just in time and our diners will never know at what expense!"

There was one more mishap involving the Olds that summer, and it occurred one day on my afternoon off. That morning I was telling Mrs. Richmond how I was going that night with my parents to see *The Children's Hour* with Shirley MacLaine and Audrey Hepburn. Mr. Fitzpatrick from next door had written the screenplay from Lillian Hellman's famous play. Mrs. Richmond told me how she had seen the original play on Broadway and had become a Hellman fan because of it. She had also enjoyed the first movie version called *These Three*.

"If I can get away, I might join you at the movies," said Mrs. Richmond.

That night, as I was crossing Main Street in Ellsworth with my parents, headed towards the Grand Theatre, I heard this loud crash from up the street. To our shock—and then amusement—we looked in the direction of the crash to see the Olds, with Mrs. Richmond at the wheel, wrapped around a parking meter. I ran up to her, laughing. The car was half on the sidewalk and half on the street. Mrs. Richmond was laughing, too.

"Well, that does it, Andy! This goddamn car was evidently engineered for self-destruction! Or maybe it was trying to tell me it was time for a trade-in! I guess I failed to judge my parking correctly. . . Damn it all, I hope to hell I haven't punctured the radiator! Don't stray far after the film—I may need a tow!"

46

The most exciting guest of 1962 arrived in the night in a drenching downpour. It must have been around nine o'clock or so, for I know it was after dinner when a taxi pulled under the *porte-cochère*. Ellen, Sally, and I were sitting around the kitchen table with Mrs. Richmond and Miss Meyer trading yarns.

"Now, who's gonna git up and see who our surprise guest might be?" asked Mrs. Richmond. "Anybody especially curious?"

"I'll go," I said.

"We'll go, too," said Ellen and Sally.

"You're all such obedient and willing servants," said Mrs. Richmond.

Ultimately, we all went, arriving in the foyer just as a knock came at the door. There in the golden light of the carriage lamps, standing against the stormy black night, was a tall, gray-haired, handsome man of middle age clad only in wrinkled trousers, a tee-shirt, and sneakers.

"Might you ladies have room for some silly summer sailors washed ashore?" he asked with an infectious grin.

"Why, yes, we have a room," Mrs. Richmond said with a chuckle. She always delighted over such novel scenes as this. "Come on in an dry off your pinfeathers. You look like a drowned rat!"

"I feel like one, ma'am," he said. "Let me first inform my wife of the good news. Please excuse me."

He stepped down to the car, opened the rear door, and said, "All ashore, sweetheart! C'mon." We could hear her mumble from inside something unintelligible and his saying, "I know, I know, it's O.K., c'mon."

We watched as he lifted her out of the car. It was a strange sight, for she had on a nice light coat and looked very dressed up, but in a rather disheveled state. She was wearing sunglasses that were askew and her hair was a mess. She was evidently too sick or tired to walk by herself, so he carried her up the stairs, past us, into the Manor's lobby. Some of the other guests were sitting around talking and reading by the fireplace and they looked up as the man carried his wife upstairs to the Number Eight or Violet Room, our only room with a double bed, and it was a brass bed. All they had for luggage was her purse, which was large and fancy looking. I was to show them the way to the room.

Just as I was starting upstairs, I overheard the cab driver, evidently all upset, saying, "This has been the goddamnedest trip! I've driven these two fools all over Kingdom Come. Bangor to Bar Harbor, Bar Harbor to here! I've got to call in. Can I use your phone?"

"Certainly," said Mrs. Richmond. "It's right here in the hall."

After the frustrated driver had made his call, most of which the guests could hear out in the living room, and driven away; and the sick-looking lady had been put to bed with some hot tea, the man who introduced himself as Captain Bartholomew Bar from Long Island came downstairs and joined us in the kitchen for a drink and something to eat.

"My wife and I are lucky to be alive, let me tell you," he said.

"It has been quite a storm," said Mrs. Richmond, "and not exactly fit weather in which to go for a sail."

"So we found out. My boat will have to be repaired. I've wanted to cruise the Maine Coast all my life. We started out from Long Island about a week ago, but I guess we simply didn't consider that there'd be any fog as bad as this. It was our dream trip, you see, and there was no room for fog in our dream. I hope the boat isn't damaged too badly."

"How come your wife is all dressed up and you're not?" asked

Sally.

"Oh, as sick as she was, she didn't want to show up any place in her wet sea togs. She's funny like that—has to always make a good appearance."

"She looked really nice being lugged in like that," said Ellen to me down at the further end of the kitchen.

"Where did ya pick up the Bangor taxi?" asked Mrs. Richmond.

"We called for it, because we thought we were going there at first," said Captain Bar. "And then, we drove over to Bar Harbor because my wife has relatives there."

"What do you do when you're not sailing a boat?" asked Mrs. Richmond.

"I'm a doctor."

"Do you have a specialty or are you a general practitioner?"

"G.P., one of a dying breed."

He talked and talked for over an hour on his theories of medicine, politics, and sailing; and ate ravenously of every snack we placed before him. Mrs. Richmond later pronounced him a charming rogue, but Miss Meyer was not quite as impressed.

"Errr. . .did he say anything about a deposit, or paying in advance?"

"No, Jean," said Mrs. Richmond. "But he gave Andy a good tip for taking the night caps upstairs. That's some indication, I'd say, that he's on the up-and-up."

But great mystery fan that she was and good judge of character, too, Miss Meyer remained suspicious of our latest, most offbeat guest and his soggy companion.

"Errr. . .even if they were forced to come ashore from their boat, which they couldn't have been if she had time to get all dolled up, wouldn't there have been some local authorities accompanying them? And I'm sure, from the whiff I caught of her, that she was more drunk than sick. The whole thing seems a bit fishy to me."

It turned out to be not just an overnight stay, either, but a several day affair. Each day, Captain Bar would make telephone calls and busy himself about the hotel. He said that he was in constant contact with the boat yard who had charge of repairing his craft and that he and his wife had friends in the area who would be dropping by to bring clothes and some of their stuff. Cars did come for him, and one time an old truck. We watched Captain Bar in his tee shirt come and go;

he did seem to know a number of different people and many of them seemed a bit strange in dress and demeanor. One or two even looked a mite sinister. "Who was Captain Bar really?" we all began to ask ourselves.

In preference to the girls, who were busy enough downstairs all the time in August, I was commissioned to wait exclusively on the Bars since they never joined the other guests in the dining room for meals. I had to take trays up, and their orders were always rather curious: hardly any food, mostly just liquid refreshment. One time, Captain Bar asked me for a six pack of beer and a bottle of cooking vanilla. And that was only a day before he returned from one of his excursions with "friends" that he brought back with him a whole case of vanilla and two full cases of beer which he wanted kept on ice downstairs.

"What's going on upstairs, Andy?" Mrs. Richmond asked.

"They keep the room dark all the time with the shades down. There are things strewn all over. Mrs. Bar is never dressed and always seems very groggy and sick."

"I would think she would if she's guzzling vanilla and beer. Sounds like a real skid row bum to me. The doctor's prescription sounds a little low-class. Something's going on up there, that's for sure. Who usually tips ya?"

"Captain Bar, if he's there. He gets his wife's purse and takes out a dollar or two. She's paid me a couple of times, but she's so out of it, she has trouble telling the difference between a penny and a half-dollar."

"I'm getting worried," my boss said. "I better check into how long they plan on staying. We can't have drunks like that here."

A couple of days later, returning from the rocks in my tee shirt and swimming trunks, I saw two State Police cars parked ever so clandestinely behind the cedar hedge surrounding the back parking lot. I wondered what was going on, as I rushed up the back porch stairs into the hotel.

"What's up?" I asked Miss Meyer who was seated by the kitchen windows puffing on her cigarette more nervously than usual.

"Errr. . .they've come for Captain Bar," she said. "Madella has taken the police upstairs to his room; they should be bringing them down any minute now."

"Why? What did he do?"

"Errr. . .he's an escaped convict, Andy. I'm not sure of his crime."

"Wow! I wonder if he's a murderer?"

"Errr. . .I hope not. Let's hope our guests don't find out about this whole awful incident. I'm afraid Mr. Titcomb did see the police."

"Most of 'em are out for the afternoon, aren't they?"

"Errr. . .yes, thank God."

"Do you think he has a gun? What if he tries to shoot his way out?"

"Errr. . .let's hope he just goes quickly and quietly. I knew there was something wrong with him the night he came; but, of course, Madella likened him to another Errol Flynn, some kind of delightful buccaneer, the type of man she likes."

"How did you find out about him?"

"Errr. . .after I overheard some of his very suspicious telephone calls, I called the State Police and he matched their description of this escaped fellow from Thomaston State Prison. The police have been very nice. I'm certainly glad they parked their cars out back."

Sadly, there was no dramatic shoot-out with lots of screaming and carrying on. Captain Bar was apprehended without a struggle or any kind of ugly scene. He went quieter than he came. Mrs. Richmond reported that when he opened the door and saw the police standing there, he simply grinned at them and said, "Well, the party's over, Mrs. Bar! Put yer panties on and pick up yer vanilla bottles. Will you boys just be patient a moment while the lady gets dressed?"

"We can wait for the lady, but we want you out here in the hall right now!" the sergeant in command said.

"I still say Captain Bar was a fine gentleman. . .and a consummate liar!" Mrs. Richmond said later. "He even thanked me most graciously for the fine accommodations and services. When I asked him how come he chose our particular hostelry, he said he always went first-class."

"Errr. . .but did he offer to pay at least some of the bill he ran up?"

"No, Jean; I'm afraid we'll have to write that one off as a tax loss, or take all of Andy's tips in partial payment."

"Who was *she*?" I asked.

"Why, it seems that Mrs. Bar was some socialite from Mount Desert who had known Captain Bar from his pre-prison days. When he jumped the hoosegow, he got in touch with her and she financed their joy ride down the coast to here. That explains the difference in attire, you see. I guess she had some money; and we might be able to get her to foot some of the bill; but she sure had her drinking and emotional problems. The police said they were going to try and get her family to put her some place where she'd get dried out."

"Errr. . .and what about aiding and abetting a fugitive? They ought to put her some place for that, too."

"Then he wasn't a real doctor?" I asked.

"No, of course not. His real name is Arthur Littlefield from some small Maine town upcountry, sort of a second-rate Great Impostor. All his life he's evidently been in the habit of duping others and pulling fast ones, and with his good looks and winning personality, he has been able to get away with it. He was in for forgery and armed robbery, poor soul."

"Errr. . .why, Madella, do you always feel so sorry for tramps like that?"

"I like tramps, Jean. I guess I'm a tramp at heart. There but for the grace of God go all of us, ya know. Daring, creative tramps like Mr. Littlefield know instinctively how short-lived will be their glorious schemes, but they make the best of 'em anyhow! And I say, that's the spirit! It'll make a nice little vignette for that book of mine I'm gonna write someday."

"Ha!" exclaimed Miss Meyer.

"Why, Jean, ya forgot to clear ya throat!" said Mrs. Richmond.

47

Even though I grew up with lobster fishermen in my family and neighborhood, and in a town with three lobster pounds where relatives worked, lobster feeds were still special occasions. Once or twice a summer, we might have lobster salad or boiled lobster; but in my family we were more likely to go buy a lobster roll at a take-out restaurant.

We did, however, do a lot of clamming; and a mess of clams steaming in a wash tub on the back of the kitchen stove was a common sight. We had fried clams, steamed clams, clam fritters, clam chowders, and clam casseroles. There was also plenty of flounder, halibut, salt fish, and "wrinkles," or sea snails which we'd gather by the potful at low tide for steaming and eating with melted butter and vinegar.

My paternal step-grandfather, Fat Moon, was a part-time lobsterman; but I don't remember his supplying us with any lobster. He brought us mackerel, clams, and wrinkles. Of course, because of our local connections, we could get lobster much cheaper than the tourists and people buying from commercial outlets.

But lobster and the Maine Coast are synonymous to most people from away and they expect lobster on the menu, even if it's only a small family diner on Route One.

When they first opened the Manor, Mrs. Richmond and Miss Miller decided to make Friday night lobster night to satisfy both the demand for that popular crustacean and because of the Catholic Church, which then required that Catholics eat fish (abstain from eating red meat) on Friday. For those few guests who didn't like lobster, and weren't Catholic, we offered broiled lamb chops, creamed cauliflower, and string beans; but always for the great majority we performed the great Downeast lobster dinner ritual. Since I was in charge of cooking and preparing the lobsters, Friday was my busiest day.

To accompany the lobster, we served tossed salad and prepared Crescent dinner rolls with the help of Pillsbury. The first course was always clam or fish chowder and for dessert we always served homemade lemon meringue pie.

After my first three years in the kitchen, and especially after Mrs. Spurling, the pastry chef, had left, my bosses let me try and make the pies all by myself, which was quite the ordeal. And for some reason, every time I tried, two or three of the five or six pies needed every Friday night would be perfect with the rest less than perfect. I could never figure out why since I tried to follow the recipe the same way each time. At least one, however, would always turn out so watery that we couldn't even serve it, so it became the help's dessert.

In the first three summers I was at the Manor, we still served gold glass fingerbowls with lemon in them for use during lobster dinners, but the last summers we used Wash 'n' Dri wet naps.

One of the main compensations of being the lobster chef and kitchen boy was that on Saturday mornings I got to pick the meat out of the leftover lobsters and any tail meat that was tainted by the green of the tamale I got to eat. The rest of the meat was packed in plastic containers, put back on the ice to be used later for salads, chowders, and sandwiches.

"Lobster night's our only real nod to Maine cuisine," said Mrs. Richmond. "We tried boiled dinners once and the plates came back full. Indian pudding laid a bomb, too. New England clam chowder is fairly popular, but no more so than Manhattan. So, we've put our *Yankee Cook Book* back on the shelf and are sticking with *Good Housekeeping* and *The Joy of Cooking*."

Despite the splitting of the claws and tail and the inclusion at every place setting of picks and nutcrackers, a number of our guests never could get all the meat out of the joints, claws, and bodies. Also, some were never sure of what to eat and too spleeny to try. So, they would send back their lobsters to me to have the meat removed for them.

Everyone seemed to have a lobster tale they wanted to share, so many Friday nights, guests would come back to the kitchen to chat with me and my bossladies about the popular scavengers of the ocean.

"Andy, my dear!" Mr. or Mrs. Gushworthy would exclaim. "Now, just HOW did you manage to make that lobster I just ate THE VERY BEST I've ever eaten anywhere? There must be some secret that only a Maine man like yourself would know. Tell me, how is it done? What's the secret?"

"Well, you boil some water. I use sea water and perhaps that's the secret; and then I throw in the lobsters and cook them for twenty minutes and then I take 'em out."

"You use seaweed, too, don't you?"

"Yes, but I'm not sure if that makes them any more sweet."

"Oh, it must! My dear boy, I've eaten lobster the world over and yours is by far the most succulent, the most tender, the sweetest meat I've ever sunk my dentures into! Positively out of this world! Say, where do you get your sea water?"

"Ah, the ocean. . .down in front of the Manor. . .off the rocks. . ."

"Oh, the water from this bay right here? Well, you must select the perfect pool where the minerals are most choice!"

"Well, I don't exactly use a Geiger Counter."

"Are you sure you don't have a built-in detector? Well, the only other time I remember having a lobster that tasted this good was during World War II when we all took our rationing stamps into New York City one weekend, and there was this plain little restaurant that was just like someone's kitchen where they specialized in seafood. . .and my God, was that lobster ever good that they served there. Of course, we were all four sheets to the wind, expecting the Nazis to shell Times Square at any moment, but the taste of that lobster that night sobered me right up. Just like tonight, I wasn't planning on having lobster. I thought I'd have the chops, but, no, this is our last night here, and before I leave Maine, I've just got to have lobster, of course, so I did, and, God, am I glad! And we thank you, sir, for helping us make our week Downeast just about perfect!"

Of course, we often offered lobster salad on lobster night, too; and that meant a number of trips to Mrs. Bishop's; and more and more that meant that Essie would prepare the salad and be there waiting for me when I came to pick it up. We'd still joke with each other, but there was a big difference. She wouldn't be touching me anymore and she wouldn't be scantily dressed. One time, she said, "I'm a good wife and mother, An-day—ain't that something?"

"I think it's great, Ess-ay." And I did, even while wondering if we would ever have sex again.

48

Every night after we had our supper in the back dining room, and while the girls were busy getting ready for the guests' dinner, I had the job of going through the house and turning on selected hall, lobby, and living room lights. Miss Meyer always wanted the place lit up even if we only had one guest in the hotel. At dusk, she'd often stroll up the front driveway and look back at her hotel to see if it looked romantic and inviting enough to anyone who might be driving by. Mrs. Richmond might have been the extravagant one with food and drink, but Miss Meyer was extravagant with lights. However, as she'd say, "Errr. . .besides the view, our lights on at night are our best advertisement. Lights are welcoming."

If it were a cool evening, I'd also be expected to light the living room fire; and after the lamps were lit and the fire was crackling, I'd have to select the dinner music for the record player. The old dinner gong was shaped like a miniature xylophone, and the waitresses had charge of ringing that. I only got to play it occasionally. The girls used to play the old "NBC Theme" on it.

Some evenings, when we weren't too busy, and when I felt like it and no guests were around, I liked to pause a while in the living room and glance through the handsome, leather-bound guest book that had been kept from when the hotel first opened after World War II. The book was kept open to the present season on the desk in the lobby, always with a pot of fresh flowers and a little brass desk lamp to either side of it. The names of the mostly northeast towns that our guests came from intrigued me, for they were snobby-sounding places like New Canaan, Greenwich, Westport, Lake Success, Tuxedo Park, Bryn Mawr, Old Saybrook, Marblehead, Scarsdale, Brookline, Wellesley Hills, Weston, Newton, Basking Ridge, and Rye. I wondered what they looked like and what living there was like. Would they be much like Bar Harbor or Northeast Harbor? Cape Elizabeth, Orono, or Falmouth Foreside?

If I were alone, I'd sometimes brazenly pretend that I was a guest and after getting a nice fire going with some of the lamps turned on, and with instrumental music playing, I'd flop myself down in one of the big overstuffed chairs in front of the fireplace and flick through some of the big picture or art books placed about the coffee and side tables. These were books on Pavlova, James Thurber's dogs, *New Yorker* cartoons, World War II, the ballet and theater, fancy homes and gardens, the treasures of the Louvre and other museums, antiques, yachts, photography, and old movies.

If I were a bit late in returning to my kitchen duties after such pleasant reveries, Ellen and Sally would come looking for me.

We'd act out different roles. I enjoyed portraying a stuffy guest with a British accent.

Sally would locate me in the living room and start in: "An-day, hon-ay! We is waitin' fo' you out in the kitchen so's we can get the melons all balled for our luscious fruit compo! We jes can't ball right without ya!"

"*An-day*?" I'd ask. "Now, who might this *An-day* be? I'm afraid you kitchen sluts are directing your attentions to the wrong personage. I'm Terence X. Crombar, the Twelfth, here on vacation with Mater and Pater making a grand tour of the Eastern Provinces. We take the waters each day at Acadia, but I must say Maine is just too provincial. Tell me, my dear, do these teeny weeny shacks you people scrounge around in have running water? Have you ever used a flush? Tell me, for I'm simply dying to know, but don't come too close! I'm planning on doing some deep sociological research for a paper on the gross inferiority of the Maine local yokel, due to casual inbreeding, for my rural landscape course at Har-vard."

"Well, Mr. Crowbar. . ." said Sally.

"*CROMBAR*! Peasant wench!"

"Oh, I do so humbly beg yo' pardon, MR. *SHITHEAD*! Would you please consider stepping out into the lowly confines of our vast culinary laboratories? We need your highly trained expertise on some tricky melons that have to be balled and then deliciously combined with the balls of other hairy fruits and their attendant juices thereof and forthwith and notwithstanding."

"Pretty please, MR. CROWBAR DARLING," said Ellen. "We woefully ignorant Downeasters do desire so to know how with only the know-how you SUPERIOR, INTELLIGENT FOLK FROM AWAY possess. We hunger for you to SHOW AND TELL."

"Yeah," said Sal. "C'mon quickly now, your liege, before the goddamn melons rot!"

"Game's over, eh?"

"You said it, Kitchen Boy! It's almost showtime!"

There were, however, many other little games which we kept up even through the serving of meals. I loved trying to make the girls break up as they left the butler's pantry with their loaded trays about to pass through the swinging door into the dining room. It delighted me to see them about to burst and be saying, "For God's sake, Andy! Stop it, you fool!"

Most of our little games were necessarily verbal with plenty of sexual innuendo. For instance, one day I told Ellen she should be more careful about using the common expression "beat it" when talking around males.

"Why?" she asked.

"Because it might turn them on and prove embarrassing. It has a certain connotation for most males, but not for many females."

"Well, can I get in on the BIG MALE SECRET so I won't embarrass any little boys?"

"I don't see why not. Haven't you ever heard of a boy beating off?"

"Ah, no. . .I don't think so. Does it have to do with fighting?"

"In a way, you might say it has to do with fighting with oneself. You know, when a male gets excited and he has to do something about it or go crazy and no one else is around to help him out of his predicament. . ."

"Oh, Andy! That's so disgusting! You can be so filthy! I think you made that up. You see sex in everything."

"Well, when you get beyond sixteen, maybe you will, too."

That day she marched away; but that night when I was busy whipping the cream for the dessert, and while the girls were busy serving the main course, Ellen came out into the kitchen with a big grin on her pretty face, leaned over me very seductively, and said in a very husky voice, "Beat it, An-day! C'mon, baby, whip that cream!"

"Beat it!" became one of our running jokes for the rest of the summer, along with other favorite expressions such as: "Eat a root!" and Mrs. Richmondisms like "Ya better slick up, kid!"

I'd drop by the girls' room when they were playing records, reading women's magazines, or primping. I loved to hear Ellen do her imitations of Brenda Lee singing "That's All Ya Gotta Do" or Theresa Brewer singing "A Sweet Old-Fashioned Girl." She'd make her voice sweet and soft-sounding at first, like those artists, and then suddenly switch to a gravelly shriek, a wonderful metamorphosis that I found insanely funny.

Outside their door in the attic, there was a collection of fancy old slop jars which were stored there. I used to accuse the girls of using them when they were too lazy to go downstairs to the bathroom, and they'd scream back, "What if we do, An-day? It's none of your business, Coastal Boy! So, BEAT IT, baby! Yeah, EAT A ROOT AND BEAT IT!"

Ellen and Sally were very willing and enthusiastic students of my continuous summer course in impromptu craziness and world absurdity, anxious to participate in all manner of off hour adventures in and around the Manor and environs. They loved the late night swims in the pool and we went even more often than I had with Morgan and Lillie. We also continued to peek into the summer people's windows, especially when they were having parties either at the yacht club or somebody's cottage. We spied on the hotel guests and our boss ladies. We played games and read many books which we would avidly discuss with each other. On rainy or foggy afternoons, we stayed mostly up in our attic rooms, resting and fooling around.

One such afternoon I was lying on my bed reading to records like "Somebody Nobody Wants," Roy Orbison's "Candy Man," and Ricky Nelson's "Poor Little Fool," sipping on a Coke, when I heard the girls coming up the stairs. As usual, they would pause in my doorway smirking at me in their shiny white uniforms and inquire, "Whatcha doin', An-day, Hon-ay?"

"Oh, re-reading my favorite passages from *Lady Chatterly's Lover.*"

"What's that?"

"Come in a little closer, girls, and I'll read you a few of the best parts."

They giggled and piled onto my bed on top of me with these oranges they were eating.

"Oh, look at the cover—a sex book!" said Sally. "I can hardly wait! Is this as good as that one you gave us about the seventy-two positions?"

"Better. This is real art."

"Yummy," said Ellen. "I only hope it's as juicy as these oranges."

"What's the story about, An-day, de-ah?" asked Sally, who often made fun of me by affecting a pronounced Downeast accent, this time by dripping orange juice all over me and my bed.

"Must you be so messy?" I asked.

"I'm an earth goddess, An-day. I just can't help it. Juice flows from every pore, and in every season. With me, it's always planting time."

"C'mon, Andy, you promised to tell us the story," cooed Ellen in my ear.

"Well, you might say it's basically the story of John Thomas and Lady Jane."

"And who might they be, O great storyteller? The main characters?"

"In a way. John Thomas is the name the hero gives to his thing, you know, his main sex organ."

"Omigod!" said Sally. "Andy, here you go again! This is just a bit too raunchy for clean cut inland girls like us! DO GO ON. . ."

". . .and Lady Jane is the name given to the heroine's comparable body part. The section I wanted to read to you was this part where she winds these flowers around John Thomas. It's a riot."

"Would you rather we brought you flowers, instead of oranges, Andy?" asked Ellen.

"Might be nice, as long as they aren't too prickly," I said.

"Prickly! Very funny, you dirty-minded college boy!" said Sal.

Needless to say, I became very excited reading such passages from D.H. Lawrence while the girls were piled on top of me or lying beside me in my bed, their tight white uniforms straining against the contours of their firm, sexy, young female forms while the rain pelted against the roof and window. I tried to arrange for as many sequels to this scene as possible.

Somehow, I thought that maybe I might be able to turn one of them into another Essie; but I didn't seem to be able to. We'd only go so far physically with each other. Also, the girls were always together; I could never be alone with either of them.

I'd holler at them passing by in the hall. "Girls! I've got a new book here!"

"Sorry, Andy. We're just reading the Bible and *Good Housekeeping* these days!"

"Yes, preparing ourselves for saintly womanhood, not for those frightening college boy fraternity parties."

They'd tee-hee down the hall, and I would return to my books, records, and fantasies.

There was a point on Granite Neck about a mile's walk from the Manor called Swanson Point, named for a Mr. Swanson who was one of the early settlers who had helped design the summer colony and some of the houses. From this point, where there was a granite bench erected in memory of Mr. Swanson, paths ran through the woods alongside the cliffs and ocean. Ellen and Sally often liked to walk down to Swanson Point at night after work and sit on the stone bench and sing duets into the night and roar of the ocean.

Sometimes we made it a trio, and one night there was a wild storm and all three of us walked down to the point in it and watched the ocean surf, which was spectacular. It was very dark and windy, and yet we could make out the white of the breakers. The rain soaked us within minutes, but we loved it. We laughed and hollered and whooped and ran in it until we reached the point where we found the tide just coming in and the surf bashing the ledges of the headlands. In the pitch dark, clinging onto each other, we ventured out onto the slippery ledges, where, with the break of each wave, a foot of water would rush up and swirl about our legs. The pull of the icy sea water was terrific and would drag us out deeper along the ledge. We screamed and laughed, loving it because of the shock and danger; but ultimately coming to the realization, particularly after one mighty wave which almost carried us under, of the foolhardiness of our thrill-seeking and we retired, numb from the cold water, from the outer ledges to the shore's edge.

Walking back to the hotel, we traded horrifying ghost, murder, and UFO stories and I raced about in the dark trying to grab at the girls and make them shriek. In turn, they would grab at me and poke me until I screamed.

Back at the Manor and into dry clothes, we'd sit around the kitchen with cups of cocoa and marshmallows analyzing our exciting venture into the dark of night and the eye of the storm, almost becoming one with the ocean.

"Why does the ocean exert such an influence over us all?" Ellen asked seriously. "It always excites me so. I love to be near it, in it, to stand and watch it, continuously changing, sloshing about."

"It's our primeval mother," I said.

"Huh?" asked Sal. "Our mother? Who's Dad?"

"God, I guess," I said. "Unless God's the Sun. Anyway, we had to come from the sea originally. Every form of life did."

"You're a form of life, all right, An-day," said Sal.

"Our ancestors were fish, and then through the process of evolution, one of them, a mutation, crawled out of the ocean and started walking around on land, breathing. That's what it said in *The Immense Journey* by Loren Eisley, anyway."

"Maybe your ancestors were fish, An-day," said Sal, "but I still prefer to think of mine as monkeys and apes."

"Well, they're certainly relatives."

"Hey, watch whatcha callin' my relatives, Fish Face!"

"Yeah, Barnacle Head!" chimed in Ellen.

"Sea worm!"

"I thought you wanted to know about evolution," I said.

"We don't want to know about evolution," said Sal. "We want to know about life!"

49

Most Maine people, even if they live on the ocean, if they can afford it, have a camp on a pond or lake in the woods, not just for the summer but also for the hunting season in November and for ice fishing trips in the winter. We were too poor to own such a place, but our friends and relatives were always very generous in inviting us to their camps; and especially summers we visited as often as possible.

During my summers at Frenchman's Bay Manor, I'd often spend my evenings off with my parents at my Cousin Merle's camp at Molasses Pond, or my father's boss's elaborate camp at Flanders Pond, or with our close friends the Barclays, Ellen's parents, at their camp at Beech Hill Pond in Otis, north of Ellsworth. The Barclays lived in Bangor where Albert Barclay ran a television station. Both Albert and his wife Anita, whom we called "Neeta," had grown up in Taunton Ferry with my parents. Albert's father was a legendary engineer on the Maine Central steamboats on which my father had worked when he was young. My father and Albert always went hunting together, so it was great fun being with them and hearing all the stories from the colorful steamboat days on Frenchman's Bay, as well as amusing hunting and fishing tales, and yarns of our parents' growing up times.

The Barclays' son Russell was my age and one of my best pals.

There were pictures of us in the same crib together. I enjoyed visiting the Barclays' camp chiefly because of him and our adventures together. There were also two younger girls in the family named Jody and Janie, who were approximately ten years younger than Ellen and Russell. "We've got two families actually," Neeta would say.

The Barclays' camp was the last one off a private dirt road at the southern end of the pond. The road was closed to the public by an iron gate erected by the half-dozen families who lived there and who wanted to keep interlopers from using their property to get to the water or beach. To open the gate, I had to get out of our car and run down to the camp to get the key to the padlock from either Neeta or Albert.

"We're here!" I'd announce, upon entering the side door by the camp's kitchen area.

"Well, let the good times roll," Neeta would say. "Want the key, or do you want to keep Frank and Eleanor out there for a while?"

"I guess I'd better get the key this time," I said.

"Hurry up, the water's still nice and warm for a swim," she said.

I loved the Barclays and our occasional get-togethers, mostly at their camp in the summers and at our house for Thanksgiving. They were solidly middle-class, however, and we were not; and this bothered me some. They had a 1959 red-and-white Oldsmobile with lots of glass, fins, and sporty upholstery, while we had the '51 Mercury. They had all the latest gadgets and good clothes. We didn't. I was still wearing hand-me-downs from a summer boy in New Jersey.

There was a private sand beach near their camp and it was a wonderful place to swim and sunbathe. While I enjoyed practically a daily swim down off Granite Neck, swimming in the frigid ocean water wasn't as satisfactory as in Beech Hill Pond where I could paddle around for hours and it was wonderful.

Russell and I would swim way out in the pond to this raft that someone had set up and we'd dive off, fool around, or just lie there in the waning sunlight, talking and laughing. Afterwards, we'd swim into shore and hold mudfights with each other, slinging handfuls of wet sand at each other, trying to make each other yowl from the sting.

The Barclays also owned a motorboat in which Russell and I went fishing, trawling, and waterskiing. We'd also just ride around the pond before it got too dark, waving at people outside on their camp porches. There was a girl named Della Brown with whom Russell was in love.

Her family owned a camp up the pond, and Russell loved to go by her place and yell to her. She went to Ellsworth High School and Russell tried to impress her with his college boy sophistication.

There was also this young fellow who lived nearby named Percy Guptill, and Russell described Percy as "being a little slow." Percy would always be rowing back and forth near the Barclays' wharf, and Russell would often engage Percy in some banter.

"Hey, Percy, where ya bound?"

"Oh, up and around the bend," Percy would answer.

"Well, don't go around the bend too far," Russell would say. "There are rapids up there, ya know."

"Rapids?"

"Oh, yes. When the current changes, and it can change fast, it gets mighty treacherous with them rapids. Suck ya right in."

"Don't 'member no rapids."

"Well, Percy, ya gotta have a keen eye. Gotta be sharp and on the lookout. Keep ya eyeballs peeled."

"O.K., I'll be careful."

"Ya better, Percy. We wouldn't wanta lose ya!"

As Percy rowed away from us, looking as dumbfounded and nervous as ever, Russell and I would laugh our heads off, feeling superior to poor stupid Percy.

It was great fun to be with Russell even if we were just driving up to the Otis General Store to get some gas for the boat.

Russell would jump into his father's fancy Olds. He would pump the accelerator a few times before turning on the ignition. We both loved the way some Maine people said "exhilarator" for "accelerator."

"Gotta pump the *exhilarator*, An-day! Got to loosen 'er up!" he'd say with a great grin, mocking the way native Mainiacs talked. "Gotta clean out the lines!"

We'd back up with the dust of the road flying. "Got to tromp down on the unit!" Russell would say, as we raced up to the store. "Somebody might get there before us!"

As twenty-year-old college boys, everything and everybody made us laugh when we were together, like the old-timer who ran the Otis General Store.

"Wha'd you boys like?" he'd ask.

"You couldn't supply it," Russell said. "But, for now, we'd like to have some of your finest gasoline."

"Well, how much?"

"About a canful, I'd say, wouldn't you, An-day?"

"Just about."

"Well, yep. That's what we'll have then, by jay-sus! A good-sized canful."

"Christ, boys, we don't measure the goddamn gas by the canful around here. How about two gallons?"

"Well," said Russell, as if giving the matter great consideration, "guess maybe that'll have to do. Can you get both of them gallons in my can?"

"Well, tell ya what I'll do," the old-timer said. "What I can't git in the can, I'll shove up ya ass, O.K.?"

"Better make that Andy's ass," Russell said. "He's more regular while I take high-test."

"I'd say you go a long ways on hot air."

"You know it, Pop. I never have to inflate my tires."

After boating and swimming some more, we'd be called in for supper which was most always beans, hot dogs, brown bread, cole-slaw, rolls, and some kind of homemade pie or cake with ice cream for dessert.

While our folks sat around gabbing and reminiscing, our fathers having a few beers, Russell and I would go out around the pond exploring; and later, if we stayed over, at night in his room in the bunk beds we'd talk and laugh over the latest *MAD* magazine, which we had both loved since high school; and we'd look at *Playboy*, other sex magazines, and talk about cars, girls, and sex. Russell was the joker and so he'd tell me the latest jokes.

Since we were both students at the University of Maine, we also talked about that, our classes, other students, the sports and social life. Russell was joining a fraternity in the fall and would be living at the frat house, while I would still be in the same dormitory I had been in the previous two years. Russell had been rushed by several of the fraternities, while I had been rushed by none. My "social life" was confined to working in the library on the weekends and going to the ten-cent movies in the Union. Russell was always promising me big times, however.

"We'll have to have you over to all the parties at Theta Chi," he'd say, both of us knowing this would never be the case. Russell was much more the fraternity type than I. He played at being the Big Man on Campus, while I was the shy, introverted bookworm. I envied him because he was more outgoing, more sure of himself as a man. He'd dare go around and pick up girls, loved flirting with them. At home, he also shared a wonderful, joking, man-to-man relationship with his father, something I never had with my father. Russell would call out to his father, "Hey, Al! How about another round?"

We'd play cards and games at the big picnic table they had in the middle of the camp, drinking Coke, beer, and whiskey that we kept hidden from our parents.

It would always bother me whenever Neeta would start comparing Russell and me. She'd praise me for my high grades and say things like, "If only Russell would get some grades like An-day. If only he'd try to amount to something besides a playboy."

At such moments, I always wanted to yell out, "What I'd give to be living the life of a playboy!" But I never said any such thing. I just tried to be a good and loyal companion whenever he and I were together; but I always knew that if our parents weren't such good friends, we wouldn't be.

Probably our funniest times together revolved around our imitations of our parents while talking with each other with their Maine accents.

"'Member, An-day," Russell would say, "that time the *Norumbega* went aground down to the Ha-buh? We sure thought she was a gon-ah that time. Knocked me ass-over-teakettle down in the engine room! Yep. Ayuh. Sure 'nuff!"

"She sure was some ship, now I'll tell ya."

"Ayuh, I know it."

"Ayuh, sure was! Won't be another like 'er. Just like I used to say to old Henry Ford and John D. Rockefeller, when they'd come down to visit me in the engine room, they don't build 'em like that anymore. Nope."

"Ayuh, I know it."

Long before I had one, Russell had his first car, a '52 green Plymouth four-door sedan, which would still keep running even when he had turned off the ignition. One time he drove down to the Manor to visit with Ellen, Sally, and me. We had a great visit driving all over the place; and Russell loved the hotel.

"Well, An-day, old pal," he said after his visit, "I'm just gonna have to do this again. You people run a nice place down here, so you can expect me to pop by for more hours of frivolity. Now, An-day, you scoundrel, you be nice to my baby sister! I'll be checking up on ya."

But, of course, he never did.

Summer 1963

50

During my junior year in college in December 1962, I went to Florida for Christmas with my parents to visit my older brother Bobber, who was working at Cape Canaveral; and during spring break in 1963, I went to Boston for a week or so with my college roommate Doug Thompson and another college pal. With that little taste of escape to the greater world, realizing by then that it really was possible, I decided for the summer of 1963 to make a change and leave my safe and routine haven at Frenchman's Bay Manor for a livelier summer job scene where there would be more college kids and hang-outs for such.

My mother had told me about a possible opening for a boy at Whitcomb Brothers' Lobster Wharf in Townsend Harbor, "Maine's Boating Capital," about a hundred miles west down the coast from Taunton. The wharf was operated by Millard Whitcomb and his brother-in-law Cecil Thornrock who were partners along with Millard's two older brothers. The Whitcomb family had built the first lobster pound in the United States back in the 19th century and as Maine's first family of lobstering had once owned pounds all along the coast, including their biggest one in Taunton where a number of my relatives and neighbors had worked.

In 1952, the Whitcombs sold their Taunton pound to the Consolidated Lobster Company of Gloucester, Massachusetts; and Millard and his wife Maxine, great friends of my parents, moved with their family to Townsend Harbor where the Whitcombs operated their wholesale lobster and crabmeat business. As an adjunct to the main concern, they had started a busy take-out service for summer tourists who could eat and drink at one of the picnic tables under the canopied roof of the Whitcomb wharf with its beautiful view of the whole harbor and town, a picturesque scene that once served as the backdrop for the movie version of *Carousel*, filmed in the mid-fifties.

Over the years, the Whitcombs had employed their own son and daughter, Cameron and Lynne, and also a number of their nieces and nephews; but most of them by the summer of 1963 had gone away to school or were employed elsewhere in full-time jobs. The girls' jobs at the wharf were now all filled by local Townsend girls; but one boy's job was still open and I wrote to Millard immediately.

He wrote back that I could have the job if I wanted it. So, as far as I was concerned, it was all set, as simple as that, except for letting Miss Meyer and Mrs. Richmond know of my impending desertion.

True to their nature, they were very nice and completely understanding about it. Mrs. Richmond wrote me, as she had all through my first three years in college, one of her typical letters punctuated with exclamation points.

> Dearest Andy,
>
> Of course, you must leave! The time is probably right; but, alas for us! Like two doting mother hens, Jean and I have been nervously expecting your leave taking. It was only a matter of time. And it's a dreadful shame for us to lose such a devoted, hard-working, and important employee (it will be hard replacing you!). More than hired help, you have been a cherished friend and such good company. We shall miss you, Andy!
>
> But I understand, perhaps better than you do at this point, why you must leave. There's growing and exploring to do, there's experiences to be gained, adventures to be had! You've got to test yourself, learn more about yourself and the world—and from a fresh location!

How exciting really to be a young man like yourself, blessed with a number of important attributes on the threshold of everything!

And don't really be down about anything at your age, Andy. "Life is fer livin'"—and take it in big gulps—its joys, its frustrations, its greatness and its meanness!

Even in your absence, we do hope that your lovely mother can be persuaded to continue to service our linen and tote our spring water, for we have grown spoiled rotten and entirely dependent upon her excellent care and quality of work. Like mother, like son!

Andy, dear, do enjoy and profit from the Townsend experience, and don't forget to come back and visit us. Do stay in touch!

Affectionately,
Madella Richmond

I wrote her back that my mother would continue with the linen and water; and right after I got out of college, the first week in June, my parents drove me one early Sunday morning down Route One to Townsend Harbor, a trip we had made several times before over the years to visit with the Whitcombs.

In 1962 before the great Florida trek, my parents had actually traded in the old Mercury for a 1959 green-and-white Ford coupe that had belonged to the Taunton Grammar School principal. So we had a car that was only three years old.

Trips anywhere with my parents were always the same: up and away before sun-up and hardly ever stopping, except for gas. I was always pleading with them to take some side trips off Route One and the by-pass roads, so that I could see more places and parts of my native state that I had never visited before, but they never did. We stuck to the same familiar route from the foot of Jonathan Buck's tombstone and the view of Fort Knox in Bucksport across the Waldo-Hancock suspension bridge to Perry's Nut House and the stench of the chicken factories in Belfast, and from the Maine State Prison, the cement plant, and the Montpelier estate in Thomaston. My mother always said how she wanted to visit the Prison Store in Thomaston where the prisoners themselves waited on the customers trying to sell their model boats, tables made out of matchsticks, and lamps made out of tongue depressors. But we never stopped there. I never saw Downtown Rockland at all, since we always took the alternate route that skirted it.

"For a lark, Dad, let's visit Downtown Rockland for once," I'd say; and he'd say, "Christ, An-day, downtown Rockland is the same as downtown Belfast and downtown Bucksport! Take my word for it!"

At Lincolnville Beach, I'd mention how nice it must be to take the ferry out to Islesboro and Vinalhaven.

"Jay-sus, An-day! The spruce trees and rocks on those islands are just as spruce and just as rocky as on Mount Desert!"

My parents seemed always bent on avoiding other people as much as possible; and while my father spent time trying to elude even the slightest hint of traffic congestion, I longed for busy streets clogged with people bustling here and there.

Camden, thankfully, had no alternate route; and we drove right through town. I was always very impressed by the houses in Camden as well as those in Wiscasset and Thomaston. In the early '60s, too, there were still elm trees lining the streets. Camden is where the young Edna St. Vincent Millay had read her poem "Renascence" at the Whitehall Inn, on the porch of which Lana Turner had appeared to be sitting years later, in 1957 when *Peyton Place* was filmed there.

Beyond Camden was Pemaquid Point.

"Can't we drive down and see the Pemaquid lighthouse?" I asked my parents that Sunday of my escape from Hancock County.

"An-day, that's twenty miles out of the way," my father said. "What do you want to see that for?"

"I've never seen a lighthouse up close before."

"There's nothing much to see."

"But I've lived on the Maine Coast all my life and the only lighthouses I've ever seen are Mark's Island, off Schoodic, Egg Rock, and Crabtree's Ledge in Frenchman's Bay; and these only from a boat. Don't you think it's terrible that I've never been to one of Maine's most famous lighthouses? I feel ignorant of my heritage."

"Well, you're ignorant of more than that," my father said.

"We really don't have time," my mother said.

"Yes, that's true," I said. "It must be nearly eight o'clock already; and we must try and step on it to get there by breakfast!"

And it certainly wasn't much later when we did finally arrive at the Whitcomb's wharf. They hadn't even opened up for the day's business when my father backed our Ford down onto the wharf where we could most easily unload my stuff from the trunk.

"Greetings and salutations!" said Millard Whitcomb welcoming us, just before showing me to my summer quarters upstairs over the shop, or main office and storeroom of the firm. Actually, where I was to live was another storage area, this one twice as large as my Manor garret, but full of cartons of Dixie cups, paper plates, napkins with red lobster designs, flat wooden spoons for ice cream, paper cups for melted butter, plastic red lobster coffee stirrers, red-white-and-blue cardboard containers for the clams and lobsters, Wash 'n' Dri packets, paper towels, and toilet paper. In the midst of all of this was a big double bed with pieced-together mattresses, along with a chair, a small table, and a portable TV set which Lynne Whitcomb was loaning me for the summer.

Near the door on the opposite side of the room from the bed were a sink with cold running water and a hot plate. I had just enough room for my clothes, books, record player, and myself. And while the place wasn't as tastefully furnished as my former attic room, I loved the idea of living in an upstairs warehouse overlooking the busy wharf and harbor scene. There was a window at either end of the room and a door with a mirror nailed to it. I loved it, for I always wanted to live in places where human residence was least expected: a quiet salon off a busy avenue, the back room of a pool hall, the corner of a shed, upstairs over a nightclub, in an office building, or under a swimming pool as 3-D Magee and Pony Tail did in an old Dick Tracy comic strip.

"You'll be the night watchman this summer," said Millard to me.

Once settled in, I joined my parents and the Whitcombs for Sunday dinner; and afterwards received a tour of the wharf and its operations. Besides the shop, which also included the take-out area for hot dogs and hamburgers, there was a separate take-out building for lobsters and clams, where I was to work. Directly across from the shop was the wharf proper with its twenty picnic tables evenly spaced and overlaid by a wooden canopy with plastic green roofing. There was a slip at the end of the wharf leading down to a float where the boats were tied up and where the clamdiggers came by boat to weigh and sell their clams to the Whitcombs. There was also a gasoline pump there where outboarders could buy gas. To the right side of the shop looking towards the harbor was more warehouse space in a long, rectangular building, its black-shingled roof whitened at the peak by the sea gulls who perched there. Inside there was also the picking room where the women picked out crabmeat and lobster meat for packing and freezing. Beside it was the tank room where the lobsters, clams, and crabs were kept alive in a series of wooden tanks filled with cold ocean water pumped continuously through them.

The take-out stand where I was to work was opposite the tank room on the other side of the wharf. It was a little clapboarded building painted white with green trim, like all the rest of the complex, and the front opened up into a counter around whose sides were hung the racks of potato chips and signs advertising the wares and prices. To one side of the little building were the outdoor tanks where the lobsters to be sold were separated by size: one pound, one-and-a-quarter pound, one-and-a-half pound, and two pounds. The prices, of course, were posted above each tank and varied with the size. There was another tank just for the clams that had to be weighed and bagged in little net bags ready for steaming. Ocean water was pumped through these outdoor tanks just like the inside ones. At Whitcomb's Wharf, there was always the sound of rushing water. Tucked into the corner of the wharf beside the outdoor tanks were the clam steamer, which looked like a converted old wash tub, and the larger wooden steamer for the lobsters, which looked like a huge freezer, painted gray.

Since the wharf was hosed down every day, the place was very neat and clean, and typically Downeast unpretentious. There were no neon signs and paved parking lots, no fancy entrances as there were just next door at Red's Wharf where part of the musical *Carousel* had been filmed. The tourist in search of Hollywood "atmosphere" with pictures of Gordon MacCrae and Shirley Jones in their *Carousel* outfits and fishnets and sea shells hanging from the ceiling paid a good price for their clam chowder or lobster stew.

In contrast, at Whitcomb's there was only one big wooden sign, painted green and white, and a dirt parking lot off Atlantic Avenue, which skirted Townsend Harbor. Everything was plain and simple and the seafood was fresh and delicious, the best-tasting in town, and people knew that. They also didn't have to dress up. Business was good and prosperous; on an average summer day, we served several hundred people, and on the Fourth of July and Sundays, we served sometimes a thousand or more. The cash registers would have to be emptied several times a day.

However, the main business of Whitcomb Brothers was not the picnic and take-out area. I was told they hardly even broke even on that. Their business was selling live, fresh and frozen seafood wholesale across the country. Trucks would be packed early in the morning for delivery to Portland's train station and airport. There were also the Consolidated trucks that went back and forth to Gloucester. In these days before jet travel had become so common, live lobsters were only shipped as far west as Kansas City, Missouri. There were always people calling, including Hollywood movie producers, trying to order fresh lobsters for some big party; but Millard would try and tell them all no.

The *Portland Sunday Telegram* once ran a story on the Whitcomb Brothers and their business entitled "Maine's Educated Lobstermen," since all four had attended Phillips Exeter Academy, and the two oldest, Mason and Morgan, had graduated from Harvard. Millard had gone to Husson Business College in Bangor, as had Cecil, his brother-in-law, who acted as bookkeeper of the Townsend operation. Cecil was a tall man with a pot belly and a close-cropped, bird-like shaped head. Cecil was fond of making jokes at other people's expense. Both he and Millard wore green or tan Dickies and both wore glasses. Often they sported L.L. Bean fishermen's boots for work around the wharf and in the tank rooms.

Millard was easy-going, whistled and hummed a lot, and favored smoking a pipe. The Whitcomb brothers were well-liked by their employees because they worked right alongside their people and they worked hard. They were also fair-minded, honest and kind folk.

Among the regular year-round employees I met that afternoon was Harold Young, who was stone deaf and lived in a neat, little, white house up Atlantic Avenue from the wharf. He was pudgy, fleshy pink, and smiled a lot. He always wore his lobsterman's boots rolled over just before the knee and a turned-up tan-colored baseball cap that complemented his tan Dickies work outfit. Harold was a nice man, kind to everyone, and always busy. He'd be there early in the morning helping the other men pack the barrels with lobster, ice, and seaweed for shipment; and throughout the day he was cooking the lobsters and crabs, then hosing down wire baskets full of the cooked crustaceans to cool them off for the picking room ladies. Before we opened for business at ten a.m., Harold would have hosed off the wharf, and run the U.S. flag up the flagpole. Around closing time at eight p.m.

at night, he'd take it down. And he'd whistle all the way. Millard used to say Harold's so happy because he can't hear a goddamn thing!

There were three regular pickers in the picking room: Gram, Pearl, and Irma. All were very obese women and all were related. Gram was the veteran and Champion Crabmeat Picker of Maine. She was also the oldest; the mother of Pearl, who was half-witted and silly; and the mother-in-law of Irma, who never said anything. Propped on her stool and bathed in the light from the wharf window coated with salt spray, Gram reigned over the picking table piled high with discarded lobster and crab shells and mountains of fresh pink meat. She was amazingly fast and efficient, particularly in view of her fat hands; and she took a great deal of pride in her work.

"There ain't no one in Maine who can outpick old Gram," she'd say with a big grin.

After I'd been there a while, and got into the routine, I used to wander over to the picking room in the dead part of the afternoon and call on the girls, who'd let me have a nice, juicy, fresh lobster tail to dunk in a cup of melted butter for a little mid-day snack.

Millard's wife, Maxine, and Cecil's wife, Virginia, helped out frequently, especially on Sundays, our busiest days, when they took turns helping in the hamburger and hot dog counter. Maxine would usually bring some homemade brownies to sell. The two wives also took turns providing me with a hot supper. Virginia's suppers were always more tasty and varied than Maxine's. Maxine tended to go heavy on the Hungarian goulash and beef stew, while Virginia prepared more well-balanced meals with meat, vegetables, and desserts. Everyone but me went home for dinner, so I got an hour out to eat mine when they returned.

The Thornrock children were still too young to work at the wharf, but the Whitcomb's son Cameron, who was twenty-five that summer, a Navy veteran, who had just completed his first year in engineering school in Boston, was employed in the tank room, guardian of the lobsters and clams, and as an all-around handyman for the business.

One of Cameron's jobs, as soon as the trucks were packed in the morning, was to take one of the company station wagons and go get the pickers; and then take them home again at night.

After having sat in the picking room draped over their stools all day, picking out tons of lobster and crab meat and packing it in plastic containers, the overweight women would literally waddle from their work area to the station wagon with the handsome young Cameron leaning out the car window, yelling at them: "C'mon, Pearl, old girl! Pick it up, baby! Let's go, girls! Lift 'em up and lay 'em down! C'mon, move it! I've got a big date tonight!"

Once in the car, the weight of the three huge women would lower the car so that the back bumper would often scrape on the driveway as Cameron stepped down on the gas.

"Christ, girls! We're scraping bottom! We're dragging the driveway with us! Hold on!"

Returning later, he'd say such things to me as: "Jesus, it would take a guy with a two-foot dick to probe that Pearl—even to feel anything at all!"

"Would you want to even try?" I'd ask.

"Well, I figure it's the man's duty to give all women pleasure," he'd say with a wink. "Remember the slogan of that men's store in Bangor—'Big or Small, Short or Tall, John Paul fits 'em all'? That's me—John Paul. I try and fit 'em all!"

At the lobster-and-clam take-out counter, I was to assist Sharon Lavert, a pretty, petite redhead, two years my junior, who had just completed a year of merchandising school in Boston and who was saving up for a trip to London in the fall. The two of us in turn were to be helped part-time by Sharon's cousin Patty Lavert, a junior in high school. When it wasn't busy, Patty was to be helping Cecil in his office.

The other take-out counter was operated most of the time by Sharon's younger sister Trudy, who would be a senior at Townsend Regional High School in the fall.

When I first met the girls, with whom I was to work most closely, I sensed their sizing me up with disapproval. They were joking around with each other at the time; and my being new, I naturally felt awkward and uncomfortable, trying to make a good first impression, but hardly succeeding, and wishing to be back down the coast at the Manor. As Sharon told me later, "That day when you first arrived here, I didn't think you'd last a week."

"Why?" I asked her.

"Because you acted like a creep."

"But now I've passed your test, right?"

"Sure. You have a great sense of humor and you work hard. You do a good job and people like you. We like you; but none of your humor and personality showed at first. It's like you're two different people. When you're feeling comfortable, you're fun to be with and great company; but if you're the least bit uncomfortable, you freeze up and get this gruesome, grouchy look on your face."

"Don't you think most people when they are new to a situation are not exactly themselves?"

"I don't know. Some people just seem to know what to do and how to act, seem to instinctively know how to take charge. And some people have such a great personality it's written all over them. But not you. At first, you seemed so unsure of yourself and afraid."

"Creep, huh?"

"No, you're a really sweet guy, but at first you acted like a creep!"

"You're such a perceptive psychologist, Sharon."

"Ain't I though?"

"Yeah, but I didn't notice it right off."

51

Even though I didn't have to be on the job until ten a.m., it was hard to sleep in at Whitcomb's Crab and Lobster Wharf, and not just because of the continuous sloshing of the ocean water coming and going with the tide, or the noise made by the men early in the morning packing up the seafood trucks. There was a floor register right by my bed, and from the office downstairs I could hear the arguing going on between Millard and Cecil, usually over Cameron and the business. One morning, Cecil was upset over finding Cameron asleep on the job in the tank room.

"Honest to God, Millard," said Cecil, "Cameron has got to stop running around to all hours of the night, so that he can be of some use to us here the first thing in the morning."

"He's here, isn't he?"

"Sure—*asleep*! Again in the tank room. He's here, but he's no good to us, the condition he's in. You've got to stop making excuses for him. He's costing us money every time we turn around. Somebody needs to kick him in the ass, and it should be you."

"How is he costing us money?"

"How much did that speeding ticket on the Maine Turnpike cost ya last week?"

"It wasn't that much, Cecil; and it's none of your damn business. What I paid came out of my own pocket."

"It certainly is my business when I see my livelihood affected this way by him—profits being eliminated by a spendthrift playboy."

"What Cameron costs me does not affect this business or your salary, for Christ's sake."

"We pay him a weekly salary, don't we? That's a waste right there, in my opinion. I don't even see how it's possible for him to still have a license and drive around, he's been picked up so much."

"Listen, Cecil, I know how you feel about my kids and me and how you could run this business so much better all by yourself, but I'm sick and tired of hearing about it. Wait till your kids get older and start running around before you start giving me advice."

It was interesting to go from working for two women to two men. Mrs. Richmond and Miss Meyer would often disagree and even argue sometimes, but never compete with each other, or try to get all their employees on one side or the other. Millard wasn't competitive either, but Cecil was. He never lost an opportunity to make fun of Millard, for one thing, and he also encouraged the girls, who were solidly on Cecil's side, to do the same. It was true that Millard wasn't exactly a dynamic businessman with lots of new and exciting ideas about the marketing of shellfish; but Millard was very honest, dependable, and trustworthy, a man of his word, who didn't play games. However, Cecil was ten years younger and full of ambition. He played golf and liked to rub shoulders with the other area businessmen. He was very involved in town affairs, while Millard couldn't care less.

As for the matter with Cameron, Cecil was probably just jealous of him. Cameron was a handsome, well-built young man, popular and lucky with women. Cecil was middle-aged, paunchy, and yet evidently considered himself something of the ladies' man, always joking and playing up to the women and girls about the wharf. Cameron was always going to parties and racing around Maine and Massachusetts with his friends, living in the fast lane. While Cameron tooled around town in a bright red Volkswagen bug, Cecil drove a conservative tan-colored Chevrolet sedan, and most nights went directly home to his wife and family.

Cecil tried one time to get me on his side against Millard and family, but I told him I didn't want to get involved in any family squabbles, that my loyalty would always be with the Whitcombs since I had known them all my life and loved them. Cecil said he understood my position, but I think he was a bit frustrated and disappointed for the rest of the summer that he couldn't make me into a disciple for his cause. Cecil paid me in cash at the end of every week. Since I received $75 per week, I made almost as much in a week there as I made in a month at the Manor. Of course, I didn't get the tips or bonuses that I did at Granite Neck, and I had more personal expenses at Townsend Harbor; but at the end of the summer, by being frugal, I would have a few hundred more dollars than usual with which to start my senior year in college. So, despite Cecil's air of reserve and coolness towards me, I was determined to make good on the job and have everyone else like me or respect me, even if he never did.

I'd get up mornings, make my bed, pick up my dirty laundry to be mailed home to my mother in the laundry box she supplied me. Since my parents could never afford to give me any money for college, they did provide laundry service, along with an occasional box of homemade goodies. I had to use the men's public toilet on the Wharf, and if I had to sit down, I'd always wash off the toilet seat. From there, I'd pick up my orange juice and milk for my cereal from the shop's refrigerator, and go back upstairs to my warehouse quarters and have breakfast.

Before ten a.m., if it was a good day, I'd usually walk "over town," which meant hiking up Atlantic Avenue for a few blocks and crossing over the harbor by way of the footbridge to the business section where I'd browse about The Fruit Store, looking mostly at the racks of paperbacks and magazines; the drugstore where I bought my favorite coffee milkshakes; the Strand movie theater where I scanned the posters of coming attractions noting which movies I wanted to see; the library where I took out a lot of books that I half-read; the appliance store which also stocked the latest rock-'n'-roll records; the A & P grocery store; and a number of the tourist gift shops which proliferated about town. Some days I'd wander about the wharves and look at the boats. There were several tour boats that went out to Monhegan and other islands. One of these boats, the *Jennie Two*, was owned and operated by Captain Dick Barclay, Russell's great-uncle. I used to visit with him a bit. Often there would be a whole yacht club from Marblehead, Massachusetts or some other place and the harbor would be packed with fancy sailboats with many people coming and going. Sometimes I'd take my milk shake or candy bar with my latest paperback or magazine and sit on one of the benches in the village green by the bandstand or down by Fisherman's Wharf where I'd observe the colorful goings-on.

Mostly, however, I enjoyed my long leisurely strolls back and forth on the footbridge, the most outstanding feature of Townsend Harbor, which I had loved ever since first walking and playing on it as a child when visiting the Whitcombs on weekends. A variety of people would always be dangling a fishing line off the footbridge, shopping at the little unpainted gray-shingled shop in the center of it, or just leaning on the railings taking in the beautiful view of the harbor and town that in the bright of a summer day seemed dazzling white in contrast with the water's sparkling blue. A few people would be taking photos or painting pictures, for Townsend Harbor looked exactly like the quaint Maine fishing village that everyone pictures as "typically Downeast."

In my morning walks I always met the same people, who evidently kept a similar schedule. One old lady I particularly recall. I never learned her name, but I would always meet her either coming or going on the bridge; and even on the hottest days she'd be all dressed up in a heavy winter suit with a fancy blouse secured at the neck by a glittering brooch. She'd also have on a large, elaborate hat with netting and ribbons and would be carrying a large fancy purse. Like most old ladies, she stepped along carefully and slowly, taking special care not to fall down and break anything. She was always heavily made-up and reeked of some kind of strong perfume. When she got close enough to me, she'd always smile this little girl smile and say in a soft, little, ladylike voice, "Good day, sir." I'd watch her pass by other people, however, and she'd never say anything to them, a fact which puzzled me. I suppose she spoke to me because she somehow sensed that I was fascinated and intrigued by her.

Just off the footbridge on the "downtown side," near where all the tour boats and private craft were moored, there was a wharf for deep-sea fishing boats; and the captain of one of them, *The Bay Bitch*, was a ruddy-faced, but youngish-looking and high-spirited fellow, who worked in the merchant marine for several months of the year, but who came home summers to run his deep sea fishing business. His name was "Doozie" and he was a native of Townsend Harbor and knew the Whitcombs. He'd often hail me from his boat as I stood on the bridge or was walking by.

"Hey, Crew Cut!" he'd yell, or "Hey, Slim Jim! How's the weather up there?" He'd call me other names, too; and even though we talked a couple of times, I never really got to know him, but I liked his rambunctious spirit and the name of his boat. Doozie took life as he found it, all right; and he was one Maine native who'd been around the world and seen everything and who could tell great yarns. I imagined that he gave his customers a good time while out on the briny deep fishing for tuna, whether they actually caught any fish or not. He asked me to come with him several times, but I never went. Stupid of me, but I was too shy. I always made the excuse that I was needed at work all the time.

"They can't bag those clams as well as you can, right?" he'd say.

At the Atlantic Avenue end of the bridge, there was a little grocery store that sold exclusively S. S. Pierce products, and so I'd often buy a can of small onions or Indian pudding that would remind me of Frenchman's Bay Manor. At the same end of the footbridge was the VFW Hall, and right inside from the side door on the ground floor stood an old upright piano which a happy-go-lucky man named "Pappy" used to play with a lot of gusto, usually after imbibing several bottles of beer. When the door was open, which was frequently the case, Pappy's piano music could be heard the whole length of the footbridge. Some nights walking back to Whitcomb's from the movies, I'd love to hear Pappy playing. There's something about music heard over the water like that is especially haunting, sad and beautiful at the same time.

One early evening on one of my days off, I went by the VFW Hall in the company of the blonde and effervescent Lynne Whitcomb, who used to play some pretty mean piano rags herself, when she asked me if I'd ever met Pappy.

"Nope," I said.

"Well, here's ya chance. He's a town character, ya know, but a damn good piano player. He can really rattle those ivories. He's played all over the world with the armed services."

We walked in the side door just before the footbridge, and there in a long dusty hall with a bar at one end sat a skinny, grinning little man astride a Sears-Roebuck catalog with his legs crossed pounding away on the piano, singing along with his music. Between tunes, Pappy would stop and take a sip from his Budweiser bottle which he had placed beside him in a chair.

"Hey, Professor! How about a little ankle action?" asked Lynne.

Pappy turned and smiled at her. "Hiya, Lynnie! You know I don't play with my ankles, girlie."

"Well, let's at least hear what you can do with your 'Five Foot Two.'"

"Your wish is my command," he said, and away his fingers flew, pounding out 'Five Foot Two' in a wonderfully raucous manner.

The piano music from the VFW Hall ended abruptly at the end of that summer when one night Pappy shot himself to death. The flag was lowered to half-mast over the side door to the hall and someone had hand-printed a crude sign and stuck it in the window. It read: "God Bless Our Pappy. We Sure Miss His Happy Piano."

There were artists' galleries and studios all over Townsend Harbor. Most of them were painters of seascapes and familiar pretty Maine pictures for which they charge high prices. One place near Whitcombs' was called The Black Rock Gallery and I'd sometimes peek in the windows to see what was on display, but there was hardly ever anything and never much activity about the place. The artist himself, a full-bearded fellow, seemed to spend most of his time in his red bikini briefs out on his sun deck. There was always much more activity going on across the street at a boatyard where a half-dozen men were always very busy putting the finishing touches on a variety of craft they were building. These boatbuilder artists impressed me more than the proprietor of Black Rock.

Near the big orange fish factory building, probably the most imposing on the water front, I'd often stop and buy some fudge from the candy lady who lived in a neat little white house with blue shutters with a white picket fence around it. On a white wooden table in the middle of the lawn would be a neatly lettered sign that read: DIVINITY FUDGE TEN CENTS. There was a small tin pan with change in it where the customer was expected to make his own change. The fudge squares were all individually wrapped in wax paper. The candy lady would sometimes be sitting out on her lawn in a rocking chair under an umbrella, and at other times one could catch a glimpse of her peeking out of one of her front windows. What amused me about her operation was the fact that her neat little place lay directly across the street from the awful smelling fish factory. When I first saw her sign, I thought it must be some kind of joke. The combination of rotten fish stench and rich fudge was enough to turn anyone's stomach; but I'd buy some anyway and save it to nibble on later when I was back in my room.

Dominating the Townsend Harbor skyline was the handsome white Catholic Church, "Our Lady of Peace," which set up on top of the hill in the middle of Atlantic Avenue with a commanding view of the whole harbor. It was to this church the summer before in 1962 that President Kennedy had come for Sunday services accompanied by his sister Patricia Lawford. They had been the guests that weekend of former boxing great Gene Tunney, who had a summer place on one of the islands. Kennedy's churchgoing was the big event from the summer before, and people were still talking about it.

"There must have been ten thousand people here to see him," Cecil told me. "What a crowd. I think we depleted the tanks that day."

"And he was so handsome," said Sharon. "Some people were afraid he'd fall through the rotten old wharf over at the Co-op, where he came ashore."

"You had a great view of him then from here?" I asked.

"Yes and no, depending on where you were and who you were. We had so many people packed in here—and we sold tons of clams and lobsters; but it was really hard for most everyone here to really get a good view—unless you were tall or right down next to the water."

"Millard was afraid, with all the people, that our wharf would collapse, like when they were making *Carousel* years ago at Red's Wharf and one of the heavy cinemascope cameras went into the drink," said Trudy.

"Some people made a lot of money on that day like the guy who sold parking places up the street for a dollar apiece. I heard he sold a few hundred," said Cecil.

"I wish I had been here to see him," I said.

"He was gorgeous, but that sister of his is a dog," said Trudy.

"I wouldn't mind being nipped by that dog with all of that money," said Cecil.

Little did I know then that I'd be getting the chance to see President Kennedy myself that fall at the University of Maine.

52

My work day began with the clams. Before the girls arrived and before we officially opened at ten a.m., I was out on the wharf picking over the clams, separating the dead and squashed ones, which stank to the high heavens, from the fresh, live ones. I'd lug the wire clam baskets out of the tank room one at a time and pick through them, throwing the stinkers off the wharf, and watch in amazement as a sharp-eyed sea gull would swoop down and catch the clam in its beak before the mollusk hit the water.

I'd bag enough of the good clams to start the day. They were placed in one-pound or two-pound net bags and weighed on a scale; then they were hung in the clam tank full of fresh salt water.

In the adjacent lobster tanks, one could tell when a storm was brewing, even it was at the moment a bright and sunny day, by how bristly the lobsters would be in the salt water. Their antennae would be sticking above the tanks and moving through the water and they would be frisky and hard to pick up.

By the time the girls arrived, I'd have the clam-and-lobster area ready for business. While Sharon got the coffee perking and was melting the butter on the hot plate, I'd be opening up the front, filling up and arranging the candy display, setting out the napkin dispensers.

Both of us would replenish the supply of plastic trays, cardboard containers, cups for both the coffee and melted butter, spoons and forks, plastic coffee stirrers, and nutcrackers and picks for the lobsters. We used canned milk for the coffee and always put a Wash 'n' Dri packet on every lobster tray. There were big bibs and napkins with bright red lobsters and WHITCOMB'S CRAB AND LOBSTER WHARF printed on them which also went on the trays. We had to make sure our trays, the nutcrackers, and picks all came back and didn't get thrown out. We washed the trays and dried them in the sun on racks on the back of the wharf. A clock design had been drawn on the side of the take-out building to which individual tags were affixed for people's lobster and clam orders that were cooking. The clams took ten minutes and the lobsters twenty. When an order was ready, we'd announce it over the P.A. system: "Number 42, your clams are ready!" Most people would have an order of clams as a first course while waiting for their lobster. Sometimes, when we'd be cooking and the wind off the water would be blowing the steam around, the P.A. system wouldn't work right and we'd have trouble notifying the customers about their orders.

When people left their picnic tables, one of us would have to run over and clean them off. Garbage pails were available all along the wharf, but many people would fail to use them. We'd both try and keep an eye on everything; and when things were very hectic, as they often were, we'd have to holler for help. Sometimes everyone would be there with us: Millard, Cecil, Cameron, Trudy, and Patty. And we'd all be crazy, running around, getting in each other's way, confusing or even forgetting the orders. We were open seven days a week and everyone got one night off a week. Of course, rainy days weren't as busy, but there were very few rainy days the sunny summer of '63.

Our first customers would be the representatives of local concerns, mostly restaurants and hotels in need of fresh supplies of seafood. One daily caller was a young, handsome, dark-haired youth from down south named Tad, who was always attired in his kitchen boy's outfit of jeans and tee-shirt. The Levi Strauss Company in the early '60s had introduced white jeans, and we boys were all wearing them, alternating with the regular blue jeans. Tad would pick up his supply of crab and lobster meat for the restaurant where he worked, but he'd also hang around and joke with the girls and me; and because he was such a good-looking and fun-loving guy, Patty would usually find an excuse the moment of his arrival to leave the office to linger by our take-out counter. I don't remember whether or not they ever went out with each other, but young Tad did take a more than casual interest in Patty. Tad worked at the Shamrock Inn, one of Townsend Harbor's most popular watering holes housed in a handsome old Victorian mansion on a hill overlooking the harbor. It was advertised as "A Wee Bit O' Erie in Maine" and the Irishman who ran it was quite a character. Tad would tell us funny stories about Seamus O'Flaherty, his huge, physically imposing boss tending bar in his kilts and other getups; and also about his wife Bridget, who could evidently drink most men under the table. Tad's tales of the Shamrock Inn would get me to reminiscing about my summers at Frenchman's Bay Manor. We'd compare notes. Both Millard and Cecil, however, after Tad had gone, would have nothing good to say about the O'Flahertys and their inn.

By 11:30 a.m. or so, the lunchtime crowd would begin to arrive and one of our most prominent regulars was a lovely, tall, blonde woman always very dressed-up who ran a gift shop called The Smiling Cow; and that's what we called her. One day, Sharon even made the mistake by announcing over the P.A. system: "Mrs. Cow, your clams are ready!"

On Sundays, an old German man who couldn't speak English very well always brought his family and a gallon jug of white wine which he'd plunk down in the middle of a table. He'd never order any lobsters or clams. Instead, he'd march back and forth to the hamburger and hot dog take-out and slam his fist down on the counter, yelling, "OMBURGER!" We called him The Old Kraut.

There was Honest John the Crook who ran a used car lot in town and came for lunch two or three times a week. He'd always say he's like a "mess o' clams" and Sharon would ask him how much a mess was.

"Now, you know, dearie."

"Not really. We sell 'em by the pound. Is a mess a pound?"

"Now look, sweetheart, you grew up in Maine, didn't ya?"

"Oh, ayuh!"

"Then you must know that when a Maine man orders a mess o' clams, he don't mean a goddamn half-dozen like ya get in some city restaurant."

"O.K., then a mess is more than six."

"Now, Missy, do I look like a man who'll be satisfied with six or seven clams?"

"You don't look like a man who's ever satisfied."

And so it would go, unless there were a number of other customers standing in line.

At least once a week, sometimes for lunch, sometimes for dinner, we'd get this couple: a handsome white-haired old man and his senile or mentally disturbed white-haired wife. She'd cling to him and giggle while he'd try to order the food. Sometimes she'd scream or run away across the wharf. She'd throw stuff, take things off other people's tables, and ask strange, uninhibited, funny questions. She'd tee hee, hum, dance around, and babble nonsense. He'd always scurry after her and try to hold onto her. One time I was out back washing the lobster trays when I heard this squeal, and I looked down from the wharf onto the water and there they were in a rowboat. He was rowing and she was in the bow all dressed up in a frilly white frock and big hat, waving her hands, pounding her feet, giggling and calling to everyone on the wharf. We named them Tard and Retard.

"Omigod! It's Tard and Retard!" said Sharon. "Now, they're coming at us from the water! She's waving to ya, Andy. Don't forget to wave back! We sure don't want to go losing any of our favorite regulars."

There was a man who came only at night, frequently just before closing. He'd drive his purple Thunderbird down on the wharf, a practice the Whitcombs did not encourage. He sported rings on nearly every finger and claimed to have Mafia connections in Boston. He smoked cigars, wore dark glasses at night, and had a crush on Sharon. He spent most of his time when at Whitcombs' hanging on our counter telling Sharon how much she reminded him of the spunky Maine gals of his youth when he was a Boston boy working on the steamboats going Downeast from Bean Town.

"Ya know, Sharon," he'd say, "you've even got a good old-fashioned name like them good-looking Stonington gals."

"Old-fashioned, huh?"

"Yup, in the good way. Those were good women, them Stonington gals. They sure could scull a dory."

"Strong, huh?"

"Strong? They'd row right out to meet the boats. And that's what we boys used to always say about them—they sure could scull a dory!"

We called him The Underworld and Sharon would always try to

pretend to be busy elsewhere if she saw him coming.

"I always seem to attract those types," Sharon would say. "The little gal with a lot of spunk! The tough Maine gal who could scull a dory! That's me! Little but mighty—the type men appreciate only after they've reached middle age and have only their memories left."

Sharon's entertainment specialty was putting lobsters to sleep. If it were a slow night, and there was a tourist who was unfamiliar with the phenomenon, Sharon would take a live lobster, stand him on his head, start stroking his back until he'd just stay there immobile in that upside down position. Some customers were so delighted they'd make her do it over and over again; and, of course, want to try it themselves.

Both Sharon and I would get to be in dozens of home movies and family pictures, Sharon with her lobster stroking and me for my cooking. The amateur film directors would have us pose with their wives and kiddies, with me or both of us holding up the lobsters about to be cooked with the steam swirling about.

There would also be the daily complaints. Some would be upset that there was no clam juice to go with the clams. Some were shocked to open up their lobsters and fine roe (they thought there was something rotten), while others especially ordered female lobsters for the roe. Even though with every order we served mats that showed how to take a lobster apart, many customers had to be shown step-by-step. Some were bothered by the pukey green tamale inside the tail and body, while still others thought eating a lobster was just like eating a big red bug. People would ask me to show them the difference between a male and female lobster. As for the asexual clams, I remember overhearing Patty one day in a serious tone explaining to one fellow how all Maine soft shell steamer clams were homosexual.

One afternoon, an imposing lady in dark glasses happened by with her young son. While talking with us, trying to make a decision about her order, she turned to her boy, who was sticking his fingers into the lobster tanks, saying, "Son, don't play with your food!"

Millard warned us to be on the lookout for the gypsies. They were a Maine summer tradition. "They'll rob us blind if ya don't watch out," said Millard. "They always travel in groups and while one of 'em distracts ya, the others steal everything that isn't nailed down."

I thought he was exaggerating until one sunny afternoon when business was slow, Sharon was gone, and I was alone; a little, dark-skinned woman with a colorful bandanna on her head arrived with two little boys. She was very friendly and wanted to know all about Maine clams and how we prepared them. As I started to show them to her, she took a handful and started cracking them and eating them raw while talking with me and pretending to listen.

"You're not supposed to eat Maine clams raw," I said. "You might get hepatitis or something. They have to be cooked."

"Oh, really?" she asked. "But I like clams raw."

After she and the boys left, thanking me for my information and hospitality, I happened to notice the counter and the candy display which was empty. Every candy bar and stick of gum was gone. The gypsies had paid us a call.

Most of the big bus tours from Boston and New York came on Wednesdays; and we were grateful for that. They were usually made up of little old ladies, often widows from the Bronx or Brooklyn. Sharon and I would line them up and take their orders, which were usually on the finicky side.

"How many clams in a pound?" one would ask, and when told, would reply, "I don't know if I can eat that many. Maybe I'll just have a bag of potato chips."

Another would ask, "Can you just get one lobster claw? Or just a tail? I don't want a whole lobster, but I'd love to have a little taste."

While I'd be running around trying to cook up the orders, Sharon would wink at me from the counter saying things like, "Say, An-day! Have ya got that little piece of tail cooked up yet?"

One awful Wednesday in August, at the height of the season, four busses pulled into the parking lot. It seemed to take forever to process that crowd. On a typical day, the noon rush would dissipate by three p.m. or so, so that we could get a break before the dinnertime rush around six p.m.; but days when the multiple tour busses arrived, we wouldn't get a break at all.

The drunks came out at night, especially on the weekends. There was one local couple, who used to arrive around supper time, monopolize one table at the end of the wharf for hours, leaving only by closing time. They were good-natured, but crude and loud. They'd often break into song and also start hollering to the other customers around them. One night, as a signal that it was time for them to leave, I was told to take the U.S. flag down; and when the overweight slob of a husband discovered this, he yelled at me, "Hey, shithead! Whataya think ya doin'? Pulling down the American flag, which I fought for!

Which should always be flying! C'mon, everybody, let's sing *The Star Spangled Banner*!"

And sing he did, one of the worst renditions of the National Anthem to be followed by equally inharmonious versions of "America" and "Mine Eyes Have Seen the Glory." His overweight wife laughed and laughed, conducting her hubby's musicale with a lobster pick and beer bottle. Finally, as they made their drunken, reeling way from the wharf to their station wagon, the husband made the car first, and as his wife stumbled up the bank from the wharf with their picnic basket, he sang "Mairzy Doats," conducting himself with his arms out the car window.

Our most famous, and one of our most welcome, customers was the late naturalist-writer Rachel Carson, who had just published her classic best-seller *Silent Spring*. Sharon's father, who was a local carpenter, had built Miss Carson's house on Townsend Peninsula. Sharon had told me that Miss Carson was then dying of cancer, a fact we found doubly awful and ironic because of the concerns in her book about what pesticides were doing to the environment. She was a lovely, shy little lady who came to the wharf with her twelve-year-old nephew who lived with her.

Almost daily, Veronique, whom I called Very Unique, but whose surname I never learned, would appear down at the end of the wharf posing amidst the clamdiggers weighing their dig. And it would always be a provocative appearance, since Veronique was one of the sexiest creatures in Townsend Harbor. With her long blonde hair, beautiful face, and curvaceous body, she would strike poses in her little, flimsy summer dresses or cut-off jeans that would have the fishermen on the neighboring co-op wharf all agog, to say nothing of Cameron, Cecil, and the other men coming and going at Whitcomb's. An exchange student from France, Veronique had spent the past school year at Townsend Regional and was due to return to her country in midsummer.

A running joke all summer between Cecil and me concerned Veronique. Cecil claimed he saw her early one morning outside my door trying to get in and peeking in my window from the outdoors landing. I didn't believe him; I felt he was making one of his usual jokes at my expense, but I couldn't help wondering. I even entertained thoughts of her returning and I would be there and she would be in one of her little white skimpy summer dresses in which she looked so sexy.

Then there was a man who obviously had serious problems with his lower extremities. Even though he wore baggy trousers to help conceal his problem, there was this incredible bulge. We referred to him as The Permanent Erection.

One especially hectic day when everything seemed to go wrong, and it was pouring rain, too, Sharon, clad in her bright yellow slicker and hat, turned to me in sudden exasperation, both of us soaked to the skin, yelling, "MY GOD, AN-DAY! You won't believe it, but BOTH The Smiling Cow and The Permanent Erection are on their way down the wharf! I see 'em comin' through the fog and rain with their umbrellas! All we need now are Tard and Retard and The Underworld to show up and drive us both insane!"

53

It was soon after the Fourth of July when I first noticed that I was going bald. I had been at Whitcomb's Wharf for nearly a month, had celebrated my twenty-first birthday by buying my first bottle of sauterne at the state-owned liquor store, and had awakened to an anxious talk between Millard and Cecil in the shop down below about some potential trouble stirring among the women in the picking room.

I was getting ready for work that morning when I first noticed that my hair was falling out. I was standing in my Levi's and tee-shirt looking at myself in the mirror nailed to the door. At 6'1" and 150 pounds, I hadn't changed much since high school. I was still too skinny-looking with a sandy crewcut and ears that stuck out. I wished I had a more muscular and tanned body like Cameron's. I was so upset over the prospect of becoming a chromedome, too, that I sat down on the edge of my bed not wanting to go to work for the fear that the girls would notice and laugh.

As I sat there, with my comb full of hair, I listened to Millard and Cecil. They had hired a new girl, Francie Brasslett, younger than the other women in the picking room, to help speed up the operation, and the veterans resented her. Francie was also thin and had her own car, so she didn't ride with them either. The men were trying to decide what to do. Through the floor register I could hear everything.

"There was a lot of tension in the pickin' room yesterday," Cecil was saying. "The girls don't want her in there."

"Well," said Millard, "the girls aren't running things around here. They better get the message that we brought in a new woman to help speed up things."

"O.K., but be aware that there might be trouble today. It's supposed to be the hottest day of the year. We better hook up the fan for the pickers."

More concerned about my becoming prematurely bald than about any uneasy situation in the picking room, I pulled myself together enough to get down to the wharf where I picked through the clams and got the take-out counter opened up and ready for another day. Everyone was talking about the heat wave and how hot it was supposed to be.

"An-day, darlin'," said Sharon, "as soon as you can separate yourself from those sweet smelling clams, I wish you'd scurry right back up to your boudoir and get me another package of napkins. You know how The Smiling Cow goes through the napkins!"

Sharon also hollered at Cameron, who was walking around, as he often did, without any shirt on. "It's supposed to be the hottest day of the year, Cameron!"

He grinned. "Hey, we might have to strip right down and go for a dip off the wharf!" He wasn't kidding. On hot days, Cameron loved to parade through the luncheon crowd at the picnic tables in the briefest of swim trunks, showing off his good build, and dive off the wharf into the harbor.

The day did get hot and we were very busy. My tee-shirt was literally stuck to my skin as I steamed the lobsters and clams. We had a big luncheon crowd and Sharon and I had hardly any time to even chat with each other or go to the toilet. Luckily, the fracas in the picking room didn't start until mid-afternoon, after most of the customers were gone and we were getting set up for the evening. Both Millard and Cecil were busy in the shop, and Cameron was helping Harold Young in the tank room. Because Harold was so deaf, Cameron was always hollering at him. "HAROLD, THESE ARE THE TWO-POUNDERS IN THIS TANK! AND THOSE LOBSTERS OVER THERE HAVEN'T BEEN PEGGED, SO WATCH YOUR HANDS!"

Sharon first alerted me to the altercation in the picking room.

"An-day! Something's going on in the pickin' room!" she yelled. "Harold, Cameron, Cecil, and Millard all just ran lickety-split in there! I think the girls are duking it out, or else Pearl's had a heart attack or something!"

By the time Sharon, Trudy, Patty, and I got across the wharf, it was all over. And what a sight, when we opened the screen door!

Cameron, Harold, and Cecil were trying to pick up the fallen pickers while Millard seemed to be assessing the damage. Pearl and Irma, these two huge women, were lying flat and helpless on their backs on the floor covered with lobster and crab meat, cardboard containers, plastic covers, lobster picks, forks, and melted butter. The stools were upended. Gram, who was Pearl's mother, was sobbing in one corner; and Francie, whom Harold was trying to comfort, was yelling and crying, "That fat bitch tried to shove my head in the crabmeat! Gawd, she was trying to smother me!"

After the men got the women off the floor, Francie went off with Millard to the office, while Cameron took the other pickers home early.

Later that evening, after it had cooled down, when we were beginning to close up for another day, Sharon asked me why I was so glum after such an exciting day.

"Did the heat getcha, An-day?" she asked.

"No, I discovered this morning that my hair is falling out. I'm going bald!"

She examined my scalp. "Oh, you've got plenty of hair yet, but if it does all fall out, we can get you a green or tan Dickies outfit and start calling you Harold Junior!"

54

Coming to terms with Cameron Whitcomb the summer of 1963, I was coming to terms with myself. Ours had always been a love-hate relationship. Growing up in Taunton, he'd always enjoyed making fun of me and putting me down in front of other kids. Once on the schoolbus, when we were both in Taunton Grammar School, Cameron mocked me for wetting my pants by singing a satirical version of "Here Comes Santa Claus."

"Here comes Droopy Drawers! Here comes Droopy Drawers! Right down Droopy Drawers Lane!"

Still, when we were kids, I loved going into his bedroom with its super-masculine decor: cowboy wallpaper, six-shooter cap pistols in fancy holsters dangling from his bedstead, model planes—one of them gasoline powered, model cars, games, and the biggest collection of comic books I'd ever seen. Cameron had everything. He was always going on Boy Scout trips with my older brother Bobber.

Our mothers were best friends, and so growing up, we were often thrown together. We slept together at his grandmother's house, at his house, in assorted Maine woods camps. He was moody, but he could be hilariously funny and make me roar with laughter. Cameron always took the lead. He was full of energy and good-looking. He drove the boat, he decided where to go fishing, he chose the games to play. I tried to follow his lead, but when I messed up, he'd mock me. My world was books, records, movies, and school. At school what he liked best was sports, and the rougher the better. When the Whitcombs moved to Townsend Harbor at the end of Cameron's freshman year at Ellsworth High School, he left the Eagles' football team for that of Townsend Regional. Once they had left Taunton, I never saw Cameron much again except for the summer of 1963. They were filming *Carousel* when Cameron was in high school, and they used the students for extras in the movie. Originally, Frank Sinatra was hired as the lead, and Sinatra had rented a place for the summer; but after only about three weeks, he quit the picture to be replaced by Gordon MacRae. Cameron said he enjoyed being around Sinatra more than MacRae, because Sinatra was so damn cool. It was easy for me to see why Cameron would admire Sinatra, for he, too, wanted to be the coolest guy, the boss, the head honcho.

After high school in 1956, Cameron went to the Maine Maritime Academy. He'd always been around boats, knew how to handle them. But something went wrong at the Academy, for he didn't finish out his freshman year. The following year, he joined the Navy.

Talking with Sharon one day, I asked her why she thought Cameron quit Maine Maritime.

"He probably couldn't take the discipline," she said. "Ya know, Cameron has had it hard trying to live up to the Whitcomb name. He'd be a great guy if he wasn't always trying so hard to be a big deal."

Throughout the summer, Cameron would often stop by our take-out area and joke with us, especially the girls. He'd pick up Sharon, Trudy, or Patty and bounce them up and down on his lap, saying, "Humpty Dumpty sat on a wall! Humpty Dumpty had a great fall!" and then drop them through his knees onto the floor. He'd sidle up to one of the girls, clutching his crotch, whining, "Nurse! I've got this awful pain right here! Something's gotta be done!"

One afternoon Cameron was visiting with us, joking around, making fun of Cecil and Millard as they both walked about the wharf whistling while they worked, when Cameron's sister Lynne happened by. She was a dental hygienist by trade and was working during the week that summer in Aroostook County, but she'd be back on the coast for the weekends. That day Lynne drove her 1961 red-and-white Plymouth convertible, which she called "Cupcake," right down on the wharf at a faster-than-safe speed, screeching to a stop less than a foot from her father, who was filling up one of the two Pepsi machines at the edge of the wharf.

Lynne, who was wearing sunglasses, hollered, "Watch out, Millard! Almost gotcha that time!"

Making a reference to the popular Bette Davis film of 1962, Cameron gestured towards his older sister, saying, "You know *Whatever Happened to Baby Jane*, well, look what happened to Baby Lynne!"

Bright, attractive, and talented, Lynne Whitcomb had excelled as both a student and athlete in high school, and had gone off to college pregnant by her boyfriend. She married him, dropped out of school, and gave birth to a son. The marriage failed after a short time, she returned to college, getting her degree in dental hygiene. Since then, she had worked for the State of Maine going from school to school as a hygienist.

Her blonde hair blowing in the breeze, Lynne greeted us by asking, "How are you guys doing since the big crabmeat picking riot?"

One Saturday night, just before closing time, Lynne arrived with a bunch of her partying friends and they took over two picnic tables at the end of the wharf and were having a high old time. I was about to boil up another batch of two-pounders for them, as Lynne had instructed, when Millard said, "Don't boil another damn lobster for 'em! We're closing up. They can stay here all night and get loaded and throw each other off the wharf, but I'm not serving her and those goddamn bums anything more!"

That was the strongest outburst of temper I'd ever seen or heard from Millard. I assume he never knew what I overheard between him and Cecil through the register. In public especially he kept his feelings to himself and always appeared calm, collected, moderate, friendly, and easy-going. He'd be puffing on his pipe and musing thoughtfully about the state of the world. He told me once that his greatest pleasure of the week was sitting down after supper in his favorite reclining chair on one of his nights off and reading *Time* magazine from cover to cover.

One night in August, Maxine invited me to a birthday party for Cameron. Others were invited, too, but I was the only one who showed up. Millard didn't come until late because it was his night on. Even Cameron himself was late; and he stayed only long enough to open his presents, which included an electric fry pan, two gift certificates from Portland men's stores, a ski sweater, a portable typewriter, and an electric shaver. Maxine told him that he would also be getting a freezer full of steaks for the upcoming school year. "He needs his time for studying, and so he eats steak a lot because it's so easy to prepare," she explained. Cameron lived in his own apartment in Boston and his mother even drove down once in a while to clean it for him. As Cameron was making a wish before blowing out all the candles on his cake, I remember wondering what it could be that he was wishing for? Cameron didn't eat any cake or ice cream because he said it was too fattening. He was also in a great hurry to be off some place; so Maxine, Millard, and I sat there eating the cake heaped high with Cameron's favorite flavor—chocolate marshmallow.

On the stormiest night of the summer, I was in bed reading, listening to the wail of the wind and the sound of the rain, when who should come knocking at my door but Cameron, standing there wild and handsome in his yellow slicker against the night and storm. He was wild eyed and yelling at me, "FOR CHRIST'S SAKE, GET YOUR PANTS ON! PUT DOWN YOUR GODDAMN BOOK, AND COME HELP ME!" As usual, I did as he commanded, but I did ask him what was going on. "Is the wharf collapsing?"

"No! But I've got to get a boat out of here tonight!"

"But it's too rough out, Cameron. Practically a hurricane. Look at the size of the waves in the harbor!"

The wind was raging and the driven rain pelted us as we made our way down the outside stairs to the wharf below.

"Christ, stop being such a whiny old lady for five minutes!" Cameron yelled at me for trying to reason with him. "In the Navy, I was on the water in much worse weather than this!"

Underneath the main wharf were several floats where punts and a couple of motor boats were secured. The floats and boats that night were bobbing up and down while Cameron continued yelling instructions to me. We had to lug an outboard motor down from the shop, and then hook it on the back of one of the motor boats. Cameron wanted me to both help steady the boat and hold a flashlight while he attached and started the motor. It was an insane scene.

"Where do you need to go on a night like this?"

"Listen, I don't ask you where you go, do I? Of course, I don't have to since you don't go any place; but I've got to get to this fucking party out on Black Island! I'm late as it is!"

"Must be quite the bash," I said.

He didn't reply, and I stood there on the bobbing float watching Cameron, his black hair hanging in his face. He had one foot in the boat and the other on the wharf, repeatedly yanking the starter cord, trying to get the motor going.

"Steady the christled boat, will ya, stupid? And keep the light shining in the right direction!"

"Kind of hard to steady anything when the float is going up and down," I said; but I got down on my hands and knees on the slippery, cold float and held onto the boat as best I could, while he continued to tug away on the cord. Finally, the motor burst into life, Cameron cast off, and I let go. He managed to back the boat out and away from the float, the angry water slapping and gurgling all about us. He took the light from me and set it on one of the boat seats.

"Take it easy!" I said.

"Are you kidding?" he asked. "I've never taken anything easy in my life! Say, Bookworm, ya wanna climb in and go with me to a party you'll never forget?"

"No thanks. I think you're committing suicide this time."

"Well, Andy Pandy, Old Boy, you just make sure they give me a first-class funeral, huh? Have a nice night reading and playing with yourself!"

And off he went into the stormy harbor. I really didn't expect to see him alive again. I stood there for as long as I could still make him out—I was already thoroughly soaked—but, finally, I trudged back upstairs to change my clothes, heat some water for coffee, and try and get warm.

Cameron survived, but he was having a run of bad luck, since the very next day, he was reaching over the tank where the big lobsters were, and an unpegged two-pounder snagged one of his pectoral muscles. I had never heard such a yelp come out of Cameron before; and he came out of the tank room bleeding and hopping mad.

"I want this goddamn lobster cooked up right now! I'm going to eat the bastard!"

All Millard said was this ought to teach Cameron to not go barechested in the tank room.

Near the end of August, I got to go to one of Cameron's notorious parties. He knew I was yearning for some kind of social life—

we had talked about it; and he had even offered me his car. One afternoon, I was busy rinsing off the lobster trays and putting them on the drying racks, when he came over to me and asked, "Ya wanna come to my party—the best party of the summer—that I'm throwing this weekend?"

"Sure," I said, "but I can't afford the ten dollar admission you're charging." He knew I was trying to save money for my last year in college.

"You won't have to pay if you do me a couple of favors. Interested?"

"Yes."

"Well, then, I need a chauffeur, and you used to do that down to Granite Neck, didn't ya?"

"Yes."

"O.K., well, look, I'll get Dad to let you off early Saturday night, so you can pick up my car and drive to the Portland Airport and pick up the best-looking stewardess coming in on the six p.m. Northeast flight from Boston. Then drive back here, go to the rear of Fisherman's Wharf and pick up José. He's the chef and he'll be expecting you. Just go to the kitchen door. Then, I'd like you to pick up one more lovely lady, a girl you might know—Claire Lizotte?"

"From the University of Maine? Pretty blonde cheerleader?"

"That's the one. Sexy little French broad with big tits."

"She's in my class. She was chosen a Sophomore Eagle, and this year she'll be an All Maine Woman."

"She's all woman all right."

"Where will she be?"

"She works over to Fisherman's Wharf, too; but lives in the big white house across from the village green. You know the place I mean—the house with green shutters. Lots of college girls live there."

"I think so."

"Then, you drive all of 'em out the Ocean Point Road to Rocky Island Lodge, O.K.?"

"O.K., thanks, Cameron."

"It's my treat. It'll be good to have ya—and good for ya. You'll have a good time, Egghead." He slapped me on the shoulder and smiled. "Give ya the juicy specifics on the stewardess later. Her name's Camille."

"Another French girl?"

"Maybe she's French. I just know she's from Texas and she's stacked."

That Saturday night, I couldn't drive Cameron's VW bug, couldn't get it in reverse, so Millard let me drive his Plymouth station wagon. I picked up Camille, who was a very lovely stewardess indeed; and also the chef, who turned out to be Cuban and who brought all his cooking equipment with him; and Claire, whom I remembered well from school but who didn't remember me at all, even though we had had classes together at Orono.

Cameron had rented the whole Rocky Lodge area, a secluded peninsula, and it was already packed with people when we got there. Cameron had special admission cards printed up with just his name on them, so we showed our cards to the guy at the gate who let us pass. I parked the car and we walked, carrying the cooking equipment, to an open area near the water where a couple of fires were already going for the barbecue. José took charge immediately; and as it ended up, I helped José for much of the evening with his cooking of the chicken, potatoes, and corn. There was plenty of beer--and I was impressed by the kegs, having never been to a fraternity "keg party" before. When the party got into full swing, there was a good-looking red haired British woman of middle-age vintage with an accordion who provided the music, along with some young guy who played the guitar. Cameron was running around collecting tickets from everyone to make sure there weren't any freeloaders. He didn't seem happy; he was in one of his grumpy moods. All of his girlfriends, including Camille and Claire, were always wondering where he was.

José laughingly referred to Cameron as the "Downeast Hugh Hefner."

At one point Cameron accosted me. "Why the fuck did you bring my old man's car?"

"I wasn't able to get the VW into reverse."

"Too complicated for ya, huh? Jesus, what a retard!"

Besides the beer kegs I was also impressed by my first view of marijuana cigarettes, which a number of people seemed to be passing around.

Of course, most of the clientele was made up of college students who worked in the Townsend area; but there were older and younger people, too. Near midnight, while José was still busy roasting chicken and hot dogs, the red-haired songstress switched from her bawdy ballads and party songs to folk music, which had couples nestling about the rocks and beach, going off into the bushes. The evening was winding down and getting very wistful when, suddenly, a very pretty blonde girl wearing a University of Minnesota sweatshirt, jumped on a picnic table and started doing a very sexy striptease to music. The tempo changed again, and people gathered around her clapping and shouting, "Take it off!" And, as she did so, other girls and guys decided to do the same; and I decided to leave.

I had drunk a lot of beer, and I stumbled down this dirt road in search of Millard's Plymouth which I had parked in a ditch near the entrance. There was no worry about José, Claire, or Camille, because they all had other rides. Getting back to Townsend Harbor, however, I had to go to the bathroom very urgently; so I drove the car right down on the wharf, got out, and rushed to the edge of the wharf near the gas pump. And there, at two in the morning, looking out across the bay and the lights of the harbor, I took one of the best and longest pisses of my life!

The next day at work, Cameron, who claimed he had a hell of a hangover, asked me if I had enjoyed myself.

"Sure. It was quite the wingding," I said.

"Just don't go blabbing to my parents about the dope, O.K.?"

"O.K."

"Christ, I'll never have another party like that," he said. "Too much fucking trouble, and I lost about three hundred dollars."

"The University of Minnesota made quite a splash. Max Shulman would have enjoyed that touch."

"What the hell are you talking about?" Cameron asked, taking a drag on his cigarette.

"The blonde with the University of Minnesota sweatshirt who did the tabletop strip—in his books, Max Shulman is always making fun of the University of Minnesota."

"You read too many books," Cameron said.

And speaking of books, Cameron had me read two for him that summer so he could get some English credit.

"Have you read *Catcher in the Rye* and *Red Badge of Courage*?" he asked.

"Yes, but a long time ago," I said. "Why?"

"Would you consider reading them again and writing me a couple of book reports I could give to my English professor this fall? I'll pay you for 'em. I'm just too busy this summer to read and write."

"Sure." And the last week in August, I went upstairs to Cameron's room and knocked on his door. He said, "Come in," and I did. He was naked, sitting in the dark on his bed with his knees drawn up to his chest and his arms hugging his legs. He looked as if he had been lost in meditation.

"Cameron?"

"Yeah, what do you want?"

"I have the two reports for you."

"What reports?"

"The two book reports on *Catcher in the Rye* and *The Red Badge of Courage*. Here, see if they're O.K." I held them out to him, but he didn't take them.

"Yeah, I'm sure they are." He didn't even look at them. "Put 'em over on top of the dresser. I'll see ya later, O.K.?"

"Yeah, O.K."

I left, closing the door behind me. The reports were never mentioned again. I never knew if he thought them suitable or if he ever used them. He never paid me for them.

The last week before Labor Day, it came off very hot one sunny afternoon. There were only a few customers on the wharf, when suddenly, Cameron appeared in his swim trunks, dashed across the wharf, and dove into the water.

Our reactions were instantaneous. "If Cameron can do it, so can we!" yelled Sharon; and so all of us kids ran and jumped off the wharf, too, with all our clothes on. The customers were surprised but they laughed along with us, as we splashed about in the freezing brine.

Cameron had scrambled back up on one of the floats and was standing there in his muscular glory flexing against the sky.

Sharon screamed at him, "Cameron! Help me out of here! I just thought of the stuff that gets thrown in here! This harbor is one of Maine's most polluted! Something just brushed my cheek that smelled awful suspicious! We've got to get out of here before we start rotting!"

But as Sharon tried to pull herself up on the float, Cameron would push her off. He did the same with the other girls, too, but not with me. As the girls screamed and yelled at him, I could see they were getting more and more upset, so I got up behind him and pushed him off. The girls loved it, and screamed, "YEA, AN-DAY! AN-DAY'S

OUR HERO!"

It was wonderful to see the shocked expression on Cameron's face when he surfaced spouting a mouthful of salt water.

"Jesus!" he said, "Old An-day's getting back at me. I gotta watch my ass from now on!"

55

Except for Cameron's big *soirée* and his much smaller birthday bash, I didn't go to any more parties the summer of 1963. Mostly my social life consisted of movie dates with Sharon. I had no car and no money, after all, and very little time off.

To make the nine o'clock show at the movie theatre, we'd really have to race, after closing around 8:30 p.m., from Whitcomb's down Atlantic Avenue across the footbridge to the other side of town. The Strand Theatre, like so many other small-town coastal movie houses, ran only from Memorial Day weekend through Labor Day and films played for only two or three days. It was possible in a summer to see all the major American films, and even some European and art films, that had been released over the past year. Inside, the theatre smelled musty and damp with creaky, worn-out, half-padded old seats. There was a big water stain on the faded stage curtain, but they did still use the curtain in beginning and ending the picture show. The theatre smelled of popcorn, too, and we always had some. Sharon and I enjoyed such films that summer as *Irma La Douce*, *Hud*, *To Kill A Mockingbird*, *Whatever Happened to Baby Jane?*, and *The L-Shaped Room*, in which I remember the unwed and pregnant Leslie Caron saying, "My virginity was becoming rather cumbersome." She also befriends a lesbian in the same dowdy London boarding house, and when Leslie finds out that the lesbian's great friend is another woman, the lesbian with a smile simply explains, "It takes all kinds, dear."

Even though I had had the one time with Essie Torrey, I could still identify closely with the "cumbersome virginity" line. I still felt and acted like a hysterical virgin. I didn't dare look at Sharon at that point, but I did wonder if she were a virgin. The pill had been invented and was first generally available in 1963. We had been talking about that, and how girls were now as free as boys to have sex.

As a good boy afraid to grope, even in the darkness of a movie theatre, I must have thought of my skinny, despised, young man's body as some kind of sacred vessel to be known only to God, an occasional doctor, and my undertaker. Pure as Grade A Maine milk, untouched by other men or women, and hardly by myself. My mother, who used to scrub me in the kitchen sink (we had no running water nor indoor bathroom when I was growing up), with her neatness mania and her own sexual hang-ups, had driven into me the need to be clean above all else. Thus, I couldn't imagine having sex in a dirty place or anywhere under less than sanitary, pristine conditions. If it had to happen, it should be as in June Allyson and Van Johnson movies in sparkling, clean, comfortable, and Technicolor surroundings, preferably bathed in a warm, golden hue with romantic music playing. But sex, of course, isn't clean. It's a very messy business; and at that overwrought and confusing point in my silly young life, still suffering from a bad self-image, inferiority complex, and terminal shyness, I wasn't ready for any kind of sex beyond furtive self-abuse, with, of course, plenty of Kleenex close by.

No matter what the film was, it was fun being with Sharon. We'd usually discuss the movie on our walk back home. When we went to see Jack Lemmon and Lee Remick in *Days of Wine and Roses*, there was a scene in which the actors are standing on a wharf and Lee tells Jack not to look down below them at the flotsam and jetsam where it's all filthy and polluted, but to look straight out at the water where it's beautiful. On our way back to Atlantic Avenue that night, we paused on the footbridge and replayed that scene.

"Don't look into the depths, An-day," said Sharon. "Best to stay on the surface."

Another night after work, Sharon and I went searching for J.D. Salinger. Rumor had it that the celebrated author, a major hero of my generation, was staying at the Village Inn in the middle of Townsend Harbor. Even though I was just twenty-one and Sharon was only twenty, and neither of us had been in a bar before, we took the chance for the sake of meeting old J.D. The Village Inn bar was jammed with tourists, but we did get a spot in a dark corner. Sharon ordered a rum-and-Coke while I ordered a Budweiser. We felt very naughty and foolish, not sure of bar protocol. When the waitress brought us our drinks, I asked her if it were true that J.D. Salinger was actually staying there.

"I honestly don't know," she said, "but I heard someone else say there was a Mr. Salinger at the bar."

We stared hard at the backs of the men's heads surrounding the bar across the room. Sharon got up at one point to see if the man we thought most likely him was him.

"I'm not sure," Sharon said, "but the guy in the plaid sports coat could possibly be an older Holden Caulfield."

Then I got up with my drink in hand, something that was then against the law in Maine. I started to walk towards the bar when another waitress yelled at me. I thought I was under arrest.

"If you're going to move around, you can't take your drink with ya. I have to bring it to ya. That's the law."

"What a stupid law," I said, feeling as if all eyes, including J.D.'s, were on me.

I sat back down again, and we finished our drinks. Deciding against a second one, we also planned on leaving by walking right by the bar where we could get one last good look to see if anything about any of the men seated there gave off any telltale hints of being the famous author.

No one did.

Back on the footbridge again, I said, "I wish I had had enough guts to go right up to the bar and ask, 'O.K., which one of you guys is J.D.?'"

"Now, Andy, do you think, if he was really there, he would have raised his hand and said, 'Hiya, boy! Say, I'm J.D., and I do wish you and the little gal there would join me!'"

"I don't know, but I would have liked to have tried; and if he had acknowledged himself, I would have asked him whatever became of Holden, Fanny, and Zooey."

"We couldn't have told him we'd been to the movies, though."

"No, that's true."

We continued to walk along talking about old J.D. and what he must really be like all the way back to Sharon's house.

I did so much walking that summer. Another night after work, Patty asked me to walk her home, since she didn't have her usual ride. She was staying with her grandmother while working at the wharf, and her grandmother's house was about two miles on the other side of the harbor.

"I'm afraid if I go home alone," Patty said, "the greasy boys will get me, An-day, so you've got to go with me and protect me."

"Who are the greasy boys?"

"Townies, ya know, local hoods. They see me with my boyfriend, and I know they just want to rape and ravish me."

"I wonder what they'll think when they see you with me?"

"Well, you're a big college man. I don't think they'd dare pull anything, but going alone I know I'd be scared."

Patty was a cute girl, and I was naturally very flattered to escort her any place. We had a delightful walk and talk, Patty pointing out to me along the way *her* Townsend Harbor, her favorite haunts and places to go. When we got to her grandmother's house, she invited me in and I had fun chatting with the older woman who swapped some good Maine stories with me. The next day at work Patty told me how much her grandmother had enjoyed my visit.

"Yep, I'm always popular with old ladies," I said.

"Hey, my grannie isn't just any old bag! And she's a good judge of people. She said you were a good guy."

"I am grateful for the fine compliment," I said.

"Well, you should be!" said Patty.

One night toward the end of the summer, I invited the three girls up to my warehouse digs for a little party. It was practically the first party I had ever thrown for anyone anywhere. I provided beer, Coke, ice, assorted crackers and peanuts. We mostly just sat around playing records, talking, drinking, and eating. It was a good time because we were all in a very good mood. Even Trudy, who could be grumpy, was on her best behavior. She had a boyfriend named Fred, and she especially enjoyed the song from the Carol Burnett show *Once Upon a Mattress*, entitled "I'm in Love with a Girl Named Fred." She made me play the song several times and broke up over it every time.

One night, I tried watching Educational Television, which is what public TV was called before PBS was born; and I remember what a hodgepodge it seemed. There was a Japanese film with sub-titles followed by a man sharpening knives followed by some discussion of the world situation. I didn't see much hope at the time for such fare. I preferred watching pro wrestling. There was a young clean-cut muscleman called "Scientific Bobby," who, try as he might with all of his scientific maneuvers and holds, couldn't win a match. Bobby proved week after week that being handsome, well-built, and wrestling by the rules didn't go for much in a world of dastardly villains.

Now an official English major and History minor, I was busy reading all the time, per usual. Besides *Silent Spring*, which we were all reading, there were *Rats, Lice, and History* by Hans Zinsser, *The Heart is a Lonely Hunter* by Carson McCullers, *Darkness at Noon* by Arthur Koestler, *Fathers and Sons* by Turgenev, *The Day of the Locust* by Nathaniel West, and the book that impressed me the most: *The Fire Next Time* by James Baldwin.

I had picked up the Baldwin book, the black and fiery Dell paperback edition, in the Townsend Fruit Store, and it scared the hell out of me. It made me realize vividly for the first time what was going on that summer in America while I was cooking lobsters in Maine. Since I did read the paper every day, and *Time* magazine every week, I did know about the March on Washington, and I thrilled to Martin Luther King's famous speech; but it took Baldwin's great power as a writer to really make me see and want to get involved in Civil Rights and the Black Revolution as much as possible. I sent away to the Dell Book Company for *Notes of a Native Son* and *Go Tell It On the Mountain*, for I wanted to read all of Baldwin as soon as possible.

As for background music for my reading, I played the popular songs like "Sukiyaki" sung by Kyu Sakamoto in Japanese; "Blowing in the Wind" by Peter, Paul, and Mary; "Hello, Muddah, Hello, Fadduh" by Allen Sherman; "Be My Baby" by the Ronettes; "Danke Schoen" by Wayne Newton; and "Surf City" by Jan and Dean. I bought the *Victory at Sea* album which I played over and over.

The weekly letter writing took up some time. I had no telephone, except for the one in the shop which I hardly ever used, so I wrote frequent letters to my mother, Cousin Lillie working in Boston as a medical technologist, Morgan working in New York for her second summer at McGraw-Hill, and to Stephanie Cartwright, a girl I had met my junior year at the University when we were both working at the library. Stephanie was a native of New York City, like Morgan, and she wore her hair à la Jackie Kennedy and dressed like the First Lady, too. She was a graduate student in English, two years my senior. We shared a similar sense of the absurd and made each other laugh all the time. We had had several dates throughout the school year, and I loved exchanging nutty letters with her. For a couple of weeks she was attending William Butler Yeats summer school in Sligo, Ireland. Stephanie had fallen in love with Yeats at Orono and now had totally enmeshed herself in the poet's world. She wrote me that before returning to Maine in September, she was going to be traveling around England and Scotland as well as Ireland.

Stephanie's cards and letters to me from Ireland were such a joy. She'd tell me of her trips to places like Lough Gill in Sligo, the River Corrib and Claddagh Bridge in Galway, and the River Shannon near Limerick City.

And I'd write back to her, telling of my imaginary jaunts around and about Greater Townsend Harbor.

> Limerick City, eh? Well, today I took a few turns about JokeTown, a small village that lies next to Flounderville, a typical Maine harbor town filled with fishy and foul-smelling folk. What's funny, though, is that even though they are so fishy, they really go for divinity fudge.
>
> One of my favorite haunts there is the Maine Stereotype Lounge, next to the Satirical Grill, where I have *whiled* away many an hour whittling wooden boats to put in old bottles, trading "tall tales" with the old fellas about all their Grand Banks fishing days.
>
> Here's where the *real poets* live doing really poetic things, tossing similes about, weaving alliterative passages, and serving up extended metaphor with every mouthful they utter.

I called her "Steph" and she called me "And," and because we also loved playing with our school French, she also referred to me as "Et." In one pre-Sligo letter, she wrote:

> Dear Et,
>
> Did I say that we, two, are "misfits"? I don't remember what I was meaning when I said so, but I can whip

> up a meaning now. I hope we ARE "misfits" in terms of not "belonging" to the human race—perhaps "misfits" was a poor word choice: the "mis" DOES suggest that I thought our not "fitting" to be a bad thing. I think, of course, that everyone-is-different-from-everyone-else and that sort of business, but I think you and I (and others, certainly) are MORE different from everyone else. This is a feeling of superiority?? Perhaps—but not necessarily—different from doesn't have to imply better-than (but then, again . . .) Actually, I haven't (as must be apparent) given this much thought. But as some indication of our unusualness, look at our friends: they're no run-of-the-mill dopes—they're crazy—most of mine anyway. I'm going to stop now and go to bed (after watching my vaccination ooze for a while).

I wrote to my male friends, too, at least once each. Barry DeGarribody, my lifelong pal in Taunton, who used to mow lawns, too, now worked at a hotel on Scarborough Beach, a much bigger hotel than Frenchman's Bay Manor; and Lester Moon, who would be a senior at Husson College in the fall, was still working at home as a caretaker and part-time lobsterman. Russell Barclay had given up summer hotel work for a job as a cameraman for Channel 5 in Bangor. Both Russell and Barry planned on being back at Maine in September with me. Doug Thompson, who was working at a popular restaurant in his hometown of York Beach, would again be my roommate in the fall. Doug and I were both majoring in English.

56

In August the State of Maine must double its population. Not only is that the busiest month for the tourist industry, but it's also traditionally the month when most of Maine's long-time summer people take their vacations. It's in August when the tennis tournaments and sailing regattas are held, along with all the big blueberry pancake breakfasts and state fairs. August is homecoming Downeast for both mainiacs and foreigners. People who've grown up in Maine, or spent all the summers of their lives on the coast or at one of the lakes at the family camp or cottage, plan to come home in August to be in familiar and beloved surroundings, surrounded by their families and friends and neighbors they've known for years.

So it was at the tail end of August of 1963 when both Morgan Carlisle and Cousin Lillie Partridge planned their vacations and would be back in Maine at the same time. I wrote to each of them to plan to come and visit me in Townsend Harbor and I'd get the afternoon off for our reunion. They agreed and set it up. I was very excited to see them both since I hadn't seen Morgan since she stopped working at Frenchman's Bay Manor in 1961, and I hadn't seen Cousin Lil since my April vacation in Boston.

While I did want Morgan and Lil to meet everyone at Whitcomb's and see where I lived, I didn't want to eat there. I wanted us to have a more private picnic outside of town, and so I selected a secluded little beach in Ocean Point a few miles away. In preparation for the big event, I went to the state liquor store to buy my first bottle of wine.

Quite the traumatic experience. Even though I had sampled a number of types of wine, I knew nothing about it. I didn't even know that champagne was a wine, until I saw it listed as such in the store. Wine then could not be purchased in the grocery store, only in the liquor emporium; and the men-in-charge acted like federal agents, or straight-laced, sour-pussed Sunday school superintendents. Every customer was a sinner to them.

The fronts of most State of Maine liquor stores were, for some reason, painted dark green; and so people referred to their local outlet as "the green front," and it was often the butt of gossip and joking. Someone would begin by saying, "Guess who I saw coming out of the Green Front yesterday?"

In Townsend Harbor, however, the liquor store was disguised as a neat little New England cottage with white clapboards and green shutters. One entered a sparkling clean lobby and faced a full-length counter behind which stood the state guardians of the grape. I approached them awkwardly. I did know that since I was serving shellfish, I must get a white wine, but which kind presented a problem. I studied the charts on the walls, and there were a number of white wines, the names of which I had never heard and most of which I couldn't pronounce. Some place, in a book or movie probably, I had heard of sauterne, so sauterne it was.

I stepped up to the counter, expecting this humorless Downeaster with a black necktie to ask me to prove I was twenty-one.

"I'd like some sauterne," I said.

"What kind?"

"French. A nice French one."

"*Haut*?"

"Hot? No, cold, I'd say."

"*Haut* has nothing to do with temperature. It's a type of sauterne, a little sweeter than the regular."

"Oh, well, that sounds good. I'll take a bottle of the *haut*."

Without changing his dour expression, he went to get my wine. Buying liquor then was like getting a book from a library with closed stacks; the customer was not allowed to browse. He returned, my *haut* sauterne wrapped in a brown bag. I paid him what seemed to be a rather high price and hurried away, elated to have been able to buy booze from a liquor store, like an adult.

Next was to get some ice from the freezer room at the wharf in which to pack the sauterne. The lunch menu consisted of lobster, clams, potato chips, and wine. I put the ice and wine in a sturdy cardboard box on the stair landing outside my room. As soon as Morgan and Lillie arrived, I would order the shellfish to be cooked.

But they didn't arrive at noon when they had written they would; and while waiting, I thought of Morgan and our four-year relationship.

Her letters from Smith College had kept me alive and kicking at the University of Maine. I could brag to my roommates that I received letters from a very smart girl from Smith. She made me feel special. She was my connection to the glamorous, greater world of the Ivy League, Manhattan, and the New York suburbs. Morgan had a sharp eye for the ironies and inconsistencies in life. She also loved to nip the pompous and the pretentious in the bud. She was usually on the side of the underdog and didn't suffer fools gladly. When we first met in 1960, and I'd make an assertion about something that I had just read, she'd snap at me, "Have you done any research on it?"

She'd make me feel stupid, and I'd retort, "I suppose if I'd gone to high school in New Jersey, I'd know much more."

"Probably so," she'd say.

I loved our times at the Manor together. Our meals especially would either be occasions of great mirth or antagonism, depending upon the topic under discussion. Once I was discoursing in great ignorance about the cheapness of Jews, when Morgan suddenly slammed down her fork, which bounced off the table, yelling, "FOR GOD'S SAKE, ANDY! MY GRANDMOTHER IS A JEW! I'M ONE-FOURTH JEW!" And she marched out of the dining room. I was crushed. I didn't know what to say to her in apology; but as time went by, the scene became a favorite butt of our on-going jokes.

"I suppose your being one-fourth a Jew, you'll take exception to this," I'd say, "but I want you to know that I have done some research on it!"

About the same time there had been the big cake-in-the-face scene. Morgan had made a chocolate cake with white frosting one night for the help's dessert; and after work, when she, Lil, and I were sitting around in the kitchen preparing to eat some of the cake with ice cream, Morgan started in insulting me in her usual manner; and I said, "You either take that back, Miss New Jersey, or I'm gonna shove this cake in your face!"

Morgan loved courting such physical threats from males, so she just laughed and continued poking fun at me, so I picked up a piece of the cake and shoved it in her face. She was so startled, because she didn't really think I'd ever do such a thing, that bits of the cake went up her nose, and she started choking, coughing, and spitting.

When she did finally get her breath, she yelled, almost in delight, "ANDY! MY GOD, YOU REALLY DID IT!" She was also laughing with bits of chocolate and white frosting all over her face.

It frustrated me when Morgan would talk about the local fishermen, some of them boys I had gone to school with, as if they were some kind of primitive gods. She seemed to envy them for their independence, their self-sufficiency, their way of talking and moving about, and their individualistic idiosyncrasies. Men against nature, or maybe she saw them as men close to nature, romantically and mysteriously different from her New York/New Jersey men.

Finally, here she was again—Morgan with Lillie—in Morgan's father's old gray '57 Plymouth. They were late, as they explained, because of my poor directions. They both looked great with their sunglasses and summer tans. Morgan had on jeans and a white blouse while Lil was in bright pink shorts with a white halter. Both were in great moods. After hugging and kissing, I took them around to meet Millard, Cecil, Harold, Cameron, the crabmeat ladies, and the girls. Millard and Cameron, of course, remembered Lillie from when they lived in Taunton.

After the seafood was cooked, we took off in the gray Plymouth to the Ocean Point picnic site.

When the three of us were together, we always tried for the big laugh. Catching up with each other, swapping story after story in rapid succession, as Morgan, her foot heavy on the accelerator, maneuvered the old Plymouth up and down the narrow winding roads. I began with my observations on life at Crab and Lobster Wharf, while Morgan added her tales of what it was like working in Manhattan in the summer heat, and Lil filled us in on the adventures of a young medical technologist in Boston.

"So what are you going to major in, Morgan?" I asked.

"Well, it doesn't look like Mandarin. . .or French."

"What happened?"

"Let's say the Chinese have proven too inscrutable for me. I'm to be an English major with a French minor; but I'll be living in the French house."

"What does that mean? Remember, I'm only a public school kid."

"That means I'll be living in a house where we will converse only in French."

"That should prove interesting."

"You'll have to come down and visit and see for yourself."

"All I'll be able to do is order *haut sauterne*!"

"What do you mean?" Lil asked.

"You'll see."

Besides college, we talked about living in the city versus living in Maine, the big march in Washington, Civil Rights, the Kennedys, mutual friends, memoirs of the Manor, plans for the future. Peppered with puns and jokes our conversation, as usual, went off in all directions. We did build up to our big laugh. I don't remember what triggered it, but I do remember Morgan almost careening off the road and all three of us laughing uncontrollably.

As for Lillie, she told us about some of her adventures in Boston. Lil had known one of the victims of The Boston Strangler; and after working as a medical technologist for a year, she had discovered that she wanted to go back to college and get a B.A. in another subject, maybe in theater.

"Perhaps you'd be willing to help me, Cousin? I might want to come home and go to the University of Maine. What do you think?"

"I think it would be great, and of course I'll help you."

At Ocean Point there was a narrow rocky beach where we laid out our lunch. The lobsters and clams were still steaming hot when we took them out of the double paper bags. There was plenty of melted butter in styrofoam coffee cups; but I had forgotten to get a cork screw. All Morgan had in the glove compartment were a bottle opener, jack knife, and screwdriver; but by using this tool combination, I managed to whittle down and loosen the cork enough so that I could push the bottom of it out of the bottle neck into the wine. So we drank our haut sauterne with bits of cork floating on top.

Then came the attack of the bees.

We had just raised our wine cups for a toast to our reunion and friendship when the bees came a-buzzing. With a whoop and in a scurry, we moved ourselves and our feast down the beach away from the wild rosebushes that we presumed was the bees' territory. For the most part, this did seem to do the trick; but for the length of our stay there, we were persistently bothered by the little yellow-jacketed beasts.

As Lil commented philosophically later, as Lil was ever wont to do, "I suppose we must always keep in mind, no matter how joyful the reunion, or how rich the friendship, there's always apt to be cork in the wine and bees buzzin' around the lobster."

"Ah, words of wisdom from the medical specialist!" I said.

Years later, when reading *The Letters of Thomas Wolfe*, I came across a few letters he wrote from Ocean Point, Maine the summer before *Look Homeward, Angel* was published; and I liked to think my hero once strode on the beach where we had our picnic.

On the way back to Townsend Harbor, we talked about our summers at the Manor.

"Don't you miss it?" asked Morgan.

"Yes, of course," I said. "It was probably a mistake to leave."

"You can go back, can't you, next summer?" asked Lil.

"I don't know, maybe."

"Andy, remember my first job at the Manor?" asked Morgan.

"No."

"Miss Meyer had me sort out the bugs from the almonds! Honest to God, I spent a good afternoon. It was a little hard, because the bugs, even though they were squiggly, resembled the almonds in both color and size. The almonds were blanched and sliced, and there was nearly a whole can of 'em. Miss Meyer had had them from the summer before, and couldn't see throwing 'em out."

"My first job was painting the back porch toilet seat," I said. "What was yours, Lil?"

"I'm not sure, but I think Miss Meyer was testing my motor skills by taking down the fancy parfait glasses from the cupboard and washing them without breaking them."

"I remember one of our last adventures together was the time when we went to see the movie *Raisin in the Sun* at a matinee in Ellsworth, and how we had a spat because I was afraid we'd be late for dinner preparations and would have to leave before the end of the film, and you wouldn't leave, Morgan!" I said.

"No, of course not. Sidney Poitier was much more important than the damn job at the Manor! Remember how I yelled at you to get your priorities straight?"

"Oh, yes."

"Do you agree now?"

"In retrospect, yes, of course. I loved the movie. It was important for everyone to see it, but I remember when I got back to college in the fall, hardly anyone even knew a thing about *Raisin in the Sun*."

"Or any other black films, writings, or artists, right?"

"Mostly just Cassius Clay's latest boxing match. A bunch of white guys grouped anxiously about a radio listening to Clay's fight. In sports, blacks are getting more and more important and visible."

"About time, wouldn't you say?" asked Morgan, forever the Civil Rights activist.

57

There are those moments and scenes from our lives that continue to trouble and haunt us because at the time we acted so stupidly or wrongly. Such moments often hint at some basic flaw within us; and it makes us cringe to remember them. One such stupid scene from my life happened at the end of the summer of 1963. I call it the Night of the Ten Dollar Error.

It was nearly closing time at Whitcomb's and it was already dark. I was very tired, and because Cecil was standing around watching every move I was making, I was more nervous than usual.

A well-dressed and good-looking summer lady came up to the counter and ordered a couple of pound-and-a-half lobsters boiled to go. Since Sharon was busy talking with Cecil, I handled the order. I boiled the lobsters and wrapped them in a double paper bag for her. She handed me what I thought was a twenty dollar bill. The lobsters came to four dollars, so I handed her back sixteen dollars.

"I only gave you a ten," she said.

And then, I don't know what made me do it; but I started to disagree with her.

"No, you didn't. You gave me a twenty, I'm sure."

"No, I didn't," she said. "I'm positive it was only a ten. It was the only money I brought with me."

At this point, Sharon and Cecil had stopped talking and were staring at me incredulously, as I kept insisting that I was correct and the customer was wrong.

"What is this, some kind of *Candid Camera* joke?" she asked.

"I insist you take the change," I said.

"Well, all right, if you insist," she said with a confused grin. "I certainly won't argue with such a bargain. I'll tell all my friends to buy all their lobsters here where one not only gets free lobsters and their money back, but a tip as well!"

She walked away and I stood foolishly firm in my belief that I was correct.

"I hope you're right," said Cecil.

"I know I am. I don't think she realized she had a twenty."

"An-day, that was the craziest scene yet," said Sharon. She was shaking her head and giggling. "Let's close up. We can't top that one tonight!"

That night in bed I began to worry about it and realized what a total fool I had been, especially in front of Cecil, my boss!

As soon as I saw him the next morning, I asked Cecil how the receipts came out from the previous day.

Without even looking up at me, he said, "We were ten dollars short."

"I'm sorry. You can take it out of my pay."

"That sounds like a good idea."

But he didn't, or they didn't. I received my last week's pay and it was the same as the others. I didn't get any end-of-the-summer bonus, though.

So I crept away from Townsend Harbor that September in bald disgrace. While I may have made one good friend in Sharon, and proven, despite the ten dollar error, that I could be a good, dependable worker in a pressured business, I also knew I shouldn't return. I didn't fit in. Acutely self-conscious and socially inept, I was beginning to get the picture of myself as primarily bookish and a loner. Whenever I thought about it, I was happiest alone in my room, reading and listening to music, keeping my journal. The library, the darkened theater, the bookstore and record shop, and occasional classrooms were the places I felt most at home. I had to find companionship from others who felt the same.

Time to return for my final growing-up summer at Frenchman's Bay Manor.

Summer 1964

58

My senior year at the University of Maine was both dramatic and harried. On October 19, 1963, President Kennedy spoke at the football stadium; and it was a grand occasion and a beautiful, warm day. Because we had had such a good time with Kennedy, his assassination a month later was even more terrible and unbelievable for those of us who had been in his presence that wonderful autumn afternoon.

In January, 1964, my parents helped me buy my first car, a white 1959 Ford Galaxie four-door hardtop, so that I could begin my student teaching at Bangor High School in February. I student taught for half-days in the mornings for sixteen weeks while carrying a full academic load in the afternoons. I worked in the library as much as possible to help support my car and drinking expenses. Since I could drink in bars now, I went all the time with my friends to the taproom at Pat's Pizza in Orono, the most popular student hangout at the time.

The Vietnam War was escalating, and all of us graduating males were required to take Army physicals. I passed! I had had two years of R.O.T.C. my first two years in college. I was busy interviewing for teaching jobs, mostly outside of Maine. Since they needed teachers at the time, it was possible with some school districts to get teacher deferments. When I accepted a position with a central New York school, I asked the superintendent if I could get such a deferment and he said yes. No problem since he was on the draft board. I signed a contract to teach English for $4,800 with $200 more for coaching the boys' cross country team.

Before I had accepted the New York job in the spring of '64, I had driven with my roommate Doug Thompson to New Milford, Connecticut where I had interviewed for another teaching position I almost took. On the way back to Maine, we stopped in Boston to have dinner with Cousin Lil and to go to the film *Doctor Strangelove*, which all three of us were very excited about.

The speaker at my graduation was Dr. Ralph Bunche, then the U.S. Ambassador to the U.N. A number of us students were very pleased to be addressed by one of the country's most prominent black leaders. Our class was very race-conscious, since we had chosen the first black homecoming queen at Maine and had accepted the first American black boy into a Maine fraternity.

The Barclays gave me a graduation dinner party at their house in Bangor. My parents and other relatives came up from the coast for the festivities.

There had been girlfriend trouble, too, in my senior year. I had expected Stephanie to return in the fall as planned, but she couldn't afford it, so she stayed home in New York, after her summer in the British Isles, for the fall semester working in Manhattan. She did return for the spring semester, but she was so poor, she was living in a shack down near the Stillwater River; she was also working at a mill in Old Town instead of in the library with me. The library job didn't pay as much as the mill. She was only taking two courses because of her busy schedule, and wasn't sure if she would ever finish her master's degree. We had a few dates, but it wasn't the same as before. She had new friends and one was a blond violin player named John. He played for the Bangor Symphony.

So, on the weekends, I was going more and more to Bangor drinking in all the bars on Exchange Street with my good friend Cato and my roommate Doug. We also found out we enjoyed strippers and frequented a couple of striptease joints along with the Air Force boys from Dow Air Base and old-time loggers from out of the woods. One night Cato and I even tried to find a whorehouse we had been told was on Ohio Street in Bangor. Instead, that night we got stopped by the Bangor Police for running a red light. I ended up in traffic court along with some men who had sold liquor to minors and a couple of prostitutes. From the Penobscot County Court House, where I paid my fine, I had to rush back to the University and take a final exam. That last semester in college was a wild time for me. I was on overload with too little sleep, too much drinking, too little studying, and too much working. I flunked one of my final exams because the night before I had tried to study with a few of my classmates, all of us having beer and pizza in an Old Town apartment; and the next morning I had a terrible hangover.

Just before my graduation, my Aunt Eller Partridge, Lillie's mother and my mother's younger sister, died in a car accident. Eller was the first of the twelve children of my Warren grandparents to die. She was only forty-six and my favorite aunt whom I loved. I took the day off from student teaching and school for her funeral. Lillie came home from Boston and was staying at our house. I stayed with her for a while after the funeral, talking quietly with her upstairs in the dark; and then drove back to the University, crying all the way.

By the end of June, I was back at my summer job at Frenchman's Bay Manor where Miss Meyer had not only welcomed me back with open arms but raised my pay and position to assistant manager. So, I had returned, but it wasn't the same. Thomas Wolfe had said it all when he wrote *You Can't Go Home Again.* While Ellen, Sally, and Mia were still there, they had learned to get on without me, and I was frustrated not to have things my old way.

I couldn't even have my old attic room back, since there was a new kitchen boy, Roderick Poors, who had taken my place the summer before. The room I was given was on the second floor with the guests, the tiny room that Parker Lawson always had at the end of the summer. It was a room that we hardly ever rented; and which, Miss Meyer told me, I might have to vacate if Parker came as usual at the end of August and the hotel was full.

Other than the fact that we were both Maine boys, Roderick, whom we called Roddy, and I had little in common. I was now a college graduate who would become a teacher in the fall, and Roddy was still a high school student at Mollusk Memorial. He had a good sense of humor, but since he wasn't much interested in books and the arts, we indulged mostly in small talk. Roddy also didn't seem to be obsessed by the dreams I had of escaping from Maine and becoming some kind of artist. He was interested in the normal pursuits of cars, girls, sports, and making money.

My conversations with him went something like this:

"Hey, An-day, you always wear Levi's. Do you like 'em better than Lee's or Wrangler's?"

"Yeah, I guess I do. I like the way they look and fit better."

"Yeah, there is something sexier about the cut of Levi's jeans."

"Now, Roddy, do you think I look sexy in my Levi's?"

He giggled. "Well, now, I guess you look O.K. for a guy. But why I was asking you that is because I respect you and your opinions. You've been to college."

"Yes, and everyone who has been to college deserves great respect. You should get down on your Wrangler-clad knees and worship me, the college grad in his Levi's."

"No, seriously, An-day, I've only known you for a few days, but I'm impressed by how everyone respects you and likes you, how you deal with the guests like you do. You know just what to say to 'em."

"Well, after five years, I should be able to."

"No, it's not just the old-time regulars who love you; it's the new people, too. You know so damn much that whatever subject they bring up, you can think of a good comment. Now, I could never do that."

"I guess, Roddy, it helps to read a lot and be interested in everything, especially people."

"Yeah, you sure do read a lot. I read a little but it never stays with me. How do you know which books are the best to read?"

"You don't at first. I just tried all the authors and books recommended by my teachers, relatives, friends, other people like Mrs. Richmond and Miss Meyer; and little by little, you find your way, the authors and books that mean the most to you."

"Could you recommend some books for me?"

"Sure, but I've got to find out what you're interested in, curious about, and want to know about. I read mostly because I want to know everything. I also read because it gives me great pleasure, like I'm part of a great big discussion or world-wide storytelling session. When I was growing up I was a lonely kid who wanted to know about the world beyond Downeast and yet I wanted to know about Maine, too, before I was born."

That reading discussion was probably the heaviest Roddy and I ever shared. Usually, it was about cars and girls.

"Hey, An-day," Roddy asked one time. "Can I ask you a question?"

"Sure, Rodd-ay, ask me anything."

"How much did you pay for that Galaxie of yours?"

"Eleven hundred, and I'm still paying."

"It's a nice car."

"I have my father to thank for that. He picked it out for me over to Ellsworth. He's a good mechanic and knows what to look for. I didn't even know enough to look under the car to see whether or not it's been in an accident, but my father did."

"Could I borrow it sometime, in case I need to go somewhere?"

"Yes, if you pay for the gas."

"Just between you and me, what I'd like most to do this summer would be to have a date with Ellen. Now, don't tell her, but, God, I think she's the best-looking girl around these parts. I get a hard-on every time she comes into the room. Do you think she'd go out with me?"

"Oh, I think she might, if you give her a good reason to, but I wouldn't mention the hard-on right off."

"Jesus, if Ellen and Sall-ay are any indication, they must have some wicked good-looking women up there in Bangor."

"They've got their share, Rodd-ay."

"The girls I get to date around these parts are nice enough, I suppose, but not as sexy and smart like Ellen and Sall-ay."

"I know."

As it turned out, Roddy did borrow my car and date Ellen once. He took her bowling in Ellsworth; and they both said it was a very enjoyable time, but that was the only date they had that summer with each other. Most of the time, Roddy went off with his local pals; and by the end of the summer, both Ellen and Sally were busy dating boys from the Navy base. After work, most evenings, I never saw any of my co-workers. I started spending my evenings and drinking with Miss Meyer. One night she taught me about the greatness of Caruso. I brought my record player downstairs and she told me to go into her office closet and get this stack of old 78 rpm records. We drank drink after drink and played record after record, which she tried to sing along with. When she was really sloshed and nearly passed out, I tried helping her upstairs to her room. She fell down and I had to pick her up and carry her upstairs. As I lay her down on her bed, she said to me that she wouldn't be down in the morning, that I'd have to handle breakfast by myself.

As assistant manager, and for many of the meals, assistant cook, I'd order the girls about a bit, and they didn't like it. We'd start having spats. I felt quite often they were taking advantage of Miss Meyer, especially in her advanced drunken states, and do sloppy work, and I'd pick them up on it.

"Sally, don't use a chipped plate for someone's meal! Get a good plate," I'd say.

Sally stuck out her tongue at me. "Oh, Mr. Bachelor of Arts! He just expects everything to be perfect!"

"I just expect you to do a good job."

"Yassuh, Boss!"

So, we'd work together, but the fun was gone. In my absence, the girls had had the charge of the Olds. Mrs. Richmond had had it repaired so it looked new, and they used it all the time. They ran the errands I used to, and at night they went out in it. Of course, I had my own car, and it was newer than the Olds. The girls didn't need me like they did in 1962. Instead of the right-hand man, I felt like the odd man out.

Things came to a head one morning when I went berserk in the cellar. I had had words with both Ellen and Sally, and Miss Meyer backed them against me. I had gone down to check the coal stoves and the girls had some of their uniforms hanging up drying by the stoves. It was raining out that day so they couldn't hang them outdoors, and we had no dryer. Frustrated and ranting to myself, I took one of the coal shovels and knocked down the uniforms which fell into the coal bin. The girls were infuriated at me, and Miss Meyer had me in her office for a talk.

"Errr. . .Andy, this behavior of yours can't go on. I was prepared today to let you go, but I hope you'll change. The girls and Roddy, too, feel that you're being too bossy with them. With your attitude and behavior you've created a lot of unnecessary tension."

So, I did try to change for the rest of the summer; and things improved. I still did the chauffeuring and Miss Meyer sent me on runs to the liquor stores in both Milbridge and Ellsworth. One afternoon in Milbridge, I drove by the funeral for Lawrence Billings, one of my classmates and friends from high school who had been killed in a car crash. He was a great-looking guy, reckless and full of life. I had run on the state championship cross country team with him and we had played on the same basketball team, too. Everyone had loved Lawrence, and there looked to be hundreds of people at his funeral. I had almost stopped the car to go and join them. Lawrence had married soon after graduating from high school and had already fathered one child. However, he had always driven too fast and taken too many chances. He had always had new cars, too, thanks to the man he worked for who supplied several of the boys in Milbridge with new cars. He had been such bright company for us at Mollusk Memorial at the games, in classes, at dances, on the bus coming and going to games. Lawrence's death, along with Aunt Eller's, and the assassination of Kennedy, combined with my worry over being drafted for Vietnam despite the promise of deferment, made me edgy, ill at ease, and more fretful than usual. I knew I wasn't being myself and knew I wasn't much fun to be with.

So, I'd drink with Miss Meyer at night, and she'd tell me stories. Once she said she had had one of Ginger Rogers' ex-husbands chase her around the Manor's kitchen telling her how beautiful she was. Another night, she told me all about her German immigrant family and even dug out her father's old *bourganmeister* jacket and medal from when he was a prominent citizen of some small German town. She told me how she had had to work to help her brother and sisters get through school. She had been a fine student but had had to work instead of going on to college. She progressed through a series of secretarial positions in Manhattan before landing her plum job at the Waldorf-Astoria.

While getting drunker and drunker, Miss Meyer would recite lines of poetry, sing bits of popular tunes. Once banging her beer glass on the table, she recited: "A knife and a fork / A bottle and a cork / That's how you spell New York!"

Her hair a frightful, frizzy mess, she'd take dramatic drags on her cigarette, sip from her drink, throw her head back, grin from ear to ear, and push her breasts upwards, sometimes massaging her breasts while recounting her tales. Sometimes she'd ask me to massage her neck and shoulders. One night, Ellen and Sally came back early, and we all danced to some rock-'n' roll records. I remember Ellen swinging Miss Meyer around the kitchen to the tune of Ray Stevens' "Ahab, the A-rab."

Some afternoons, the girls and Roddy would accompany me down to the rocks; but it was no longer a regular habit. When they were done with their work, they no longer hung around the place like they used to. The late-night swims in the pool were over, too. Roddy told me he couldn't swim; and so on my off-hours I was mostly by myself.

As for Mia Jones, she was still the chambermaid and still her beautiful, warm self. Since 1962, however, she had learned to drive; and so when she wasn't needed at the hotel, she went home to her family. She told me, though, how glad she was to have me around again. She was also relieved that Hedy Smith's husband Herman had been transferred to New York, so that she didn't have to put up with "Hedy the Nazi" anymore.

Of course, I was most curious as to whatever had happened to Essie. Mia told me that she didn't live with her husband's grandmother in Summer Harbor anymore, that they had bought a house in nearby Cold Harbor. Mia said that Essie was still the same and that she went lobstering with her husband.

"Zey have hiz and herz boats!" Mia said, "and she makes a very good lobstervoman. You know, how she loves to be down on the varves vith all zee men."

"Oh, yes, how well I know."

I spent the summer trying to see her, but I only got to see her once. I ran into her in the grocery store, and there she was shopping with her boys.

"See my two little dinks, An-day! Wild as their mom and dad! Vaughn says they'll be lobstering themselves by next summer; and that'll be good because I'll be laid up for a while." She patted her stomach.

"Another baby?" I asked.

"Yep. 'Fraid so. Earth Mother, ya know. Remember how you always called me the Mermaid? Well, I might be a good piece of tail, but somehow I keep getting caught in the trap! Now, what about you? You're now a college graduate, right?"

"Yes; and I've got a teaching job for September in New York State."

"So, you really are leaving Downeast? Somehow I thought you never really would. It'll be strange not having you around."

"Oh, I'll be back vacations and summers."

"Well, you say that now; but maybe you'll finally meet someone and get married and settle down; and your goddamn wife will want you to stay in New York with her, and I'll never see you again!"

"Well, if that does happen, it won't be for a while."

"Don't you have a love life yet?"

"Not really," I said.

"For God's sake, An-day! After I went to all that trouble of breaking you in! What's the matter with you? Get after those gals down to the Manor. They must like you!"

"They've got boyfriends."

"Jesus, when we were kids, you were all concerned about getting good grades and money enough for college; now you're concerned about what? Everyone needs a little regular nookie, An-day! Makes everything better."

"I'll be working on it, O.K.?"

"You'd better! Now, have you seen my lobster boat?"

"No."

"You're in luck. I happened to come grocery shoppin' in 'er! She's tied up down at the town dock. She's a beaut! Wait till you see!"

I walked down from Guilford's to the dock, helping her with her groceries; and when we got there, she asked me to pick out her boat from the ones in the harbor.

"Ess-ay, how am I supposed to tell which one is yours?"

"Read the names on their rear-ends, College Man!"

I looked at them all, and there on the stern of a handsome green-and-white boat was boldly lettered FISH BAIT.

"There, see, you named my boat!" She left her groceries and boys, and came over to me and hugged and kissed me. "You put your brand on this cowgal a long time ago; and even though you've never felt about me the way I felt about you, I'll always love ya! Now, go find someone else to love, even thought she'll never be as good as me!"

We were standing in the middle of the dock with cars and trucks coming and going, fishermen with their gear going to and from their boats. One man even grinned at Essie, and said, "For God's sake, Ess-ay, you making love down here on the wharf again today?"

"Oh, fuck you, Hollis! You're just jealous, as usual!" Essie yelled.

"Seriously, An-day, you've got to come lobstering with me some morning so we can talk. But if you can't, and I don't see ya, you have a great time in New York, and a great teaching career, and for God's sake, GO GET LAID! And have some great orgasms! GOTTA

GO! C'mon, boys! Help Mummer with the groceries!"

I watched her row her sons and groceries out to the boat, start the motor, and cast off; and as I trudged up the hill back to Main Street in the village, she gave me a good blast from the horn on the FISH BAIT.

59

To add to Miss Meyer's worries, she had received a call early in the summer from Mrs. Richmond in Greenwich. Mrs. Richmond had fallen in her office at the hospital and broken her ankle. She was getting around on crutches, and would be laid up for a spell; but she still planned on coming up to Maine. As the summer wore on, however, it became clear with each phone call back and forth that Mrs. Richmond would not be coming, even though her ankle was healing slowly. We all got to talk and joke with Mrs. Richmond on the phone, and she was as hilarious as ever; but more and more, Miss Meyer talked about selling the Manor. She even had "Buzzie" Bradley, Mrs. Bradley's son, and other prominent Granite Neck residents in to talk and appraise the value of the place.

"It's been almost twenty years," Miss Meyer said, "and I can't run this place for much longer by myself."

Business seemed pretty good in 1964. Most of the regulars like the Wertzes, the Titcombs, Mrs. Lawson, the Fidelsteins, the Hillocks, Mrs. Chittendon, Rosie Talbot and Ruth Tainter, Mrs. Gay & Co., Betsy Jane Rousseau, Belle Kane, Erastus Bull, and the Pettengills all showed up; and the dining room was busy with special parties and Sunday afternoon dinner guests.

Among the newcomers were three interesting women, two of whom I had to chauffeur.

One was a tiny French woman named Mrs. Martin from Long Island. She was accompanied by her twelve-year-old grandson whom she was taking to all the national parks in one summer, starting with Acadia in Maine. She was a pretty and jolly lady and I enjoyed our chats as I chauffeured them about. They stayed for a week and each day I'd drive them to another place with a picnic lunch and leave them until later in the day when I'd pick them up. Mrs. Martin would always give me a good-sized tip every trip; and it was through her that I learned about a local man, Phil Alley, a service veteran and part-time lobsterman, who had started a ferry boat service between Granite Neck and Mount Desert Island. I drove up to his house on the back road to Summer Harbor where he had a dock and a small boat that he used to take people across the bay.

"In the old days, there used to be regular ferry service from Summer Harbor to Bar Harbor, you know," he told me.

"Yes, I know," I said. I asked him about his charges and times when he could take our hotel guests across. Mrs. Martin and grandson were the first passengers from the Manor, and they pronounced his service wonderful.

"He's just perfect as a Maine guide," said Mrs. Martin. "He's got a lovely accent and is a good storyteller. He's not hurried, and he points out so many things of interest. He knows his bay and this area well. He has a charming sense of humor, and he arranged for us to be met at the dock by a taxi."

So for the rest of the summer, the Manor advertised Phil's ferry service with great success.

Another guest who loved Phil and his boat tour was Miss Connie McNeil, a schoolteacher, also from Long Island. She was practically the most appreciative and effervescent guest we ever had. Rain or shine, she had the best time. She got up very early and went hiking everywhere. She walked regularly around the oval after dinner with Julie Lawson, she was friends with all of us and the other guests. I chauffeured her a lot, too; but one day, she confessed that she had run out of money.

"This is so terrible, Andy," she said. "I've always dreamed of summering on the Maine Coast, and so this summer I just had to come, and it's even better and more wonderful than I could imagine; but I'm not going to be able to pay my bill nor give any of you wonderful people the tips you deserve. I'm very embarrassed."

"I think Miss Meyer will make a deal with you. Don't worry about it," I said.

Miss Meyer did make a deal, and, as I delivered Connie to the Bangor Airport to return to New York, she said to me, "Andy, do please let the girls know that I will be sending you all tips as soon as possible. You have been just great. Thanks for helping me have the best summer vacation I could imagine!" And she kissed me good-bye.

She was as good as her word, for a few days later we all received thank-you cards with ten dollar bills.

Miss Meyer's only comment was that "Connie McNeil is that type of old-maid schoolmarm who gets her energy and optimism from some mysterious source. I'm from another regiment of old-maid office girls; but we're all from the same Plain Jane Army."

"Oh, you're not so plain, Miss Meyer!" I said. "You're pretty damn colorful! Complicated, too."

"Errr. . .well, I like to think so."

The third of the memorable female guests was Sylvia Gordon, wife of the American Ambassador to Germany. She was one of the most beautiful women I had ever seen. I didn't have to chauffeur her, because she came in a rent-a-car from the airport. She was on her way from Arizona, where they lived, to Bonn, Germany, stopping in Maine to see how the youngest son was doing at the Three R's School for Rich Boys. She was wearing a light yellow linen suit and dark glasses. She had dark brown hair. I followed her into the hotel with her bags. It was the afternoon and Roddy was gone when she arrived. As she stepped into the lobby, she said, "Why, it's simply breath-taking here! Why haven't I been here before?" And turning to Miss Meyer, standing by, she asked, "May I have a cocktail out on the terrace right away?"

"Errr. . .indeed you may," said Miss Meyer. "What would you like?"

"I'd like a very dry martini with a twist of lemon."

"Errr. . .fine. Andy, will you take Mrs. Gordon's bags to the Number One Room, and then come out to the kitchen for her martini."

"How wonderful!" said Mrs. Gordon. "Could you also let me know the number of the Three R's School? I do want to let my son know I'm here, and that I'd like him to join me for dinner."

"Errr. . .yes, of course. As soon as you see your room, you may use the telephone in the hall off the foyer. The number of the school is posted right above the telephone stand."

"Thank you so much, Miss Meyer. You have granted all my wishes, and I am very grateful."

"Errr. . .anything else you want, just let Andy know, or me directly—I'm usually right out in the kitchen—and we'll do what we can."

I showed Mrs. Gordon to the Number One room, which was downstairs off the library with a full view of the bay and mountains. She loved it. I placed her bags on the luggage racks and she gave me two dollars.

Back out in the kitchen, Miss Meyer was having trouble locating the gin for the martini.

"Errr. . .Andy, have you seen that half gallon of Poland Spring Gin I had here in the liquor cabinet?"

"Probably Berter Fickett has been snooping around."

"Errr. . .I hope not. Look around and see if you can find it, while I get a tray and some crackers for her."

I did find it, and I watched my boss make a whole pitcherful of martinis. I knew then that Mrs. Gordon must be someone special, because Miss Meyer didn't provide mixed drinks like this for just anyone.

"Who is she?" I asked.

"Errr. . .her husband is the American Ambassador to Germany. Here, hurry all of this to her."

"Certainly an important post," I said.

I found Mrs. Gordon out on the terrace, and served her the drinks and crackers.

"Thank you so much, Andy," she said. "I can't tell you how I wished I had planned better so I could stay longer. My son failed to let on in his communications what a gorgeous place this is."

Her son with his suitcoat and tie on joined her for dinner; they visited, and then she took him back to the school. She returned before it was dark and sat again nursing a drink out on the terrace. I was picking up around the place, when she spoke to me.

"Oh, Andy, I'm staying out here until the sun goes down. Then, around nine p.m. or so, would you bring some wood to my room and start a fire in my fireplace? I should like to read in bed this evening."

"Sure."

I'll never forget the sight of her in bed in that room. I was on my hands and knees getting the fire going, when I looked up and across the room at her propped up against the pillows with her dark hair down. She had put her book down, too, and was smiling at me. She was bathed in golden lamplight and had on a silky nightie. She was so sexy and the scene was so sexy. I stood up like a goon, and she said, "This is so beautiful."

"Yes, it is," I agreed.

"You're a very nice young man. Thank you."

"Thank you, Mrs. Gordon. Good night."

"Good night."

60

Mrs. Richmond had always referred to artists as the "true aristocracy" of the human race; and I had known all along that that was the elite group to which I wanted to belong. In college I had had a creative writing teacher who had encouraged me to write; for a time I even had my own column for the college paper. I was forever scribbling in my journal; and the summer of 1964, I started putting together a tentative collection of my stories. I kept changing the title. Beginning with *Summer Set-Ups and Kitchen Dreams*, I changed to *The Dreams of Kitchen Boys* and to *Portrait of the Teacher as a Young Kitchen Boy*. The working title for most of the summer, though, became *More Truth Than Poetry*.

I needed an audience for my work, and I thought of Lizzie Guilford, grocer Wyman Guilford's daughter, my high school classmate who had also just graduated from college and was home for the summer. I called her and asked if I could see her. She said of course, and told me to come down that afternoon and we'd go out on her boat.

I drove to her huge white house overlooking the harbor of Summer Harbor Proper. Lizzie had gone to a private Catholic college and majored in math. She was planning to be a teacher, too. After a pleasant reunion and talk, we started walking from her house down the hill which led to the town wharf.

"I thought we might row to the other side of the harbor where there's a little beach and there you can read to me."

"Sounds great."

"Do you want to row?"

"Well, I'm not very good at it, but I'll try."

The town wharf was a local hangout, a working area for fishermen. Lobster traps and gear were packed all about the wharf and floats. A few men were standing around as we made our way down the slip to the float where Lizzie's rowboat was tied up. I knew that some of the men must have been amused by my awkward efforts at rowing the boat. I could paddle a canoe all right, but I had never learned to row well, even though I had grown up on the coast. I was embarrassed at such times not to be what a Maine boy was expected to be. On the way back, Lizzie rowed.

At the little beach, I did read to her, and she seemed to like my initial efforts at scribbling.

"You always wrote such funny essays in high school," she said. "You have a gift for humor. My essays are always so serious."

I tried out some of my titles on her, too.

"What do you think of *Preliminary to Leave-Taking*?"

"Instead of leaving Maine, it sounds like you're dying, leaving life," she said. "I don't think it's a good title for what you're trying to do."

I read a quote from Thomas Wolfe: ". . .he was like a man who stands upon a hill above the town he has left, yet does not say 'the town is near,' but turns his eyes upon the distant soaring ranges."

"What about 'distant soaring ranges?' It's from *Look Homeward, Angel*."

"Well, it's very dramatic, but I think you see more 'distant soaring ranges' down in North Carolina than here on the Maine Coast."

"What about *Hot Flashes and Cold Chills*?"

"Why that?"

"Well, isn't that what life is—sometimes hot and sometimes cold? I don't see existence as very moderate."

"But aren't hot flashes what women have when they're going through menopause, ya know, the so-called middle-aged crisis?"

"I don't know. I don't know about menopause."

"You'd better check."

"How about the *cold chills*?"

"Oh, I think the cold chills is fine. That's life in Maine all right."

"What about *Summer People and Some Are Help*?"

She laughed, but said, "No, too cute. Too gimmicky. I think you better just get your stories written first and then think of a title."

Luckily, Hattie Pinkham was still working next door for the Fitzpatricks. She had just returned from spending the winter in Hollywood, and I visited her one night when the Fitzpatricks were out to dinner over to Bar Harbor and she was baby-sitting the kids.

"So, Hattie, how was life among the stars? Get to eat at the Brown Derby?"

"No, but Mr. Fitzpatrick rented Jack Webb's house and I had my own little cottage across the pool. It was very nice."

"Was Sergeant Friday around?"

"He happened by one day, but I didn't meet him. The only celebrity I got to wait upon was Hal Wallis, the movie producer; and, oh yes, there was Peter Lawford—I passed him a cracker."

"Served with a smile, I bet."

"You bet your little lobster-cracking ass. I did get a couple of dates that were worth remembering."

"With Peter Lawford?"

"Oh, sure. Him and John Wayne. No, there were a couple of nice working class Joes who serviced Beverly Hills and they took me dancing—my favorite hobby, you know."

While we talked, and I was looking, once again, through Mr. Fitzpatrick's books, records, and bound movie scripts, I asked her what movie he was writing now.

"Oh, something with Steve McQueen in it. I think it's a modern day western."

Hattie didn't want to talk about Hollywood, though; she had something to tell me about herself.

"You're not the only one going to New York, ya know," she said.

"You are? With the Fitzpatricks?"

"Nope. On my own. I'm leaving this job come September."

"What are you going to do?"

"I've got a chance to work in Manhattan, and while there taking care of this old lady, I am planning on getting my high school diploma and go to nursing school. I'm going to have a whole new career and life!"

"Hattie, that's great. I'll be able to come down and visit you from Upstate."

"You better."

We jumped off the couch when we heard a car drive in. It was the Fitzpatricks who had come home early.

Mr. Fitzpatrick, who was very ebullient as usual, said they were having dinner at this restaurant when someone ran over a skunk outside the place and the windows were open. He sat and visited with us for a bit, but Mrs. Fitzpatrick went upstairs.

Even though I could have talked with him then about being a writer, and about writing for the movies, I was afraid to, so I said goodnight to both Hattie and him, and went back to my room at the Manor.

In my readings that summer, I was most impressed with *Lie Down in Darkness* by William Styron, another southerner I loved. I was also reading my last Carson McCullers book, *Reflections in a Golden Eye*; as well as more James Baldwin, Albert Camus, John Updike, more Wright Morris, and Theodore Dreiser. At the East Coast Shop, this little store next door to the barber shop/pool room in Summer Harbor run by a little old lady, I had bought an old high school literature text that I thought might make a good survey for me before teaching. I also ordered a book from Betts' Book Store in Bangor on the coaching of cross country. Wanting to look more muscular, I had started buying magazines like *Mr. America* and *Muscular Development*. I didn't own a set of weights, but I was exercising regularly, trying to do as many push-ups and sit-ups as I could do to put some muscle on my still skinny frame.

I was invited for dinner one night by the Carlisles, Morgan's parents, to join them and the grandparents, the Morgans, at Eastward in Cold Harbor. Grandpa Morgan, white-haired with twinkly blue eyes, was an art teacher, painter, and illustrator. Some of his students had also established summer homes in the area along with galleries and studios. I loved hearing both Mr. and Mrs. Morgan reminisce about their early days on the Maine Coast when they knew the famous artists like John Marin, Marsden Hartley, and Waldo Pierce. In turn, Mr. Morgan loved to hear me talk and tell my tales of my Maine. I felt like an adopted son in the presence of both the Carlisles and the Morgans. With them, more than any other summer family I had gotten to know, I felt comfortable and accepted for myself.

Another memorable evening at the end of the summer I spent in the company of good friend and high school and college classmate, Robin Noyes. He had been living in New York for some time, but he always tried to make it home summers for his beloved sailing. He was one of the best native sailors who had once been the Maine State Sailing Champ. He had a lot of trophies, and had taught a number of summer folk how to sail. Two years older than I, Robin was handsome, athletic, and had grown up as part of a summer colony. He was from an old Maine family that had once owned a great chunk of the Downeast coastline as well as several islands. He loved the arts, loved to read, and liked being up on current affairs. He had left the University of Maine in my sophomore year when he should have graduated but didn't have enough credits to do so. In a letter to me written from a YMCA in New York City, he had confessed that he was a homosexual and then went on to describe the impressive physique of his first New York lover, a blonde Marine from Alabama. I remember how I read it over and over and then went and threw it in the incinerator. I hadn't seen him much since 1962 and didn't know quite what to expect when I drove to his parents' large house. I was directed by his mother, who had gone to high school with my mother, to the enclosed front porch where I met Robin playing Schubert records with his black friend William.

"William is a graduate of Julliard," said Robin, "and a classical pianist of some repute."

"Oh, I'd like to hear you play," I said.

"Not on our piano!" said Robin. "Mother hasn't had our piano tuned for years!"

I asked them what was playing, and after they had told me, they started talking about "good Schubert and bad Schubert." Since I couldn't participate in such a debate, I spent the evening asking Robin banal questions like had he been sailing much.

I had never met an effeminate black male like William before. He was also very intelligent and witty and I enjoyed hearing him and Robin telling me about their lives in New York. They dropped a lot of names, a few I knew.

"Did you hear Aaron Copland lecturing on modern composing?" Robin asked William.

"Many times," said William.

Robin asked me if I knew the poet W.H. Auden, and when I said yes, he told me about hearing Auden read at the New School. "His readings were awfully pleasant, but never profound," said Robin. "Auden wore scrubby shoes and he addressed himself to the back wall."

Mary Treat was living in New York, too, and Robin claimed she tried to make advances towards him.

They interspersed their talk of all the famous people they had met or heard with stories about the homosexual hustling scene.

"Remember that U.N. official who picked up John in a chauffeur-driven limo?" William asked.

"Oh, yes," Robin said.

Robin had heard Henry Morgan lecture on comedy at some Hebrew center, Edward Albee at Columbia University, Mark Van Doren at N.Y.U., Katherine Anne Porter read from *Ship of Fools*, and the Archbishop of Canterbury at Trinity Church on Wall Street, among many others.

I was most impressed, however, by his having heard Martin Luther King preach at Riverside Church. "King was very moving," Robin said. And by his having met and talked with James Baldwin. "He gave me his phone number, but I never followed it up," said Robin.

Life in New York seemed such a dizzying whirl with so much going on.

Upon my leave, I shook hands with William, and he said, "Look, after you get settled in with your teaching job, take a weekend and come down to the city and we'll show you a good time."

"I'd like that," I said; but as I drove away, it occurred to me that I hadn't any idea of what Robin actually did for a living. Did he have a job in New York, or was he just a hustler? Did he just live in the Y and go around to lectures, recitals, and concerts? Did he ever get his college degree? He seemed to be having a great time with his life, and very happy, however it was that he was situated.

Robin had walked me out to my car and I had said to him, "You've now become a summer person."

He laughed, and said, "And next summer, you will be, too."

61

Throughout the whole last summer I had trouble sleeping almost every night. I was so restless and horny. I had written in my journal: "What is a virginal twenty-two-year-old man but a thing possessed?"

For even though I had had sex once, I still felt like a virgin. I thought about Essie all the time and almost called her several nights. One night I even went so far as to drive to Cold Harbor and go by her house, imagining myself in bed with both her and Vaughn.

Since I couldn't sleep, I'd get out of bed in the middle of the night and go naked into the world. I was like a crazed beast stalking the halls of the Manor, as well as the surrounding grounds, and even the paths and roads of Granite Neck, and on my evenings off, the paths, the fields, the woods, and shores of my hometown of Taunton. The shy, withdrawn bookworm had become a flaming exhibitionist! By day, a mere kitchen boy; but by night, a Tarzan of the dark.

One night I got out of bed and tip-toed buck naked down the backstairs, down the cellar stairs to the door that led out to the back lawn around which I ran and then made my way somehow through the rocks and bushes down to the rocky shore where I plunged into the cold ocean water. I did a furious set of push-ups on the ledges and I stood like a young Hercules up by the old tea house hurling rocks into the sea, bouncing boulders off the beach. I covered myself with seaweed.

I yelled into the dark blue night, "O LOST, THOMAS WOLFE! O LOST! OR MAYBE: O FOUND! O FOUND AT LAST, THOMAS WOLFE! AT LAST!"

I spoke to my literary heroes: "Hey, Mark Twain! You had your brown Mississippi River, and I've got my black Frenchman's Bay!"

"Hey, Thoreau, whataya know! I'm hugging the trees and planting my seeds in the Maine puckerbrush all in a row! New Growth!"

After my romp and soliloquy, I made my way back up the overgrown path to the Manor. Examining my body in my bedroom, I was surprised that the scars were minor. The bottoms of my feet were filthy, and there were bits of grass and dirt between my toes; but I was surprised I wasn't bloodier and dirtier than I was.

With each of my subsequent forays into the summer night, I grew bolder and crazier. I ran naked around Granite Neck. One night I was naked in full view of the streetlight at the playground doing chin-ups on the exercise bar and swinging in the swings. On the tennis court, I had myself a naked game of shadowball. I rolled around on the grass calling out, "HEY, WALT WHITMAN! I'M NOT ONLY LYING IN THE GRASS; I'M FUCKING THE GRASS! I AM ONE WITH THE GRASS! SPARSE AS IT IS ON THE GRANITE COAST!"

Some nights I would walk nude around the kitchen making myself a peanut butter sandwich and drinking a beer. William Burroughs had his *Naked Lunch* while I had my *Naked Midnight Snack*. A late-night visitor to the Manor might turn on the lights in the living room or library to find me lying nude on a couch or window seat. While I never slid down the banister in the altogether, I did walk up and down the main staircase naked as a jaybird. One night, I had the inspiration to do some nude weightlifting with a couple of the huge decorative vases or urns that adorned the grounds. I had to dump the rainwater out of them first, and then I lifted them high above my head.

On one of my nights off near the end of August, I was home in Taunton Ferry. It was very warm and I couldn't sleep. I had a wonderful erection, but instead of doing something about it right then, I decided to get out of bed and see how far I could run down the road sustaining this condition. Quietly, without disturbing my parents, or the neighbors with their windows open on a summer night, I went downstairs, opened the front door, and ran out the driveway, down the road to a field which led to the shore road and ocean. The field, which belonged to my uncle Oliver, and had been used for haying by my grandfather, was soggy and squishy in places, but I ran through it as fast as I could, then dashed across the dirt shore road, down the grassy bank and beach and plunged into the freezing waters of Warren Cove, an inlet of Frenchman's Bay named for my Warren ancestors. I remember thinking, "Thank God, it's high tide!"

The freezing water brought me to my senses immediately. Needless to say, my erection had long since withered; and I paddled quickly ashore, not daring to look up at my summer neighbor's cottages in case my splashing may have awakened them.

I had dashed down the road and field as if I were trying to break a track record, but I walked back home like a defeated and spent marathon swimmer. This time, I discovered, by my bedroom light that I had cut my feet and legs in several places. I was a mess. I had to go downstairs to the bathroom and patch myself up.

One night driving from Ellsworth to Summer Harbor, the urge to commit nudity came over me again. I drove off Route One up to Flanders Pond where I used to swim and camp a lot as a child. I parked the Galaxie by the public beach and stripped again, greatly enjoying for once a warm fresh water swim in the moonlight, until I happened to remember that the whole pond was full of bloodsuckers.

At the tail end of August, I had a few beers one evening with my friend Lester Moon, who had just accepted a banking position in Augusta, and upon driving back to the Manor, I went by the Granite Neck swimming pool, and decided to cap my Frenchman's Bay Manor years with one more dip in the forbidden pool. And this time, instead of trying to hide, I drove boldly into the pool parking area and left the Galaxie under the streetlight.

Precisely because it was so forbidden, because I had enjoyed so many secretive swims there with the girls, and because it was so dramatically situated, the Granite Neck pool was the most special pool in the world. I paddled about, remembering the first clandestine dips with Lillie, Amanda, and Morgan. I floated on my back, looking up at the stars twinkling above the dark ocean waters, the cliffs, the treetops, and the lights of Summer Harbor across the way. I was thinking of how in just a week or so now, I'd be leaving Maine to become a teacher in Central New York State. Just that morning, in fact, Mrs.

Lawson had given me a red Brooks Brothers tie as a going away gift, and another summer woman had admonished me about giving my students too much useless homework.

I was just about to swim to the side of the pool and crawl out, when suddenly, the high beams of a car's headlights appeared in the drive which led up to the pool!

The shadow of a man in a cop's uniform appeared with a flashlight. "HEY! WHAT DO YA THINK YA DOING IN THIS POOL?"

"Why, I believe I'm taking a little swim."

He came closer and I could see it was Teddy Lambert, with whom I'd gone to high school. He was the rent-a-cop the summer people had hired for the summer to police the Neck. Summer Harbor had no police department.

"Well, An-day Harrison, I'm shocked!" he said.

"How come?" I asked. "Don't you think I have a right to swim in this pool when no one else is using it?"

"Well, you're not exactly a member of the club."

"Are you?"

"Of course not. I don't live on Granite Neck. I'm a local like you."

"Teddy, you should take off your clothes right now and jump in this pool with me!"

"Oh, I couldn't do that. You know, I could have you arrested."

I was out of the pool by this point, trying to get my clothes on, while he kept shining the flashlight on me.

"Oh, Ted-day, don't be so foolish!" I said. "I wanted one more swim before I left Maine for good."

"Where are ya going?"

"New York, where I'm going to teach school."

"Well, you always were smart. I don't blame you for trying to get away."

"Ted-day! You're smart, too. Why didn't you go to college?"

"I had to stay here and help my mother with the laundry."

"And do a job like this one guarding our oppressors' property! Preying on your own kind?"

"I don't think the summer people are so bad. They provide a lot of jobs."

"Yeah, and all of them low-paying."

"Not all of 'em."

"No, they've gotta have wardens, gate-keepers, yacht captains, chauffeurs, and head caretakers! Boy, am I glad to be leaving! A servant no longer to the summer people! You can have it, Ted-day!"

I started walking away, carrying my sneakers.

"An-day, don't try swimming in here again," said Teddy.

"Don't worry. That's my last swim on Granite Neck!"

I drove back to the hotel, went up to my room, took off my soggy clothes and lay down on my bed. Sometime after midnight I realized the hall light just outside my door was still on, so I got up to turn it off. I was naked, and I opened the door. Just as I stepped out in the hall, I saw a figure moving toward me. It was Mrs. Lawson! She was in one of her summer frocks, looking all disheveled but still lovely. I was shocked that she'd see *me naked*! The tables were turned. All I could gasp was, "Oh, Mrs. Lawson!"

She smiled as she tip-toed by in her worn-out satin slippers.

"Good night, Andy," she said.

Epilogue
1965-1975

62

In the years that I taught school in New York, I'd always try and get down to New York City once a year to drop by to see Miss Meyer at her apartment on East 77th Street. I remember the first time I went there. The lobby and halls were very dark and the elevator was very small and slow. Miss Meyer was waiting for me at the end of the hall on her floor. Her apartment, where she had been living since the 1930s, was only one room. She had a window that looked out on an old courtyard. She had lights over the old paintings she had on her walls, but the ceiling in her bathroom was falling down. As with most of my visits, we'd have a drink at her place, and then she'd take me to dinner to an Italian restaurant that she loved because of the waiters with names like Victor and Benedicto, who would always make much of her. She ate there regularly where she could be the belle.

Before we'd go to dinner, she'd always have me call Mrs. Richmond in Greenwich, who would, in turn, invite me for weekends in Connecticut, but I never went.

Over the years, there would always be Christmas cards and occasional letters from them both.

One time I met Hattie Pinkham in New York. She had completed her nurse's training as planned and was working at St. Vincent's Hospital. We met for a drink at the Commodore Hotel and then went to Miss Meyer's for dinner.

In 1969, I was in the big city for a weekend before flying to Florida for Christmas with my parents, my brother Bobber and his family. I showed up at Miss Meyer's and she told me that Mrs. Richmond had just had her leg amputated at Greenwich Hospital. It was the leg with the ankle that had never healed.

I called her. "Mrs. Richmond? It's Andy."

"Oh, Andy, dear, it's so good to hear your voice. How are you?"

"I'm fine, Mrs. Richmond; but I just learned from Miss Meyer about your leg."

"Oh, hell, water over the dam is water over the dam, ya know. Say, Andy, I've got a joke for you: what did the little cricket say the first time she got laid?"

"I don't know."

"Tsk, tsk. . .and that's about how I feel after having my leg off. . . tsk, tsk. . .they'll be fitting me for a prosthesis, ya know, a wooden leg, next week. . .and you can bet it'll be a shapely one!"

She was forever joking, asking me about my schoolteaching, asking me if I had read some current essay in the latest *Atlantic Monthly*; as I tried to talk and laugh with her through my tears.

"Listen, you stop that blubbering over me and enjoy your weekend in New York. I only wish I could be there with you and Jean. Live it up, Andy! It's a wonderful life, a gift really, despite the little pitfalls. . .and even some of those little pitfalls can be fun! My love to you."

By 1970, I had been a veteran teacher for six years, had gotten fired from the first job, and moved on to a school in Syracuse, where I had experienced my first race riot. I had founded a couple of literary magazines for my students, and had been granted tenure. I had been to New York City many times, seen Broadway shows and all the sights, and was near the end of completing work on my master's degree from Syracuse University.

Every summer I'd go home to Maine, where I'd always make a visit to the Manor and Miss Meyer. In the summer of 1967, she even employed me for a week or so to help instruct the new kitchen boy, a tall, blonde kid who played basketball for Mollusk Memorial and reminded me of myself.

During the course of my first year of teaching, I had found another Essie in the person of a lovely, blonde science teacher my age named Marilyn. She was half Polish, half German and from Herkimer, New York. She had one leg a bit longer than the other which gave her a wonderful walk. She had a musical laugh. We both loved to go drinking and dancing and had a great time together, laughing all the time.

The summer of 1970, I was delighted to read in the *Bangor Daily News* that Essie Bishop had become the first woman to win a Summer Harbor lobster boat race. She was posed in a picture with Vaughn and their four sons on board the winning craft, a brand-new boat built by the Bishops themselves, called *The Torrid Essie*.

In 1971, Mrs. Richmond returned to the Manor in a wheelchair. Miss Meyer called me; and my girlfriend, Betty, a pretty brown-haired French teacher from Syracuse, my mother, and I all drove down to the Manor for a visit.

We met in the living room and hugged and kissed. The most shocking thing about seeing Mrs. Richmond again after all those years was not her being in a wheelchair, but her being so thin. She had lost a great deal of weight and was about half the size she used to be; but her great fun-loving spirit was intact, and we had a great time reliving the past. Betty only met Madella and Jean that once, but she never forgot them.

The Manor had actually been sold by 1970 to our former guest, Mrs. P. Canfield Gay, who had restored it to a one-family summer home. Both my mother and Miss Meyer had been employed that summer taking care of the place and Mrs. Gay.

In December 1970, Mrs. Richmond died from a severe stroke. In her last letter to me, she wrote: "Oh, Andy, it was all such fun! I wish I could relive those years, although I must say I probably wouldn't do anything any different. I say again it was all such fun! I remember especially when I was there alone that year. You and Lillie and I in the kitchen discussing everything—books, people, moral codes, parental influence, etc. I often quote your saying, 'Have an opinion of your own and you are called disrespectful!' Of course, one has to become an adult to see the humor of this! You mention Thomas Wolfe. I always loved his style and he never wrote a truer book than *You Can't Go Home Again*. Isn't it true? Once launched on one's own—the saying 'for better or worse' is one's slogan. You should write, Andy—your letter put me back years and I lived it all again.

As you say, Morgan, all the waitresses, the music, the wild running to the store, Lillie, Ellen and Sally and the everlasting giggling that went on! Yes, it was a golden time—put it all in a story, Andy! You and the girls on the rocks at the bay—you never knew, Andy, I used to take a look at you all through my opera glasses! Dear Andy, I got such a laugh about your innocence 'being gone these many years' and it started to go at the Manor!"

I wrote to Miss Meyer after Mrs. Richmond's death, and she wrote back: "I miss her gay laughter which still prevailed the day before her stroke, for I spoke to her twice on the phone that day. But I guess she couldn't take any more. She was having trouble with her left leg and went to see her doctor on the Friday before the stroke. She was a smart cookie and I suppose surmised what was happening. The director of nurses who was a friend of hers told me the leg had—or rather the foot—had started to turn black. So it goes, and will with all of us. But why, why, why did she have to suffer so for seven years?"

In the spring of 1974, I took some of my stories about the Manor to New York to read to Miss Meyer. She was drinking then even before noon. We went to a nice Upper East Side restaurant called The Raveled Sleeve for brunch; and then later back in her apartment, I tried to get her to sit down so I could read the stories to her. But she was more concerned about my trying to fix her refrigerator, which had turned into an ice block. She did sit down and listen, though, and when I had finished reading, I asked her what she thought.

"Errr. . .you make me sound too Jewish," she said, "and you've over-emphasized the eccentricities of the guests. You make it sound like a collection of circus freaks. Take some of 'em out. I think you also make some of the summer people sound like royalty. Also, you mustn't repeat yourself too much. The trouble with repetition is that is ceases to mean anything."

"Well, besides all of those objections, do you think it will make a good book?"

She took another drag on her cigarette and another slug of her scotch, and she looked straight at me.

"Errr. . .your manuscript is very interesting. It just lacks professional polish."

Being and sounding professional was everything to Miss Jean Meyer. It was her credo, how she achieved her own position as executive secretary at the Waldorf-Astoria.

After I left her that day, I never saw her again. Mrs. Richmond had died in December 1970, and Miss Meyer, whom I learned was 75 in her obituary, died in December 1975. Both of them were as old as the century, and just as lively.

THE END